J. J. Connington and The Murder Room

>>> This title is part of The Murder Room, our series dedicated to making available out-of-print or hard-to-find titles by classic crime writers.

Crime fiction has always held up a mirror to society. The Victorians were fascinated by sensational murder and the emerging science of detection; now we are obsessed with the forensic detail of violent death. And no other genre has so captivated and enthralled readers.

Vast troves of classic crime writing have for a long time been unavailable to all but the most dedicated frequenters of second-hand bookshops. The advent of digital publishing means that we are now able to bring you the backlists of a huge range of titles by classic and contemporary crime writers, some of which have been out of print for decades.

From the genteel amateur private eyes of the Golden Age and the femmes fatales of pulp fiction, to the morally ambiguous hard-boiled detectives of mid twentieth-century America and their descendants who walk our twenty-first century streets, The Murder Room has it all. >>>

The Murder Room
Where Criminal Minds Meet

themurderroom.com

T0351825

J. J. Connington (1880–1947)

Alfred Walter Stewart, who wrote under the pen name J. J. Connington, was born in Glasgow, the youngest of three sons of Reverend Dr Stewart. He graduated from Glasgow University and pursued an academic career as a chemistry professor, working for the Admiralty during the First World War. Known for his ingenious and carefully worked-out puzzles and in-depth character development, he was admired by a host of his better-known contemporaries, including Dorothy L. Sayers and John Dickson Carr, who both paid tribute to his influence on their work. He married Jessie Lily Courts in 1916 and they had one daughter.

By J. J. Connington

Sir Clinton Driffield Mysteries
Murder in the Maze (1927)
Tragedy at Ravensthorpe (1927)
The Case with Nine Solutions (1928)
Mystery at Lynden Sands (1928)
Nemesis at Raynham Parva (1929)
  (a.k.a. Grim Vengenace)
The Boathouse Riddle (1931)
The Sweepstake Murders (1931)
The Castleford Conundrum (1932)
The Ha-Ha Case (1934)
  (a.k.a. The Brandon Case)
In Whose Dim Shadow (1935)
  (a.k.a. The Tau Cross Mystery)
A Minor Operation (1937)
Murder Will Speak (1938)

Truth Comes Limping (1938)
The Twenty-One Clues (1941)
No Past is Dead (1942)
Jack-in-the-Box (1944)
Common Sense Is All You Need (1947)

Supt Ross Mysteries
The Eye in the Museum (1929)
The Two Tickets Puzzle (1930)

Novels
Death at Swaythling Court (1926)
The Dangerfield Talisman (1926)
Tom Tiddler's Island (1933)
  (a.k.a. Gold Brick Island)
The Counsellor (1939)
The Four Defences (1940)

Common Sense Is All You Need

J. J. Connington

CONTENTS

Introduction
by
Curtis Evans

During the Golden Age of the detective novel, in the 1920s and 1930s, J. J. Connington stood with fellow crime writers R. Austin Freeman, Cecil John Charles Street and Freeman Wills Crofts as the foremost practitioner in British mystery fiction of the science of pure detection. I use the word 'science' advisedly, for the man behind J. J. Connington, Alfred Walter Stewart, was an esteemed Scottish-born scientist. A 'small, unassuming, moustached polymath', Stewart was 'a strikingly effective lecturer with an excellent sense of humor, fertile imagination and fantastically retentive memory', qualities that also served him well in his fiction. He held the Chair of Chemistry at Queens University, Belfast for twenty-five years, from 1919 until his retirement in 1944.

During roughly this period, the busy Professor Stewart found time to author a remarkable apocalyptic science fiction tale, *Nordenholt's Million* (1923), a mainstream novel, *Almighty Gold* (1924), a collection of essays, *Alias J. J. Connington* (1947), and, between 1926 and 1947, twenty-four mysteries (all but one tales of detection), many of them sterling examples of the Golden Age puzzle-oriented detective novel at its considerable best. 'For those who ask first of all in a detective story for exact and mathematical accuracy in the construction of the plot', avowed a contemporary *London Daily Mail* reviewer, 'there is no author to equal the distinguished scientist who writes under the name of J. J. Connington.'[1]

Alfred Stewart's background as a man of science is reflected in his fiction, not only in the impressive puzzle plot mechanics he devised for his mysteries but in his choices of themes and

i

depictions of characters. Along with Stanley Nordenholt of *Nordenholt's Million*, a novel about a plutocrat's pitiless efforts to preserve a ruthlessly remolded remnant of human life after a global environmental calamity, Stewart's most notable character is Chief Constable Sir Clinton Driffield, the detective in seventeen of the twenty-four Connington crime novels. Driffield is one of crime fiction's most highhanded investigators, occasionally taking on the functions of judge and jury as well as chief of police.

Absent from Stewart's fiction is the hail-fellow-well-met quality found in John Street's works or the religious ethos suffusing those of Freeman Wills Crofts, not to mention the effervescent novel-of-manners style of the British Golden Age Crime Queens Dorothy L. Sayers, Margery Allingham and Ngaio Marsh. Instead we see an often disdainful cynicism about the human animal and a marked admiration for detached supermen with superior intellects. For this reason, reading a Connington novel can be a challenging experience for modern readers inculcated in gentler social beliefs. Yet Alfred Stewart produced a classic apocalyptic science fiction tale in *Nordenholt's Million* (justly dubbed 'exciting and terrifying reading' by the *Spectator*) as well as superb detective novels boasting well-wrought puzzles, bracing characterization and an occasional leavening of dry humor. Not long after Stewart's death in 1947, the Connington novels fell entirely out of print. The recent embrace of Stewart's fiction by Orion's Murder Room imprint is a welcome event indeed, correcting as it does over sixty years of underserved neglect of an accomplished genre writer.

Born in Glasgow on 5 September 1880, Alfred Stewart had significant exposure to religion in his earlier life. His father was William Stewart, longtime Professor of Divinity and Biblical Criticism at Glasgow University, and he married Lily Coats, a daughter of the Reverend Jervis Coats and member of one of

Scotland's preeminent Baptist families. Religious sensibility is entirely absent from the Connington corpus, however. A confirmed secularist, Stewart once referred to one of his wife's brothers, the Reverend William Holms Coats (1881–1954), principal of the Scottish Baptist College, as his 'mental and spiritual antithesis', bemusedly adding: 'It's quite an education to see what one would look like if one were turned into one's mirror-image.'

Stewart's J. J. Connington pseudonym was derived from a nineteenth-century Oxford Professor of Latin and translator of Horace, indicating that Stewart's literary interests lay not in pietistic writing but rather in the pre-Christian classics ('I prefer the *Odyssey* to *Paradise Lost*,' the author once avowed). Possessing an inquisitive and expansive mind, Stewart was in fact an uncommonly well-read individual, freely ranging over a variety of literary genres. His deep immersion in French literature and supernatural horror fiction, for example, is documented in his lively correspondence with the noted horologist Rupert Thomas Gould.[2]

It thus is not surprising that in the 1920s the intellectually restless Stewart, having achieved a distinguished middle age as a highly regarded man of science, decided to apply his creative energy to a new endeavor, the writing of fiction. After several years he settled, like other gifted men and women of his generation, on the wildly popular mystery genre. Stewart was modest about his accomplishments in this particular field of light fiction, telling Rupert Gould later in life that 'I write these things [what Stewart called tec yarns] because they amuse me in parts when I am putting them together and because they are the only writings of mine that the public will look at. Also, in a minor degree, because I like to think some people get pleasure out of them.' No doubt Stewart's single most impressive literary accomplishment is *Nordenholt's Million*, yet in their time the two dozen J. J. Connington mysteries did indeed give readers in Great Britain, the United States and other countries much diversionary reading pleasure. Today these works constitute an estimable addition to British crime fiction.

After his 'prentice pastiche mystery, *Death at Swaythling Court* (1926), a rural English country-house tale set in the highly traditional village of Fernhurst Parva, Stewart published another, superior country-house affair, *The Dangerfield Talisman* (1926), a novel about the baffling theft of a precious family heirloom, an ancient, jewel-encrusted armlet. This clever, murderless tale, which likely is the one that the author told Rupert Gould he wrote in under six weeks, was praised in *The Bookman* as 'continuously exciting and interesting' and in the *New York Times Book Review* as 'ingeniously fitted together and, what is more, written with a deal of real literary charm'. Despite its virtues, however, *The Dangerfield Talisman* is not fully characteristic of mature Connington detective fiction. The author needed a memorable series sleuth, more representative of his own forceful personality.

It was the next year, 1927, that saw J. J. Connington make his break to the front of the murdermongerer's pack with a third country-house mystery, *Murder in the Maze*, wherein debuted as the author's great series detective the assertive and acerbic Sir Clinton Driffield, along with Sir Clinton's neighbor and 'Watson', the more genial (if much less astute) Squire Wendover. In this much-praised novel, Stewart's detective duo confronts some truly diabolical doings, including slayings by means of curare-tipped darts in the double-centered hedge maze at a country estate, Whistlefield. No less a fan of the genre than T. S. Eliot praised *Murder in the Maze* for its construction ('we are provided early in the story with all the clues which guide the detective') and its liveliness ('The very idea of murder in a box-hedge labyrinth does the author great credit, and he makes full use of its possibilities'). The delighted Eliot concluded that

Murder in the Maze was 'a really first-rate detective story'. For his part, the critic H. C. Harwood declared in *The Outlook* that with the publication of *Murder in the Maze* Connington demanded and deserved 'comparison with the masters'. 'Buy, borrow, or – anyhow – get hold of it', he amusingly advised. Two decades later, in his 1946 critical essay 'The Grandest Game in the World', the great locked-room detective novelist John Dickson Carr echoed Eliot's assessment of the novel's virtuoso setting, writing: 'These 1920s [. . .] thronged with sheer brains. What would be one of the best possible settings for violent death? J. J. Connington found the answer, with *Murder in the Maze*.' Certainly in retrospect *Murder in the Maze* stands as one of the finest English country-house mysteries of the 1920s, cleverly yet fairly clued, imaginatively detailed and often grimly suspenseful. As the great American true-crime writer Edmund Lester Pearson noted in his review of *Murder in the Maze* in *The Outlook*, this Connington novel had everything that one could desire in a detective story: 'A shrubbery maze, a hot day, and somebody potting at you with an air gun loaded with darts covered with a deadly South-American arrow-poison – *there* is a situation to wheedle two dollars out of anybody's pocket.'[3]

Staying with what had worked so well for him to date, Stewart the same year produced yet another country-house mystery, *Tragedy at Ravensthorpe*, an ingenious tale of murders and thefts at the ancestral home of the Chacewaters, old family friends of Sir Clinton Driffield. There is much clever matter in *Ravensthorpe*. Especially fascinating is the author's inspired integration of faerie folklore into his plot. Stewart, who had a lifelong – though skeptical – interest in paranormal phenomena, probably was inspired in this instance by the recent hubbub over the Cottingly Faeries photographs that in the early 1920s had famously duped, among other individuals, Arthur Conan Doyle.[4] As with *Murder in the Maze*, critics raved about this new Connington mystery. In the *Spectator*, for example, a reviewer hailed *Tragedy at Ravensthorpe* in the strongest terms, declaring of the novel: 'This is more than a good detective tale. Alike in plot, characterization, and literary style, it is a work of art.'

In 1928 there appeared two additional Sir Clinton Driffield detective novels, *Mystery at Lynden Sands* and *The Case with Nine Solutions*. Once again there was great praise for the latest Conningtons. H. C. Harwood, the critic who had so much admired *Murder in the Maze*, opined of *Mystery at Lynden Sands* that it 'may just fail of being the detective story of the century', while in the United States author and book reviewer Frederic F. Van de Water expressed nearly as high an opinion of *The Case with Nine Solutions*. 'This book is a thoroughbred of a distinguished lineage that runs back to "The Gold Bug" of [Edgar Allan] Poe,' he avowed. 'It represents the highest type of detective fiction.' In both of these Connington novels, Stewart moved away from his customary country-house milieu, setting *Lynden Sands* at a fashionable beach resort and *Nine Solutions* at a scientific research institute. *Nine Solutions* is of particular interest today, I think, for its relatively frank sexual subject matter and its modern urban setting among science professionals, which rather resembles the locales found in P. D. James' classic detective novels *A Mind to Murder* (1963) and *Shroud for a Nightingale* (1971).

By the end of the 1920s, J. J. Connington's critical reputation had achieved enviable heights indeed. At this time Stewart became one of the charter members of the Detection Club, an assemblage of the finest writers of British detective fiction that included, among other distinguished individuals, Agatha Christie, Dorothy L. Sayers and G. K. Chesterton. Certainly Victor Gollancz, the British publisher of the J. J. Connington mysteries, did not stint praise for the author, informing readers that 'J. J. Connington is now established as, in the opinion of many, the greatest living master of the story of pure detection. He is one of those who, discarding all the superfluities, has made of deductive fiction a genuine minor art, with its own laws and its own conventions.'

Such warm praise for J. J. Connington makes it all the more surprising that at this juncture the esteemed author tinkered with his successful formula by dispensing with his original series detective. In the fifth Clinton Driffield detective novel, *Nemesis at Raynham Parva* (1929), Alfred Walter Stewart, rather like Arthur Conan Doyle before him, seemed with a dramatic dénouement to have devised his popular series detective's permanent exit from the fictional stage (read it and see for yourself). The next two Connington detective novels, *The Eye in the Museum* (1929) and *The Two Tickets Puzzle* (1930), have a different series detective, Superintendent Ross, a rather dull dog of a policeman. While both these mysteries are competently done – the railway material in *The Two Tickets Puzzle* is particularly effective and should have appeal today – the presence of Sir Clinton Driffield (no superfluity he!) is missed.

Probably Stewart detected that the public minded the absence of the brilliant and biting Sir Clinton, for the Chief Constable – accompanied, naturally, by his friend Squire Wendover – triumphantly returned in 1931 in *The Boathouse Riddle*, another well-constructed criminous country-house affair. Later in the year came *The Sweepstake Murders*, which boasts the perennially popular tontine multiple-murder plot, in this case a rapid succession of puzzling suspicious deaths afflicting the members of a sweepstake syndicate that has just won nearly £250,000.[5] Adding piquancy to this plot is the fact that Wendover is one of the imperiled syndicate members. Altogether the novel is, as the late Jacques Barzun and his colleague Wendell Hertig Taylor put it in *A Catalogue of Crime* (1971, 1989), their magisterial survey of detective fiction, 'one of Connington's best conceptions'.

Stewart's productivity as a fiction writer slowed in the 1930s, so that, barring the year 1938, at most only one new Connington appeared annually. However, in 1932 Stewart produced one of the best Connington mysteries, *The Castleford Conundrum*. A classic country-house detective novel, Castleford introduces to readers Stewart's most delightfully unpleasant set of greedy relations and one of his most deserving murderees, Winifred Castleford. Stewart also fashions a wonderfully rich puzzle plot, full of meaty material clues for the reader's delectation. *Castleford* presented critics with no conundrum over its quality. 'In *The Castleford Conundrum* Mr Connington goes to work like an accomplished chess player. The moves in the games his detectives are called on to play are a delight to watch,' raved the reviewer for the *Sunday Times*, adding that 'the clues would have rejoiced Mr. Holmes' heart.' For its part, the *Spectator* concurred in the *Sunday Times*' assessment of the novel's masterfully constructed plot: 'Few detective stories show such sound reasoning as that by which the Chief Constable brings the crime home to the culprit.' Additionally, E. C. Bentley, much admired himself as the author of the landmark detective novel *Trent's Last Case*, took time to praise Connington's purely literary virtues, noting: 'Mr Connington has never written better, or drawn characters more full of life.'

With *Tom Tiddler's Island* in 1933 Stewart produced a different sort of Connington, a criminal-gang mystery in the rather more breathless style of such hugely popular English thriller writers as Sapper, Sax Rohmer, John Buchan and Edgar Wallace (in violation of the strict detective fiction rules of Ronald Knox, there is even a secret passage in the novel). Detailing the startling discoveries made by a newlywed couple honeymooning on a remote Scottish island, *Tom Tiddler's Island* is an atmospheric and entertaining tale, though it is not as mentally stimulating for armchair sleuths as Stewart's true detective novels. The title, incidentally, refers to an ancient British children's game, 'Tom Tiddler's Ground', in which one child tries to hold a height against other children.

After his fictional Scottish excursion into thrillerdom, Stewart returned the next year to his English country-house roots with *The Ha-Ha Case* (1934), his last masterwork in this classic mystery setting (for elucidation of non-British readers, a ha-ha is a sunken wall, placed so as to delineate property boundaries while not obstructing views). Although *The Ha-Ha Case* is not set in Scotland, Stewart drew inspiration for the novel from a notorious Scottish true crime, the 1893 Ardlamont murder case. From the facts of the Ardlamont affair Stewart drew several of the key characters in *The Ha-Ha Case*, as well as the circumstances of the novel's murder (a shooting 'accident' while hunting), though he added complications that take the tale in a new direction.[6]

In newspaper reviews both Dorothy L. Sayers and 'Francis Iles' (crime novelist Anthony Berkeley Cox) highly praised this latest mystery by 'The Clever Mr Connington', as he was now dubbed on book jackets by his new English publisher, Hodder & Stoughton. Sayers particularly noted the effective characterisation in *The Ha-Ha Case*: 'There is no need to say that Mr Connington has given us a sound and interesting plot, very carefully and ingeniously worked out. In addition, there are the three portraits of the three brothers, cleverly and rather subtly characterised, of the [governess], and of Inspector Hinton, whose admirable qualities are counteracted by that besetting sin of the man who has made his own way: a jealousy of delegating responsibility.' The reviewer for the *Times Literary Supplement* detected signs that the sardonic Sir Clinton Driffield had begun mellowing with age: 'Those who have never really liked Sir Clinton's perhaps excessively soldierly manner will be surprised to find that he makes his discovery not only by the pure light of intelligence, but partly as a reward for amiability and tact, qualities in which the Inspector [Hinton] was strikingly deficient.' This is true enough, although the classic Sir Clinton emerges a number of times in the novel, as in his subtly sarcastic recurrent backhanded praise of Inspector Hinton: 'He writes a first class report.'

Clinton Driffield returned the next year in the detective novel *In Whose Dim Shadow* (1935), a tale set in a recently erected English suburb, the denizens of which seem to have committed an impressive number of indiscretions, including sexual ones. The intriguing title of the British edition of the novel is drawn from a poem by the British historian Thomas Babington Macaulay: 'Those trees in whose dim shadow/The ghastly priest doth reign/The priest who slew the slayer/And shall himself be slain.' Stewart's puzzle plot in *In Whose Dim Shadow* is well clued and compelling, the kicker of a closing paragraph is a classic of its kind and, additionally, the author paints some excellent character portraits. I fully concur with the *Sunday Times'* assessment of the tale: 'Quiet domestic murder, full of the neatest detective points [. . .] These are not the detective's stock figures, but fully realised human beings.'[7]

Uncharacteristically for Stewart, nearly twenty months elapsed between the publication of *In Whose Dim Shadow* and his next book, *A Minor Operation* (1937). The reason for the author's delay in production was the onset in 1935–36 of the afflictions of cataracts and heart disease (Stewart ultimately succumbed to heart disease in 1947). Despite these grave health complications, Stewart in late 1936 was able to complete *A Minor Operation*, a first-rate Clinton Driffield story of murder and a most baffling disappearance. A *Times Literary Supplement* reviewer found that *A Minor Operation* treated the reader 'to exactly the right mixture of mystification and clue' and that, in addition to its impressive construction, the novel boasted 'character-drawing above the average' for a detective novel.

Alfred Stewart's final eight mysteries, which appeared between 1938 and 1947, the year of the author's death, are, on the whole, a somewhat weaker group of tales than the sixteen that appeared between 1926 and 1937, yet they are not without interest. In 1938 Stewart for the last time managed to publish two detective novels, *Truth Comes Limping* and *For Murder Will Speak* (also published as *Murder Will Speak*). The latter tale is much the superior of the two, having an interesting suburban setting and a bevy of female characters found to have motives when a contemptible philandering businessman meets with foul play. Sexual neurosis plays a major role in *For Murder Will Speak*, the ever-thorough Stewart obviously having made a study of the subject when writing the novel. The somewhat squeamish reviewer for *Scribner's Magazine* considered the subject matter of *For Murder Will Speak* 'rather unsavory at times', yet this individual conceded that the novel nevertheless made 'first-class reading for those who enjoy a good puzzle intricately worked out'. 'Judge Lynch' in the *Saturday Review* apparently had no such moral reservations about the latest Clinton Driffield murder case, avowing simply of the novel: 'They don't come any better'.

Over the next couple of years Stewart again sent Sir Clinton Driffield temporarily packing, replacing him with a new series detective, a brash radio personality named Mark Brand, in *The Counsellor* (1939) and *The Four Defences* (1940). The better of these two novels is *The Four Defences*, which Stewart based on another notorious British true-crime case, the Alfred Rouse blazing-car murder. (Rouse is believed to have fabricated his death by murdering an unknown man, placing the dead man's body in his car and setting the car on fire, in the hope that the murdered man's body would be taken for his.) Though admittedly a thinly characterised academic exercise in ratiocination, Stewart's *Four Defences* surely is also one of the most complexly plotted Golden Age detective novels and should delight devotees of classical detection. Taking the Rouse blazing-car affair as his theme, Stewart composes from it a stunning set of diabolically ingenious criminal variations. 'This is in the cold-blooded category which [. . .] excites a crossword puzzle kind of interest,' the reviewer for the *Times Literary Supplement* acutely noted of the novel. 'Nothing in the Rouse case would prepare you for these complications upon complications [. . .] What they prove is that Mr Connington has the power of penetrating into the puzzle-corner of the brain. He leaves it dazedly wondering whether in the records of actual crime there can be any dark deed to equal this in its planned convolutions.'

Sir Clinton Driffield returned to action in the remaining four detective novels in the Connington oeuvre, *The Twenty-One Clues* (1941), *No Past is Dead* (1942), *Jack-in-the-Box* (1944) and *Commonsense is All You Need* (1947), all of which were written as Stewart's heart disease steadily worsened and reflect to some extent his diminishing physical and mental energy. Although *The Twenty-One Clues* was inspired by the notorious Hall-Mills double murder case – probably the most publicised murder case in the United States in the 1920s – and the American critic and novelist Anthony Boucher commended *Jack-in-the-Box*, I believe the best of these later mysteries is *No Past Is Dead*, which Stewart partly based on a bizarre French true-crime affair, the 1891 Achet-Lepine murder case.[8] Besides providing an interesting background for the tale, the ailing author managed some virtuoso plot twists, of the sort most associated today with that ingenious Golden Age Queen of Crime, Agatha Christie.

What Stewart with characteristic bluntness referred to as 'my complete crack-up' forced his retirement from Queen's University in 1944. 'I am afraid,' Stewart wrote a friend, the chemist and forensic scientist F. Gerald Tryhorn, in August 1946, eleven months before his death, 'that I shall never be much use again. Very stupidly, I tried for a session to combine a full course of lecturing with angina pectoris; and ended up by establishing that the two are immiscible.' He added that since retiring in 1944, he had been physically 'limited to my house, since even a fifty-yard crawl brings on the usual cramps'. Stewart completed his essay collection and a final novel before he died at his study desk in his Belfast home on 1 July 1947, at the age of sixty-six. When death came to the author he was busy at work, writing.

More than six decades after Alfred Walter Stewart's death, his J. J. Connington fiction is again available to a wider audience of classic-mystery fans, rather than strictly limited to a select company of rare-book collectors with deep pockets. This is fitting for an individual who was one of the finest writers of British genre fiction between the two world wars. 'Heaven forfend that you should imagine I take myself for anything out of the common in the tec yarn stuff,' Stewart once self-deprecatingly declared in a letter to Rupert Gould. Yet, as contemporary critics recognised, as a writer of detective and science fiction Stewart indeed was something out of the common. Now more modern readers can find this out for themselves. They have much good sleuthing in store.

1. For more on Street, Crofts and particularly Stewart, see Curtis Evans, *Masters of the 'Humdrum' Mystery: Cecil John Charles Street, Freeman Wills Crofts, Alfred Walter Stewart and the British Detective Novel, 1920–1961* (Jefferson, NC: McFarland, 2012). On the academic career of Alfred Walter Stewart, see his entry in *Oxford Dictionary of National Biography* (London and New York: Oxford University Press, 2004), vol. 52, 627–628.
2. The Gould-Stewart correspondence is discussed in considerable detail in *Masters of the 'Humdrum' Mystery*. For more on the life of the fascinating Rupert Thomas Gould, see Jonathan Betts, *Time Restored: The Harrison Timekeepers and R. T. Gould, the*

Man Who Knew (Almost) Everything (London and New York: Oxford University Press, 2006) and *Longitude,* the 2000 British film adaptation of Dava Sobel's book *Longitude:The True Story of a Lone Genius Who Solved the Greatest Scientific Problem of His Time* (London: Harper Collins, 1995), which details Gould's restoration of the marine chronometers built by in the eighteenth century by the clockmaker John Harrison.

3. Potential purchasers of *Murder in the Maze* should keep in mind that $2 in 1927 is worth over $26 today.

4. In a 1920 article in *The Strand Magazine,* Arthur Conan Doyle endorsed as real prank photographs of purported fairies taken by two English girls in the garden of a house in the village of Cottingley. In the aftermath of the Great War Doyle had become a fervent believer in Spiritualism and other paranormal phenomena. Especially embarrassing to Doyle's admirers today, he also published *The Coming of the Faeries* (1922), wherein he argued that these mystical creatures genuinely existed. 'When the spirits came in, the common sense oozed out,' Stewart once wrote bluntly to his friend Rupert Gould of the creator of Sherlock Holmes. Like Gould, however, Stewart had an intense interest in the subject of the Loch Ness Monster, believing that he, his wife and daughter had sighted a large marine creature of some sort in Loch Ness in 1935. A year earlier Gould had authored *The Loch Ness Monster and Others*, and it was this book that led Stewart, after he made his 'Nessie' sighting, to initiate correspondence with Gould.

5. A tontine is a financial arrangement wherein shareowners in a common fund receive annuities that increase in value with the death of each participant, with the entire amount of the fund going to the last survivor. The impetus that the tontine provided to the deadly creative imaginations of Golden Age mystery writers should be sufficiently obvious.

6. At Ardlamont, a large country estate in Argyll, Cecil Hambrough died from a gunshot wound while hunting. Cecil's tutor, Alfred John Monson, and another man, both of whom were out hunting with Cecil, claimed that Cecil had accidentally shot himself, but Monson was arrested and tried for Cecil's murder. The verdict delivered was 'not proven', but Monson was then – and is today – considered almost certain to have been guilty of the murder. On the Ardlamont case, see William Roughead, *Classic Crimes* (1951; repr., New York: New York Review Books Classics, 2000), 378–464.

7. For the genesis of the title, see Macaulay's 'The Battle of the Lake

Regillus', from his narrative poem collection *Lays of Ancient Rome*. In this poem Macaulay alludes to the ancient cult of Diana Nemorensis, which elevated its priests through trial by combat. Study of the practices of the Diana Nemorensis cult influenced Sir James George Frazer's cultural interpretation of religion in his most renowned work, *The Golden Bough: A Study in Magic and Religion*. As with *Tom Tiddler's Island* and *The Ha-Ha Case* the title *In Whose Dim Shadow* proved too esoteric for Connington's American publishers, Little, Brown and Co., who altered it to the more prosaic *The Tau Cross Mystery*.

8. Stewart analysed the Achet-Lepine case in detail in 'The Mystery of Chantelle', one of the best essays in his 1947 collection *Alias J. J. Connington*.

1

SALVAGE

As he neared Ambledown, Wendover turned in his driving-seat and cast a regretful glance at the mass of books and papers which overspread the rear space of his car. The last load! Earlier consignments had been transported in one of the estate farm-carts, but to-day he was using his car for official business and it might as well carry whatever still remained to go. Besides, he had arranged to save some petrol by killing two birds with one stone: calling at Friar's Pardon on his way to Ambledown and picking up some of Collingbourne's salvage also.

For ten days or more, he had been going through his extensive library at the Grange, weeding out everything that he could bring himself to contribute to this paper salvage. It had not been a congenial task for one who loved old things even if they had long fallen out of current use. He had done his best to stifle sentimental feelings, but his library would never be the same to him hereafter, with those ugly gaps breaking the continuity of the long tiers of books which had been accumulated on the shelves by generation after generation of his forebears.

All over the district, the same thing was going on. Even that dilettante bibliophile Collingbourne had been stirred to discard some of his magpie hoard, but Wendover gave the credit for that to Collingbourne's niece who lived with him at Friar's Pardon. She seemed to have thrown herself heart and soul into this salvage affair during her holiday from her secretarial work in that confounded dynamo factory which was drawing those air-raids upon Ambledown. Where did she get the petrol for all her scurryings up and down the countryside in her car? Perhaps the W.V.S. supplied it, since in these days paper salvage was, in its way, a national service.

Wendover interrupted his speculation and turned his car off the highway through the dilapidated-looking gates which led to the drive up to Friar's Pardon. The old house crowned a height; and the tree-fringed approach to it, designed to give an easy gradient to the horse-drawn carriages of an earlier age, wound upward in long undulating zigzags across the sloping lands of the estate. On either hand, there was a file of stones set up at short intervals to form a border between carriage-way and turf. But even here, in this secluded place, the influence of the war was manifest. The turf by the parkway was growing rank for lack of attention, and the stones had been roughly whitewashed to mark the breadth of the road for the benefit of anyone driving in the black-out.

As he drew near the house, Wendover's curiosity was aroused as he glanced to the right of the carriage-way. A whole series of small plots of ground had been outlined by streaks of whitewash and fenced off by wire, evidently to protect them from grazing animals. What fresh hobby was this which had captured Collingbourne's inconstant fancy? Wendover shrugged his shoulders in tolerant contempt. Though he had been acquainted with Collingbourne for years, he had never "taken to him." What could one make of a creature like that, always dashing from one whim to another, dropping out of one wild-goose chase merely to join a fresh one, a man smitten with the Curse of Reuben? The only hobby which had ever held his attention for long was this one of collecting books and manuscripts and even in that field, Wendover shrewdly guessed, Collingbourne's dealings were more extensive than profound. And every one of these fads cost money. The man must be feeling the pinch nowadays, with this war taxation. High time for him to draw in his horns and show some common sense.

The car rounded the last bend in the avenue and came out on the wide gravel sweep before the house. Originally, Friar's Pardon had been a long, low, two-storied building, not unpleasing in its design, but now it was thrown completely out of balance by an extension built on to the western end: a square squat tower surmounted by a dome which housed a telescope and rose higher than roof-level. Another "folly," Wendover reflected; but it could not be imputed to Collingbourne. His father had erected it. All the family seemed alike feckless.

Wendover drew up his car before a portico, in the shelter of which he saw a pile of books and packages evidently intended for the salvage collection. A smartly-dressed, good-looking maid appeared in answer to his ring.

"Mr. Wendover?" she asked, pertly, looking this stranger up and down with frank curiosity. "Miss Diana's expectin' you. She'll be 'ere in a minute or two, an' Mr. Collingbourne said would you just step inside an' 'ave a chat with 'im w'ile she gets 'erself ready."

Unceremoniously she stepped past the visitor and glanced into the car.

"You've got a tidy bunch already," she commented. "But don't you worry. There'll be room enough for our little lot 'ere. Plenty."

Her vowels betrayed her origin more clearly than her missing aitches.

"You come from London, don't you?" asked Wendover, pleasantly.

She was not the type of maid he employed at the Grange, but he liked to put people at their ease, and her unstudied familiarity was so natural that it amused him. Evidently she was one of those girls whose most salient characteristic was inquisitiveness.

"Yuss! Evacuee. I 'ad enough of the bombing, after a bit. You should see our street at 'ome, Mr. Wendover. Coo! This is a dead-alive 'ole after London, but anythin' for a quiet life, nowadays. No panic, 'ereabouts, except you goes to the pitchers in Ambledown. By the w'y, that was a bit of a Brock's Benefit there, last night. I was watchin' the newsreel when they began to come down . . . But I'm forgettin', lettin' my tongue run on like this, with Mr. Collingbourne waitin' for you. Will you step this way?"

She led Wendover along the hall and ushered him into a big roomy study.

"Mr. Wendover's come, Mr. Collingbourne."

A tall, heavily-built, rather stupid-looking man rose from an armchair. He did not come forward to greet Wendover, but stood peering uncertainly in the direction of the visitor. Evidently Collingbourne's sight had degenerated markedly since the last time Wendover had met him, a few months earlier.

"Good morning, Collingbourne. How are the eyes?"

"Oh, pretty bad, nowadays, pretty bad," explained the host, making a vague motion of his hand towards a chair and reseating himself. "I wouldn't have recognised you, if I hadn't been expecting you. Blind as a

4

bat, almost, nowadays, except when I drop atropine into my eyes, and even that's not much help."

"Can you read? That always helps to pass the time."

"Read?" said Collingbourne in his rather flat tone. "I haven't been able to make out large print for weeks, months really. There's nothing to do but sit about and think, and that's a dull business when one's cut off from all one's normal interests. It's very depressing after a while, very."

He peered in Wendover's direction, obviously too blind to see the sympathy in his visitor's face.

"It must be. But they promise you your sight will be as good as ever, after they operate," said Wendover, comfortingly. "And in the meanwhile you're free of your work as J.P. People can't come worrying you to sign papers for them. I'm flooded out with that sort of thing, nowadays, with all these new war regulations."

"But they do; they come to me still. I can manage it, if I drop in atropine to dilate my pupils. But even with that help it's hard to make head or tail of some of the forms they bring me. I really think I'll have to refuse to do it soon. One doesn't like putting one's name to some document that one can't read properly. One might be countersigning all sorts of lies, for all one can tell."

"Then I should drop it, if I were in your shoes."

"I really feel I ought to," Collingbourne admitted. "But that's not what worries me most, nowadays. It's these incendiary raids. I funk them, there's no hiding it. This house is just tinder, with all the wood in it; and if we had a fire on the premises I'd be completely helpless, now that I can hardly see farther than my nose. You've never had a fire at the Grange, have you?"

Wendover shook his head; then, remembering that

his host would probably not see the movement, he supplemented it.

"No, never."

"I've been in terror of a blaze all my life," Collingbourne confessed frankly. "When I was a child, my nursery went on fire: nurse in hysterics, wood crackling, smoke choking one, people shouting and rushing all over the place, firemen in strange uniform coming clumping in, water all over the shop, and the rest of it. Bound to make an ineffaceable impression on a youngster at the sensitive age, you know. It often comes back to me in nightmares, and sometimes, when these air-raids are on, I can't get to sleep for thinking about it. Silly, of course, you know; but that's how one's built."

"I don't wonder," said Wendover, soothingly. "But really, out here, you don't run much risk."

"I know that as well as you do," retorted Collingbourne, "but I get into a blue funk all the same. It's no good arguing about it. It just *is* so. There's that nephew of mine. He doesn't understand, just sneers at the old boy with the yellow streak and tells me not to think any more about it. As if one could help thinking about it. He suggested buying a stout rope and keeping it ready in the hall upstairs outside my bedroom, so that I could get at it and slide down from my window, if there was any trouble. Not a bad idea; so the other day I got a rope—sent in to Ambledown for it—and had a cleat fixed up for fastening it. And then, of course, he made fun of the whole thing, waxed facetious about the new Jacob's Ladder and a stout angel in pyjamas sliding down it. Oh, very funny, by his way of it— side-splitting, in fact. *He* never had the fright I got when I was a child, or he wouldn't be so cocky."

Collingbourne relapsed into silence, brooding on his grievance. He was a pathetic object, sitting slackly in his chair and gazing dully in front of him with inattentive eyes. Wendover, seeking something to divert the conversation into a new channel, glanced around the room crammed with odds and ends surviving from some of Collingbourne's discarded hobbies: a glass-fronted case holding objects which might be—but probably were not—neolithic relics, another displaying butterflies, a cabinet of old coins, a few volumes containing an abandoned philatelic collection, on the mantelpiece some Japanese *netsukés* and sword-hilts, and upon a table by one of the windows, a large binocular microscope under a glass bell. Nothing there to help; Collingbourne had lost all interest in them long ago. But as Wendover's eyes ranged over the walls, they lighted upon an oil-painting which was obviously fresh.

"Where did you get that picture over there? That one of the St. Rule's Abbey ruins, I mean."

"Oh, that!" said Collingbourne, without turning his head. "That's one of my nephew's efforts. He's taken up painting, lately. I can't see the damned thing myself, properly, of course; but Diana says it isn't bad, and she persuaded me to hang it up there. What do you think of it?"

Wendover rose from his chair and went over to examine the picture at closer range.

"Not bad, really," he reported after a thoughtful inspection. "Young Denis seems to have a touch of his own, though it's not my style. He seems to have caught the shadows in the red of the sunset pretty well."

"Colour means nothing to me, nowadays, you know," grumbled Collingbourne. "The whole world is sepia, so far as I'm concerned. I can't see any difference between a tea-rose and a geranium except for the shapes of the flowers."

"Has he dropped his astronomy? He used to have a craze for that, I remember."

"Who? Denis? No, he still potters about with that old refractor in the dome—the five-inch one my father had. He's got some bee in his bonnet about minute changes on the surface of the moon due to land-slides or something of that sort; but if you want to know anything about it you'll need to ask him, for I never could scrape up any interest in the business. He seems to make scores of drawings for comparison, and they ought to be accurate enough for there's no denying that he's clever enough in that line."

Wendover moved a step or two farther along the study and paused before something else which attracted his attention.

"What's this thing you've got hung up here?"

Collingbourne peered in his direction to see what he was examining.

"Oh, that map, you mean? Diana drew it for me, and I got it framed and hung up so that it would be handy to consult. It's an experiment I've been trying —or *was* trying, rather, before my eyes began to give out. You must have seen something of it as you came up the avenue. Didn't you notice some bits of the park fenced off?"

"Yes, but that didn't suggest much to me. I wondered what it meant."

"It's rather interesting, really," Collingbourne explained. "There are quite a number of plants in this country which never seem to spread beyond their own districts. They may be dying out, or else they don't manage to spread their seeds to a distance, or else, again, they can't multiply except on certain soils. So it occurred to me to transplant some of them here and watch the results."

"I suppose you had to bring some of their native soils with them, as a control?"

"Oh, yes, of course. It came a bit expensive to start with, but once it was done it was done."

"It *would* be expensive," agreed Wendover, dryly, as he remembered the areas which he had noticed as he drove up to the house.

"I've managed to get quite a number of them together. Fringed heath from Cornwall; some upright clover from Lizard Point; Lloydia Alpina from the Snowdon district; centaury from Newport; cut-grass— they call it *Leerzia*—from Surrey; and pipewort from Skye. The last two need water, but luckily there's a brook running down to my experimental strip. And there are other plants as well as those I've mentioned. Something's bound to come out of it all."

"I see you've turned your map into a sort of *hortus siccus* by gumming dried leaves and seeds on to the different patches."

"That was Diana's notion," explained Collingbourne. "She said it made the thing look more learned. I suppose it's her idea of a joke, for she never takes these things seriously."

Wendover glanced again at the framed map and was inclined to sympathise with Diana. The thing was just another of Collingbourne's many wild cats. In a problem of that sort, it would take years to reach definite results; and long ere that, Collingbourne would have lost interest in it and would be off on the track of something else.

"Do you get many visitors nowadays?" he asked, merely to change to a fresh subject.

Collingbourne shook his head rather despondently.

"Not many. People have stopped coming to see me, since the war. Quinton drops in now and again, but he always airs this Baconian craze of his, and I find it a bit wearisome—very. I get the other side of the argument from Pickford, that librarian in Ambledown, when he pays me a visit. He's as pro-Shakespeare as Quinton is pro-Bacon, and the two of them fight like cat and dog over it. They've made it almost a personal matter; they hate each other like poison, and yet they can't keep away from each other. Nowadays they've both taken up this old local tradition that Shakespeare lived for a time in this neighbourhood in his latter days."

"There certainly was *a* Shakespeare hereabouts at one time," interjected Wendover. "I've seen the name in an old rent-roll. But I don't suppose he was related to the Bard, except perhaps through Adam."

"Anyhow," Collingbourne continued. "Quinton is all out to prove that this specimen was a boor and a blackguard, whilst Pickford wants to make out that he was the man who wrote *Hamlet*."

"I steer clear of that subject," declared Wendover. "Are these your only callers?"

"I'm expecting an American sometime soon," Collingbourne volunteered. "He wants to look over my collection of manuscripts, it seems."

"Have you picked up anything fresh, lately?"

"Not recently. With these eyes of mine, it's growing more and more difficult to read even catalogues, and a manuscript in crabbed handwriting is beyond me altogether. Tibberton's a great loss."

"Tibberton? You mean the second-hand bookseller in Ambledown? The man who was killed in one of the raids a while ago, when he was on A.R.P. duty?"

"Yes, that's the man. He had a wonderful nose for hunting out rare books and manuscripts. I could never get him to tell me where he picked them up. On that side he was as close as an oyster. Perhaps he was afraid I might grudge him his commission and deal direct with the original sellers, though of course that never entered my mind."

"What became of Tibberton's stock after he died?" asked Wendover. "There must have been quite a lot of books in that shop of his."

"If you think you're going to pick up anything of Tibberton's," said Collingbourne, dampingly, "you're a day or two behind the fair. His executors knew nothing about books and cared less. They seem to have sold the lot to the first man who came along and made them a cash-down offer. They don't know even his name, much less his address. If I'd had my eyesight, I'd have been on the spot and might have picked up a lot of rarities from his stock; but I'm as blind as a bat nowadays, when it comes to print and manuscripts, so I put off going to the shop until the damage was done. By the time I got there, every volume was gone. They'd even sent his loose papers to the salvage collection and were trying to let the empty shop."

Wendover was about to reply when the door opened and Diana Herne appeared.

"Sorry to keep you waiting," she greeted him in an offhanded tone which expressed no regret whatever.

If he had been put to it, Wendover could hardly have said whether he liked her or not, though he had seen her often enough. When he happened to have guests of her age at the Grange, she was always ready to come across and help to entertain them, and she seemed popular enough when she came. She had outdoor tastes, could play golf or tennis rather better than the average, was a very fair shot, and, on wet days, could play a good hand at bridge. But she puzzled him. One never really knew what she was thinking about, even in her frankest moods. Those grey eyes gave nothing away, and her slightly statuesque looks had the impenetrability of marble when one attempted to see deeper than the surface. "You'd like to know, wouldn't you? But you shan't!" That was the impression she made upon Wendover. Another thing jarred on him: she was careless with her make-up. She had beautifully-cut lips; but they were on the thin side, and she evidently preferred to disguise this slight defect by a lavish application of lipstick which wholly spoiled the fine lines of her mouth.

She turned from Wendover, glanced at the hearth in which some coals were smouldering, and swung round accusingly on her uncle.

"A fire at this time of the year!"

"Well, I must keep warm," retorted Collingbourne tartly. "I get no exercise nowadays with these eyes of mine. It's no pleasure to go out, when all I could do would be to trudge up and down the avenue, seeing nothing. And one gets chilly, even in this weather, if one has nothing to do but sit about in the house."

Wendover had enough imagination to sympathise with his host. In earlier days, Collingbourne had been a great walker, delighting to get off the beaten track and roam over the countryside. That big frame needed brisk exercise to keep its blood circulating properly, and now the man was cooped up in his house, unable to venture off the road lest he should stumble on rough ground, and cut off from all the pleasures of fields and woods. No wonder that he felt the change and insisted on a fire in his study, even if it were too small to do more than yield him a moral support and not any physical warmth.

Diana glanced at her wrist-watch.

"Time we were getting along, isn't it?" she pointed out.

"Can I help you to put your stuff into my car?"

"That's all done already."

"Then we'll go."

2

THE MITCHAM LIBRARY

"How are you getting on in that dynamo factory?" asked Wendover as he drove down the undulating avenue. "You're a secretary, aren't you?"

Diana nodded.

"It's easy enough now," she explained, "easier than it was at the start, anyhow."

"I suppose it took some time to find your way about?"

"It wasn't altogether that. There are two ways of dealing with documents, you see: the filing system and the piling system. In the first of them, you put each paper into its proper file and index it; in the other, you simply pitch the documents on to a table, higgledy-piggledy as they come in, and trust to finding them somehow, if they're wanted later on. The girl before me went on the piling system, and it took a while to clear up the mess she left when she went away."

"But you've managed to get things shipshape by this time?"

"Yes. Luckily I knew something about filing systems. When Uncle's eyes began to give him trouble, he turned me loose on his collection. Such a mess! He's an old muddle-head. Everything was at sixes and sevens, and I had to start from scratch. I read up everything I could lay hands on about methods of filing and cataloguing before I began to wade through that jumble. It just shows how even the most futile occupation may prove useful in the end."

"You seem to be putting a lot of vim into this salvage work in your spare time."

"It's a foul job—physically dirty, I mean. You may have noticed that I'm not attired like the Queen of Sheba when she went to pay a call on Solomon. These are the oldest things I have in stock. You've no notion of the dust that gathers in the libraries of some of these old country houses round here. You should see my bath water after a day of it."

"I hear that you and that fellow Oakley of the Mitcham Library are hunting in couples."

"You seem to hear a lot," Diana retorted acidly. "I drive him about to examine and collect printed litter; and we come back looking like a pair of blackamoors. Very romantic, isn't it? 'Two souls with but a single thought'—salvage! Are you suggesting that his charms have overcome my maiden modesty? Or what?"

"He may be making a fool of himself over you," said Wendover, seriously.

"Not with my help. I can't see myself leaving the church-door with him under an arch of library-ladders. I'm not particular, but he's about the last person I'm likely to take a fancy to. I don't like swarthy skins. I'm not inclined to fall for a pair of Rudolph Hess eyebrows. Nor do I care for an over-sized Adam's apple

14

sticking up above a stiff collar," said Diana, cruelly. "As for his conversational style, it's so 'refined' and stilted that I couldn't think where he picked it up, until one day he let out that his favourite reading was in bound volumes of old penny novelettes which he gets in the Mitcham Library. If he had £10,000 a year, one might put up with things like these; but love in a slum on £225 per annum is not my cup of tea."

"Aren't you rather hard on him?"

"Oh, he has his points," Diana admitted. "He's very ambitious, in a grubby sort of way. He dreams dreams, apparently, and confides some of them to me: shows me round his castles in Spain when we're out hunting salvage. Very pretty—in the penny novelette style. He seems to think that if he had £5,000 a year he could buy up all the world and half of heaven as well. He's got a lot to learn, in some ways. 'I'd give almost anything, Miss Herne, to have £5,000 a year!' Free of income tax, I suppose. Really, he's rather pathetic; but a bit of a nuisance, too."

"He's not the only one who dreams dreams. Your uncle hasn't dug up the lost treasure yet, has he?" Wendover inquired without troubling to hide a certain derision in his tone.

"You mean the one that the Abbot of St. Rule's was supposed to have buried at the time of the Visitation of the Monasteries under Henry VIII? You never believed that fairy-tale, did you?" .

"One never can tell with these old traditions. Sometimes there's a substratum of truth, but it's seldom quite the kind of thing one has been expecting," declared Wendover, half seriously. "So he's given up looking for it, has he?"

"He's not done much about it since his eyes cracked

up," said Diana. "Not that it wouldn't be a good thing if he could find it, considering the state of his finances nowadays. It gives me an ache when I think of the amount of cash he's muddled away since I came to Friar's Pardon. Nowadays, when I try to make a touch, it's like squeezing blood out of a stone. I'm giving away no secrets. You must have a pretty good idea of how he stands."

Wendover nodded sympathetically.

"He's managed to inoculate someone else with this treasure mania," Diana went on, scornfully. "It seems to me most men are either children or fools."

"Who's the guinea-pig?"

"Mr. Pickford of the Mitcham Library. They're both quite moonstruck on the subject; you can't tell t'other from which, on that matter. Quite harmless, of course; but a total loss in the brain department when that topic pops up. I always pack up and leave the room when they start any chat about it. By the way, would you mind going by Smith Street? The road the buses take, you know. I want to call at a shop."

"Certainly," agreed Wendover. "Here's your factory"—he made a gesture towards the buildings—"if you happen to want to drop in for a minute. No? Then we'll go on."

A few minutes later, Diana gave a sharp exclamation of warning. "Look out! There's a new bomb-crater in the road!"

A bomb had fallen on one side of the highway, throwing a huge spurt of clay mingled with tarmac right across the road and on to the opposite pavement so that although the street was still practicable for passengers afoot it was completely blocked to any vehicular traffic.

"That must have been done in last night's raid,"

added Diana. "I went along here yesterday in the bus. You'll have to reverse and take a side-street to get past."

"Nasty place to blunder on in the black-out," Wendover commented. "Even at this time of year with the long evenings. That's what your wretched dynamo factory produces, for evidently that was what they were trying for."

"It produces aeroplane dynamos, too," retorted Diana tartly. "This is only a by-product."

Wendover ran his car back, got into the side-street, and so past the crater and back into Smith Street.

"Stop!" ordered Diana. "I won't be a minute in this shop."

Her errand did not take her long, and in a few minutes Wendover drew up before the Mitcham Library, a memorial to a former citizen of Ambledown. Wendover was one of the trustees. At the moment, the place was busier than usual, since it served as the headquarters for the local paper-salvage organisation, and a cart was at that moment being unloaded by voluntary helpers. Among them, marked out by his flaming red hair, was Diana's cousin, Fearon.

"Denis seems to be making himself useful," Wendover remarked to the girl as he nodded to Fearon.

"I persuaded him," Diana replied. "Off his own bat, he'd have done nothing. Thanks for the lift. Denis and I will unload this stuff here at the back. You needn't bother to lend a hand. I know you have some business inside with Mr. Pickford."

Wendover took the hint that he was not wanted, and, leaving his car, he went up the steps to the library door. The entrance hall was littered with parcels and packages of the salvage collection and he had some difficulty in

17

making his way to the room which the librarian used as a private office. Even when he penetrated into it, he had to pick his steps, for the floor was obstructed by piles of books and papers untidily stacked, and evidently awaiting examination.

Pickford was a fussy, worried-looking little man in his fifties, with a drooping mouth and a querulous voice which suggested that he had a grievance against the world in general without having the vigour to react against it. His grizzled hair was rumpled, his clothes unbrushed, his tie askew, his hands and shirt-cuffs soiled with dust from the books. He seemed to have no order or system in his work, yet somehow he managed to find his way through the chaos which his methods created. He had a genuine knowledge of books: rarities, old editions, book-prices current, and binding-costs, which redeemed his more obvious faults; and, though no scholar, he had an enthusiasm for Shakespeare which put him above the level of a mere library hack.

Pickford acted as secretary to the trustees, and Wendover had come to make an inquiry about some matter which was on the agenda for that afternoon's meeting. This point settled, he glanced at the disorderly stacks which encumbered the floor.

"Have you made any find amongst all this stuff?" he asked. "Anything worth keeping?"

"More than I expected; people seem to know nothing and care nothing about what they have in their libraries. That's their look-out, of course; if they don't bother to learn, we're quite entitled to snap up anything they let us take away. There are five volumes of the first edition of Gibbon's *Decline and Fall* over there; pity the third volume was missing. I found an Elzevir edition of Livy, too, 1652; and a first edition of *The Wind in the*

Willows. Then there's something I must consult the trustees about: the first bound edition of the *Pickwick Papers*—I thought of suggesting it should be handed over to the Dickens Museum. And we found a copy of a limited edition—250 copies—of Lucian's *True History*; but I haven't had time to look it up, yet. The best thing so far has been a copy of Boccaccio's *Amorous Fiametta*, translated by Bartholomew Yong in 1587. I know of only four other copies supposed to be in existence. But that needs checking; it's not the Navarre Society reprint, at any rate."

"Mr. Collingbourne tells me that you've got all the loose papers from Tibberton's shop. Anything interesting among them? According to Mr. Collingbourne, Tibberton was very sharp in the book-finding line."

Pickford seemed to consider for a moment before answering.

"No," he said finally. "I've got nothing of Tibberton's that would be worth showing you. The papers we got from his executor were mostly old accounts and back correspondence, not worth the saving, except for salvage. I was rather disappointed to tell you the truth. I expected something better from his stuff."

"Is Mr. Quinton giving you a hand with this business?" asked Wendover.

"He is *not*," said Pickford with undisguised acerbity. "I have enough worry on my hands already with this salvage affair without having Mr. Quinton at my elbow all day long, talking and talking about his silly Baconian notions. He offered his help and I refused it. I'm bothered to death as it is, lest I let anything really valuable get past me; and I simply couldn't stand a lot of Baconian chatter on top of that! All this 'Hang hog' rubbish! I'm sorry to seem knaggy, Mr. Wendover, but I've got so much on my hands just now that it would try the patience of Job. And there's this meeting of trustees coming on this afternoon . . ."

"Well, I mustn't detain you," said Wendover hastily. "I'll leave you to get on with your work."

As he walked out to his car, he could not keep his thoughts from dwelling on Pickford. Poor devil! No wonder he was worried. Wendover never sought to hear gossip, but he was that type of sympathetic man to whom gossip comes even against his will. And Pickford's private affairs were almost common property. What could the man have expected when he married that wife of his, a young termagant of half his age, ready to throw her handkerchief at any man who gave her a glance. A thoroughly bad lot!

3

THE GARAGE

THE enemy had been paying some attention to Ambledown in the previous day or two, and Miles Bartram was—as he put it—"damn well fed to the teeth with them" when the Alert sounded and he had to don his steel helmet and air-raid warden's coat before going out on duty.

He had had a heavy day of it, ending with an un-necessary trip with his lorry to Trendon and back, because some fool had forgotten to include a bale of castings in the previous load. As a result, he had reached home with a smouldering grievance which was accentuated by the meagreness and quality of the rations which awaited him there. And then, while he was having a quiet pipe and drowsing over the newspaper, the Alert had sounded at ten to nine calling him out on duty when he ought to have been in bed, trying to make up the sleep he had lost in the last couple of nights. "England expects . . ." of course; and so far as he was concerned she would not be let down. Still . . . Then his normal good-temper came into the ascendant. It might have been worse. It was a summer evening with the sky still all aglow with red and gold in the west. If it had been winter-time, he might have been trudging through snow and slush, chilled to the bone.

The raid was a brief one, hardly more than a tip-and-run affair. Bartram stolidly made his patrol, ordering a few venturesome people to get under cover, taking shelter himself for some moments during a burst of machine-gun fire, noting the fall of a couple of bombs which seemed as if they might drop in his district, and keeping a sharp look-out for incendiaries. In about half an hour, it was over, and the drone of the All Clear told him that the raiders had gone. On his way home he made a conscientious search of the gardens and yards to which he was able to gain access lest any suspicious objects had been dropped by the raiders. He found none.

Incendiaries were the things which worried Bartram most. In an earlier raid, he had encountered a time-bomb, and since then he had ruminated on the possibility of a delayed-action incendiary—something which would show no activity at the moment of impact, but which would blaze up some hours later when precautions had been relaxed and the wardens had gone off duty.

As he turned into Goodman's Row, this notion of a delayed-action incendiary recurred to his mind. Say that a thing of that sort fell through the roof of an empty house, it would not be spotted until the fire raised by it had taken a firm hold. And suddenly, farther down the row, his eye caught just the kind of building he was thinking about: a small one-storied brick shed which served as a garage for somebody's car. It had no windows in its walls and was lighted by a skylight in the roof. The very place where a delayed-action incendiary might fall without attracting notice, and from which a fire, once kindled, might easily spread to the adjoining property.

As he approached it seemed innocent enough and he felt inclined not to bother about it, but to go straight home. Still . . . one never knew! If he did not take a look at it now very likely he would begin to worry about it as soon as he got into bed. Better to be on the safe side and spare himself anxiety later on.

He crossed the street and went up to the door of the shed.

"Anybody here?" he demanded loudly.

No answer from inside the shed. He sniffed once or twice: no odour of a burning fuse came to his nostrils. A false alarm, evidently. His imagination had run away with him. Half ashamed, he knocked heavily on the door and, getting no reply, he was about to turn away when, almost without thinking, he tried the handle and found the door give. There was a Yale keyhole alongside the door handle. Apparently someone had pressed up the catch inside and had forgotten to bring the lock into action again on leaving the place.

Involuntarily, he turned the handle and pushed that section of the running door open. Since he could make an entrance, he might as well satisfy himself about the safety of the premises. He stepped inside and found himself between the wall of the shed and the body of a car. A jack and some tools were scattered on the floor just in front of them. Then he raised his eyes and halted, transfixed.

Over the roof of the car, a face stared at him, a horrible bluish-skinned thing with a protruding tongue which seemed to mock him. The head was awry on the neck, and its sidelong tilt suggested some ghastly coyness, a macabre ogling at the intruder. Bartram's glance passed upward to the rope which rose to a cross-beam above, over which it ran. A puff of air drifted through the open door, and the head swung gently, pendulum-like.

In the course of the raids on Ambledown the warden had more than once seen death in forms far more shocking than this which faced him now. A momentary pause of surprise, and then he stepped gingerly over the scattered tools and passed along to the back of the car so as to get a view of the body.

Should he cut it down? He decided against that after a swift consideration. Artificial respiration was the only thing he could try if he did cut the body down, and Bartram distrusted his own ability in that line. Quite likely he'd bungle it. Still . . . he'd like to feel sure the fellow was really dead. He felt one of the hands. It seemed to be hardly up to normal temperature, but that was not very convincing. Then he thought of the iris, and taking out his flash-lamp, he held it close to the eyes of the dead man. The pupils remained unaffected and to him that seemed a fairly sound proof of death.

"Better leave him alone," Bartram reflected.

Then another consideration crossed his mind and turned the scale definitely. In his leisure hours, Bartram was an eager reader of detective stories, and from his studies he had acquired an exaggerated respect for Clues. (He spoke of them with such reverence that a listener

could detect the capital letter without any difficulty.)
Never risk destroying a Clue! Stupid people, ignorant
people, thoughtless people—these came blundering in and
perhaps obliterated some Essential Clue without having
even enough sense to realise the damage they were doing.
Never tamper with anything on the scene of a crime; that
was the golden rule for the layman. Leave it all to the
police. It was up to them, after they got the office. No,
it wasn't his job to butt in and mess things up; that
was clear. His duty was to lodge information, and be
quick about it. He retreated past the car, closed the
door-flap behind him, and set off at a run in search of a
constable.

He had not far to go. Almost as soon as he got out
of the garage, he saw Constable Fleming crossing the
end of Goodman's Row, and pursued him, shouting to
attract attention.

"That garage down there," panted Bartram as he
overtook his quarry. "A man's hung himself in it!"

Constable Fleming was a man of few words who
prided himself on never betraying surprise. When he
encountered a novelty, he invariably reacted in three
stages. First came a show of mild incredulity; then
followed a pause for reflection; and at last came action.
He treated this situation according to his normal method.

"Is that so?" he responded in a tone which suggested
courteous scepticism.

Then after a moment's rumination he added:

"Umph!"

This monosyllable was one of Fleming's idiosyncrasies.
It committed him to nothing. It gave him time to think.
It exercised a damping effect upon an excited witness.
And it could be voiced in so may different tones that it
served in almost any circumstances.

Finally, he ejaculated, "Come on!" and began to run towards the shed, with the air-raid warden at his heels.

On reaching the garage, Constable Fleming unceremoniously pushed open its door and picked his way to the back of the car, avoiding the litter which obstructed the restricted passage-way: a low wooden stool against the whitewashed wall, some scattered bricks, a car-jack, an empty petrol-tin. On the end wall, behind the body, were shelves bearing tins of grease and oil, a portable foot-pump, an electrical battery-charger, dusters, and other odds and ends which accumulate in a garage. A short pair of folding steps, with four treads, had evidently served to reach the higher shelves, but now lay upset on the concrete floor. Fleming examined the body and made a jotting in his notebook.

"Things just as you left them?" he demanded from Bartram, who gave an affirmative nod.

"Umph! His feet are three feet off the ground. He must have made his noose in the rope, flung it over that beam, and then tied the end to the car bumper. Then he could climb the steps, put his head in the noose, and kick the steps away. Suicide. Plain as the nose on your face. But why did he do it? Who is he?"

Bartram shook his head.

"I never saw him before; don't know him from Adam. I didn't search his pockets. I just went straight off to get hold of you."

"What are you pawing me for?" asked Fleming, crossly. "Can't you see I'm busy?"

"I was just trying to brush some whitewash off your tunic," explained Bartram, apologetically. "You must have rubbed your shoulder against the wall as you went by."

"Umph! All right!" said Fleming, ungraciously.

He squeezed himself between the body and the shelves.

"I wasn't the only one," he grumbled. "This fellow rubbed against the wall too. There's quite a patch of whitewash on his coat—right across the shoulders."

He came round to the front of the body again and lifted one of the wrists.

"No pulse that I can feel," he reported after a minute or so. "Looks dead enough. Still, we can't take chances. We'll have to cut him down and try artificial respiration. Umph! See any paper or sacking or anything of that sort about the place? Something to put on the floor before we lay him out flat?"

Bartram saw nothing suitable on the floor or on the shelves, and was about to say so when, glancing through the car window, he noticed, thrown down on the back seat, an open newspaper.

"This might do," he suggested, opening the door and picking up the paper.

"It'll have to," grunted Fleming, taking the sheets and spreading them out on a clear space of the floor. "Not big enough, but we've got nothing else. Now I'll hold him steady and you can cut the rope. Here's a knife. Cut about six inches above the knot. You'll need to get up on these steps to do it."

They laid out the body on the newspaper. Then Fleming scribbled a note on a page of his notebook which he tore out and handed to his assistant.

"Run and ring up the station—here's the number. Ask for Inspector Loxton, if he's in. Tell him about this business and say I'm in charge—Fleming. Then you'd better come back here. He'll want to speak to you when he comes. Go on, now. The nearest callbox is in Brent Street. And, by the way, you'd better tell them the number of the car while you're at it; then they can look up the owner. Go on. I'll try artificial respiration now. Not that it looks like a dog's chance."

Bartram set off at once, eager to have something to do. Fleming, left alone, loosened the noose about the dead man's neck without untying the knots, and then set about his attempt at resuscitation. He was still unsuccessfully engaged in this when Bartram returned, breathless, from his errand. Almost immediately after, a police car drew up before the garage and several people got out. A couple of constables were left outside, posted at the door to keep away the little group of neighbours who, now the raid was over, had come out to look round and had been attracted by the sight of the uniformed men in the police car. Inspector Loxton, followed by the police surgeon, came into the garage and closed the door behind them.

Inspector Loxton was a tall lean-faced man, with deep-set eyes and not a superfluous ounce of flesh on his body. His habitual air of gloom and boredom suggested—wholly deceptively—that he suffered acutely from dyspepsia and took not the slightest interest in things about him, an impression which was intensified by his deep, toneless voice. He acknowledged Fleming's presence by a curt nod. The inspector was not loved by his subordinates; he had no gift of friendliness. Nor was he hated by them, for he was invariably ready to give credit where credit was due and was ever fair—but no more than fair—to delinquents.

"You can drop that," he said to Fleming, who was still toiling at his attempted resuscitation. "Dr. Massinger will examine the body now."

Fleming rose to his feet and made way for the doctor. Loxton turned to Bartram and took out a notebook.

"You're the man who found him? Tell me about it."

Bartram was not a bad witness. He told his story succinctly whilst the inspector occasionally jotted down a note.

"That'll do for the present," Loxton informed him when he had finished his tale. "You can go now. We'll need you again—to-morrow. You'll hear from us. Good night."

The intonation of the last word was enough to show Bartram that his hopes of seeing detectives actually at work were vain. Rather reluctantly, he took his departure. Meanwhile, the police surgeon had finished his preliminary examination of the body. Loxton turned to him with a glance of inquiry.

"He seems to me dead as a door-nail, but one never can tell in a case like this," said the doctor. "You'd better go on with artificial respiration, on the off chance. Keep it up for an hour."

Fleming stepped forward, but Loxton checked him with a gesture.

"Not you; you've had your whack. Get one of the two at the door to relieve you."

He turned back to the doctor.

"Can you tell when he died?"

"If he *is* dead, he must have died within the last couple of hours or so. If he doesn't come round in an hour, you can inform the coroner and put him in the mortuary. I'll send in a report. That's all I can do for you at the moment, so there's no point in my hanging about here, is there?"

"None that I can see," said the inspector, tersely. "Good night, Doctor."

When the police surgeon had gone, Loxton called on Fleming for an account of his share in the discovery, to which he listened without interruption. At the end he put a question.

"Why did you cut him down? Any grounds for supposing he was still alive?"

"No, sir. But he might have been, for all I knew, and I thought I'd better give him all the chances."

Loxton's only comment was non-committal in both words and tone.

"Just so."

Then he added, after a pause:

"I've rung up Professor Dundas. He was out at dinner somewhere. They're to get hold of him. He'll be here, by and by. No doubt he'd have preferred to see things just as they were."

"I'm sorry, sir, but——"

"Just so. I don't say you're wrong. After all, the fellow may come round even yet. That would be a feather in your cap. Meanwhile, since he's been shifted, we may as well have a look over him. Go through his pockets. That can do no harm."

With the help of Fleming and the other constable, Loxton made a careful search of the body's clothes. The first thing which came to light was an identity card in a transparent cover.

"George Pickford, 23 Laurel Grove," the inspector read out. "That's not far from here. Pickford . . . Isn't that the name of the librarian at the Mitcham Memorial? I never met him. Either of you two recognise him? No? Well, it's a start, anyhow. Look in the door-pockets of the car, Fleming, and see if you can find a driving-licence or an insurance certificate."

Fleming went through the car-pockets but found neither of these documents.

"Probably the car's laid up," commented Loxton, "and the owner has his papers at home."

The only other thing of interest on the body was a

key-ring carrying half a dozen keys of the Yale type, and by trial Loxton was able to identify in turn the key of the garage, the key of the car, the ignition-key. Another looked like the key of a door, and there was a small flat one which might be that of a desk.

Loxton then turned his attention to the garage. The bricks and the jack suggested that somebody had set out to jack up the car and had been interrupted or had abandoned the task before it was well begun. The electric light had not been switched on; but in the earlier evening there would have been enough illumination from the skylight to make artificial light unnecessary. It was now deepening dusk, and the inspector switched on the single lamp which lit the place; then, recollecting the unobscured skylight, he switched off again on account of the black-out. But while the light was on he had noticed some marks on the garage floor which he now began to examine with the help of his torch.

They were, apparently, footprints made by someone who had stepped on some clay on his way to the garage, and as the clay was still moist they evidently were quite recently made. They did not outline the whole foot, so Loxton was unable to guess even at the size of boot which had made them. In any case, they could wait. Professor Dundas would be all over them, Loxton reflected. Deliver a full-dress lecture on them, no doubt. Better let him tackle that job.

The thought of Dundas made the inspector glance at his watch. The expert could not arrive for a while yet; he had to be found and notified, and then it would take him some time to drive over from Trendon to Ambledown. Laurel Grove was only a five minutes' walk. Loxton decided to fill in the time before the arrival of Dundas by paying a call at No. 23. The news would have to be broken to the man's family sometime, and the sooner the better. He gave some instructions to his subordinates about putting a tarpaulin over the skylight so that the electric light could be used, and then he set out on his errand.

4

MAY PICKFORD

INSPECTOR LOXTON had never been gifted with much sympathetic imagination, and during his career he had broken bad news so often that he had become almost wholly dulled to the emotional aspect of the procedure. Breaking bad news was just a job like any other: nothing to worry about in advance. So as he walked to Laurel Grove the inspector neither hurried nor dawdled reluctantly. Nor did he lose himself in speculation over the motives which had led a grizzled little man of fifty to go into a garage and hang himself. There would be time enough for that when more facts were available; at present there were too few data to make it worth while to spend time over conjectures. Loxton put the problem out of his mind and turned his thoughts to his springer puppy which was down with distemper and needed nursing. Filthy business, a dog with distemper. Smelly, too.

The inspector turned into Laurel Grove, a straight, drab road which bore the stamp of some long-dead speculative builder who had repeated the same dreary house-design again and again to save himself the expense of fresh plans. On either hand stretched a vista of semi-detached dwellings, each identical with its neighbours.

The two little houses in each block were mirror-images of each other, with entrances at opposite ends, and in front of each was a rectangular garden-plot too small to hold a garage.

The iron gate of No. 23 creaked shrilly for lack of oil as Loxton pushed it open. Catmint borders had been allowed to straggle untidily over the short path which led to the front-door steps. On the left was a patch of grass which should have been mown at least a month earlier. The only visible flowering plants were a few perennials which had survived, untended, from previous years. Evidently the householders took but little interest in their surroundings.

The inspector switched on his torch and mounted the steps to the front door. They, at least, were clean, he noted as he stood waiting for an answer to his ring—not a footmark on them. The house was too small to suggest a maidservant; probably a charwoman came in to do the rough work, Loxton guessed. She would be gone, long ago; and when the door opened he would be confronted by Mrs. Pickford, if there was a Mrs. Pickford. He would have to start his explanations on the doorstep. He hoped he wouldn't have a middle-aged woman in hysterics on his hands, attracting the attention of passers-by. That had happened to him before, and even the memory was unpleasant. There might even be children.

A few light steps sounded inside the house, and then the door was opened by a woman whom he could see only dimly, since she had switched off the hall-lamp on her way to answer the bell.

"I'm Inspector Loxton . . ."

"Oh! Is there something wrong with our black-out? I'm sorry," answered a pleasant voice which surprised him by its youthfulness. "Will you please come in and let me see what's wrong? We really are very careful, usually."

Judging from the voice, Loxton inferred that Pickford's daughter had come to the door. She stood aside with a gesture inviting him to enter, closed the door after him, and then switched on the hall-light. With another gesture she led the way into the room from which she had come, where an electric reading-lamp still burned beside an easy-chair. Loxton found himself facing a tall, dark-haired graceful girl, not more than twenty-five, he guessed, with a curiously attractive welcoming smile which showed beautiful teeth. She did not get her looks from her father, Loxton reflected.

"There's nothing the matter with your black-out," Loxton hastened to explain. "It's your father. I'm sorry to tell you that he's had a mishap, Miss Pickford."

The girl's lips lost their original friendly expression.

"I'm *Mrs.* Pickford—Mrs. May Pickford," she corrected him, rather sharply. "What's happened to my husband?"

Loxton felt that he had put his foot in it.

"He's had a mishap."

"Don't repeat things like a parrot," snapped the girl. "What kind of mishap? Was he hurt in the raid? Or knocked down by a car? He was always a jay-walker. I've told him so dozens of times, but he paid no heed. Where is he? In hospital?"

"He's been looked after," explained Loxton, diplomatically.

One load was off his mind: there would be no hysterics with this girl. Her tone suggested vexation or resentment rather than anxiety. No great acumen was needed to guess that she and her husband were not infatuated with each other, and that she had a temper.

33

Loxton glanced round the dingy room, more like a library than a woman's drawing-room, with untidy bookshelves and a closed roll-top desk in one corner. Not a flower anywhere. Shabby armchairs which advertised by their looks that they had been inexpensive even when new. One of them, beside the reading-lamp, had an open book on its seat. Facing it was a second armchair, on the arm of which was an ash-tray with ash and a couple of cigarette-stubs in it. The inspector recalled that he had found no cigarette-case on Pickford's body when he searched it, nor any pipe. What a cheerless setting, he mused, for a woman like this: young, good-looking above the average, and gifted with a certain charm. Sheer waste! No great wonder if things did not run smoothly in such a *ménage*.

He turned his eyes back to the girl again. Evidently she knew what suited her, and she could carry the outfit well when she had bought it. This thing she had on now looked simple, but the inspector could recognise expensive simplicity when he saw it. It must have cost her a fair penny. But, to his taste, she spoiled the effect by wearing too much cheap jewellery: elaborate ear-rings, a diamond clip on her dress, a jewelled wrist-watch, and —yes—a sapphire and diamond marquise ring as a keeper to her wedding-ring and two other rings on her right hand. Synthetic stuff, no doubt. They did that kind of thing very well nowadays. But a girl with her face and figure might have been content to rely on her natural gifts and not to compete with a jeweller's shop-window.

May Pickford made a gesture of impatience, as though resenting the inspector's deliberate survey.

"What's happened?" she demanded sharply. "Was he drunk?"

34

Both words and tone were enough to show Loxton that further equivocation was needless.

"We found him hanging in a garage in Goodman's Row," he answered with equal curtness.

"Ah!"

Loxton tried to interpret the intonation which she gave to that long-drawn-out monosyllable. Assuredly it betrayed not a trace of regret. Surprise was in it, perhaps; a certain relief, also. But the main component was something else: a note of perplexity was there as well. And her eyes seemed to lend further evidence. Loxton got the impression that she was not thinking of the news itself but of some problem which had flashed into her mind when she heard his message. The inspector could not guess what this might be, but it evidently preoccupied her completely for a moment or two. Then, recovering herself, she stared Loxton straight in the face.

"I suppose you've come to ask questions?"

The inspector nodded, still puzzled by that queer interval of introspection. Evidently there was something behind all this, if he could but get down to the root of things. She seemed to have been sobered, anyhow, for she appeared to have forgotten her show of ill-temper completely. Perhaps a few questions would elicit the thing which was puzzling her. He pulled out his notebook and assumed his official air.

"When did your husband come home this evening?"

"About a quarter past six, just as usual. We had supper at seven. It's our ordinary time."

"What did he talk about after he came in?"

"We never talked much to each other. I don't remember him saying anything special."

"You had no disagreement? Nothing which might have put him off his balance?"

"Nothing that I can remember."

"Did he seem depressed about anything?"

"I noticed nothing out of the common. He always made a long face over everything. No, I didn't see anything unusual in his manner."

"When did he leave the house after supper?"

May Pickford considered for a moment.

"I can't tell you to a minute. It would be about a quarter past eight, I think. He went out without saying anything to me, but I heard him close the front door."

"Had you expected him to go out?"

"Yes, I did, for he mentioned—not this evening— that to-night he was going to lay up our car. We haven't used it for months and he was getting fussy about leaving the weight on the tyres, since there's no chance of our getting any more petrol so long as the war lasts."

"Were you dressed like this at supper-time?"

"Of course not," she retorted with a flash of contempt. "I had to wash up the supper-things. I had an old dress on."

Loxton had a mental vision of that supper-table. On one side of it that shabby, grizzled little man; on the other, this girl young enough to be his daughter, wearing an old dress. A conversation reduced to the merest commonplaces with long gaps of silence between the dull remarks. And so it must have gone on, day after day, week after week. Under his official mask he could not help being sorry for the girl. What a life! They could hardly have one interest in common, and financial stringency must have cramped them at every turn, judging from the look of the house.

"Then, after you had washed the supper-things, you changed into what you're wearing now?" continued Loxton.

"Yes, of course," answered the girl.

"Were you expecting a visitor this evening?" Loxton asked.

It seemed unlikely that she had gone to the trouble of decking herself with all this jewellery, merely to sit alone in that dingy house; but to his surprise she hesitated for a moment or two before answering his question, as though it required consideration. Then, as he stared pointedly at the ash-tray with the two stubs on it, she followed his gaze and apparently decided that prevarication would be useless.

"I thought someone might come in."

"Who came to see you to-night?"

This time the pause was longer. She covered it by going to the mantelpiece and taking a cigarette which she lighted while weighing her answer.

"It was Mr. Oakley, my husband's assistant at the library."

"When did you expect your husband back? It doesn't take long to jack up a car."

An expression of disgust flitted for a moment across the girl's face.

"No, it doesn't, of course. But when he goes out at night he generally finishes the evening in some hotel bar and comes home only after closing-time. I never expect him till fairly late."

So that was why her first thought had been that Pickford might have been drunk, reflected the inspector.

"Did Mr. Oakley come here to see your husband on business?"

"He asked if he was in," Mrs. Pickford replied, ambiguously.

"When did he come?"

May Pickford seemed to ponder for a moment.

"It was before the All Clear went. We were in this room when it sounded, I remember."

"When did he leave again?"

"I don't remember exactly. About half an hour before you came to the door, I think."

"About half-past ten, then. So he stayed for about an hour. You know him quite well, I suppose?"

"My husband used to bring him here at first to talk about literary things—Shakespeare and all that. That was how I came across him."

"And after that he became a family friend—I mean, he came to see you as much as to see your husband?"

"I suppose that was so," May Pickford admitted with a certain reluctance.

"To-night, for instance, he knew that he wouldn't meet your husband here?"

"Perhaps."

Her fencing was so obvious that it began to irritate the inspector. Suspicions arose in his mind which had not occurred to him before this stage. "I suppose so . . . Perhaps . . ." Why be so studiously non-committal if there was nothing to hide? It didn't look well, somehow. Struck by an idea, he glanced at the carpet, but he could see no traces of footmarks on it.

"Now tell me," he continued in a harder tone, "exactly what terms were you on with Mr. Oakley?"

He could see from her face that she understood the suggestion under the words, but instead of flashing up as he had hoped, she paused to consider her answer.

"I think he sympathised with me. Is there any harm in that? Not much wonder if he did, is there?"

Loxton realised that he had failed to force any self-betrayal out of her on the spur of the moment, whether there were grounds for it or not. Nothing was to be gained by bullying a woman of this type evidently. But his suspicion remained; she had not been clever enough to throw dust in his eyes completely. There was something behind this, if he could only get at it. Well, there were other ways of finding out things of that kind, even if some people thought they were very cool and clever. Meanwhile, he had other work to do.

"I have some keys here," he said, producing them and changing his tone with the fresh subject. "Have you any objection to my looking over his papers? They may throw some light on this affair. I'd like to go through his desk over there; and I think this Yale key will probably fit it."

May Pickford gave him permission with an indifferent gesture.

"Search it, if you like," she said. "I've no idea what's inside. He kept his papers under lock and key; and I never bothered about them."

"It may take a little time," Loxton explained. "You'd better sit down, hadn't you?"

He drew a chair before the desk and sat down, after giving her this broad hint; for he had no wish to have her looking over his shoulder. But May Pickford seemed to have no desire to hamper him. After a moment or two she evidently realised that he meant to go methodically about his task and that he was not inclined to hurry merely because she kept on her feet. She lifted the book from the armchair and seated herself, pulling at her cigarette from time to time and keeping a listless watch on the inspector's doings.

The first thing which caught Loxton's eye when he opened the desk was a row of uniform quarto volumes standing at the back. He picked up one of them and found, as he half-expected from the look of them, that it was part of a diary, written in a tiny, rather crabbed hand not very easy to decipher. That might be useful he decided; but for the present it could wait until he had gone through the loose papers in the desk drawers. There were a good many of these; and as they were very untidily arranged it took him some time to skim through them, but before he had completed the task another aspect of Pickford's life lay plain. Cheque-book stubs showed that the man seemed to have wavered always on the border of solvency, with an occasional overdraft at the bank. Some letters revealed that he had got into the hands of a moneylender and was not always punctual in his payments of interest. On the other side, there was some correspondence with a lawyer concerning an estate out of which a small legacy was due to Pickford. There were no traces of personal correspondence, even with relations. Several drawers of the desk were filled with untidy piles of notes, written in Pickford's crabbed fist and dealing with literary topics which failed to interest the inspector, who replaced them after a cursory glance.

"Had he a deed-box or anything of that sort?" Loxton demanded, turning to May Pickford when he had completed his examination of the various documents.

"I never saw one. All his stuff was in that desk."

"I shall have to take these volumes with me," said Loxton, pointing to the diary. "No objection? Thanks. And I wonder if you could give me a bit of stout twine to tie them up with. They'd be awkward things to carry loose."

"I'll see if I can find some," said May Pickford, getting up without any show of zeal. "Wait a minute."

As soon as she had left the room Loxton examined the two stubs on the ash-tray and compared them with the cigarettes in the box upon the mantelpiece.

"Same brand," he noted. "And she smokes herself. H'm! Not much proof that she really had a visitor to-night. I wonder . . ."

His reflections were interrupted by May's return with some twine, and he devoted himself to making a neat parcel of the diary.

"Any objections to my putting a seal on the lock of that desk?" he inquired in a casual tone. "It'll save bother, really."

"Just as you like."

Loxton put a rough seal over the keyhole and then made a further request.

"I ought to look over the rest of the house. Just to be able to say I've done it. Any objections?"

"None, if you think it's worth while. I'll show you over it if you want to see it."

But if Loxton expected to find anything of interest in the other rooms he was disappointed. The whole house had a faint air of slovenliness, as though no one cared to keep it tidy. Evidently husband and wife used different bedrooms. In one, May Pickford's day-dress was flung down anyhow, as if she had changed in a hurry that evening; in Pickford's room, a jacket had been left slung askew on the back of a chair, as if the owner had been too lazy to put it into the wardrobe, and on the top of a tallboy lay some articles back from the laundry which no one had taken the trouble to put into the drawers. In the dining-room, though the dishes had been removed, it was plain enough that crumbs still remained on the table, and no attempt had been made to prepare for next morning's meal. Apart from those two cigarette stubs Loxton could see no trace whatever of the presence of any visitor except himself that evening.

41

When he had finished his exploration of the premises the inspector followed May Pickford down the crooked little stair to the hall, where he had left the diary.

"You'll not be bothered again to-night," he said in parting. "Meanwhile, you can get to sleep. Best thing, if you can manage it. Likely enough we'll need you as a witness to-morrow, perhaps. You may be able to remember something else before then. Good night, Mrs. Pickford."

As he passed the garden of the house adjoining Pickford's his eye was caught by a dim, crouching figure moving under its front windows and a wandering spot of light on the flower-bed.

"Here! What are you after?" Loxton demanded suspiciously, laying down his heavy parcel and pulling out his torch.

The figure straightened itself and came across the little grass plot to the hedge. A flash of Loxton's torch revealed a spick-and-span little man armed with a steel knitting-needle and a pickle-bottle holding some liquid in which small etiolated things were writhing.

"Inspector Loxton, isn't it?" queried the apparition, with a gesture of friendly recognition. "It's all right; don't worry; I'm not burgling my own house."

"Slug-hunting, eh?" returned the inspector, discarding his suspicions. "How do you come to know my name?"

"I'm not very good at faces, but I never forget the way a man walks or the sound of his voice," explained the slug-hunter, leaning over the hedge with an air of taking Loxton into his confidence. "I saw you at the police station a while ago, when my dog got lost after one of the raids. Someone told me who you were. And I spotted you to-night by your walk when you went in next door. Anything wrong there?"

"I had to leave a message."

The slug-hunter put down his pickle-bottle and leaned both arms on the hedge. Evidently he was in a conversational mood. Not an unusual phase with him, Loxton surmised from his manner.

"Ah? Didn't get your head snapped off, did you? My name's Elam, by the way. Terrible temper that girl's got—simply terrible. Not on speaking terms with the wife nowadays. Picked a quarrel over some trifle or other—I don't remember exactly what it was—some trifle or other. Pity it's dark—my garden's looking well just now. I'd like you to have seen my lupins."

"Not very pleasant neighbours, then?" asked Loxton, sympathetically.

"Pleasant? No, indeed—far from it. That's the worst of these semi-detached houses—one hears far too much from next door—our sitting-room's wall-to-wall with theirs. We don't like all the noise—we don't like it at all—we hate it, the wife and I. Often I've wondered if we couldn't get an injunction or something. Cat-and-dog, those two, just cat-and-dog. Loud voices, quarrels, broils—it goes on all the time when they're in the house together. I think he's afraid of her—she's a termagant —a real termagant. I've a suspicion he drinks more than's good for him at times."

This was the very man for the inspector's purpose, a guileless slanderer whose muddy flow of detraction might contain a pearl or two worth fishing out. Elam paused to draw breath and then continued.

"Most disagreeable to have them next door. You can tell what people are from their gardens—and their garden's a disgrace to this road. You've seen it? A downright disgrace! After all, it only needs a little trouble, and you have colour all the year round. Nothing like a bit of colour when you look out of your windows, is there? Cheers things up. And it helps to brighten the inside of the house, too. The wife says it makes all the difference—even to have a bit of gypsophila to put amongst the flowers on the dinner-table. Makes it look daintier, she thinks."

"They don't seem a very well-matched pair," suggested Loxton, stolidly pursuing scraps of information amid all the irrelevance.

"May and December," said Elam, sententiously. "May and December. Or May and October—anyhow, he must be double her age, double her age at least. Quite ill-assorted, that pair. Now the wife and I are just of an age—in fact, she's a year older than I am. And they say, too, that Pickford's got a weak heart—not at all the sort of man to marry a youngish piece like that. She's too young and too lively for him—far too young—and a bit of a flibberty-gibbet, too, if you ask me."

"Fond of men?" asked the inspector, crudely.

"Likes male society," amended Elam, with a slightly shocked air. "Let me give you a button-hole, Mr. Loxton."

"Don't trouble," said the inspector hastily.

He loathed a flower in his coat, even at weddings; but Elam would take no denial.

"No trouble at all—you're quite welcome. After all, it's something to have enough flowers to be able to give one away whenever one feels inclined. Wait a moment and I'll pick something that'll please you."

He wandered hither and thither with his dimmed torch and soon returned with a trophy.

"There! Let me fix it for you—I've got a pin here. Lupins are doing well this year—I wish you could see mine. And phlox—you can't go wrong with phlox.

Roses, sweet peas, delphiniums—always something to decorate the house with. Very pretty on the hall-table, the wife thinks. You'll like that button-hole when you see it in a proper light."

"Then I suppose the Pickfords have plenty of visitors, from what you say?" pursued Loxton, patiently.

"Oh, yes, quite a lot. I don't pry, of course. But working in the garden here, I can't help seeing them go in next door, you know. The wife sees them in the afternoons, too—coming to take that young piece for an airing when Pickford's away at the library."

"Men or women?"

"Very few women callers—hardly any, one might say. But that's not surprising, really."

"Why? Because she's a termagant?"

"Well, that may be it—partly. But my own idea's different. You see, Mr. Loxton, nobody knows much about her. She's not a local girl. No one knows where she's sprung from. Pickford brought her here one day—introduced her as his wife—first we'd heard of it—no invitations, you understand?—no wedding cake or cards. A curious affair altogether, the wife thought, and I agree with her there. The wife called on her—they didn't seem to hit it off, somehow. No doubt other people up and down the road found it the same. Don't you find bulbs difficult to get nowadays? I do. This war's cut off the Dutch supply. Tulips, gladioli, hyacinths—much scarcer than they used to be."

The inspector sourly reflected that most of the bombs had fallen near the dynamo factory. None had dropped in this district. If this little gossip had had his house knocked to bits, he'd have worried less over his wretched flowers.

"Then it's mostly men who come to call next door?"

he put in, stemming the horticultural stream of the conversation. "I suppose they drop in singly?"

"Oh, yes. Sometimes one, sometimes another. I've seen the same man come along here—week after week —and then he disappears and somebody else turns up calling. She tires of them—or they tire of her—I'm sure I don't know which it is. The only 'steadies' I've noticed are young Mr. Quinton—the rich one—gentleman farmer—you know him—out Talgarth way. He's one. And there's Oakley, the sub-librarian at the Mitcham Memorial—junior to Pickford. He used to be round here often and often."

"To-night, for instance?"

"No, I didn't see him to-night—but I was working round at the back, part of the time, so I may have missed him if he did call. But he hasn't been so regular a caller lately—there seems to have been a cooling-off or something. Just as well for him if he didn't come to-night—he'd have found her in a temper. The wife and I heard a fearful row at supper-time—her and Pickford. Most uncomfortable neighbours, they are—most unpleasant. The wife and I are all for quietness, you know, and that sort of thing—well, it's disagreeable to people like us, most distasteful. We were glad to see him go out, afterwards—a guarantee of some sort of peace, once he'd taken himself off."

"About what time was that?"

"Let's see . . . It was before that air-raid warning —a good while before that."

"The sirens went at ten to nine," prompted Loxton.

"Did they? Well, then, I'd say Pickford went out about half an hour before that—just about half an hour. Call it somewhere between a quarter and half-past eight —yes, there or thereabouts."

46

The inspector had now secured enough information for the present, and a glance at his watch reminded him that time was passing.

"I'll have to be moving on," he announced, picking up his parcel.

"Pity. I've enjoyed this little chat with you—enjoyed it very much indeed. If you're passing—any other time—I'd like you to see my garden in daylight. By the way! You don't know anything that's good for slugs? Terrible, the quantities of slugs hereabouts—ruin everything, ruin everything. I've tried every cure I can hear of, but I've come back again to the knitting-needle and the pickle-bottle with salt water in it—it's really as good as anything. Loathsome job, though—hate it. Well, good night, Mr. Loxton, good night. Any time you're passing . . ."

He returned to his pursuit of slugs.

Loxton walked towards Goodman's Row. As soon as he was out of sight in the dusk, he pulled the flower from his button-hole and dropped it thoughtfully in the gutter.

5

THE KEY OF THE FIELDS

WHEN Loxton reached the garage again, he found that the constables originally in charge had been replaced by two new men.

"Anything fresh since I left?" he demanded, laying his parcel on one of the shelves.

"He hasn't revived, sir," said one of the constables,

with a nod towards Pickford's body. "Seems to me he's growing colder."

"Better go on pumping until Professor Dundas turns up. Any word of him?"

"He phoned up the station, sir. They'd managed to get hold of him at his friend's house, and he went straight home to change and pick up some things. He may be here almost any minute, sir; he's coming over in his car from Trendon."

"Good!" said the inspector, laconically. "Anything else?"

"Nobody was seriously hurt in that collision at eight o'clock, sir: the one between the Trendon bus and a private car, near the dynamo factory. Slight affair, it turns out to have been. The car radiator's damaged and the front axle of the bus was a bit twisted. The bus passengers got off with no worse than a shaking. There's some dispute as to how the accident happened; but we've got the names of six witnesses. Here's the list; Sergeant Malpas gave it to me. Sarah Coplestone, cook at Friar's Pardon; Jacob Hare, 61 Bush Lane, Ambledown; Ray Lyons, 17 Palmer Street, Trendon; Denis Fearon, Friar's Pardon; Bill Lidgate, Archer Street, Talgarth; and a child, Margaret Mowbray, 10 Tanner's Alley, Ambledown."

"We'll have to make some inquiries," said Loxton. "What about the raid? Any damage to the factory? That's what they were after, as usual, evidently."

"Nothing serious, sir. So they say. But there's one man killed and a woman and a child rather badly hurt by bombs that fell near the factory."

"No bombs in our district?"

"None reported, yet, sir."

"Any fires?"

"A lot of small ones, sir; but they've all been put out by now. They say our fighters got one of the bombers on the way home; but that's only a rumour, so far."

"Wish we'd fried the lot," grunted Loxton, turning away to unpack his parcel.

He inspected the volumes in turn, grouping them in chronological order. Then selecting the most recent of them, he seated himself on the stool beside the car and began to go through the manuscript. The light was poor and Pickford's handwriting was crabbed, so Loxton made no attempt to read every line; he contented himself with a cursory survey, skipping when he found difficulty in deciphering a sentence and leaving it for a more minute examination later on, under better conditions. At the moment, all he wanted was a rough notion of the diary's contents. Dundas might drop in very soon and interrupt his reading.

To a mind gifted with sympathetic understanding, these volumes of Pickford's journal might have made painful reading. Quite unconsciously, their author had painted a picture of himself: a self-centred, unlikeable little man beset by troubles ever growing in number and intensity until they sapped his resistance and left him a tormented creature swept by gusts of fear, hatred, suspicion, hope deferred, and despair. But Loxton cared for none of these things. He read purely in search of facts, and the little tragedy embodied in the diary left him wholly apathetic. To the inspector, Pickford had ceased to matter as a human being and had become merely "a case" which had to be "cleared up" if possible.

Opening a volume and glancing down a page, his eye was caught by a reference to May Pickford, and he paused to read it. "May's extravagance is as bad as ever. Noticed her to-day with a new bit of artificial jewellery. Told her I could not afford trash of that sort. She broke out, as usual. Violent quarrel. Why did I ever marry such a woman?"

Further entries followed in the same strain: some chronicling petty disputes, others setting down more serious disagreements, a constant flow of bickering between two people who had lost all respect for each other and in which the man always seemed to have the worst of it.

Next there came a series of jottings from which it appeared that Pickford's finances were causing him anxiety. The war taxation had evidently hit him hard. He had been forced to use up all his little savings in paying for his wife's extravagances and he was becoming seriously embarrassed in his money affairs. He had tried to sell his car, but found no buyer owing to the petrol shortage.

Following on this came a statement that he had been forced to resort to a moneylender, Grindal, in order to tide himself over a difficulty; and apparently this had eased his position temporarily. Only temporarily, however; for shortly after this a long overdue bill seemed to have come in for dresses bought by Mrs. Pickford. Apparently it had been rendered several times, but she had managed to keep it from his knowledge until the firm threatened to take proceedings to recover its money. The payment of this account swallowed up the small credit balance he had gained by his resort to the moneylender. Evidently there had been a battle-royal between husband and wife over this incident.

Here a fresh apprehension appeared in the pages of the diary: the terror of bankruptcy. Apparently Pickford began to fear that if he went bankrupt it might affect his position at the library; and he dwelt on this possibility until he persuaded himself that he would be dismissed from his post if he failed to meet the demands of his creditors. Soon he was grasping at anything which seemed to offer a chance, no matter how faint, of pulling himself straight.

At this stage, a fresh theme appeared: the legend of the St. Rule's Treasure which local tradition declared to have been buried by the monks when Henry VIII plundered the monasteries. Loxton was an Ambledown man and had heard the tale as a child. It was part of the mythology of the countryside, handed down from generation to generation through three centuries: a piece of folk-lore with as much credibility as stories of local witchcraft and demonology. The inspector read the entry with contemptuous surprise. "Looked into a book presented to the library by old Sidworth. Curiously circumstantial account of the St. Rule's Treasure tradition. Almost convincing. Refers to an earlier book, *Annals of the Abbeys of Ambledown, Faircross, and St. Rule's*, for details. Must ask Tibberton to get me a copy if he can." Loxton raised his eyebrows as he read this. Pickford must have been touched if he took that old yarn seriously. Even if there were anything at the back of it the secret had been lost ages ago.

The air-raids had evidently begun to shake Pickford's nerves. He noted down the casualties, raid by raid, dwelt on any morbid details he could learn, and his comments betrayed only too clearly the trend of his thoughts. It was not long before he seemed to have been going in hourly terror of the next attack.

In a further entry he returned to the subject of his wife after one of their ever-recurring quarrels. "Why did I marry that woman without knowing about her previous life? And to-day she actually taunted me because, she said, she had made a bad bargain by taking me!"

A few pages later Loxton came again upon the St. Rule's Treasure. "Tibberton has managed to get me the *Annals of the Abbeys* (privately printed, 1639). A copy with margins full of curious MS. annotations, some dealing with the St. Rule's Treasure and its location. Tibberton put a higher price on the book on this account. Much too dear, but bought it." His purchase seems to have diverted Pickford from his troubles for a short time. There were several entries full of grumblings at the difficulty of deciphering the MS. notes, owing to the illegibility of the script and the way in which it was cramped in the margins of the pages.

A little farther on came a fresh name. "I wish I had never brought Quinton to my house. As if his absurd Baconian notions were not enough, May compares us continually, always to my disadvantage. His looks, his manners, his money, his dress, his personality: she harps on these things. It is unbearable."

Ere this, in the diary, there had been hints that Pickford was seeking solace in alcohol; and now came querulous complaints about the increase in the price of whisky and the difficulty of obtaining a stock to keep in his house. Apparently it was at this period that he fell into the pub-crawling practices about which Loxton had learned from May . Pickford. The worries of the librarian were keeping him awake at night, and alcohol had become necessary as a night-cap. One entry suggested that even alcohol had not been sufficient, and that he had taken to the use of some drug to put himself to sleep.

Farther on in the volume came a long reference to the death of Tibberton the bookseller during an air-raid.

Up to this point the casualties had all been among strangers; and the fact that one of his acquaintances had been killed seemed to accentuate his terrors. Thereafter, the air-raids bulked even more largely in the diary, and evidently Pickford had worked himself into such a state of mind that he was beginning to wonder if life was worth living, under such a strain. "He that cuts off twenty years of life, cuts off so many years of fearing death." Apparently the fear of fires from incendiary bombs grew in Pickford's imagination. "I might be burned alive in the night. What a death! Must buy a rope so as to be able to escape from my bedroom window if the house catches fire."

Almost immediately after this, however, Pickford made a discovery which, for a time at least, put the enemy raids almost entirely out of his mind. He had at this stage become so hard up that he had taken to betting in shillings and half-crowns, but without any marked success. One day he was without any ready money at all; he would not be able to pay his habitual evening visit to the public-house; and, final exasperation, he had been given what he regarded as a certainty for a race on the morrow. In desperation, he laid hands on a small pendant belonging to his wife and took it to the nearest pawn-shop, hoping to raise a shilling or two. "I handed it over the counter without saying anything," the diary recounted, "and to my amazement the man offered me £15 on that security. He saw my surprise, looked at the pendant more carefully and then repeated his offer, saying that was the most he was prepared to advance. I took the money and went off, trying to conceal my astonishment. If he made a blunder, that's his own look-out. But has he made a blunder? He didn't look like a man who'd advance more than a thing was worth—far from it. Very puzzling. He had a very careful look at the thing before he repeated his offer. It must be genuine."

Some further entries suggested that he was brooding over the affair and that it was troubling him more than a little.

Then came the episode of the caretaker at the library. Pickford, apparently, dismissed this man summarily for some slight fault, and Rusthall had gained a good deal of sympathy. "I hear a lot of ill-natured criticism of my action in sending Rusthall about his business. Wendover seems much put out by it and asked me to take the man back; but I refused, point-blank. It is a matter for me to settle, and I will not be dictated to by anyone. Oakley also tried to put in a word for the fellow. I refused to listen. It seems the man's wife is seriously ill. What has that got to do with the rights and wrongs of the case? Some readers have spoken to me about it. Everybody seems against me nowadays."

Close on the heels of this came a specially violent quarrel with his wife. "I questioned her about the pendant that I pawned. She was furious; I thought she was going to strike me. She says it is a bit of jewellery she inherited from her mother. Of course it is genuine! I don't believe her. Something in her manner made me suspicious, and in any case I can't trust her word. I'll take steps to find out if the rest of her things are genuine or not. She can hardly say she inherited them all, for I know some of them are quite new."

This project, however, fell through, as a later entry made clear. "I have tried to get hold of her jewellery, but she seems to be afraid of my laying hands on it and she has hidden it away somewhere or other. This makes me sure that it is genuine, like the pendant I pawned.

But where did she get all this genuine stuff? Has she been taking presents from Quinton? And from other men as well? I could believe anything about her."

Subsequent dates were occupied by jottings which merely chronicled Pickford's growing suspicions of May, without adding any actual evidence. Apparently he had deliberately picked a quarrel with Quinton over some literary point, so as to deprive the man of any excuse for paying calls at Laurel Grove. Tied as he was to the Mitcham Library during the hours when it was open, he seemed to have spent these times in tormenting his imagination with pictures of what might be happening at home during his absence; and he was evidently working himself up into a state bordering on helpless fury.

"Consulted my lawyer, Goodge, as to divorce procedure and costs. Goodge says I have no case on the evidence available. I might employ private detectives to watch the woman. But I have no money for this; it is as much as I can do to keep afloat at all, just now. My salary is all spent long before I draw it."

His financial worries seemed to have taken a turn for the worse. "Grindal is pressing me for interest on his loans. I shall have to borrow from other people, by hook or crook, to raise enough to tide me over. But where can I get it? No one seems inclined to do much for me. I hate these fair-weather friends."

At this stage, the diary became a mere stream of complaints and more complaints, showing a growing desperation, unhappiness, suspicion, and impotent rage. "Everyone is against me! Everyone!"

Then, like a flash from a lowering sky, came a sinister quotation: "The sweetest gift nature has bequeathed to us . . . is that she has left us the key of the fields."

Loxton had no difficulty in guessing which way Pickford's mind had been tending in his search for a way out of his troubles.

6

COMMON SENSE IS ALL YOU NEED

LOXTON was still brooding over the implication of Pickford's quotation when the garage door opened to admit a newcomer: a sharp-nosed, sharp-eyed, quick-moving man carrying a large leather case in his hand. With his finger between the pages of the diary to mark the place, the inspector rose from his stool and greeted the new arrival cordially.

"Good evening, Professor."

Howard Dundas held the Chair of Chemistry in Trendon University College, but for some obscure reason he disliked the title Professor. "People think all professors are Dry-as-dusts," he explained to justify his whim. "I'm not a Dry-as-dust and don't want to be mistaken for one. It's even worse to be addressed as 'Professor' *tout court*, for then some folk confuse me with a conjuror or a chiropodist. Or even a palmist, at times. I don't mind 'Dr. Dundas.' After all, I have a D.Sc. degree. But then there's the bother of explaining that I'm not a medico and can't give advice on ingrowing toe-nails. And when they hear I'm a chemist, they seem to think I wear a white apron and serve behind the counter in a druggist's shop. Troublesome, isn't it?"

Quite oblivious of having rasped Dundas's suscepti-bilities, the inspector opened the diary and pointed to the quotation.

"This seems to suggest something, Professor."

Dundas set down his leather case, took the diary, and glanced at the page.

"H'm! Montaigne, eh? So you think it's suicide? Why bother me then? The nearest medico would do all you need if this fellow hanged himself."

"I only got this diary after I'd rung you up," Loxton explained hastily. "Even now I'd feel safer if I had your opinion, Professor."

This rather grudging admission did no more than justice to Dundas, for not only had he instituted un-official courses of training at his laboratory in which local detectives could learn the application of science to their craft but he had also brought his own technical skill and knowledge to bear on some puzzling cases, and he was now a valued consultant on criminal matters in the county.

"Hedging, are you?" Dundas commented in a tone of genial contempt. "Never hedge. Either you know or you don't; there's no half-way house. Very well. Since you wish it, I'll have a look round. Though why you want me, I can't see. Common sense is all you need in these affairs. What one fool can see, another can also, if he'll take pains enough. Let's begin at ground-level."

He opened his leather case in readiness and then began a minute scrutiny of the garage floor, using a pocket torch to help him in his examination and going down on his knees at some points. After crawling hither and thither for a time he rose to his feet again and mechanically dusted his trousers.

"What do you make of these clay marks on the floor, Professor?" demanded Loxton, who had watched the attention paid to them by Dundas. "I couldn't find a decent footprint amongst the lot."

"Neither could I," Dundas assured him, blandly.

"Neither could I. We have that much in common. The clay's moist; that's all one can say at first sight."

From his case he took some little glass containers into which he transferred some of the clay from the footprints, affixing labels to each specimen as he scraped it up.

"Just pass me that stool, will you? No use getting a crick in the back if one can help it."

He planted the stool beside the car and, lifting the jack gingerly, examined it meticulously in search of fingerprints. Evidently he found none. Then, in turn, he picked up the bricks which had evidently been intended to support the car when the wheels were off the ground; but here he drew blank also, for the bricks were rough-surfaced and could have taken no prints of any value.

"Now let's have a look at these steps."

Taking a tape-measure from his case he measured the height of the top tread—four feet from the ground when the steps were opened out. Then, again using his torch, he inspected the patches of clay on the treads and took some further specimens.

"No clear prints on the steps either," the inspector ventured to comment. "Just blobs."

Dundas, who had taken a little glass apparatus from his case and gone to the garage water-tap, eyed him with owlish solemnity.

"Just as you say, blobs."

He turned again to his case and extracted from it a microscope and some slides; then he placed the microscope on one of the shelves, adjusted the mirror to catch the light, put a dab of clay on a slide, and examined it. After this he returned to his glass apparatus through which the tap water had been flowing.

"What are you doing with that, Professor?" demanded Loxton.

"Washing its face," explained Dundas with the same air of gravity.

After a time he seemed satisfied and ran something out of the glass apparatus on to a new slide which he took to the microscope and examined.

"Here!" He invited the inspector to look down the tube. "See that dark grey-brown stuff where I've put the pointer? Turn the stage of the microscope—this thing here. See it change colour—going yellowish and then coming back again as you turn the stage round? That's tourmaline. See these black objects? They suggest something you're familiar enough with on a bigger scale. Another thing, there's no sign of any fragments of vegetation, bits of leaves or blades of grass. And I could find none with my pocket-lens either. That's all I care to say just now. It's enough to suggest something; but I want to make a more careful examination in my lab. Now let's have a look at the rope."

He ignored the body and stepped over to look at the remains of the rope which still hung from the beam overhead.

"They must have meant to put a floor on top of these joists when they built this place, but they never bothered to finish the job," Dundas surmised. "Now let's see."

He put the steps in position and very carefully removed the rope from the beam, handing the cut end to the inspector to hold.

"I suppose one of your men cut him down. Had he the wit to measure how far his feet were off the ground before he started in with his knife?"

"Three feet, he said. He measured it."

"Give him a good mark for common sense. Common sense is all you need. I've said that often. Now we'll look at the other end." He examined the knot. "A clove-hitch round the bumper. That's interesting. And now what about the knot at his neck. Three grannies, one on top of the other. Anyone could tie that."

He untied the rope from the bumper of the car and handed the end to one of the constables, ordering him to take it to the other end of the garage so that the rope was stretched between him and the inspector. Dundas examined it minutely, making measurements with his tape-measure and using his pocket-lens at some points. Taking some tie-on labels from his leather case he tied them to the rope, marking each of them with a number and making a jotting in his pocket-book to correspond.

"This will need to be very carefully packed. You'd better send for a long box and some twine. I'll pack it myself. In the meanwhile we'll hang it up clear of everything with some twine at each end."

Loxton dispatched one of his men on the errand. Then he came back to find that Dundas had fixed the rope in safety and was dusting his hands.

"Well, Professor?"

"I don't know whether it's 'well' or not. It's plain murder, anyhow. You can drop your suicide notion out of mind."

The inspector was loath to give up the idea of a suicide which he had gathered from reading Pickford's diary.

"How are you going to prove that it's murder, Professor?" he demanded, with unconcealed scepticism.

"By Goddefroy's method," retorted Dundas. "I'll explain, by and by. You should have attended my lectures, Loxton, and then you'd have seen it for yourself. Common sense, you know, just common sense."

It rankled a little with Dundas that Loxton had sent his subordinates to attend the criminological courses at Trendon but had not thought it dignified to go there himself; and he was not sorry to have the chance of rubbing the point in.

"Now we'll have a look at the body," he continued. "The fellow's clothes don't seem to have been disarranged by a struggle. Pity they had to manhandle him in all that artificial respiration attempt, which hasn't done a ha'porth of good in the end. Help me to turn him face upwards, will you? By the way, he must have been sitting on that stool."

"How do you know that?"

"Because even yet you can see traces of whitewash from the wall across the shoulders of his jacket; and if you could look at your own back you'd find the match of them on your own. You were sitting on the stool and leaning back against the wall when I came in."

The inspector stripped off his jacket and examined the cloth; then he beat off the whitewash powder which had marked the fabric.

"Plain enough in your case, eh? So I looked carefully at his jacket. Most of the stuff has been brushed off when they were working at their artificial respiration, but there's a trace or two left if you look for it. I did. Just common sense. It's all you need."

He kneeled down and examined the soles of the body's shoes.

"No clay on these, not a trace," he reported, after a careful scrutiny with torch and magnifying-glass. "You'd better let me have the shoes, though, later on. Sometimes one can get things out by scraping the space between the sole and the welt. See my lectures," he added with an impish grin at the inspector.

Dundas moved farther up the body and lifted the hands, one after another, taking specimens by scraping under the nails and examining these under the microscope.

"Nothing there," he reported. "I didn't expect it since there are no signs of a struggle. That saves you the bother of looking for a murderer with a scratched face. By the way, did the police surgeon give you any estimate of the time of death? I suppose he took the temperature of the body?"

"He took it at about half-past ten," explained Loxton, "and he said death might have occurred a couple of hours or so before that. He didn't put a closer figure on it."

"Wise man! I never trust these temperature guesses. Too many factors come in for any accuracy. I'll leave him to do the swearing on that subject, so I don't need to bother taking the temperature again. Let's try something else."

Again he kneeled beside the body and sniffed delicately at its open mouth.

"You have a try, Loxton," he suggested, beckoning to the inspector.

Loxton obediently went down on his knees also and bent himself to smell in his turn.

"Alcohol?" he asked, preparing to get up again. "There's not much in that. I've been reading his diary and it makes plain enough that he was a soaker in his last days."

Dundas checked him with a gesture as he was about to rise.

"Try again. See if you spot anything else besides the alcohol. Sniff slowly and gently."

Loxton obeyed and then looked up.

"There seems to be a trace of something else," he admitted. "I don't know the smell. Something sharpish."

"Try to remember it. I can let you smell the stuff

itself another time. It's important. That's all just now. I don't suppose his neck's broken. In any case, the P.M. will fix that. We needn't worry over it to-night. Now tell me what he had in his pockets."

"It's all here," said the inspector, pointing to a neatly arranged series of objects on one of the shelves. "Handkerchief; identity card; fountain-pen; reading spectacles in case; pocket-knife; note-case with single £1 note and one ten-bob note in it; six and fivepence in silver and coppers."

"No Crœsus, evidently," commented Dundas. "Unless he had more in his note-case and the thief left this for a blind. In which case it wasn't a tramp, I imagine."

"I gathered from his diary that he was hard up," Loxton explained. "I doubt if he had any more on him than we've found."

"No cigarette-case, holder, lighter, flask, or anything of that sort?"

Loxton shook his head.

"No, it's all there—absolutely all."

Dundas pondered for a moment,

"That's interesting," he said after a moment or two. "Even suggestive. I'd have expected more than that."

He stooped down and examined the newspaper on which the body was lying.

"Where did this come from?"

"It was on the back seat of the car. We'd nothing else we could use to keep his clothes from getting soiled by the floor."

"To-day's Trendon *Telegraph*," said Dundas, musingly. "Third edition. When does that reach Ambledown, usually, Loxton?"

"About eight o'clock, most days. Never before half-past seven, Professor."

"Ah!" Dundas went off on a fresh track. "You visited his house. What sort of place is it?"

"Shabby little den," explained the inspector. "Neglected, both house and garden. His wife's twenty years younger than he was; handsome piece of goods; cool enough when she chooses; decked out with gew-gaws. I thought they were sham stuff, but some of them were real, I gather from his diary. She liked male society and led the poor little devil a dog's life. So a neighbour says, and the diary confirms that—frightful temper. He took to drink towards the end—pub-crawler."

"A suburban idyll, eh?" said Dundas. "The wife sounds like a Doll Tearsheet. What do you make of it, Loxton?"

"It looks like suicide to me, Professor," declared Loxton, stubbornly.

"Have another look, then," Dundas advised. "Common sense is all you need. But I think I said that before. It bears repeating."

He paused for a moment as if marshalling his arguments in logical sequence; then he began slowly.

"That clay on the floor is moist; therefore these prints were made quite recently. They're not old ones. There's no clay on the soles of Pickford's shoes; therefore he didn't make the prints. Ergo, two men were in this garage to-night, and one of them is dead. Pass that?"

"Nothing against it," admitted Loxton, rather grudgingly.

"Next point," went on Dundas. "We found no fingerprints. You've got all Pickford's belongings on the shelf there. I asked you if there was anything more. What I wanted to know was if you had found a pair of gloves. You hadn't. Therefore Pickford didn't handle the jack; and the man who did handle it had gloves on."

"Wearing gloves isn't a felony," objected the inspector. "And besides, the first thing a lot of motorists do before starting on any job about a car is to put on an old pair of gloves."

"True, O King! All the same, it reinforces my argument that two men were here together to-night. Now we come to this copy of the *Telegraph*, which you found on the back seat of the car. That suggests that the owner of this newspaper arrived before the other fellow, and sat down to read his paper to pass the time while he was waiting for the other chap. And this first arrival must have had a key to open the door so, as it's Pickford's garage, one may infer that Pickford was the man who came first. Further, since he sat about, instead of getting to work on the car, he must have been expecting the other chap; and the meeting had been prearranged. And, finally, since Pickford had that newspaper with him, he can't have died until after it was being sold in Ambledown. When did his wife tell you he left home?"

"About a quarter past eight."

"That seems to fit well enough. We proceed. The man with the gloves began to work at the car. Meanwhile Pickford sat on that stool, with his back against the wall, and looked on. That's plain from the patch of whitewash on the back of his jacket. Admit that?"

"Nothing against it," repeated Loxton.

"Thanks for your hearty concurrence," said Dundas ironically. "Most gratifying. Lest we should disagree on a minor point, I refrain from asserting that the person who was *not* Pickford made these clay prints on those steps when he was climbing up to throw the rope over that joist up there. It's twenty feet from the floor."

"How do you know that?" demanded Loxton. "I never saw you measure its height."

"I measured it on the rope," retorted Dundas. "One thing at a time, please. We'll come to it later. In the meanwhile, you'll note that there's no sign of a struggle. But no normal man would let a friend tie a rope round his neck and hang him up without making some slight resistance. *Ergo*, I infer that Pickford was drugged or stupefied before the operation. You tell me that he was an habitual soaker. A man of that sort isn't likely to go blotto with a couple of quick ones. If he was stupefied, it was a drug that did it, and a quick-acting one at that, I imagine. You sniffed his lips before. Have another try."

The inspector did so.

"There certainly does seem to be something there beyond whisky," he admitted glumly, as he rose to his feet again.

"A peculiar tang, eh? My guess is that it's paraldehyde. You can buy it from any druggist. It has a pretty ghastly nip, but a steady boozer would probably swallow it in whisky without a blink. As for its speed of action, I've tried most of these stuffs on myself. I once took a dose at bedtime, and before I could get my clothes off, I was knocked out. I woke up later to find myself on my bed, only half-undressed. I'm not going to bet on paraldehyde merely on the strength of the whiff I got from his lips; but tell your P.M. expert to look out for it in Pickford's stomach. It's easy to identify."

"Pickford may have administered it to himself, Professor," suggested Loxton. "I noticed in his diary that he was taking sleep-stuffs for insomnia."

Dundas shook his head sceptically.

"Paraldehyde's a liquid. If he brought it in his pocket, where's the bottle he had it in? He couldn't have dosed himself before he came here, or he'd have fallen asleep in the gutter on his way here from his house. My own idea is that the other man had a flask of doctored whisky in his pocket and invited Pickford to have a quencher before work started on the car. Afterwards, he'd take the flask away with him. That accounts for your finding nothing that would hold liquid."

"It might be so," conceded Loxton. "I'll admit you're plausible, Professor. And what comes next?"

"This 'good hempen cape,' as Swift calls it. Also a slight digression or excursus on Goddefroy's method, intended to prove that this is a case of murder and not suicide. Come over and have a look at the rope. Here's the end which was cut away from the noose. Then you see my label, marked A, tied on about 11 feet from where the noose was. Beyond that, there's a stretch of about 8½ feet, which brings you to my label marked B. Finally, another 16½ feet brings you to the end that was hitched to the bumper of the car. Like this."

He pulled a notebook from his pocket and made a rough sketch (Diagram I) which he showed to Loxton.

"Now," Dundas continued, "if you'll take my magnifying-glass and look at the stretch of 11 feet from the noose end to the label A, you'll see that the surface fibres sticking up from the rope are roughly vertical to its axis—I've drawn them roughly in that sketch so that you'll know what to look for. See that?"

Loxton examined the rope carefully and then nodded.

"Now take the next portion, 8½ feet long, between the labels A and B," Dundas directed. "You'll find that on one side of the rope the surface fibres stick up vertically as before; but on the other side they're flattened down

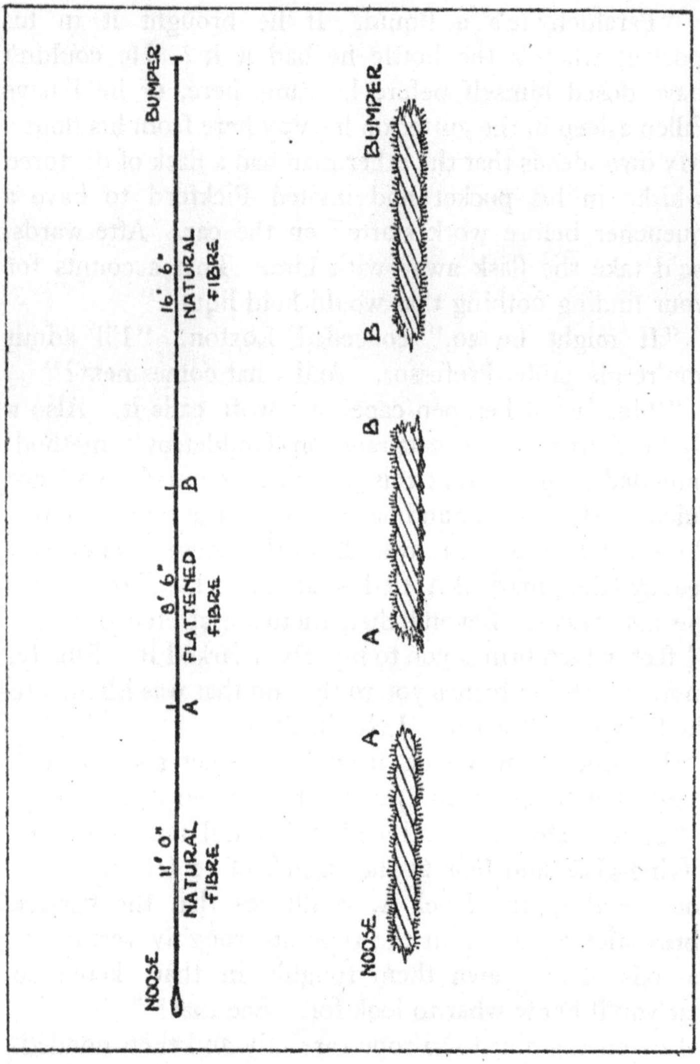
NOOSE
11' 0"
NATURAL
FIBRE
A
8' 6"
FLATTENED
FIBRE
B
16' 6"
NATURAL
FIBRE
BUMPER
NOOSE
A
A
B
B
BUMPER

DIAGRAM I

and their ends lie pointing towards the noose, as I've drawn them in the sketch. See that? Good. And lastly, if you look at the remaining 16½ feet of the rope which ran from label B to the bumper of the car, you'll see the rope fibres are all vertical again, as I've drawn them in the sketch. There's the evidence."

The inspector meticulously compared the actual rope surfaces with the sketches in the notebook.

"Yes, I see that all right," he admitted.

"Now for the interpretation," Dundas continued, taking back the notebook and making a fresh sketch. "To start with, Pickford—unconscious under a dose of narcotic—was lying flat on the floor. Mr. Not-Pickford, whoever he was, tied the rope round Pickford's neck. The rest of the rope hung over the joist up there, and the other end was loose. That's how things were at this stage. There had been no heavy friction on the rope to disturb the lie of the surface fibres in any way."

Dundas handed the notebook back to the inspector who examined the new diagram. (Diagram 2.)

"Well, go on, Professor," said Loxton, whose pretence of a lack of interest was now wearing thin.

Dundas took back the notebook and drew a final sketch. (Diagram 3.)

"Having got the noose round Pickford's neck," Dundas continued, "Mr. Not-Pickford took hold of the other end of the rope and began to haul the body off the ground until its feet were 3 feet from the floor. That meant he had to pull the rope over the joist for a distance equal to the length of Pickford's height plus 3 feet. Pickford was 5 feet 6 inches in height, so that makes 8½ feet in all. In rubbing heavily on the joist, then, a bit of the rope 8½ feet long was subjected to heavy friction; and the surface fibres of the rope in contact with the joist got

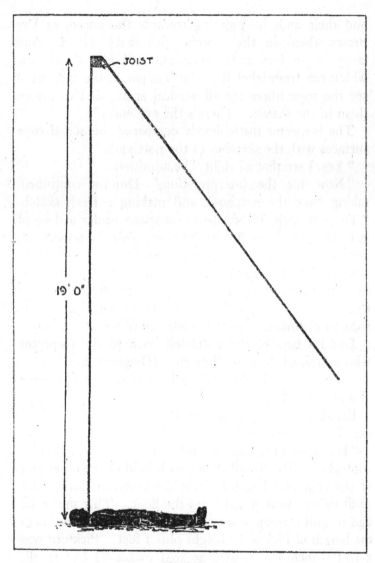

DIAGRAM 2

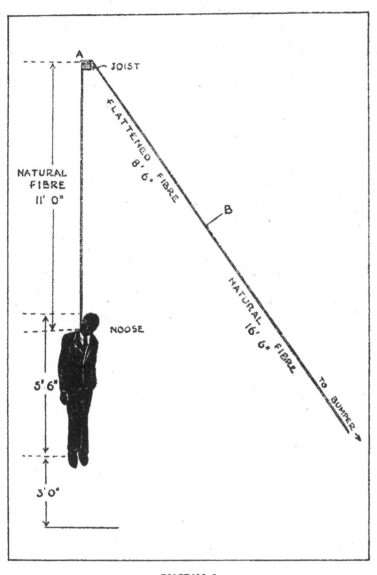

A

JOIST

FLATTENED FIBRE 8' 6"

B

NATURAL FIBRE 11' 0"

NATURAL 16' 6" FIBRE

NOOSE

TO BUMPER

5' 6"

3' 0"

DIAGRAM 3

flattened down, whilst the fibres on the other part of that bit of the rope were left unaffected, since they didn't bear on the joist. That's the section between my labels A and B. You can see the A and B in the third diagram. Then Mr. Not-Pickford hitched the rope to the bumper of the car, so as to leave Pickford hanging. Common sense, you see, Loxton. Just common sense and a pair of eyes in one's head."

"Something in that," admitted Loxton. "But what would it have looked like if Pickford had suicided?"

"Quite different. If it were a case of suicide, Pickford would have made his noose first of all. Then he'd have flung the rope over that joist and hitched the end to the car bumper so that the noose hung at a height which would allow him to stand on the steps, put his head through the noose, and kick off into Eternity. In that case, the only bit of rope where the fibres would be flattened would be the six inches actually in contact with the joist, when the weight of the body put a strain on. The state of the rope shows the absurdity of that hypothesis. Satisfied?"

Loxton gave a grudging nod.

"It sounds all right," he conceded. "What about the rope itself? Do you see anything special about it?"

"No," Dundas replied. "It's good hempen stuff. I've seen it on sale—fire-escape for people nervous about incendiary raids. Anyone could buy it. You'd better make some inquiries."

"In his diary, Pickford talked about buying a rope just for that purpose," interjected the inspector. "I'll look into the matter. But it's your murderer we want. Can you give me any tips about *him*?"

"I don't profess to be a necromancer, able to tell you he's got a squint in the left eye and a taste for cheese.

Try a crystal-gazer, if you want that sort of thing. All the evidence suggests is that he may be left-handed or ambidextrous. He might be a seafaring man."

"How do you make that out?" demanded Loxton, startled.

"The noose round Pickford's neck was made with three granny knots, one on top of the other. A left-handed man ties a granny knot differently from a right-hander like myself. His knot and mine come out as mirror-images of each other. These knots at the noose are left-handed grannies. That's as far as I care to go. As to the seafaring, if you had to tie the rope to the bumper, you'd probably make a granny or a reef knot. What the murderer used was a clove-hitch, which is what a seaman would be more likely to use. But you can lay whatever stress you like on that evidence. It seems to me a matter of opinion. I don't press it. It may be useful, once you lay hands on the man. Till then, I don't think it's going to be much help to you. You can't run about asking everyone to make granny knots and clove-hitches, just on spec."

"I'll admit you've thrown light on how the thing was done, Professor. But what we want to know is: who did it? Can't you suggest anything about that, beyond this knot business?"

"Would it be any use to you if you found the route he took on his way to this place?"

"It might help."

"Well, you've seen the evidence. Use common sense. That clay had no vegetable fibres in it. It had some black specks. I haven't had a chance to examine them thoroughly, but to the naked eye they look like bits of tarmac. What does that suggest to you?"

Loxton considered for a moment or two.

"A bomb-crater on a street?"

"Yes, with the underlying clay splashed about," amplified Dundas. "There aren't so many recent bomb-craters exactly on a street. And the clay contains tourmaline. That limits the thing further. The street's still passable to foot-traffic, or Mr. Not-Pickford wouldn't have walked past the crater and got clay on his boot. That limits it still further. Now it's your turn. Get me samples of clay from the craters in town which don't verge on to gardens but keep on the road area. When I've had a look at them, I may be able to tell you something more; for tourmaline doesn't occur all over Ambledown."

He was interrupted by the return of the constable with a long box; and for the next few minutes Dundas occupied himself in packing the rope so that there should be no further displacement of the surface fibres. When he had completed this, he put all his apparatus back into his leather case.

"Seems to me you're a bit ungrateful, Loxton," he said as he closed the case. "You were quite set on the idea that it was suicide, before I looked in. Not much credit for the police in a suicide case. Now I've proved to you that it's murder. Plenty of credit for a smart inspector if he runs down a murderer. All you have to do now is to catch Mr. Not-Pickford. Good mark waiting for you there. By the way, what's your idea of a likely motive?"

"It wasn't robbery, anyhow."

"Ah? Indeed?"

The sceptical tone nettled the inspector.

"Well, he was down and out. I know that from his diary. And there was as much money in his pockets as he was likely to own."

"You can lose other things than money," said Dundas with a return to seriousness. "I've seen a man robbed of his reputation, and if you'd put him on the scales you wouldn't have found him an ounce lighter. And once a good colleague stole an idea of mine; but if you'd gone through our pockets you'd never have found a trace of the theft. Besides, you don't *know* what he had in his pockets before the murder, so you can't tell if anything's missing now."

He picked up his case and with a farewell nod to Loxton, walked out to his car. The inspector glanced at his watch and sent one of his men to telephone for an ambulance to take the body to the mortuary. Then he seated himself on the stool and settled down to read the remainder of Pickford's diary.

7

THE REST OF THE DIARY

AFTER he had written the quotation from Montaigne in his diary. Pickford's mood seemed to change. The entries immediately after that dealt with the paper-salvage campaign and the difficulty of recruiting volunteers who knew anything about old books and their values.

"Miss Herne has been very useful," Pickford wrote. "She drives Oakley about in her car looking for salvage. She knows a good deal more about books than he does, owing to her experience with her uncle's collection. Quinton has made it up with me, and he is giving a hand, too. I believe he hopes to come across something among the salvage which will serve his absurd Baconian craze."

Owing to the extra work entailed by the salvage campaign, Pickford had less time to study his annotated edition of the *Annals of the Abbeys*, but he was still poring over it at times. Once he had taken the book to Collingbourne, hoping to draw some ideas from him; but after listening to him, Collingbourne had offered no information worth having, and had merely given him permission to visit the Abbey ruins freely.

A little later Pickford tried to pursue with Oakley the same policy as he had used in Quinton's case and, by quarrelling with him, to keep him away from the house in Laurel Grove. To his relief, however, he found that Oakley seemed less interested in May than he had been before.

"More by his manner than anything, I gathered that he has cooled off. I spoke pretty bluntly. He turned red and muttered something about 'better fish in the sea than ever came out of it.' But this may be merely to throw dust in my eyes. I don't trust either of them."

Then followed a period of depression. His financial troubles seemed to grow more acute; the dismissal of the caretaker cropped up again and made him feel his unpopularity; his relations with Oakley grew worse, apparently, till at one time the two men were barely on speaking terms; whilst to judge from some cryptic remarks, he seemed to have been reduced to embezzling trifling sums from the library funds to tide himself over immediate difficulties; and his handwriting suggested that he was not altogether sober at times when he confided his grievances to his diary.

Suddenly came a burst of optimism. His great-aunt by marriage died, and under her will he inherited a few hundred pounds. Loxton came upon an entry in the month of March.

"Saw Goodge, who was my great-aunt's solicitor. It is O.K. about my legacy. He says it will take some time to settle up the estate, but then I shall have enough in hand to pay off all my debts and start square. There will even be enough to collect evidence and divorce that miserable woman. Once quit of her and her extravagances, I shall be on an even keel so far as money matters go. Meanwhile I must tide over things temporarily till my ship actually comes home."

Thus relieved in mind, he seems to have cast back to the St. Rule's Treasure. There were several entries indicating that he was again studying his copy of the *Annals of the Abbeys*. He was still grumbling about the difficulty of deciphering the handwriting in the marginal references and conjecturing their meaning.

"*Something* is there," Pickford wrote. "That's plain enough from what I have already made out. But it is all intentionally so obscure that perhaps only a happy guess will clarify it."

He had gone to see Goodge more than once about his legacy and the possibility of a divorce; but the solicitor had put him off. It was quite a big estate; there were many legacies, of which Pickford's was one of the smallest; these things took time; and so forth. Goodge had not offered to advance any money, and the possibility of raising funds elsewhere on the strength of the legacy had apparently not occurred to Pickford. There followed some further entries dealing with his efforts to solve the riddle of the *Annals of the Abbeys*.

Then, on 15th June, in sprawling handwriting showing the trembling of intense excitement, there came a single word: "EUREKA!"

Three days later there was a cryptic entry, mentioning a talk with Oakley about something described merely as

"It." More friendly relations between the two men seemed to have been established in some way.

"I have succeeded in getting Oakley to lend me £100 to tide me over and to pay some urgent debts. But £100! Even at that, he was hard to persuade. May must have been telling him how hard-pressed I am. Some more of her unexpected bills came in on me yesterday, and we had another violent quarrel. I shall never know a moment's peace till I am rid of that woman. Oakley demanded security, and, of course, I have no security to put up nowadays. Finally, at the end of a long argument, he insisted on taking It as security for his miserable hundred. I agreed to this, but I have regretted it ever since."

At this point, Loxton interrupted his reading and tried to surmise what this valuable It could be. Clearly it was something worth more than £100, or Oakley would not have accepted it as a guarantee of repayment. More than £100? Perhaps a good deal more than that; for the amount of the loan would depend on the money Oakley had available, and he was not a rich man. He was only a sub-librarian in a small library. Rack his brains as he might, Loxton could not guess what It was. At last he gave up the problem temporarily and continued his reading of the diary, hoping to find further on an entry which would give him some plainer information.

One thing was evident: some of the borrowed £100 went in drink, for the next entry was made in handwriting which betrayed only too clearly the effect of alcohol. It was only half-legible, but at last the inspector managed to make it out.

"Have written to goldsmith to-day. Should soon have some definite idea of what It is worth."

A goldsmith? Loxton's eyebrows went up in surprise.

Had Pickford really unearthed the St. Rule's Treasure, that almost mythical hoard which had defied discovery for centuries? If he had, then one could see his reason for applying to a goldsmith. Perhaps he had abstracted some object from the cache he had discovered, and was trying to get an expert opinion as to its value. In such circumstances, naturally, he would not turn to any Ambledown tradesman, since that might lead to gossip and put other folk on the track. Hence the need for writing a letter to some non-local expert. That hypothesis seemed to cover the ground, if one assumed that Pickford had actually come upon the Treasure of St. Rule's.

But if one granted this, then what was the mysterious It which Pickford had pledged with Oakley as security for his £100 loan? A man could not carry the treasure of an abbey about in his pocket and hand it over as if he were offering a cigarette. If all the references to It had been made in the diary on a single day, Loxton would have put the whole thing down as a drunken delusion; but the repeated references seemed to exclude that. There must be something, something quite definite, behind these entries in the diary, made on different days. For a time the inspector scratched his head in vain.

"No, it beats me," he had to confess to himself at last. "Perhaps there may be something clearer farther on."

He continued his study of the diary, but he found no further mention of It, or of the St. Rule's Treasure, or of the goldsmith. The next entries chronicled a fruitless attempt on Pickford's part to find a purchaser for his car. Then he apparently decided to jack up the vehicle, for there was a lament over the state of his heart, which prevented him from doing the job himself. Evidently the borrowed £100 had flowed away in paying off pressing debts, for he obviously rejected the idea of getting help from a garage, for which he would have to pay.

The diary ended on this note, the final entry being on the day preceding Pickford's death.

Laying the volume on his knee, Loxton began to run over in his mind some of the things which he had learned since he came into the case, little more than three hours earlier. It galled him to remember how completely he had been deluded at the start. Everything—even Pickford's diary—had pointed to suicide. Even the presence of a second man in the garage would not have conflicted with this, since he might have gone away before Pickford hanged himself. Dundas, however, had proved beyond doubt that it was a murder, ingeniously disguised as *felo de se*. But the very cleverness of the camouflage indicated that the murderer knew all about Pickford's private affairs, even his domestic troubles and his state of mind. *Ergo*, the assassin must be someone well acquainted with Pickford, or May Pickford, or possibly with both of them. Initially, then, mere casual acquaintances could be left off the list of suspects.

This led the inspector to Pickford's domestic affairs. Here, the dominating factor was May Pickford with her looks, her temper, her extravagant nature, her carelessness in amassing debts, and the retinue of men whom she attracted about her: Oakley, Quinton, and more besides. Where had she come from? What was her history before she encountered Pickford? Nobody seemed to know, if one swallowed Elam's evidence. Assuredly it could hardly have been a case of love at first sight on her side of the match.

Here Loxton was led on to speculate upon possible motives for the crime. The most obvious one was that May Pickford might have wanted to get rid of her husband at almost any cost. For all one could say, *she* might have been the second person in the garage that night. Still, it was hardly the sort of murder one would expect a woman to commit, cool though she undoubtedly was. It was possible that she had used one of her paramours as an instrument—Oakley or Quinton or another of her string. Some men got so besotted with a woman that they would even commit murder to retain her favours. And she was an attractive woman, despite her temper. It was probably Quinton who had given her some, at any-rate, of that valuable jewellery which she had tried to pass off as sham; and if he spent money on her so freely, he must be keen on her.

That was how the thing looked if one assumed that May Pickford was the moving spirit in the crime. But there was another aspect: May Pickford might have had no hand in the affair, and might even be ignorant of the murderer's identity. A lover might have got rid of Pickford merely in order to set May free, so that he might have her entirely to himself.

There was a third possibility, the inspector reflected. The affair might have arisen out of the St. Rule's Treasure, and be a case of murder for profit, pure and simple. Who knew about that side of the thing? Oakley for one; Collingbourne for another. Quinton had plenty of money and so was less suspect on that side; but the other two were hard up, each in his particular social grade. The state of Collingbourne's eyesight seemed to put him out of court. The man was notoriously as blind as a bat, and could hardly have carried out a crime of this sort, with his eyes in that state. Oakley seemed more likely, if it came to a choice between the pair.

But then there was this mysterious thing which

Pickford called "It." What was "It"? Obviously something connected with the Treasure of St. Rule's; it could be nothing else. Even so, that left one pretty much where one was, unless one could get some inkling about the nature of "It"; and there was nothing in the diary which threw a clear light on the point. "It" was something portable, since Pickford had given "It" into Oakley's hands as security for this £100 loan. It might be some part of the treasure itself: a golden chalice, a jewelled crosier, or something valuable like that. Something worth a good deal more than £100 anyhow, since Oakley parted with his money on the strength of it.

That brought to Loxton's mind the reference in the diary to a goldsmith. If one could get hold of this man, Pickford's letter to him might suggest something. But how many goldsmiths were there in the country? Especially now with this gold-shortage and new gold-chandlers springing up like weeds all over the place. It might be any one of them. A pretty hopeless job, searching through all that lot. Not much to be hoped for there.

It occurred to the inspector that Oakley's name seemed to be cropping up at the end of every line of speculation which he followed. The first mention of the man had been in May Pickford's statement; and all she vouched for was that he was with her when the All Clear sounded, which was about 9.30 p.m. That did not give Oakley a clear alibi, for Pickford's death might have occurred at any time between 8 p.m. when he left home and 10 p.m. when Bartram discovered the body. But, after all, what was May Pickford's word worth? Not much, in the inspector's opinion, in view of her reputation. As for confirmatory evidence, Elam had not seen Oakley that evening, either going to or coming from Pickford's house; and the two cigarette-stubs in the ash-tray might have been put there by May Pickford herself. So there was no confirmation of her tale, whether it were true or false.

Loxton shook his head rather despondently. Not an easy case, after all. He took out his notebook and jotted down notes of the points which would have to be followed up. First of all, he could try to ferret out something more definite about May Pickford, her various cavaliers, and her career previous to her marriage. Something might come out of that. Then he could get hold of Pickford's copy of the *Annals of the Abbeys*, and see if it suggested anything to him. But most probably it would not, he reflected sourly. Pickford has worked on it long enough before he wrote "EUREKA!" in his diary; and he was almost a monomaniac on the subject. There was not much chance of Loxton stumbling on the truth after a mere superficial study of the volume, starting from scratch so far as information about the tradition went. That line of inquiry could wait its turn. Thirdly, he could set his machinery to work and find out something about the purchase of the rope with which Pickford had been hanged. But plenty of people had been buying ropes in these days of incendiaries; and this line might easily lead to a blank end. Fourthly, there were these samples which Dundas wanted—clay from the bomb-craters. They could be got, easily enough. After that, it was up to the professor.

All these were matters of routine which could be handled by the staff at Loxton's disposal. He was bound to get some facts merely by persistent inquiry; but the three remaining matters seemed the merest wildcats. What chance was there of discovering where a common sleep-drug was bought? Was it likely that one would hit on Dundas's ambidextrous sea-faring man except by the purest accident? As for the goldsmith, the only chance of recognising him was the arrival of a letter from him, addressed to Pickford; and probably Pickford had received that letter and destroyed it, before he died.

8

A CLOUD OF WITNESSES

INSPECTOR LOXTON summoned a constable who was accustomed to take down statements, looked over his own notes, glanced regretfully out of the window at the sunshine, and then issued his directions for the introduction of his witnesses in a prearranged order. Among them were some who volunteered their evidence as soon as the news of Pickford's death had become public. Loxton wondered what light they could throw on the matter. Not much, likely, he guessed. Busybodies, probably. Still, one had to listen to them.

"Bring in number one."

This was Bartram, who had discovered the body in the garage. Except for one or two minor details, his story was the same as that which he had already told. The sirens sounded at ten minutes to nine, and he had gone out on patrol almost immediately. He noticed nothing peculiar about the garage when he passed it on leaving his house. The door of it was closed. He would have remembered it, had the door been even ajar, he was sure. No, he had not seen Pickford on the street; the first time he saw him that night was when he found the body in the garage.

"Did you notice anyone near the garage while you were on patrol?" demanded the inspector.

"There weren't many people about, of course, during the raid," Bartram explained. "I saw Mr. Oakley in the street about ten past nine; he was walking away from the direction of the garage. I shouted to him to get under cover, but that was all the talk I had with him, for he was on the other side of the street. I know him because I read a lot from the Mitcham Library and I've seen him there often."

"Anyone else?" Loxton inquired.

Bartram hesitated for a moment before replying.

"I noticed young Mr. Hicks—Mr. Cyril," he answered at last, with evident reluctance. "He was hanging about Goodman's Row when I came out of my house; but he was on the other side of the road and I didn't speak to him. I know him quite well by sight. He's one of the boss's sons and I see him at the factory."

"You didn't caution him to get under cover?"

Bartram shook his head. The inspector could understand his diffidence. Young Hicks was one of his employers and Bartram had evidently no desire to raise trouble in that quarter by any officiousness. Least said, soonest mended: it was Hicks's own affair if he chose to run risks.

"When did you see him in Goodman's Row?"

"It would be about five to nine."

"And how long did he hang about?"

"That I can't say," Bartram declared frankly. "I know he was gone by the time I went to look at the garage. I saw nothing of him then."

Bartram had nothing to add to this evidence, and the inspector dismissed him after he had signed the sheet.

May Pickford was the next witness: cool, wary,

volunteering nothing, and inclined to answer in mono-syllables to any questions. Loxton's attempts to elicit facts about her earlier life were met by a blunt refusal to furnish information. "I don't see what that has to do with the case," was her favourite parry. The inspector learned nothing of the slightest value from her, certainly nothing which incriminated any of her friends. She described Oakley's visit without varying in a single detail from her previous account. She knew nothing about any purchase of a rope by Pickford. He might have bought one, for all she knew. He was always talking about the risk of incendiaries falling on the house and setting it afire. She had never seen any rope in the house; and he had none with him when he left to go to the garage, so far as she knew.

Finally, she produced Pickford's copy of the *Annals of the Abbeys*: an old leather-bound quarto much the worse for wear, its margins scribbled over with almost illegible notes in faded ink. "A most unsatisfactory witness," was Loxton's mental comment when she left the room. He glanced over the book which she had left with him. A nice prospect, having to wade through all that stuff, he reflected in disgust.

"Send in the next one," he directed. "She seemed a bit full of herself, over the phone. The kind that'll talk for hours, if they're let. It's to be hoped she can give us the goods."

When the new witness was ushered in, Loxton found that his estimate had not been far off the mark. She was, indeed, "a bit full of herself," and was evidently prepared to make the most of her temporary position at the centre of the stage. The inspector made a gesture towards a chair, then sat down himself and gazed glumly at the girl before him.

"What's your name? The constable here will write down your answers. Don't be in a hurry."

"Lizzie Sparrick. I told you that over the phone. Elizabeth's what I was christened."

"I guessed as much," said Loxton, with the air of a man who has heard bad news. "What's your occupation?"

"I told you that over the phone," said the girl indignantly. "Don't you listen to w'at people say? I'm the 'ousemaid at Friar's Pardon."

"Let's see your identity card . . . Thanks . . . How long have you been with Mr. Collingbourne?"

"Four months, an' I'm leavin' at the end of next month. I'm goin' into the A.T.S. There's more money there."

"And more work," amplified the inspector, dampingly. Then, noting a slight Cockney twang in her voice, he demanded abruptly. "Why aren't you in one of the Services already? Not been called up yet?"

"They can't call me up. I was born in Ireland. Lived most of my life in England, though."

"You've volunteered your evidence in this case," Loxton went on. "You know something about Mr. Pickford and Mr. Oakley, you say?"

"Yes, I do know somethin' about 'em," Lizzie Sparrick said perkily. "It's this way. Miss 'Erne, she's very keen on 'elpin' on this waste-paper campaign. She wants the town to do well an' she wants everybody to 'elp. She got me and Mr. Fearon—'er cousin, that is—persuaded to go down an' give an 'and at the Mitcham Library, an' if I'd known w'at dirty work it was—'andlin' a lot o' musty ole books an' papers—I'd 'ave seen 'er further, first. But she got me talked over into a start, an' once I'd begun, I just went on. Back-breakin' it is, though, carryin' piles o' 'eavy books about."

"No doubt, no doubt!" interjected Loxton without much sympathy.

Lizzie Sparrick evidently resented the implied criticism.

"I'm tellin' you this thing *as* it 'appened. If you don't want to 'ear me, don't. It won't worry me, you can bet."

"Go on," said the inspector stoically.

"I'm tellin' you," continued Lizzie with some asperity. "Well it was there that I come across this Oakley man, first of all. 'Im an' Miss 'Erne an' Pickford—'im that's dead—an' Mr. Fearon an' a lot of other people was doin' the sortin' of the books an' papers to see nothin' valuable got chucked away by mistake. Miss 'Erne an' this little Oakley man seemed to 'unt in couples, always. More 'is doin' than 'ers, I could see. It didn't take 'alf an eye to spot that 'e'd fallen for 'er. Pathetic it was, a feller like 'im gettin' keen on a girl like 'er. She didn't even seem to notice w'at was wrong with 'im when 'e 'ung round with 'is eyes about poppin' out of 'is 'ead as if 'e couldn't see too much of 'er. Gave me a good laugh, sometimes, at the silliness of it all. She'll want somebody like 'erself—good-lookin', good class—with a tidy bit o' money, too. Fancy 'er lookin' twice at a common little snipe like that Oakley, with no money, no manners, gawky, with an accent fit to set yer teeth on edge. But 'e 'ad it bad. It was 'im as arranged to go an' look over books in the libraries of the big 'ouses round about, an' 'e got 'er to drive 'im out to 'em in 'er car. 'E didn't get much change out of 'er on those trips, I bet, w'atever 'e expected. Strictly business."

"Quite so," said the inspector, moodily. "Did he ever go up to Friar's Pardon to see her?"

Lizzie shook her head decidedly.

"I never seen 'im, not that I remember."

"This doesn't amount to a row of pins," said Loxton. "What about Pickford? You say you know something about him."

Lizzie Sparrick was obviously nettled to find her observations dismissed in this cavalier manner. However, she had more evidence in store and she now produced it.

"There was one thing," she began, rather haltingly as if she felt she had fallen below expectation. "I once saw Oakley an' the 'ead man at the library—Pickford, 'im that's dead—talkin' by themselves, an' they seemed a bit excited over somethin'. I didn't go for to listen specially . . ."

"Oh, no. Of course not," muttered the inspector. "You haven't got ears longer than the ordinary."

He inspected Lizzie's ears as though he expected to find them abnormal and was disappointed.

"They talked a bit loud in parts, that was 'ow I come to 'ear them, 'ere an' there," Lizzie explained snappishly. "You've no cause to say anythin' about my ears. Pickford 'ad a paper in 'is 'and, an' 'e tapped it with 'is finger now an' again, as if 'e was excited a bit—nervous-like, you know. They was talkin' about some man 'Icks —'that cod 'Icks' was w'at Oakley said. An 'Pickford said, 'A hundred thou'' an' somethin' else about a second-'and bed or somethin' like that. It seemed all mixed up and like rubbish to me; an' that's w'at made me listen—just out o' curiosity. Then one of 'em, I can't rightly remember w'ich it was, said somethin' about Russians an' anatheway . . ."

"What?" interjected the inspector, evidently sceptical.

"Well, it sounded like that to me," retorted Lizzie, resentfully.

"Anathema, perhaps?"

"It might 'ave been. I never 'eard of either, an' I'm just givin' you it as best I can remember. An' that reminds me; one of 'em said 'Testament,' meanin' the Bible, I suppose. An' I 'eard somethin' about a new place, too. It sounded all cock-eyed to me an' I couldn't make out w'at they were so excited about. Oh, yes, an' Oakley, he said somethin' about 'is B.M. or somebody's B.T.M., w'ich was just like a common little twerp like 'im."

"Do you mean 'bottom'?" asked the inspector, gravely.

"Well, that's not a word I use in mixed company, but I suppose that's what he meant. B.M. was what he *said*, I know that."

"Put down B.M. and write 'bottom' with a query after it in brackets," directed Loxton, turning to the constable who received the order with a broad grin. "Anything else you can remember? When did you hear all this?"

"It would be ten days ago—Friday before last, I think. Thursday's my night out an' I wasn't at the library that evenin'."

"Now about this Hicks," continued the inspector, aspirating the initial with care. "Do you know anybody of that name?"

Lizzie reflected for a while before answering.

"There's the 'Ickses of the factory 'ere. I don't know anyone else with that name in this neighbour'ood. No, I can't call any to mind."

"You spoke as if Miss Herne has plenty of money. Has she?"

"All I meant was that she wouldn't want to step down in the world by marryin' a little guy like Oakley. I

wouldn't myself, if I was in 'er shoes. W'y should she?
'E's not 'er sort, nohow. No class at all, if you see w'at
I mean."

"Anyone else keen on her besides Oakley?"

"Yes, there is!" said Lizzie, triumphantly. "An' you
needn't go outside the 'ouse to find 'im. 'Er cousin
would marry 'er to-morrow, if she'd 'ave 'im, that 'e
would."

"Oh, indeed? You think so? What's his name?"

"Fearon—Denis Fearon. 'E's desperate keen. Anyone can see that, to look at 'em together. I'll bet 'e's
asked 'er already, an' more than once, too. But she won't
'ave 'im—anyone can spot that. 'E 'asn't any money,
for one thing. An' for another, 'e's got a temper . . .
My word! I saw 'im thrash a dog once, 'cause it
disobeyed 'im. Somethin' cruel, it was. Oh, no, you
can write 'im off. Just wastin' 'is time, 'e is. But
jealous! W'y, 'e 'ates to see 'er so much as talkin' to
another man, as I've seen often. Not that it prevents
'im tryin' to take liberties with other girls, as I well know.
'Come up an' have a peep at the moon, Lizzie.' No,
thank *you*! This fly goes up no windin' stair to 'is little
parlour, even if 'e 'as a telescope in it, an' you can kiss
the Book on that!"

"He's got no money, you say?" asked the inspector,
with a complete indifference to these revelations.

"'E tries to bite 'is uncle's ear time an' again. I've
'eard 'im complainin' 'ow 'ard up 'e gets. But gettin'
cash out of the old man's like squeezin' blood out of a
stone. Every penny 'e 'as to spare goes on that litter of
old books and papers 'e buys. It's a cryin' shame to see
the way 'e keeps Miss 'Erne short, w'en she's so fond of
pretty things."

"H'm! Anyone else after her that you know of?"

"There's always flies round 'oney," declared Lizzie sententiously. "She 'asn't a ring on, though."

The inspector seemed to weary of Miss Herne's affairs. He suddenly recurred to a previous topic.

"Did you happen to overhear any other conversations between Pickford and Oakley?"

"I remember 'earin' Pickford say to Oakley: 'It's quite safe. I 'ave it 'ere.' But I can't just be sure w'ether that was a bit of the other chat or not. I only remember that because I wondered what 'it' was, at the time."

"Had anyone besides yourself the chance of overhearing these bits of talk?"

Lizzie considered carefully for a moment or two.

"Mr. Fearon was givin' me an 'and with some old books at the time. We was in the next room, but the door was ajar-like. If I 'eard them, 'e may 'ave, too. An' there was people comin' out an' in all the time, bringin' in more books an' papers. Mr. Quinton was one of 'em. If they'd been listenin' they might 'ave 'eard, same as I did. They didn't seem to be payin' any attention, if I remember right."

"Anything else you can remember about that first conversation you mentioned?"

Lizzie evidently racked her memory to the best of her ability before answering.

"Well, there was some foreign word come in, now I think of it . . . Synie-something or other, it was. But it didn't mean nothin' to me, then or since; an' I'd almost forgot it."

"Were Pickford and Oakley good friends, from what you saw of them?"

"Sometimes they were, sometimes they weren't. I got a notion it was a case of *shershay la fam*, if you see w'at I mean. Some woman in the case."

"Do you know Mrs. Pickford?"

Lizzie shook her head decidedly.

"Not me! If she was like 'er 'usband, she must be a snuffy ole piece. No, I took it as Pickford was chippin' Oakley over fallin' for Miss 'Erne. Not fair, that. But that Pickford 'adn't a fair mind. Look 'ow 'e treated pore ole Rusthall, the library attendant. Turned 'im off, 'e did, without a thought; an' 'im with a sick wife. Most unpopular, it made 'im. I 'eard lots o' talk about it. An' quite right, too. Downright brutal, it was."

"Did you happen to hear any more of Pickford's private conversation?"

"Not so much of your 'private conversation' if *you* please," said Lizzie indignantly. "No conversation's private w'en it's bawled out loud enough to 'ear next door. There was one thing. It come to my mind w'en I 'eard about 'im bein' found dead in 'is garage. 'E was talkin' about puttin' up 'is car—storin' it away, you know, since 'e wasn't goin' to use it. 'E was talkin' to Mr. Fearon about it an' sayin' 'ow 'e 'ad a weak 'eart an' couldn't tackle the job hisself. Fearon said, careless-like: 'I'll give you an 'and with it, if you like.' But Fearon would say a thing without meanin' to keep 'is word. You couldn't count on 'is promises; they was just words, w'en it came to the pinch. I don't expect 'e ever meant to lend an 'and with that car at all. Not likely."

"When did you hear this?"

"It would be a week or ten days ago," said Lizzie, vaguely. "I don't go about like you with a notebook, writin' down names an' dates all the time. I just remember 'earin' it sometime."

"Anything else you remember? . . . No? . . . Well, you can sign this paper and that'll be all for to-day. If you call to mind anything else, you can let me know."

The next witness on Loxton's list was Oakley, and as he came into the room Loxton examined him searchingly. Lizzie Sparrick had described him as 'little,' but apparently the adjective was a mere grace-note, for he was of average height. He was black-visaged, and his most noticeable features were a pair of very dark eyebrows, darker even than his hair. He seemed to Loxton rather nervous in his manner and very much on his guard. When he spoke it was with a faint touch of pedantry like a not very well educated man trying to 'carry it off' by using a stilted vocabulary.

"You're James Oakley, of 10 Speranza Street; and you're assistant-librarian at the Mitcham Memorial Library?" Loxton began formally.

"Yes, that is accurate."

"George Pickford was head-librarian. Did you like him?"

This opening seemed to surprise Oakley, as the inspector meant it to do. He pondered for a moment or two before answering:

"No, I was not greatly attracted by him, on the whole."

"But you used to visit his house in Laurel Grove?"

"Yes, he invited me there to converse about Shakespeare. I found him a bore. He and Mr. Quinton were always arguing about the Shakespeare-Bacon controversy, which did not interest me."

"You knew his wife?"

Oakley's manner grew still more wary.

"Yes, I met her at his house."

"What were your feelings about her? Were you attracted?"

"I was sorry for her," replied Oakley, evading the second question.

"Were you intimate with her?" demanded Loxton bluntly.

"I knew her," answered Oakley, ambiguously.

"Do you still visit her?"

"There was a certain friction, from time to time, between us," Oakley admitted, with an ill grace. "I decided to break off with her. That was why I went to his house last night. She had informed me that he would be out."

"Was this friction between you and Pickford your sole ground for breaking off relations with his wife?"

Oakley hesitated for several seconds before answering this.

"There were other reasons," he said, "but they do not concern this case in the very slightest."

Loxton, recalling Lizzie Sparrick's evidence, had no difficulty in surmising what these reasons might be and he forbore to press the point.

"You live in Speranza Street. The shortest way from your house to Pickford's takes you down Goodman's Row, doesn't it?"

"That is the way I went last night."

"Past the garage? Did you notice anything there as you passed?"

"Nothing out of the common. I saw a man Bartram wearing a warden's coat and helmet. He shouted to me to get under cover. I observed another man loitering about, but he was a stranger to me. I mean I am not acquainted with him even to the extent of nodding to him in the street."

"When did you leave home and when did you get to Pickford's house?"

"I left home just before the sirens sounded—about a quarter to nine; I must have been in the vicinity of the garage about nine o'clock; and I reached Pickford's house about a quarter past nine. I stayed there till about half-past ten."

The inspector recalled that these times agreed roughly with those which May Pickford had given him in her evidence. If she and Oakley were not telling the truth they had taken pains to concoct definite details for their story. Loxton left it at that and turned to a fresh field.

"How were you dressed last night?"

"Just as I am now, exactly."

"Same hat, same suit, same socks and shoes?"

"Exactly the same."

"Did you ever discuss with Pickford some man Hicks?"

"Hicks?" repeated Oakley, evidently surprised. "I may have spoken to Pickford about him in the course of business. Miss Herne once brought a man Hicks—one of the dynamo factory people—to the library. He wanted to know if waste paper from the factory was of any interest to us in this salvage campaign. Naturally, it wasn't. The library isn't handling ordinary waste paper. And that reminds me, it was Hicks I saw loitering about in Goodman's Row last night about nine o'clock."

"Can you remember, in any conversation with Pickford, the words 'Anathema' and '£100,000' cropping up?"

"Anathema?" Oakley paused to reflect. "No, I don't recall saying that to Pickford or hearing it from him. No, nothing of the sort."

"And 'a hundred thou''; did you ever say anything like that?"

Again Oakley seemed to ponder for a few seconds before answering.

"Are you sure about the figure?" he asked. "Couldn't it have been 'a hundred *pounds*?' I once lent him £100 to get him out of a difficulty. He was always in deep water over money."

This seemed not improbable to Loxton, who recalled the entry in the diary about a £100 loan from Oakley. After all, 'a hundred thou" and 'a hundred pound' sounded very much alike.

"What about a word 'synie-something-or-other'? Does that remind you of anything in your talks with Pickford?"

"Synie-something?" Oakley was manifestly puzzled. "No, I can't say I remember anything like that. Synie-something? . . . Ah! Wait a moment! Could it have been something like 'Sign an IOU'? When I lent him the £100 I made him sign an IOU for the money. Here it is; I thought you might want to see it, so I brought it along with me this morning."

He felt in his pocket, took out a note-case, and extracted a paper which he laid on the desk before the inspector, who read: "IOU. £100, G. Pickford." He recognised the dead man's writing. Apparently Lizzie Sparrick had misunderstood what she had overheard when she listened to that conversation.

"What security had you for your £100?"

"He told me some tale about a legacy which was coming in to him. It sounded all right."

"Did he ever talk to you about the St. Rule's Treasure yarn?"

Oakley made a gesture of impatience.

"Didn't he! He was demented about that—almost as bad as the Shakespeare-Bacon affair. I told him it was all a mare's nest, and he lost his temper over the subject. He was really a very tiresome person to live with, what with this crank and that. Of course, I never had the slightest belief in that treasure tale. It's just talk."

"Did he ever speak to you about something he called 'It'?"

"Never heard of it!" said Oakley, abruptly.

"Did he ever speak to you about a goldsmith?"

"No. Why should he?"

"You can't throw any light on that? It suggests nothing to you?"

"I've never discussed jewellery with him in any shape or form," declared Oakley, tartly.

Loxton's mind went back to May Pickford's display of jewellery and he wondered if Oakley had contributed any of it. That might account for his evident desire to avoid the subject.

"There's just one thing more," said the inspector. "Have you any objection to one of my men running over you—searching you, I mean?"

Oakley seemed frankly surprised at this proposal, but gave his permission without hesitation.

"If I had anything to conceal, I'd have got rid of it long ago," he pointed out. "But if you want to go through my pockets, you're entirely welcome."

"Thanks," said Loxton. Then to the constable he added: "Get Sergeant Eyre. He can do the job,"

Sergeant Eyre was one of Dundas's pupils. Let him tackle the business since he was trained by the professor. That would shut Dundas's mouth if the thing wasn't done to his satisfaction. So Loxton reflected as he watched Eyre set to work. Oakley submitted with a good grace until the sergeant began to deal with his shoes.

"I've been perambulating about a good deal," he pointed out with a certain asperity. "What do you anticipate from this operation? There may be a good deal more adhering to my foot-gear than there was last night."

"It's just the usual routine," Eyre assured him, as he began to scrape the sole of one shoe with a knife and collected the resulting dust on a sheet of paper. "We always do it."

He wrapped up the dust in the paper and turned to scrape out the groove between sole and upper. Oakley watched him with evidently growing suspicions and finally an impatient movement of his foot took the knife out of the furrow so that it made a long scratch across the leather of the upper.

"Look what you're about!" Oakley protested in annoyance. "A pretty mess you're making of my shoe!"

"Sorry, sir," Eyre said apologetically. "It's done now."

He made a neat packet of the scrapings and, his work ended, he went out of the room, leaving Loxton to pacify the witness.

"Is that *really* necessary?" Oakley demanded truculently. "I see no point in it. You're not going to charge me with murder, are you?"

"I shouldn't be asking you questions if I were," retorted the inspector. "You've admitted you were near the scene last night. We've got to check things up. That's all there is in it. And now, will you please sign these notes of what you've said? . . . Thanks. That's all. If we need you again we'll let you know. There may be an inquest. Or there may not be one for a while."

The next witness obviously belonged to a higher social class than his predecessors. He seemed to be between twenty-five and thirty, well-featured, blue-eyed, fair-haired, well set up, with a hint of the open-air type about him. There was something in his manner which suggested coolness and a certain easy authority. A good man to have with one in a tight corner, the inspector reflected, looking him up and down with approval.

"You're Mr. Cyril Hicks? You live at 15 Holly Hill? A partner in Hicks, Mordant & Co.?"

"Not a partner," Hicks corrected him in a pleasant voice. "My father's a director; I'm only a manager of one of the departments. What can I do for you? I'm rather in the dark."

"You were in Goodman's Row last night, I think?" said Loxton.

"That's so."

"What I want to know is whether you noticed anyone you knew there. It's the death of George Pickford that we're concerned with. Did you know him?"

"I came across him only once," Hicks explained. "I called at the Mitcham Library to ask if they wanted to look over our waste paper. Apparently our stuff from the factory was no use to them, so we send it direct to the dumps. When I went to the library, Miss Herne introduced me to Pickford and another official—Oakley or Oakdale, or some name like that."

"You know Miss Herne?"

"She's a secretary at the factory. Very efficient."

"When were you in Goodman's Row last night?"

Hicks considered for a moment before answering.

"About a quarter to nine, I think," he said after a pause. "I didn't see anything of Pickford, if that's what you want to know. Oakdale or Oakley passed down the street, away from the garage, about nine o'clock, I remember. I don't know where he came from; I'd been round in Brent Street and came into Goodman's Row when he was between me and the garage. I recognised him as he passed on the opposite pavement, but I didn't speak to him, of course. I also saw an air-raid warden, one of our workmen—Bartram is his name—but I didn't speak to him either. These are the only people I can remember noticing."

"How long were you in Goodman's Row?" asked the inspector.

"Till about a quarter past nine, I think. The All Clear went as I was on my way home. But I ought to say that part of the time I was round the corner in Brent Street."

"What took you to the neighbourhood of the garage in Goodman's Row?" demanded Loxton. "You seem to have been hanging about there for quite a while—half an hour, say."

"I was keeping an appointment. Someone wired me to meet them there. I waited for them, but they didn't turn up."

"Who wired you?"

"That has nothing to do with this case," Hicks declared bluntly, with a change in his manner.

"You have this wire?"

"No, I tore it up."

"You can't remember seeing anyone else near the garage?"

Hicks shook his head decidedly.

"No, there was a raid on. People were under cover."

"Just one more point," said Loxton. "Are these the shoes you wore last night? They are? Then would you have any objection to one of my men looking them over?"

"My shoes?" exclaimed Hicks, in apparent surprise. "What on earth do you expect to learn from them? But if you want to examine them, you're welcome."

"Thanks, it's only a formality, but I might be asked about it," Loxton explained. "If you'll sign this statement, Sergeant Eyre will do his trick in another room."

As soon as Hicks had gone, the inspector ordered a constable to ring up the post office and find out about the wire which had brought him to Goodman's Row. The next two witnesses were Grindal the moneylender and Pickford's solicitor, Goodge. Both were taciturn, merely answering questions and volunteering nothing. Neither added anything to what Loxton already had learned from Pickford's diary, though their evidence confirmed its accuracy. As soon as they retired, the constable brought in a copy of the telegram.

"CYRIL HICKS, 15 HOLLY HILL
MEET ME 8.45 P.M. BRENT STREET CORNER OF
GOODMAN'S ROW
URGENT DON'T FAIL DI."

"So when he said 'them' he meant 'she,'" the inspector mused, as he consulted the constable's notes. "This must have reached him during dinner. Dispatched by D. Herne, Friar's Pardon. 'D' for Diana. Handed over the counter at the G.P.O. by some man they can't describe in detail. But if she wanted to get hold of Hicks in a such a tearing hurry, why didn't she telephone him direct from Friar's Pardon? Or at least send her wire over the phone to the Ambledown post office, instead of sending a messenger to hand it over the counter? A bit queer that. Of course, she may have been in town during the evening."

The final witness on Loxton's list turned out to be a very ordinary-looking youngish man with a ready smile and a careless manner. Flaming red hair was his only striking feature. His eyebrows were even fairer in tint, so fair, indeed, that they might have been shaven off without making any noticeable change. His grey tweed suit was old and rather shabby, but it had been well cut.

"You're Mr. Denis Fearon, residing at Friar's Pardon? A nephew of Mr. Collingbourne? You volunteered your evidence in this case? Well, I'm here to listen."

Denis Fearon had nodded assent to each of the questions, his smile broadening a little each time. He seemed very well pleased with himself, Loxton thought. Certainly shyness was not his weakness.

"This is where I begin, is it?" he inquired, with hardly-masked insolence. "I began to think *you* were going to do all the talking from the way you started off. My mistake. But now that I can get a word in, I'd better mention that I wasn't burning to intrude on you; it was your Sergeant Eyre who rang me up this morning and suggested my coming to say my piece."

"Let's see your identity card, please," interrupted the inspector, brusquely. "You're not in the Forces? Munitions, perhaps?"

"They all say it!" Fearon made a mock-weary gesture. "No, I'm not in the Forces. Nor am I in munitions, either. Not my war, you know; I'm an Eire citizen. Dev would be horribly distressed if he heard I wasn't keeping strictly neutral."

The inspector's tone grew even less cordial.

"We're rather busy. Cut it short, please."

"Well, I've answered all the questions you've asked," Fearon protested. "Now you give me a free hand, eh? So kind! Well, I had a little chat with Pickford last week. The library had just closed; I'd been on this salvage stunt all afternoon and my throat was full of dust, so I invited him out to the Green Lion. After three double whiskies, he turned confidential, poured out his woes like a burst dam. No reticence whatever. The burden of his song was his domestic affairs. Mrs. P. was a regular Cressida—at which point he threw in a few quotations from Shakespeare not to be found in Mr. Bowdler's edition, I fancy. His assistant, Oakley, came in for a remark or two also. It may have been merely the whisky, but he left me with the impression that he was afraid of those two, actually afraid they might do him in, between them. Persecution mania it sounded like. He certainly wasn't happy about it. Naturally, at the time, I paid no attention to his ramblings; but now he's dead, I thought I'd better give you it for what it's worth. Not much, I suspect. Why should they bother to get rid of him when they seem to have been able to do pretty much what they liked without asking his permission? It doesn't make sense, does it? At last I got him to change the subject, and then he wandered on to talk about the St. Rule's Treasure. But I've had enough on that matter from my uncle in my day. More than enough. Much more. Pickford seemed to think he might be on the track of it; but I never was keen on fairy-tales, even as a child."

"You don't seem to feel his loss much," commented Loxton sourly.

"Why should I? No bosom friend of mine. I hardly even spoke to him until I got run in for this paper-salvage stunt. I've met people I liked better. He had his points, of course. Full of them—like the nearest hedge-hog. Bad-tempered little devil, really. I don't wonder his wife went after more attractive game. Not that I'd hunger much for Oakley's charms myself, if I were a girl. Must be an acquired taste."

"Did you offer him a hand in jacking up that car of his?"

"I may have done," Fearon replied after a moment's thought. "Mere polite gesture, though, if I did. I never had the slightest intention of dirtying my paws in his service. Why should I? Mean little devil! Any garage would have done the job for him for a bob or two, but he preferred to sponge and get it done for nothing."

"As a matter of form," said Loxton, "where were you between eight and ten o'clock last night?"

"Gosh! He suspects everybody!" exclaimed Fearon with a mock-tragic gesture. "Well, well, well! As it happens, I've got a cast-iron alibi in my vest-pocket. Just as well, perhaps, with so much suspicion running round off the leash. Last night, from 7.45 to 11 p.m., I was enjoying the company of your Sergeant Mike Eyre. You can ask him now, if you like. I'm trying to write some detective short stories and I draw from the wells of his experience, to keep me straight on legal points. A very useful man, that sergeant of yours. Look at my notebook and you'll see the sort of stuff I get from him."

He pulled a notebook from his pocket and tendered it to the inspector.

"See here! 'Do you need a warrant to search premises in a murder case?' 'Can you get a trunk out of a Left Luggage Office and examine it?' 'Can you force a man to let you take his fingerprints if he objects and you've brought no charge?' 'What powers of detention have you if you suspect a man?' And so on. One needs to know these things when one starts writing tec yarns."

"Have you ever met Mrs. Pickford?" asked the inspector as he glanced over the pages of the notebook and verified Fearon's story.

"No, I never actually met her. Young, fair, and frisky, from all I've heard, though. Pity I don't know her. I might go and console her, in these dark days. An easy job, no doubt. But I might run into Oakley if I did. Wiser not to, perhaps."

"Much wiser," agreed the inspector morosely, handing

back the notebook. "Did you ever hear Pickford speak of a goldsmith?"

"A goldsmith?" repeated Fearon, evidently puzzled. "No, he never mentioned a goldsmith to me. Goldsmith? . . . I say, you don't think he . . .? The St. Rule's Treasure, I mean. 'O my prophetic soul, my uncle!' Sad blow to *him* if someone else tumbled on that myth. It's supposed to be buried on his ground, you know. What did the little beggar say about a goldsmith?"

"Nothing one can make head or tail of," Loxton admitted in a grudging tone. "Did you ever hear Pickford say anything about 'Anathema'?"

Fearon shook his head decidedly.

"No, never. I've heard him curse, plenty; but not in the high-falutin' style. Just plain bad language and lots of it, when he talked about his wife and Oakley."

"Do you know anyone called 'Di'?"

"Di? No. My cousin's Diana Herne, but nobody calls her anything but Diana, not even in the family."

"Was she at home last night?"

"Search me! How should I know? Haven't I just told you I went to see Mike Eyre. She'd gone to bed by the time I got home in the last bus but one. But I didn't hear of her having been out."

"Sign these papers, please. If you remember anything else, you'll let me know?"

"You don't seem to think much of my evidence," grumbled Fearon as he put his signature to the notes. "It's the best I can give you. I'm no Hans Andersen . . . Good morning to you," he added, rather huffily, as he went out.

As soon as Fearon had gone, Loxton summoned Sergeant Eyre.

"You've had a look at those samples you got from Oakley's shoes? What do you make of them?"

"Under the microscope, sir, they look to me the very spit of the stuff from the garage: no grass blades, black specks of tarmac, some stuff that might be tourmaline. I can't be sure of the tourmaline, though, for our microscope has no Nicol prisms in it. But apart from that, I'd say the two sets of samples are identical."

"Pack up the Oakley lot and send them to Professor Dundas."

"Very good, sir."

Eyre was about to leave the room when Loxton seemed to remember something.

"By the way, has anyone asked you lately if you could get a trunk out of the Left Luggage Office to examine its contents?"

Sergeant Eyre stared at his superior in some surprise.

"Why, yes, sir. Mr. Fearon asked me that last night when he was round at my house. He comes from time to time to ask me all sorts of puzzlers because he's writing crime stories. He's very free with getting beer sent in, and there's usually five bob at the end of the evening. I hope there's no harm in it, sir. Of course, I never tell him anything he shouldn't know. I'm very careful about that."

"What time did he turn up last night?"

"It would be about eight o'clock, sir. He'd a whole host of questions he wanted to ask. Sometimes I had to look up my copy of the *Police Code* to get him an answer. He kept me at it till I had to remind him he'd a bus to catch, unless he wanted to walk all the way back to Friar's Pardon."

"You advised him to see me?"

"Yes, sir. He seemed to know something about

Pickford, and every little helps. Did he tell you anything?"

"Not much," answered Loxton, moodily. "No one seems to know much except Professor Dundas."

"*He's* a wonder!" the sergeant affirmed admiringly. "He can always spring something fresh. That rope trick, now; it was new to me. He never mentioned that to us in those lectures of his. *That* was a clever one, that was."

"Oh, he got that from some foreigner," said Loxton disparagingly.

9

BLACKMAIL

ON the following afternoon, Inspector Loxton, having received reports from the police surgeon, Professor Dundas, and his own subordinates, sat down to go through the sheaf of papers on his desk. The first document he picked up was from the coroner, giving his agreement to a postponement of the inquest upon Pickford. That would avoid any premature disclosure of the evidence in the hands of the police and gave them a breathing-space for further inquiries. The inspector put the letter on his file with a nod of approval.

The next communication was the police surgeon's report on the results of the post-mortem examination which he had made. Dr. Massinger found that Pickford had died of strangulation. There was no dislocation of the vertebræ in the neck, such as a drop might have produced. An examination of the stomach contents showed that digestion probably stopped a couple of hours after Pickford's last meal, and the temperature of the body might indicate that death occurred about 9 p.m. After a short mental calculation, Loxton noted that this fitted May Pickford's evidence fairly well; so apparently she had told him the truth on this point, at least. Pickford's stomach, Dr. Massinger found, contained alcohol and a notable amount of paraldehyde. The inspector had to admit to himself that this gave support to Dundas's guess that Pickford had been drugged before he was hanged. The rest of Dr. Massinger's report was purely technical and yielded nothing suggestive to Loxton's mind.

He turned next to the police reports concerning the rope with which Pickford had been hanged. Apparently only two shops in Ambledown were selling this particular type of rope; and people had been buying it freely, owing to its usefulness as an emergency fire-escape. Loxton glanced through the list of identifiable customers: Allen, Acton, Brindley, Collingbourne, Forston, Hewlett, Nailour . . . people who had accounts with the shop-keepers and whose addresses were known. Collingbourne was the only one whose name the inspector recognised, and he made a mental note of it. There were also, however, two or three other people who had paid cash down and taken the rope away with them; and these purchasers could not be identified at the moment. No one had paid much attention to them at the time. One shop-assistant recalled that among them was a man with a dark complexion and heavy eyebrows; but his purchase had been made after the murder and it hardly seemed worth following up. Loxton added these documents to his file and dismissed them from his mind.

When he took up Professor Dundas's report, however, the inspector raised his eyebrows. Evidently there was something in this scientific stuff after all! He read it through quickly, marking the points by an unconscious tapping of his pencil on the desk as he proceeded. Dundas had examined samples of clay from the various bomb-craters in the Ambledown streets. Only one of these contained tourmaline—the crater in Smith Street. This sample appeared to be identical in nature with the clay found on the floor of the garage. *Ergo*, the murderer must have passed along Smith Street on his way to the scene of the murder. That seemed sound enough, Loxton reflected; but it did not take one very far; plenty of people must have passed along Smith Street, and how was one to pick out the person one wanted from such a collection? But as Loxton read further he found that there was something more to be learned. According to Dundas, no tourmaline occurred in the sample obtained by Sergeant Eyre from the shoes that Hicks had worn. That seemed to give Hicks a clean bill. But Oakley's case was quite different. "The scrapings from his shoes, supplied to me by Sergeant Eyre," wrote Dundas, "contain tourmaline in approximately the same percentage as that in which tourmaline occurs in the sample supplied to me from the bomb-crater in Smith Street. I have therefore submitted to a more precise examination:

(*a*) Samples of clay from the Smith Street bomb-crater.

(*b*) Samples of clay which I took myself from the garage floor.

(*c*) The samples obtained by Sergeant Eyre from the shoes of James Oakley.

As a result, I am able to state definitely that the materials (*b*) and (*c*) are identical beyond the slightest doubt; and in my opinion they are both derived from the same source, viz. the bomb-crater in Smith Street."

"Well, that finishes it!" was the inspector's first reaction to Dundas's statement. His second thoughts, however, were not so optimistic. "It's a moral cert that Oakley's the man we want—but there's a damned jury to satisfy. Would they hang him on the strength of that evidence? Not they! They'd want to know a lot more that I can't prove, yet."

But before he could spend further thought on the matter, he was interrupted by the entry of a constable.

"Well, what is it?"

"There's somebody here, sir. He says he wants to see the highest official on the premises—that's you, sir, just at the moment. I asked his business, but he wouldn't tell me anything about it. He said he'd discuss it with nobody but you. He seems very worried. A gentleman, by the look of him, well dressed. He wouldn't tell me his name, but he gave me this envelope to hand to you."

Loxton tore open the sealed envelope, out of which fell a visiting card:

> Mr. W. Penywerne Inderwick,
> Chastelnau,
> Fenton Abbas.

Fenton Abbas was a village some miles away; and the inspector wondered why Mr. Inderwick could not have contented himself with applying to the police station there, instead of troubling to come all the way to Amble-down.

Mr. Penywerne Inderwick proved to be a man in his fifties, with an emotional eye, a slack mouth, and clammy hands. In dress, he leaned towards a style which was a colourable imitation of the clerical. "A poor type, with just enough looks to be dangerous and not enough self-control to keep clear of mischief at times," was the inspector's first impression. "Badly worried about something."

"Well, sir, what is it?" Loxton demanded curtly, as he tried to catch his visitor's rather evasive eye.

Mr. Inderwick seemed to find difficulty in beginning his tale. He hummed and hawed; embarked on a sentence and dropped it in the middle in order to make a fresh start; coughed to hide his embarrassment; cleared his throat and made another plunge. At last, stimulated by an impatient tapping of the inspector's pencil on the desk, he managed to convey his meaning through a mist of words.

"Ah!" said Loxton, frigidly scanning the loose lips and terrified eyes. "It's a case of blackmail, is it? You'd better give me the particulars."

"Well, as a matter of fact, it is," Inderwick confessed, evading Loxton's glance. "I'm being blackmailed by somebody, and I must have a stop put to it. But on no account must there be a case in court over it; anything rather than that, anything. You can understand that, of course. But I want you to frighten this fellow away; you no doubt have the means to do that. But no publicity, please; at any cost, no publicity. That would be fatal, quite fatal."

"Tell me your story, please," interrupted Loxton, with a touch of impatience. "Cut it short. I'll ask any questions as you go along."

His mind was still full of the Pickford case, and he felt a certain vexation at having his consideration of it interrupted by this interlude.

"Well, this is how it was," Inderwick began, fixing his eyes on the desk to avoid meeting Loxton's gaze. "Some months ago a housemaid left us to go into the Wrens as a steward. It upset things at home, and my wife made up her mind not to have that happen again. If we engaged a British girl, she would have been called up, sooner or later, and it would have been the same thing over again, you see. Unquestionably. So, unfortunately as it has turned out, my wife decided to advertise for a maid from Eire. I had nothing to do with the matter, nothing whatever; I leave all these affairs to my wife. Entirely. She does not consult me about domestic matters. The girl arrived eventually . . ."

"What was her name?" interjected Loxton.

"Rachel Murneen. She was twenty when she came to us; a pretty girl, rather shy, and a nice speaker, with a touch of a brogue. I liked the look of her; she had gentle manners, almost lady-like, if you see what I mean. Attractive. I'm afraid my wife is inclined to be rather harsh with maids; she's apt to treat them like machines; and the girl was homesick. I felt sorry for her and used to talk to her at times. Once I found her crying, after my wife had been finding fault with her over something or other. I did my best to cheer her up; she seemed grateful for that. She was always looking about to find little things to do for me, and I did my best to make her feel she had a friend in the house . . ."

At this point in his story Inderwick hesitated, but the inspector showed no desire to help him.

"Give me the plain facts, please," he said, dryly.

Inderwick made a gesture of despair. Evidently he found the atmosphere chilling.

"Well . . . as a matter of fact . . . I got quite fond of her, in a way, and . . . I went to her room one night . . . It was the only time, that I'll swear."

He broke off, flushed and out of countenance, but the inspector showed no inclination to ease the explanation.

"Go on, please."

"A few weeks later," Inderwick continued with a gulp, "she came to me one morning when I was alone and told me about her condition. I was thunderstruck. It was . . . it was . . . a dreadful position for me, dreadful. Just one lapse in twenty years—and now, this! It threw me right off my balance. The complete unexpectedness of it! And I was in terror lest my wife should come into the room. If she had found me with this girl whimpering beside me, it would have been hard to explain, you see, very difficult, indeed. A terrible state of affairs! My wife would never understand my temptation; she's not very sympathetic at any time. She'd have been wounded, deeply wounded, both in her self-esteem and her trust in me. And there's my daughter, too. She's in the W.A.A.F. What would she think of me, if she heard about it? It's very hard, bitterly hard. Just an hour's folly . . . and this falls on me!"

"What did you do?" demanded Loxton, who evidently had no sympathy with these excursions into side-issues.

"Well, what *could* I do?" retorted Inderwick with a giggle which betrayed how near he was to hysteria. "I paid the girl a solatium on condition that she gave notice to my wife at once and kept her mouth shut about what had happened; and I promised to look after her and see her through her trouble. I'm not a rich man; my wife has the money: but I was as generous as my means allowed. I wanted her to go home; but she wouldn't do that. She didn't like the idea of her trouble being talked about over there, I think. She was very obstinate about that, quite immovable; I couldn't persuade her. The end of it was, she took lodgings here in Ambledown and posed as the wife of a dead soldier. I paid her so much a week to keep her going."

"What's her address?"

"Twenty-nine, Jerusalem Street. I never visited her there except once. It was better not to risk the slightest chance of any gossip connecting my name with hers; and I sent my remittances to her in postal orders with no covering letters."

"I understand perfectly," said Loxton, without troubling to hide his opinion of all these precautions. "Now get on to this blackmail business, please."

"I'm just coming to that," protested Inderwick. "The first thing was a letter. I've brought it to let you see it."

He fumbled in his pocket and took out an envelope which he pushed across to Loxton. It bore the Amble-down postmark and was addressed to:

> Mister Inderwick,
> Branch Secretary, A.N.C.M.,
> Chastelnau,
> Fenton Abbas.

The enclosed letter was typewritten and brief.

"Please meet the writer of this note at the seat north of King William's Oak on Dewberry Common, at 11 a.m. on Tuesday, 8th June, when you will hear something of interest to the A.N.C.M."

The paper was cheap and plain, without even an embossed address; but Loxton noted that it had been perforated for filing.

"Were you surprised to get a thing of this kind?" he asked, looking up from the letter after reading it.

"As a matter of fact, I wasn't," Inderwick explained. "What I mean to say is, I'm secretary of the local branch of the A.N.C.M.—the Argus National Council for Morality—and we often get information anonymously. People want to draw our attention to something: an immoral book, a shop selling suggestive pictures, an obscene performance, or anything of that sort, but they don't want to appear personally in the matter. So they write to put us on the alert and we take the thing up if it falls into our particular field. You can understand that, as local secretary, I get quite a number of these communications. There was nothing suspicious about this one; I put it in my file and went to keep the appointment as a mere matter of course. And then this man turned up . . ."

"How did you recognise him?"

"As a matter of fact, I didn't know him; he knew me. I'd hardly sat down on the seat before he strolled up and nodded to me as if he knew me at the first glance."

"Probably he's been watching your house and getting to know you by sight, before that," commented the inspector. "Go on."

"He plunged right into the business of this girl. That threw me off my balance, badly; you can guess as much. He knew all about it, everything. What's more, he knew all about *me*, too . . . I mean he knew that I'd lose my position with the A.N.C.M. if this affair came out; I'd have to resign, and my income would go. And he knew a good deal about my wife, too. 'If you won't pay,' he said, 'then I'll have to see what Mrs. Inderwick has to say about it all—*and she has the money!*' He knew that. He's a foul-mouthed blackguard, that man. I loathe bad language; it goes quite against the grain with me: but he took a delight in it and used most horrible expressions when he was describing the thing to me. He said I was a . . . No, I won't repeat it. Nor some of the other things he called me. I felt degraded, just listening to a fellow like that. It was a dreadful experience, to be plunged all unsuspecting into a position like that.

He was there, he said, to see the girl's wrongs righted, so far as that was possible now; and he'd see I treated her better than I had meant to do. I'd taken advantage of her innocence and her ignorance of the world, he said; and I'd thrown her out with a miserable pittance to keep herself afloat in her trouble. But he could put *that* straight, he said, anyhow; and he was going to do it. If I didn't behave generously—'*very* generously,' he said with a sort of gloating smile on his face—then the whole miserable affair would come out: I'd lose my secretary-ship; he'd see that my wife knew all about it; and my daughter would learn what kind of a father she had. 'Not one of your Puritan friends would lift a finger to help a thing like you, you hypocrite. And serve you right, too!' And he ended up by demanding £200 for the girl."

"Were you to pay him, or send the money to the girl?" interrupted Loxton.

"I was to pay him, and on the nail," Inderwick explained. "I was very shaken, you know, all of a tremble, in fact; and I couldn't hide it. It was all so . . . all so . . . I didn't know which way to turn. And he gave me no time to pull myself together, no time at all. He had me driven into a corner; I just had to do as he told me. I went to my bank, with him shadowing me all the way; and I drew £200 in one-pound notes. I had to make up a tale of some sort to account for that. He hung about in the background, even in the bank, listening to what I said to the teller; and then he followed me up the street and took the money from me with another torrent of vile language. I was terrified, I assure you, lest anyone passing should overhear what he was saying about me. I was shaking all over, just with nerves and the shock of it all. At last he left me, after I'd managed to get him to promise not to trouble me again. . . ."

The inspector gave a short bark of laughter at this.

"And you believed him?" he demanded, contemptuously.

"Yes, I must say I did," Inderwick confessed. "I thought he meant it. After all, £200 is a lot of money to part with; and he seemed fairly content, so far as that side of the thing went."

"Go on, please," said Loxton with a shrug which he did not trouble to conceal.

"I was horribly upset," Inderwick continued. "I tried to hide it, but my wife noticed that I was agitated, and that made things difficult at home. Next day, I managed to make some excuse of having business in Ambledown; and I came here to see Rachel at Jerusalem Street. I was very careful to say nothing about the thing to her, and I could see she knew nothing about it, nothing at all. She was just the same as ever, rather grateful to me for my kindness to her. Evidently the man had not had time to get at her and tell her what he had been doing. That visit relieved my mind, I don't quite know why. I came home again in much better spirits. It was like the lifting of a nightmare, somehow; my wife even noticed the change. I felt the worst was over and the thing was behind me. It had been a terrible experience, but it was over and done with. So I thought. That lasted for a week, only a week. Then the man came again . . . to my house, this time . . . and without warning. He just came in, like an ordinary caller. Of course, I was afraid lest my wife should come in and find us talking and want to know who he was and what business he had with me. She's rather inquisitive about such things. I was on pins and needles all the time; and if I tried to argue, he lifted his voice till I was in terror lest someone in the house should overhear him."

"The usual technique," commented the inspector. "When was this?"

"A fortnight ago, exactly, on the sixteenth," Inderwick explained. "This time, he was even more brutal. 'I know all about your affairs,' he said. 'You'll have to pay up. Let's have no more of your squalling; it's just wasting my time. I want £300 this shot, and it's cheap at the price. Come along to your bank now. Or else . . .' and he went and put his finger on the bell-push. I had to go to the bank with him again; he wouldn't take a cheque. That £300 cleared my current account almost to the last penny. I told him so; I explained it was no use his coming back for more; he'd drained me dry. He seemed disappointed at that. When he went away, I really thought I was rid of him at last, though it had cost me £500, just for that single slip. Really, it makes one doubt Providence, when one thinks of it."

"Leave Providence out of it," said the inspector, brusquely. "Finish your story, please."

"I had ten days of peace," Inderwick went on. "I was quite light-hearted, as day after day went past and nothing happened. My wife noticed the improvement in my spirits. I was able to throw myself into my work again, with a real interest. And then, last Saturday, back came that vampire once more to suck me again. This time he wanted £500. Five hundred pounds! I had no money to give him; he knew that from what I'd told him on his second visit. But he intimidated me completely, threatening to ring the bell and ask to see my wife; he cross-questioned me about my affairs and screwed out of me that I had some saleable securities that I could raise money on. I persuaded him to wait for a day or two, so that I could do this. 'You can't get blood out of a stone,' I said. 'You'll just have to wait.' He saw I was telling the truth, for he said at last that he'd come back. He wouldn't fix a day. . . ."

"Naturally," interjected the inspector. "Only a fool would come blundering into a trap laid for him at a fixed time."

"Well, there it is," said Inderwick, with a gulp, for he seemed on the verge of tears. "I've taken the week-end to think it over, and now I've come to ask your help. I can't afford to pay him any more; I simply can't, and that's all about it. I must have the thing stopped. Can't you lay a trap for him and frighten him off? I'm quite ready to let him keep what he's got out of me already, so long as I'm freed from this torture, never knowing when he'll turn up and intimidate me. I want it stopped. I must have it stopped. I can't stand it any longer. I can't. I *can't*!"

Inderwick's voice rose to a pitch which was almost a shriek. The inspector was unimpressed by this appeal for urgency. He took a sheet of paper from a drawer, spread it before him on the desk, gave it a fastidious touch or two to adjust it, unscrewed his fountain-pen, tried the nib, and prepared to take notes. His aloof deliberation had the effect of damping Inderwick's incipient hysteria, and when Loxton spoke, his tone completed the work.

"You don't seem to know much about the law, Mr. Inderwick. I'll explain the position to you. Extracting money by menaces is a felony. That's what *he* did. Concealing a felony is called compounding it. That's what *you've* been doing. It's a misdemeanour, punishable by fine or imprisonment. That's what *you're* liable to. The only thing you can do now is to prosecute the fellow."

"But *still* you don't understand!" cried Inderwick. "I

can't prosecute him. That's the very thing I've done all I can to avoid! Just look at my position. I've no money of my own except my salary as secretary to the A.N.C.M.; and if this came out, they'd sack me out of hand. I live in a big house; but it was bought with my wife's money and it's kept up out of her private income. She's rich, and she's very strict, rather hard and unforgiving. If even a whisper of this affair came to her ears, she'd insist on a divorce—or a separation, at the least. And what would become of me then? What would become of me? It would be complete ruin. I'm too old to make a fresh start in the world. This thing must be hushed up. It *must*, I tell you! What would my daughter think?"

"You should have thought of that before you tampered with another man's daughter," said the inspector, impatiently. "You don't seem to be worrying much about *her*. Pull yourself together and answer my questions. You're just wasting my time, with this kind of thing. What's your full name?"

"Can't my name be kept out of it?"

"Most likely it won't come out in open court," said Loxton indifferently. "In blackmail cases, the judge usually allows the prosecutor's name to be suppressed. You'll probably be called Mr. X or Mr. A, or something like that. Of course, that doesn't keep people from talking; but that's no affair of mine. What's your full name?"

Inderwick made a hopeless gesture.

"Wallace Penywerne Inderwick."

"This man visited you on the 8th, 16th and 26th June; and by threats of exposure he extracted from you first £200, then £300; and finally he demanded £500 which you could not pay?"

"Yes," confirmed Inderwick, sullenly.

121

"Describe him, please, as accurately as you can."

Inderwick considered for a moment or two.

"He was about average height," he said hesitatingly. "He was shabbily dressed . . . I mean his clothes looked old. I don't remember what they were like . . . a lounge suit . . . brown, or something like that . . . not noticeable, particularly. He was swarthy . . . with dark hair and very marked eyebrows. . . . His hair was very untidy. . . ."

"To prevent you seeing how he parted it normally, no doubt," interjected Loxton.

"His hands looked rather dirty," Inderwick went on. "But that may just have been his dark skin. He spoke hoarsely, as if he had a sore throat; and he wore no collar . . . just an old muffler round his neck. . . . That's all I can remember."

"Eye-colour? Any warts or moles on his face or hands? Scars? Irregular teeth?" prompted the inspector.

"I don't remember," Inderwick confessed helplessly. "I had other things to think about."

"Did he leave anything behind him, either intentionally or by oversight?"

"I thought of that," said Inderwick. "On his last visit to my house, he took out a bus time-table and looked up the times on the route back to Ambledown; and when he'd done that, he put it down on my study table and forgot to pick it up again when he went away. This is it."

He produced a dirty, much-folded sheet of paper, which the inspector took from him in a very gingerly fashion.

"This is for February," he said, glancing at it. "Well, I don't suppose they've changed the bus times since then. You've fingered this, of course, so I'll need to ask you to register your fingerprints, so that we can distinguish between yours and the other man's on this time-table.

One of my men will look after that before you leave. He's quite an expert in that line, is Fleming."

He laid the time-table aside on his desk and took up his pen again.

"Now, about this girl, Rachel Murneen, who's now at 29 Jerusalem Street. Whereabouts in Eire did she come from?"

"I really can't remember," Inderwick admitted. "She used to talk to me about her home sometimes, but I wasn't much interested. . . .. Oh, yes, it was somewhere near a place Sneem, in Kerry, I think. And her father's farm was on an estate. . . . Castle-something-or-other . . . I can't recall it."

"Had she any relations in this country?"

"She never spoke to me of any."

"Did anyone come to visit her while she was in your service?"

"One man used to come, very occasionally."

"A sweetheart of hers?"

"No," said Inderwick after thinking for a moment or two. "He didn't give me that impression. More like a brother, I'd have said; but he wasn't a brother; his name wasn't Murneen, though I can't remember what it actually was. I heard it only once, I think, and I've forgotten it."

"What sort of man was he?"

"Very ordinary-looking, but not in the least like this blackmailer, though. He was always quietly respectful. He might have been in the Army by his manners. If he was sitting in the hall waiting to take the girl for a walk, he always stood up if I passed; and he always said 'Sir' if I spoke to him."

"Has he come back to your house since the girl left?"

Inderwick shook his head.

"Not that I've heard."

"So he must have been in touch with her and knew she'd left Fenton Abbas," mused the inspector, half aloud.

Despite his temporary concentration on Inderwick's affairs, the Pickford murder still hung continually in Loxton's mind and prompted him to put a question.

"This blackmailer of yours had marked eyebrows, you say. Was he beetle-browed, or were his brows shaggy, or was it simply that the hair was dark and so showed up? For example, a man Oakley at the Mitcham Library has noticeable brows. Perhaps you know him. Were your man's brows like Oakley's?"

"I never met Oakley," answered Inderwick. "He's been at my house over this salvage scheme, but I was out at the time, and he just took away a pile of old books I'd left out for the collectors. The blackmailer's brows struck me because they were dark, I think, not because they were specially prominent or bristly; at least, that's my recollection of them."

The inspector added a line or two to his notes and then passed the paper across the desk to Inderwick.

"Just read that over, please, and sign it if it's correct. You haven't given us much to go on, but we may be able to lay hands on the fellow, by and by. When we get him, you'll be called in due course to give evidence."

"But I can't, I tell you!" Inderwick protested. "Don't you understand what it means for me? I simply can't afford to have this thing dragged out for everyone to know about. It would be the end of me. . . ."

"I'm afraid that's not our business," said Loxton, unsympathetically. "We're not interested in your affairs. What we want is a conviction. It's out of your hands now."

Then, as Inderwick showed signs of continuing to protest, the inspector rang a bell.

"I've called one of my men, Fleming. He'll take your fingerprints. He's our expert in that sort of thing."

10

THE CHIEF CONSTABLE

"No chess till later on, Squire."

Wendover reluctantly laid down the box of pieces which he had picked up as he came into the smoking-room after dinner. He had been looking forward to his game ever since Sir Clinton Driffield had arrived at the Grange earlier in the day; but clearly the Chief Constable had other views.

"I want to tap your local knowledge," continued Sir Clinton.

He took a voluminous file from the table, extracted something from it, and handed the file to his host.

"Read over these reports, will you, and let me know what you make of it all? Some of the stuff will be new to you."

Wendover had many hobbies, but amateur criminology stood high among them; so, nothing loath, he opened the file and began to go through its contents while Sir Clinton smoked in silence. When he had finished his task, Wendover laid the file down beside him.

"Loxton arranges his material neatly," he said, approvingly.

"Yes," agreed Sir Clinton. "He does. Everything in its place—except the solution. Unfortunately, it's the solution we want."

"The solutions, you mean," corrected Wendover.

"You've got two cases here: a blackmail one and a murder."

Sir Clinton ignored this.

"Take the blackmail business first," he said. "I'm handicapped in a case of this sort. I don't know these people and their acquaintances; and probably I'm overlooking some point which would be clear to anyone with local knowledge. That's why I want to pick your brains, Squire, since you take a friendly interest in the affairs of this countryside."

"Tell me how it appears to you," said Wendover. "Then I'll have a better notion of what you want."

Sir Clinton reached out and took back the file of papers.

"When you read over the evidence that Loxton has collected," he said, "one thing stares you in the face: and that is the intimate knowledge this blackmailer has about Inderwick. He knows the man's vulnerable point—the fact that he's secretary to these Argus people, with their itch for setting other people's morals right. But that could have been learned from a reference book. What's more suggestive is his familiarity with Inderwick's private affairs. He knows that Inderwick depends on his wife's money. He knows, too, that Inderwick is afraid of his wife. He knows that Inderwick thinks more than a little about his daughter's opinion. And he knows, quite definitely, about the seduction of this girl Murneen. That's all 'inside information'; and the obvious source of it is the girl herself, who served in Inderwick's house and could hardly help picking up these things."

"It looks as if she and the blackmailer were hand-in-glove, and she primed him with the facts," said Wendover. "That's what I took out of the evidence."

Sir Clinton shook his head dubiously and turned over the pages of the file.

"I know Loxton," he objected. "He's not gifted with much imagination, but he's a good judge of character and he knows when a witness is probably lying, in most cases. Now when he interviewed Rachel Murneen, he got the impression—you see he mentions it in his report—that she was a completely truthful girl. She was surprised to hear about the blackmail business—quite genuinely surprised, according to Loxton. He was satisfied that it was all news to her and that she wasn't mixed up in it. Further, when he asked if her people knew about Inderwick's slip from virtue, she got into a panic and begged him not to communicate with them as she didn't want them to know anything about her trouble. It was the very last thing she wanted to have spread about at home. Loxton thought that was genuine, and I'm inclined to think he's right on that point also."

"The blackmailer may have been a lover of hers," Wendover pointed out. "She refused to name the man who used to pay calls on her at Inderwick's house. Perhaps she got into trouble with him, and then the two of them planned to involve Inderwick so as to lay the blame on him."

"That's possible," Sir Clinton admitted. "But in any case it doesn't clear Inderwick. He confessed to Loxton that he tampered with the girl. That's a fact: your suggestion's only an hypothesis, Squire. I'm not bothering about that side of it. Inderwick must take what he's earned. What does seem to me important is that the blackmailer didn't return to see Inderwick again, just when we had a chance of trapping him."

"The girl may have tipped him off," suggested Wendover.

"I don't think so, judging from what Inderwick himself said about his visit to her after the blackmailing had begun. I'm inclined to trust Loxton and assume that she's honest insofar as the blackmail affair goes. But I want to hear more about Inderwick and his circle. You know everybody round about here, and that's why I came to you about it. What's the family like?"

"Pretty much what you'd gather from the evidence on the file," Wendover replied. "Mrs. Inderwick has the money. She's one of those hard, narrow-minded, obstinate women who were commoner in the last generation. She may have had some looks in her younger days, but not now; and she looks older than Inderwick. Perhaps that's what makes her jealous. Certainly she is. And she orders him about, even in public, as if he were a dog. Power of the purse, I suppose; he's got to do as he's bid. It's the sort of *ménage* that makes one thankful one's a bachelor. I know next to nothing about their daughter, but I believe she's fond of her father."

"I inferred as much from the evidence," said Sir Clinton. "It doesn't take us far. Is there anyone who might know about the Inderwicks' affairs?"

"I don't think our local people have taken them up much," Wendover explained. "We're a conservative lot, hereabouts, you know; and we didn't take to them, somehow. The good lady's temper led to trouble at the very start, and people gave them a wide berth after that. I've no use for Inderwick either; he's not my sort. When the Hernes were in Chastelnau, it was a popular place; nowadays, things have changed."

"Were these Hernes any relations of Diana Herne?" asked Sir Clinton.

"Her parents," explained. "After they died, the place came into the market. Collingbourne was a trustee for Diana and he may have had some acquaintance with the Inderwicks when they—or Mrs. Inderwick, to be exact—

128

bought Chastelnau; and he may have kept that up, for all I know."

"You're not as helpful as usual," grumbled the Chief Constable reopening the file on his knee and glancing at the contents. "Let's try another line. Have you any documents—typewritten ones—emanating from any of the people mixed up in this business: stuff from the Mitcham Library, or from young Hicks, or from Chastelnau, or from Friar's Pardon? I'd like to have a look at anything of that sort."

Wendover got up and went across to his desk where he rummaged for a time and then returned with some papers in his hand.

"There's nothing confidential about these," he said, "so there's no harm in showing them to you. Here's a letter from Collingbourne, asking me about some book in my library. It teems with misprints, so evidently he typed it himself and the blunders come from his eye trouble. He never learned touch-typing. And here's one from young Fearon, about some point in local natural history. This one's from Diana, dealing with this paper-salvage affair. They're all quite recent, as the dates on them show."

"All typed on a Remington," said the Chief Constable after a glance at them.

"It's the only machine they have at Friar's Pardon. They all use it."

"Well, it's not what I want," said Sir Clinton, to the obvious relief of Wendover. "Have you anything else?"

"Nothing from Inderwick or young Hicks, but here's a letter from the Mitcham Library about some committee business."

"Typed on an old Corona," said the Chief Constable, after examining it. "Is that the only machine they have?"

"They have two, but both are Coronas. What are you looking for?"

"The blackmailer used an Imperial machine," explained Sir Clinton, exhibiting the threatening letter on the file.

"That's not much help. It's a very popular make."

"No doubt about that," agreed the Chief Constable. "I use one myself. These reports of Loxton's are typed on the Imperial at the police station in Ambledown. Dundas uses one too. So did the writer of the telegram signed 'Di.' Of course, every individual machine has its own peculiarities. I can spot some of them myself, but I think I'll hand that part of the affair over to Dundas. He's got the apparatus for examining things like this, and why do one's own barking if one has a dog handy?"

"May I have a look at that file for a moment?" asked Wendover, holding out his hand. "Thanks."

He studied the papers for a few minutes and then passed the file back to the Chief Constable.

"There's a difference between the blackmailer's type and the type in the 'Di' telegram," he pointed out with some pride. "The 'e's' and 'o's' aren't identical. They're blotched in the blackmailer's letter and sharp in the 'Di' telegram and in Loxton's reports. Dundas has a habit of striking 'y' instead of 't' and correcting it by simply using his back-space key and printing a heavy 't' on top of the faulty 'y' without erasing the error."

"Quite right, Squire," agreed Sir Clinton, after comparing the documents. "But we'll leave these points to Dundas. He revels in that sort of thing. Loxton's rather old-fashioned. He's inclined to scoff at the Dundas technique. Perhaps he may get a sad shock before we're done with this affair. I shouldn't be surprised. But let's leave typewriters and get back to people. What about 'that cod Hicks' who appeared first in Lizzie

Sparrick's evidence. He seems very friendly with Miss Herne, judging from one or two things."

"He's engaged to another girl, though," commented Wendover with a touch of disapproval in his tone. "Joan Morant. She's the daughter of the other partner in Hicks, Morant & Co., who run that dynamo factory in Ambledown."

"That brings us to the telegram signed 'Di.' Young Hicks wouldn't say who sent it; but if he's engaged to another girl, one can quite understand that Miss Herne denies that she sent it; and it wasn't typed on the Friar's Pardon Remington. It was handed in at the post office by a man who would fit the description of either the blackmailer or Oakley. Miss Herne is called 'Diana' by all her relations, and yet this wire is signed 'Di.' I suppose you see what that might imply, Squire?"

"Oh, I see what it implies to *you*," said Wendover, rather crustily. "You mean that Diana Herne and young Hicks are on a Christian name footing, although he's engaged to another girl. Well, what of it? It's common enough in these days."

"You've hardly got the point," explained the Chief Constable. "To me, it implies a shade more than that. If young Hicks were on ordinary familiar terms with Miss Herne, he might call her 'Diana,' as her friends and relations do. But he seems to have a pet name for her, which nobody else uses. That's not quite the same thing. Further, if it's a pet name between themselves, then somebody must have heard Hicks using it in speaking to the girl."

"Well, Oakley admitted in his evidence that he met Hicks and Diana Herne together at the library, once; and Hicks said something in his deposition which confirms that. Quite possibly Hicks may have called her 'Di' in front of Oakley."

"It's not impossible," admitted Sir Clinton. "And I'll make you a present of something else. Lizzie Sparrick in her evidence asserted that Oakley is very keen on Miss Herne. In that case, he'd be inclined to be jealous if another man betrayed familiarity with the girl; and he'd remember it. A casual acquaintance probably would think nothing of it, since it wouldn't matter a straw to him personally."

"That's true enough," Wendover agreed. "I hadn't thought of it in that light. And, while we're on the subject of Oakley, I noticed a bit of evidence on the file which was new to me—I didn't know that the local dustmen reported finding a bit of half-charred rope in the dustbin of the house where Oakley lives. It matched the rope that hanged Pickford, didn't it?"

"Yes. Does it suggest anything to you, Squire?"

"Well, if I were going to hang a man myself and leave the rope round his neck, I don't think I'd leave *exactly* the length of rope that I bought for the job. The coincidence in length would be a bit hard to explain away, wouldn't it? I'd be inclined to buy a longer bit of rope, use part of it, and destroy the rest. And burning it would be the safest way of getting rid of it."

"Just as well, Squire, that you haven't taken to crime," said the Chief Constable, mockingly. "We'll have to look more carefully into these purchases of rope, evidently. But for the present, let's go on with your local Who's Who. Why is it that I've never come across this man Collingbourne in my visits here, since he's a neighbour of yours?"

"I don't come across him myself, more than once in a blue moon. He's always been a bit of a recluse, and since his eyes began to give trouble, he hardly goes about at all. They're a queer lot, that family."

"Are they?" said Sir Clinton, lazily. "In what way?"

"They have a trait which has run through three generations. It's curious how they collect things—mostly rubbish and liabilities. Especially liabilities. Matthew Collingbourne—Philip's grandfather—was before my time. He collected South Sea shells, carved coco-nuts, phormium, feather cloaks and so forth. He lost most of his money—he must have had a lot at one time—by dabbling in blockade-running during the American Civil War. Then came his son John. Astronomy was his hobby. To house his telescope, he built a hideous dome on to the old Friar's Pardon and completely ruined the look of the place. *He* collected comets, double stars, and worthless investments. He pretty well completed the financial debacle that his father had begun."

Wendover took a cigar from the box beside him, and lighted it before continuing.

"That brings me to our own generation. They were a futile lot. Philip, who owns Friar's Pardon, has dabbled in all sorts of hobbies: geology, botany, local archæology—I think he still has hopes of finding a treasure that's supposed to be buried in his ground—and he has an infallible nose for artists with falling values. A lot of his money has gone on worthless canvas. But his real craze has been his collection of old books and manuscripts. He spends every penny he can afford on that, and often a bit more. He prides himself on his flair; but I wouldn't care to buy his stuff at the valuation he puts on it—or even a tenth of that.

"His sister Eve collected samplers, embroidered bookmarkers, and old cookery-books. She married an Irish squireen, Jasper Fearon; but it wasn't a success, and Eve left him after a bit. You couldn't expect any woman to stand it. Here's just one sample. Jasper seduced the daughter of his lodge-keeper; and after Eve's son was born, Jasper brought his boy to live in the house as a playmate for young Denis. The girl from the lodge married, later on, and settled down on the estate with her husband, so that Eve never got a chance of forgetting the affair. That's only one example. I've heard there were other offspring about the place as well—a regular Mormon settlement without the Mormon sanction."

"Sounds a bit patriarchal," interjected Sir Clinton. "Whereabouts was this Agapemone?"

"You know Waterville, in Kerry?"

"Yes, I've been there, once or twice, just before the war. There's both lake- and sea-fishing within a mile of each other. Quite good. Now I come to think of it, I heard about the place from one of Loxton's men—Eyre's his name. He comes from somewhere in that neighbourhood and he knows the district. When I was across there, I picked up some acquaintances amongst the Eire police—Civic Guards, they call them."

"Well, this place of Fearon's was a bit east of Waterville; Castlecarney, I think it's called. But Fearon and his wife are both gone. Eve died in the flu epidemic after the first big war. Fearon scattered his money between Ireland and Paris and died before the start of the second German war. The Castlecarney estate was sold, and there was nothing left, except perhaps £50 a year, for young Denis Fearon. So he came over here. He's had no training of any sort. He spent the whole of his youth in fishing, hunting, shooting, sailing an old coble on the Kenmare estuary—and in some less reputable ways. He's got no notion of industry. He'll do anything for money, except an honest day's work. He bets, goes in for newspaper competitions, and that kind of thing; but mainly he lives at Friar's Pardon as a parasite on his Uncle Philip. To be fair to him, he's not a complete dud; he's got natural abilities. He paints a bit—not my kind of stuff, though. He plays the fiddle up to average amateur standard; in fact fiddling seems to be his line in life, even without an instrument. He took up golf over here and plays to a six handicap. He's a reversion to type, for he dabbles with his grandfather's telescope at Friar's Pardon, and his loafing gave him a taste for the beasts and birds of the countryside. Sometimes he bothers me with inquiries about our local fauna. They say he's in love with his cousin, Diana. If so, propinquity hasn't done much to help him; she has no use for drones, I gather."

"What about her?" inquired Sir Clinton, watching smoke curl up from his cigarette. "Where does she come in?"

"Philip Collingbourne's other sister, Esther, married a man Herne," continued Wendover. "He was 'passing rich with'—a good deal more than '£40 a year'. In her case, the Collingbourne family mania took the form of collecting old pewter, wedgwood pottery, Chelsea ware, and that kind of thing. Herne came to grief in some speculations, and just about then Esther and her husband were killed in a motor smash. Chastelnau was sold to the Inderwicks. Philip was trustee for the estate and Diana is his ward until she's twenty-five; so he brought her to live with him at Friar's Pardon. She's in the same boat as young Fearon: just enough money to scrape along."

"What's she like?" asked Sir Clinton. "I gather she's a good-looking girl, but that's merely the outside."

"She seems to be the only normal one of the lot," said Wendover. "The only things she collects are golf-clubs and fishing-flies. She's got open-air tastes; swims, shoots, fishes, rides when she gets the chance. As a girl, she was brought up in moderate luxury and well educated.

It must have been a bit of a change for her when her father lost his money. She helps her uncle in his muddling over his collection of books and manuscripts; but she doesn't trouble to hide a faint contempt for the futility of it all."

"What will happen to her and her cousin when Collingbourne dies?"

"Goodness knows. There won't be much left, I expect. Philip wasn't a millionaire to start with, and he's frittered away most of what he had. The estate wasn't entailed, so he could mortgage it up to the hilt. And that reminds me. You've had a glance at this book on the local abbeys. Do you think, if Collingbourne got hold of it, that he'd stand any chance of finding the St. Rule's Treasure? For that fairy gold is about his only hope of pulling straight financially in this world, so far as I can see."

Sir Clinton shook his head.

"He'll be a cleverer man than I am, if he makes either head or tail of it. It might have been written by a syndicate of the Sphinx, the Delphian oracle, and a sibyl or two, so far as finding the St. Rule's Treasure goes. But that's enough on the Collingbourne family, Squire. Do you know anything about the man Quinton, whose name bobs up occasionally in this business?"

"Quinton? I know him, of course, as one knows people about the countryside; but that's all. He's a gentleman-farmer with just enough money not to care whether he makes much out of his farming or not. Something of a scholar, too, in a cranky sort of way: believes that Bacon wrote Shakespeare's plays and that Nausicaa wrote the *Odyssey*, and all that kind of thing. Morally, he's a rather erratic devil, I'm told: a kind of throw-back, in a way. He ought to have lived in the days when the

Lord of the Manor had the *droit de seigneur* and held the power of high, middle, and low justice over his serfs. He used to keep a small yacht before this war, but it must be laid up, I suppose. That reminds me, Clinton, I was reading a book lately which maintained that the *droit de seigneur* never existed as a legal affair. . . ."

"I don't suppose it mattered whether it did or not, in theory. The practice must have been where the shoe pinched, I imagine. But let's leave feudal affairs, Squire, and come back to the present. What do you make of this affair? You have the local knowledge that I haven't got. Suppose you go over your views. They may suggest something more."

Wendover was silent for a minute or two while he arranged his ideas.

"It's far from clear," he admitted. "You insisted on coupling the blackmail case with the murder, so let's start with the first appearance of the blackmailer. From Inderwick's description, the blackmailer might have been Oakley, slightly disguised. He had Oakley's marked eyebrows, swarthy skin, and dark hair. He was about Oakley's height—that's to say average. Nothing much in that. What *does* strike me is the fact that he pretended to have a sore throat—to disguise his voice, no doubt— and, to add to the pretence, he was wearing a muffler on a summer day. Why the muffler? Well, Oakley has a very prominent Adam's apple, and the muffler would hide it."

"But suppose the blackmailer was someone who wanted to throw suspicion on Oakley," suggested Sir Clinton. "Then the muffler would serve just as well to hide the *lack* of a prominent Adam's apple. It cuts both ways, Squire, and you're no further on. As a matter of fact, you seem to have missed the really important point; but perhaps it's coming later. Take your own way."

Wendover shrugged his shoulders at this, but he knew only too well that he would gain nothing by asking questions when the Chief Constable was in this mood.

"Turn to the murder, now," he went on. "We don't even know the motive yet. Pickford's wife may have been at the root of it; or perhaps the St. Rule's Treasure came in, along with this mysterious It, whatever It was. What we *do* know, on the strength of Pickford's diary, is that he made an unfortunate marriage; that he was hard up; and that his wife was taking jewellery from other men. You can put your own interpretation on that last item."

"I put the one on it that most people would," said Sir Clinton, dryly.

"Oakley was one of her hangers-on," Wendover pursued. "His alibi depends wholly on her word and his. They may both be lying about his visit to Laurel Grove on the night of Pickford's death. The only evidence we have from independent witnesses was that Oakley was seen in the neighbourhood of the garage at the crucial time."

"Admitted," agreed the Chief Constable. "But one must remember that his appearance near the garage is natural enough if his visit to Mrs. Pickford actually took place. Goodman's Row is on the direct road between Oakley's house and Pickford's residence in Laurel Grove. I'm afraid we're no further on yet."

"And we aren't helped by that inspector of yours," said Wendover, crossly. "He seems to have made a complete mess of things when he examined Oakley. Lizzie Sparrick is evidently a twin sister to Paul Pry, but making allowances for mishearing there's very fair support to her evidence. She talks of 'a hundred thou',' and Oakley admits that he spoke of 'a hundred pounds.' She mentioned 'a cod Hicks,' and sure enough we find a man

Hicks mixed up in the business. And the 'synie-some-thing-or-other' turns out to be 'Sign an IOU.' On the negative side, she heard nothing about 'It' or a gold-smith; and Oakley declares that he knows nothing about either of these. But she mentioned 'Russians,' 'anathema' and 'Testament'; and your brilliant subordinate left it at that, without even speculating on what the real words may have been, since she probably misheard them. I admit that he fastened on 'B.M.' and put his own inter-pretation on it . . . just the sort of interpretation one might expect, I suppose! But there was one phrase he ought to have fastened on: 'new place.' I'd like to know if Pickford had been prospecting for the St. Rule's Treasure in Collingbourne's ground and, failing to find it at his first attempt, meant to try in 'a new place' next shot."

"We can't all be perfect," said the Chief Constable in characteristic defence of his subordinate. "But you're quite right, Squire. These things will have to be cleared up. Nothing like tidiness. But, merely *en passant*, Squire, I think you've missed one point here. And, on the whole, I don't think all this goes far towards incrimin-ating Oakley. What next?"

"I'm not trying to incriminate Oakley," protested Wendover. "I'm merely going over the evidence to see where it points. And the next thing seems to be that telegram signed 'Di.' No one ever called Diana Herne 'Di,' that I know of; and the wire was obviously a fake. But it brought Hicks to the rendezvous, so he must have known Diana as 'Di.' Who else had a chance of knowing that pet name? Oakley may have overheard it, the day that Hicks and Diana went together to the Mitcham Library over the paper-salvage affair."

"And so might a lot of other people, too, if a mere acquaintance like Oakley overheard it."

"Well, the wire was handed over the counter at the post office by a man with eyebrows like Oakley's. That limits it down a bit," grumbled Wendover. "One must take what one finds."

"Lots of people have dark eyebrows, Squire. It's quite legal."

"These are minor points," said Wendover, slightly ruffled. "But now we come to something you can't wriggle out of. What about the fact that clay was found on Oakley's shoes identical with the clay on the garage floor? And he didn't tramp on that particular clay accidentally, either on his way to his work at the library or on his way to Pickford's house, because there's no such clay on either route."

"Highly significant, Squire, I admit; though he may have gone to look at the bomb-crater out of curiosity. I'm told it's the biggest yet, in Ambledown," said Sir Clinton in a tone which showed that he had no faith in his own suggestion.

"Pigs may fly," said Wendover, tartly. "In fact, nowadays, there's nothing to hinder anybody taking one up in a plane. If that's the best you can do, I don't think much of it."

"Ah, well," Sir Clinton admitted with a sigh which did not sound quite genuine. "Sometimes we miss things under our very noses. Still, there's something in what you say, Squire. It's quite the most valuable bit of evidence you've mentioned yet. I'm not disguising that. I'm just looking at it from a different point of view. But continue."

"Well, you can throw in the fact that Oakley's dustbin contained burnt fragments of the same kind of rope that hanged Pickford."

"A serious thought!" said the Chief Constable with

mock solemnity. "But I think I've played advocate for Oakley quite long enough now. Here's something which I kept back."

He picked up the object which he had removed from the file before handing it to Wendover: a dirty piece of printed paper carefully sealed in a cellophane covering to protect it from handling.

"This is the bus time-table which the blackmailer left on Inderwick's table when he visited him. You see we've been trying it for fingerprints. Well, these are Oakley's prints beyond a shadow of doubt. Now you see why I've been playing advocate for Oakley? I wanted to hear how the rest of the evidence struck you before you saw this thing. If I'd shown it to you at the start, you wouldn't have taken so much interest in the other points."

Wendover examined the paper carefully.

"These prints are very clear," he said at last. "There's no fake about them. And they really are Oakley's prints?"

"Oh, quite certainly," Sir Clinton assured him. "In addition to the normal pattern, Oakley has a slight scar on the ball of one thumb; and you can see it quite clearly if you look at that time-table. If you laid a million pounds to a penny on it, Squire, you'd get the best odds of your lifetime."

11

THE AMERICAN EXPERT

THE moon, just past its first quarter, was hidden at the moment behind a patch of heavy cloud, but there was light enough to make near-by things visible. Dr. Oliver

Goldsmith rose to his feet, automatically dusting the knees of his trousers as he did so, and stared down at the body which lay with outspread arms on the avenue leading up towards Friar's Pardon. Nothing in the dead man's pose suggested a struggle for life; he might merely have been drunk, stumbled, and come down with his limbs asprawl.

A chill and steady wind blowing from the north made Goldsmith shiver despite his light summer rain-coat; and suddenly there came a shower—the first that day—sharp and heavy though it lasted for only a minute or two before the pattering of its drops on the avenue foliage died away. Almost immediately afterwards, the moon sailed out from behind the cloud and lit up the surroundings clearly.

Goldsmith glanced about him. At this point the empty avenue curved sharply, so that he could see only a short distance up or down its course, marked out by the unbroken files of white stones which flanked it on either side. A few yards away lay one of them, apparently detached from its place. Goldsmith made a movement to pick it up; and then, on second thoughts, he checked himself. Better to let it lie, he reflected. That was the affair of the police; let them make what they could out of it. It would be safer to say he had never touched it.

In peace-time he had found the English constabulary very helpful and friendly; but this was his first visit since the outbreak of war, and he wondered, rather uneasily, if they would still be the same. A country after four years of hostilities is apt to develop rough-and-ready methods; and in the case of a foreigner like himself they might not put on kid gloves. There was no denying that he was in an awkward position, an alien found alone with a dead body in a strange countryside where he had not a single acquaintance to vouch for him from personal knowledge; for even this man Collingbourne, whose invited guest he was, did not know him by sight. Evidently he would have to step cautiously and give away as little as possible until he saw how the police actually behaved in a case of this sort. Dr. Goldsmith prided himself on being a good poker player; he could put on a mask of imperturbability as well as the next man; and he resolved to fall back on this attitude until he found out where he stood.

Picking up the suit-case which he had set down in the roadway he continued his walk up the avenue, shifting his burden from hand to hand as he went, for he had already carried the thing over a mile and his palms and fingers ached with the unaccustomed friction of the handle. Ere long, he emerged from the avenue and found himself on a wide, shrub-fringed stretch of neglected gravel with Friar's Pardon looming up in the moonlight: a long rambling building whose blacked-out windows and lightless front lent it a gloomy and inhospitable air.

He crossed the gravel sweep, mounted the few broad steps which led up to the front door, and rang the bell, setting down his suit-case with a sigh of relief. As he did so his ears caught a distant rumbling sound which lasted for some seconds. Goldsmith had never been in an air-raid, but the noise suggested descriptions of the reverberations of distant bombs which he had heard from acquaintances. He glanced skyward but saw nothing towards the south; and the bulk of the house hid the northern horizon.

For a few moments he waited impatiently; then the door opened, but no welcoming light shone out. In the moonlight he caught sight of a uniformed maidservant, framed against the darkness of the hall. On the spur of the moment, Goldsmith came to a decision: his news was not the kind of thing one should break to a girl standing in the dark and confronted by a complete stranger. For all one could tell, she might lose her head, scream, faint, or something of that sort; then he would be faced with people running to her aid; and the situation would be complicated by the necessity of explaining two episodes instead of one which was awkward enough in itself. Much better to keep his tale for the ears of his host when he met him, and to insist on seeing him immediately.

"My name's Goldsmith. Mr. Collingbourne is expecting me, I think."

The maid moved aside to let him pass in. Then she closed the door and switched on the lights in the hall.

"If you'll leave your suit-case 'ere, sir, I'll take it up to your room, by and by. The cloakroom's this way."

She examined him inquisitively as she spoke. By listening to the family conversation, she had gathered that the visitor was an American expert on books and manuscripts, and she had pictured him to herself as something very different from the slim, wiry, keen-faced man who now confronted her. He was not a bit like the Americans she saw in the kind of talkies which she preferred.

After a momentary hesitation, Goldsmith followed her to the cloakroom, where he hung up his hat and rain-coat.

"Perhaps you'd like to go to your room first, sir?" the maid suggested.

Goldsmith shook his head impatiently.

"No. Show me in to Mr. Collingbourne at once, please. There's no time to lose."

The maid was obviously surprised by this, but she led him along the hall and ushered him into a rather dingy study, where two people were sitting. Goldsmith knew Philip Collingbourne only through correspondence, and he was a little thrown out to find that the heavily-built, rather stupid-looking man who rose to greet him was only in his fifties. He had expected someone much older.

"Glad to see you at last, Dr. Goldsmith," his host began in a slightly fussy tone, dropping the newspaper which he had been reading. "This is my nephew, Mr. Fearon. Now I must apologise for not sending a car to meet you at the station. But we've no petrol, nowadays, no petrol; it's most annoying, in cases like this, aggravating, indeed. But I hope you got a taxi; there's generally one to be had at this time of night."

Unlike his host, Goldsmith had the knack of putting his meaning into the fewest possible words.

"I got a taxi," he explained. "It broke down a mile from your gates. I walked the rest of the way. That's why I'm so late. But you'll have to ring up the police immediately. I found a dead man in your avenue as I came up."

"A——?" ejaculated Collingbourne, as if he doubted his ears.

"A dead man," repeated Goldsmith, patiently. "At least, he seemed quite dead. If he isn't, then the sooner he's attended to the better. I could do nothing."

"What was he like?" interjected Fearon.

"The moon was behind a cloud when I came upon him," Goldsmith explained, restraining his impatience. "I nearly stumbled over him. My torch battery's almost exhausted. He's dark-haired, clean-shaven, dressed in tweeds, rather cheap-looking. Hadn't you better go out and see if you know who he is?"

"No! No!" cried Collingbourne, apparently horrified

by this suggestion. "That would never do. We might obliterate footprints or ruin some invaluable clue. That would never do at all! Let the police have their chance first. They know all about that sort of thing; it's their affair. He's dead, you say? We could do nothing for him."

"You didn't go through his pockets?" Fearon demanded. "I mean in search of anything to identify him?"

"Of course not," retorted Goldsmith, with a touch of asperity at the suggestion. "That's a police job. I was careful not to disturb the body in any way. And now, if you'll be good enough to show me your phone, I'll ring up the police and tell them about it."

"I'll look after that," Fearon volunteered. "You sit down, Dr. Goldsmith, and I'll send in a drink. You'll need one, after a shock like this. Scotch or Irish? Scotch? All right. I'll see to that; and I'll ring up the police at once. Don't worry. They'll want to see you later on, of course," he added as he left the room.

Collingbourne, instead of resuming his seat, began to shamble up and down the room in an agitated fashion.

"Very disturbing, this," he commented. "Very disturbing indeed. I hate to be disturbed; hate it. I've got enough to worry me already, you know, without this sort of thing. My eyes . . ."

A fresh idea seemed to occur to him, and he broke off to consider it as Goldsmith sat down in the chair which Fearon had offered to him.

"A cheap-looking fellow, you said?" Collingbourne resumed. "And dark-haired? I wonder . . . You see, I had a man like that calling on me to-night, after dinner. By the way, you'll need some sort of meal, won't you? You've had a tiring journey and I don't suppose there

146

was a restaurant car attached to your train. No? I thought not. You'll want something now . . . a few sandwiches, say, or——"

"A couple of sandwiches will do, thanks, if it's not giving you too much trouble," Goldsmith admitted.

"No trouble, no trouble at all," Collingbourne assured him. "Some cold chicken? Tongue, perhaps? And salad, eh? Things are difficult, very difficult with all this rationing; but we'll find something for you."

"Sandwiches will be ample, thanks," said Goldsmith, definitely.

Under his mask of imperturbability his nerves were on edge, and this rambling chatter was not soothing them. He was trying to keep clearly in mind the story which he had to tell to the police, and it was a strain to listen patiently to the trivialities of his host. Collingbourne took no notice of his guest's apparent preoccupation, but darted off to a fresh topic.

"I'm looking forward to showing you my collection," he went on, apparently forgetting all about Goldsmith's creature comforts. "You'll enjoy looking through it. Many of the things are good, I know. I've got three of John Milton's letters, an unpublished poem by Burns, a page of Bunyan's manuscript—something he cut out of his final draft of *The Holy War*, rather interesting—and a letter from James VI to the Master of Gowrie which might throw some light on the Gowrie Mystery. These are just samples, you know, just samples of the things I have. Just come this way for a moment."

He threw open the big folding doors in one wall of the study and led his guest into a smaller apartment lined with filing cabinets.

"You won't have the slightest difficulty in finding anything you want to examine," he pointed out. "Here's a complete card-index to my collection. I'll leave you to look at it for a moment if you'll excuse me; the fire's very low. I'll make it up. It's a cold night, isn't it? Just take a look round."

He turned back into the study and began noisily to rake out the embers and add more fuel; but even from his invisible position he continued to pour out his stream of loquacity. Goldsmith examined the card-catalogue, making one or two visits to the actual files in the wall-cases as some item took his fancy.

"I'll be glad to have your opinion on some of my latest acquisitions," Collingbourne continued, raising his voice to compete with his clattering of the fire-irons. "My eyes are the trouble. I've got cataract, and it's growing worse. It always does, you know. The fact is, I can hardly read at all nowadays, except headlines in the newspapers. It's a great deprivation to a man of my tastes, a great deprivation."

"I'm sorry to hear that," said Goldsmith sympathetically.

"Oh, one gets along, you know, one gets along. One can alleviate it a little by dropping atropine into one's eyes to dilate the pupil and let in more light. I always keep a solution of atropine beside me—it's here on the mantelpiece. I've just been using it to see if I could read a paragraph in to-night's newspaper. It's nothing; it's nothing, really," he added cheerfully. "Only a case of waiting till an operation can be done. I'm still able to stumble about in daylight, though I can't see much after sundown, except by strong artificial light. But I can't read. I've had to buy manuscripts lately without being able to examine them; just taking a chance, you know, like buying a pig in a poke. But you'll tell me about them when you've seen them, of course."

Dr. Goldsmith came back into the study to find his host still fumbling on the hearth-rug.

"That's a very neat card-catalogue," he said.

"My niece made it for me—under my direction, of course. Quite a clever girl. She's doing war work in Ambledown, a secretary of some sort in the dynamo factory there. She lives here with me like her cousin, young Fearon, whom you saw a minute or two ago."

Collingbourne got to his feet again, paused for a moment, and then went off again at a tangent.

"By the way, what do you think of marriages between first cousins? Some people say it's unwise; others seem to think it doesn't matter. Something to be said on both sides, perhaps. I know nothing about it myself. Heredity and all that, it's off my line. Besides, of course, it may never come off. I've no idea what she thinks about it."

He was interrupted by the entrance of the maid with a tray.

"Ah! Here's your whisky, Dr. Goldsmith. Sandwiches, too," he added in a slightly puzzled tone. "I don't remember ordering sandwiches."

"Mr. Fearon told me to bring them, sir."

"Quite right, quite right! Efficient fellow, that nephew of mine, when he chooses—which isn't often, I must say," he added, turning to his guest. "Here you've been letting me ramble on, forgetting all about the sandwiches. I've no head for details, none at all, never had. You must go to my niece for that sort of thing. She's the really efficient one of the family. Got her head screwed on right. My nephew's a lazy devil, what they call 'an afternoon farmer' hereabouts."

The visitor helped himself from the tray which the maid had placed at his side. Tactfully ignoring Collingbourne's latest remark, he started a fresh topic.

"I see that book collecting isn't your only hobby," he commented. "You take an interest in astronomy as well. I noticed the dome on your roof as I came in."

"Dome? Oh, yes, of course. There's a telescope in it—five or six inches aperture—I forget which. It belonged to my father. I take no interest in it myself. You'll have to ask Denis about it; he fusses with it quite a lot, quite a lot, making lunar drawings and that kind of thing. He used to pester me to buy him some spectrographic attachment for it, as if I had money to spend on such things. I keep him, you know; what more does he expect? Any spare cash I have goes to enlarge my collection. That's a sensible way of laying out money. Don't you think so? I'm going to leave it all to the British Museum when I'm done with it. If I left it to those two youngsters, they'd put it up to auction and scatter it, after all the pains I've taken to gather the things together. Did you hear Denis at the phone? No? Well, of course it's in the cloakroom, a good way off. I didn't hear anything myself."

Dr. Goldsmith lent his host only an inattentive ear. He was hungry, and devoted himself to his sandwiches. But the thought of the coming interview with the police was still worrying him; and he wished that it were well over and that he knew where he stood. He had only the vaguest ideas about the powers of the English police. For all he knew, they might want to hold him as a material witness, and that would be awkward. His speculations were interrupted by the return of Denis Fearon, who broke brutally into the trickle of his uncle's volubility.

"I rang up the police," he reported. "An inspector's coming up. His name's Loxton, I gather. I've come across him before—a gloomy artist with a secret sorrow or something. Dyspepsia, perhaps. He may be here any minute now."

He turned to Goldsmith with a slightly sardonic smile.

"Ever been mixed up in a murder before? No? Neither have I. I'm told that if the police show any sign of suspecting you, the best thing is to make a noise like an oyster and refuse to say anything until you've consulted a solicitor."

"I'll bear that in mind," retorted Goldsmith, with an answering smile. "But I'm a mere amateur. Murders, to me, have been just things I read about in the newspapers."

"Same here," said Fearon. "But if things go on like this, we'll get a bit blasé of them, hereabouts. This is the second one we've had lately. It's only a fortnight since the head librarian of our local public library got his touch. Rather a rum affair, that was, in its way. Or so I gather. Earnest bookworm, without an enemy in the world, so far as one can tell. The police have a clue, as usual; but they're very reserved—which means they know either nothing or everything . . . Hullo, Diana! Where have you been?"

A graceful, fair-haired girl in a tweed coat and skirt had come into the room while Fearon was speaking. By Goldsmith's æsthetic standards, she was a shade thin-lipped; but he thought that she had hardly improved matters by a careless use of lipstick which blurred the contour of her mouth and contrasted with the evident care which she had spent on the rest of her appearance. Collingbourne hastened to introduce his guest.

"This is Dr. Goldsmith, Diana. My niece, Miss Herne . . . That's not the dress you were wearing at dinner, is it?" he added, peering at her doubtfully as though his eyes hardly allowed him to be sure.

"No, I've been out for a walk."

Goldsmith surprised a swift glance which Fearon threw at the girl; but he thought he understood when a question followed it.

"You didn't come back by the avenue?"

Denis Fearon, apparently, was afraid that his cousin had come upon the dead body as she returned to the house. For some reason, Diana seemed to resent the question; and after a momentary but noticeable hesitation, she countered it with another.

"Why do you ask that?" she demanded, sharply.

Her tone suggested that what she really meant was: What business is it of yours?

"Oh, just curiosity," returned Fearon, with a pretence of carelessness which was hardly convincing. "I wondered if you'd seen a new ghost about the premises, that's all. You see, my dear, Dr. Goldsmith found a dead man lying in the avenue as he came up."

"A dead man," the girl echoed. "What are you talking about, Denis? Is this one of your jokes, or what? It's not very funny."

She turned to Goldsmith, and to his surprise he read in her expression not merely astonishment but something else as well: an underlying blend of suspicion and dismay.

"Who was he?" she demanded.

Goldsmith shook his head.

"I've no idea," he explained. "I was careful not to disturb anything, and just came straight up to the house to give the alarm."

"What was he like? You must have seen *that*, at any rate," Diana persisted, with a touch of impatient contempt in her tone.

Goldsmith racked his memory and doled out the details, one by one.

"He was clean-shaven . . . dark-haired . . . a scraggy neck . . . not what you'd call a Hercules . . . dressed in dark tweeds . . . a rather shabby turn-out . . . and he'd a cap, for I saw it beside him, near a white stone. Your avenue's lined with white stones; this one was lying on the roadway . . . and he wore a starched white collar. I noticed that specially, for so few people seem to wear them nowadays over here . . ."

His final descriptive touch produced two effects which he had not expected. Diana Herne seemed to flinch momentarily; then, with an obvious effort, she regained her surface composure, though a bitten lip betrayed her repressed agitation. Collingbourne's intervention rescued her from the need for comment.

"A starched collar?" he ejaculated in some excitement. "If you'd only said that before! You hear that, Denis? It's that fellow . . . Beechwood . . . Oaklands . . . What's his name? . . . Oakley, yes, Oakley . . . the fellow who was here to-night just after dinner. You know: the sub-librarian at the Mitcham Library. That's the man! That's evidently the man. He came here to-night . . ."

An abrupt movement by Diana caught his dim eyes and suddenly he broke off his explanation.

"Yes, that's the man," he ended, lamely.

Goldsmith began to feel even more uncomfortable than before. Manifestly these three people had some knowledge which they did not wish to share with him. He turned the corner as tactfully as he could.

"The police will want to know all about this affair. Better wait till they come," he proposed. "If we begin telling our various stories to each other now, we'll merely confuse ourselves."

"That's sound," agreed Fearon, heartily. "Once we've finished with the police, it'll be time enough to compare notes among ourselves. Meanwhile, as you say, we'd better keep our tales quite separate from each other."

Goldsmith, turning to Diana for concurrence, realised that her make-up was slightly disarranged. For a moment, he put this down to her having bitten her lip; but then his memory went further back and he recalled that when she first came into the room he had, almost unconsciously, noted a faint streak of red across her cheek. Apparently she was quite unaware of it herself. She was not the sort of girl who is always glancing at the nearest mirror. Somehow, although it was only a few minutes since he first set eyes on her, she had left a curiously mixed impression. Good-looking she certainly was, the sort of girl who, even in a crowded street, would draw more than a passing glance. But when one disregarded the physical envelope, the personality behind it was fascinating in a different manner. There was an apparent hardness in her which jarred on Goldsmith; she was too cool and collected for his taste. She must have been taken wholly by surprise at the ugly news of the dead man in the avenue, yet she had, almost instanter, repressed any outward display of her feelings. That argued a rather abnormal strength of character and a surprising self-control. And there was something else: the faintest touch of contemptuous arrogance in her manner. "Is this American worth bothering about, or is he just a fool?" It was not the sort of attitude to put one at one's ease with her.

Again came that uncomfortable feeling that he was an intruder before whose uncomprehending eyes some latent drama was being acted by these three people. His mind went back to Collingbourne's blundering references to marriages between cousins. "I've no idea what she thinks about it." But Collingbourne was an egocentric type, Goldsmith reflected, and hence the last person to notice the obvious in matters which did not concern him. One had only to see the two cousins together in order to understand the state of affairs. Fearon wanted the girl, wanted her badly. That was plain almost at the first glance. But Diana's unconcealed resentment at her cousin's questions about her doings seemed clear proof that he had no privileged position with her; it suggested, rather, that she took his inquiries as an attempted infringement of her liberty, though they were harmless enough in themselves. Fearon must have noticed that smudge of lipstick, and perhaps he had jumped to the conclusion that some man had been kissing her. That would rouse his jealousy, of course. But the actual disturbance of her make-up was hardly the sort of thing which would result from a casual kiss. In any case, that was not where the key to the drama lay. Collingbourne also was in the secret, if secret there were. There was something else behind all this.

"Isn't it about time the police turned up?" demanded Collingbourne, fretfully.

"They're here already," said Fearon. "I heard a car drive up a few minutes ago."

"Then why haven't they come to see me?"

Fearon shrugged his shoulders as though the police were no affair of his.

"How should I know? Probably they're interviewing Sparrick to start with, since she let them in."

"I wish I had your ears," grumbled Collingbourne. "I've heard nothing. What could they want with Sparrick, anyhow? She's got nothing to tell them."

"She'll have plenty to tell them," retorted Fearon with a smile. "Whether it's worth hearing or not is another matter. She's too inquisitive for my taste, that same girl. I came upon her listening at a door the other day."

"Did you?" said Collingbourne waspishly. "I won't have that sort of thing in my house. You'll have to get rid of her," he added, turning to his niece.

"It's not worth while," said Diana indifferently. "She's going to leave in any case. She told me she was going into the A.T.S. as soon as they'd take her; so you needn't worry. The bother will be to find someone to replace her here."

"Well, that's your affair, that's your affair," retorted her uncle. "Look about and find somebody."

"I'm doing so. It's not so easy as you think, uncle."

"This war's upsetting everything," declared Collingbourne with the air of a man making an important discovery. "Those air-raids . . . I'll have to take steps to safeguard my collection. I ought to have done it before this. Priceless things in it, priceless. But somehow," he added, turning to Goldsmith, "I can't bear to be separated from them. It would be like parting with old friends, you know. A hateful business."

"Have you had heavy raids hereabouts?" Goldsmith thought it only polite to inquire.

He had never been in a raid himself, but he had gathered that those who had endured them were apt to grow boring when they discussed their experiences. What he wanted, at this moment, was to see the police and get it over.

"Oh, so-so," Collingbourne declared. "Only a stray bomb once in my grounds. Ambledown got it much heavier, and that was a disaster from my own point of view. A man Tibberton was killed in one of them, and I used to depend on him a good deal. He was a second-hand bookseller with an extraordinary *flair* for discovering old manuscripts . . ."

Goldsmith suddenly became alert.

"Robert Tibberton? I've heard about him. I didn't know he'd been killed."

"Oh, yes," explained Collingbourne. "He was on A.R.P. duty. Killed instantly. I shall miss him, you know. He often picked up just the sort of things I wanted. I used to give him a list of the stuff I felt inclined to buy, and he hunted about; took a long time over it, sometimes; but had a wonderful knack of scenting books out. Naturally, he kept his thumb on the names of the people he bought from. He'd have been a fool if he'd done anything else. But I never grudged him his middleman's profit, and he treated me very fairly, I think, very fairly indeed. I suppose I shall have to find some other dealer to take his place. But it was very convenient, you know, having him on my doorstep, almost, and always ready to let me look over his stock and give me the first chance at anything good that he came across. A curious creature in some ways, was Tibberton. People gave him a bad reputation in morals; said he was rather too fond of the women; but that was no affair of mine. I liked that dingy little shop of his. One could always spend an interesting hour or so in it. And now the shutters are up. His relations had no turn for bookselling; they simply let the premises to someone else—I think it's a milk-bar now."

"Ah!" said Goldsmith in a wholly non-committal tone.

Apparently Collingbourne took the interjection as a symptom that his guest was bored by the subject. He cast about for a fresh topic.

"Our local people have been running a book-salvage drive," he rambled on. "For the war, you know, to get paper for munitions. My niece lends a hand, driving about and collecting discarded books and papers. Of course, they're all examined before being passed for pulping, lest any good things should get destroyed. My nephew takes a hand, too. The Mitcham Library people have been doing the sifting. I'd have helped myself, but . . . these eyes of mine, you know. One or two things have turned up, mostly from the libraries of country houses: a black-letter folio Hakluyt; the Dublin edition of Percy's *Reliques*—badly foxed, though—and the French edition of *Vathek* in fair condition . . ."

He broke off abruptly as the door opened and the maid announced dramatically:

"The p'leece, sir!"

12

THE POLICE ARRIVE

EVEN when things went smoothly with him, Inspector Loxton rarely showed it in his face. Now, sitting beside the police chauffeur, with a kit-bag at his feet, he looked even gloomier than usual. In the ordinary run of events, he would have been at home, nursing his sick dog which had taken a turn for the worse that morning; but a sharp influenza epidemic had depleted the Ambledown police staff and had thrown extra duty on his shoulders. And so, after a heavy day, here he was with a fresh affair on his hands. Just what one might have expected: it never rains but it pours. There was the Pickford murder still unsolved; the Inderwick blackmail case was not cleared up yet; and now came this business which was taking him post-haste to Friar's Pardon. Loxton was sufficiently human to speculate glumly on his chances of getting home and to bed before morning.

To put the lid on it, the Chief Constable happened to be staying at the Grange, as he sometimes did; and when Loxton had passed the news to him, Driffield had said that he'd drive over and lend a hand. Intellectually, Loxton admired his superior; but he had a distrust of the Chief Constable's sense of humour and he would have felt happier if he had been left to handle this latest affair himself, without assistance from above. Not that Driffield would take the credit; that wasn't his way. But the inspector hated interference, especially when it was a cleverer man who intruded. It made one feel such a fool when one missed a point and had it indicated to one later on.

The police car slowed down and took the turn through the Friar's Pardon gates, but it had hardly gone more than a few yards up the avenue when a curt order made the driver pull up. Loxton's glance had caught a figure lurking amongst the trees which fringed the roadway.

"Here! Who are you?" hailed the inspector, leaning out of the car window. "Come out of it! I want to see you."

There was no reply, and the figure vanished among the shadows.

"Get out and see who that is," ordered Loxton, turning to the men in the rear seats. "Over there!"

Two constables slipped out of the car and hastened in the direction indicated by the inspector. Evidently they ran their quarry down almost at once. There was a sound of talking, evidently some protests, and then they returned, leading a woman with them. As the group came up to the car, Loxton recognised the captive as May Pickford.

"What are *you* doing here?" he demanded in some surprise. "Have you been up at the house?"

"No."

"Then what are you here for?"

There was a marked hesitation before the reply came.

"I'm waiting to see someone."

"Oh, indeed. Who is it?"

"That's no business of yours, Mr. Loxton," retorted May, who had recognised him as he stepped out of the car. "I'm not doing any harm here, am I?"

"You're trespassing."

"That's not a criminal offence. I've been doing no damage. I know all about trespass. I once was a member of a Rambling Club."

"Did you go up the avenue?" demanded Loxton, brushing this aside.

"No, I didn't," rejoined May Pickford. "And I didn't come down it, either. I've been for a walk. Is there any harm in that?"

"I'm not going to argue with you. I'm going to detain you for the present. Something has happened, and everyone we find hereabouts is under suspicion just now. You'll have to give some account of yourself, Mrs. Pickford. Think that over. The Chief Constable will be here in a few minutes. You can explain to him, if you like. That might be better."

May Pickford considered for a moment or two before answering.

"Very well," she said at last. "But if I miss the last bus you'll have to send me home in a car. I can't walk to Ambledown at this time of night."

"You'd better get in here," said the inspector, pointing to the empty rear seats. "It's growing cold, with this wind. You'll be more comfortable."

May Pickford shivered slightly and decided to fall in with the advice. The two constables also took their seats and the car moved on up the avenue for some distance.

"Stop!" ordered Loxton as they came near the house. "The car can wait here. I don't want to have its tracks all over the place. Sergeant Eyre and I are enough to start with; the others stay here till we want you."

Walking slowly and turning the rays of their torches on the ground, Eyre and the inspector made their way along the avenue, but it was not until they had rounded several bends in it that they came upon the dead man.

"Looks dead enough," said Loxton, kneeling down beside the body. "Blood oozing from the ear. That's fracture of the skull, I expect. Hit from behind with something heavy. At least, that's what I'd say. But no doubt if they call in Professor Dundas he'll tell us the man was drowned and then dropped out of a plane."

Sergeant Eyre sniggered sycophantically. Loxton's staff knew his distaste for Dundas's methods and were quite prepared to play up to it when that seemed the easiest course. But Eyre was saved from any verbal comments by the sound of a motor horn not far away, down the avenue up which they had come.

"That'll be the Chief," said Loxton, morosely. "Well, we haven't touched anything. Off you go and wave your torch at the corner, so that he'll know to drive slow as he comes up. Hurry!"

In a minute or two a car crept round the corner, with Wendover at the wheel and Eyre standing on the running-board. Loxton waved his torch to show his position, and the motor came to rest some twenty yards away. Sir Clinton got out and came cautiously forward, followed by Wendover and the sergeant.

"Good evening, Inspector. Dr. Massinger hasn't

arrived yet? That must be his car we hear now, down by the gates. Just go back and stop him, Sergeant, please. Ask him to walk up."

The Chief Constable pulled a torch from his pocket, knelt down, and examined the body.

"You haven't touched it? All the better. There'll be more of us to spot anything that turns up when we begin to look him over."

A second car came up and drew to a halt behind Wendover's motor. The police surgeon got out of it and advanced to join the group. Sir Clinton looked up and nodded.

"Good evening, Doctor. We've disturbed nothing, so you can start in at once. We'll do our share when you've finished."

He rose to his feet and drew aside so as to give the police surgeon plenty of room. Dr. Massinger produced his torch, opened his surgical bag, and fell to work while the others watched.

"The man's quite dead," he reported after a while. "I can't put an exact time on it. Not more than an hour or so before this, I'd say. It's plain enough. Someone hit him from behind, on the right-hand side of the head, and fractured his skull."

"Murder, then?" asked Wendover.

To his surprise, Dr. Massinger did not confirm this at once.

"Manslaughter, perhaps," he said in a doubtful tone. "You'll have to wait till I do a P.M. before I can say much about that. But so far as I can tell now, the fellow has an abnormally thin skull. It's gone just as the shell of a boiled egg does when you tap it with a spoon. A twelve-year-old boy could have struck that blow. Or a girl, either. A man with a normal thickness of skull night only have been stunned by it; but this man's skull is so thin that it would have been fractured if he'd slipped on a banana-skin and hit his head on the pavement in falling."

"I think we can rule out the banana-skin at this stage in the war," said Sir Clinton. "But I see what you mean. The assailant, whoever it was, may merely have meant to stun this fellow and then rob him; killing may not have been in the plan?"

"That's the notion," confirmed Massinger. "You'll need to be sure of a motive, or a smart lawyer might get your man off."

"If it is a man," qualified Sir Clinton. "By your account, it might be a boy or a girl. Even a cripple might have done it. Well, we'll bear that in mind, Doctor. Finished? Then we'll get the body down to the mortuary and you can make a fuller examination tomorrow. There's nothing else that strikes you?"

"Nothing at present."

"Then there's no reason why we should keep you here when you might be in a less draughty spot. We'd better say good night."

"Good night!" returned Massinger; and picking up his bag, he went off to his car.

Sir Clinton made a gesture to Loxton and the sergeant.

"Now that the doctor's finished with him, we can do as we like. Turn him face upward, please. I'll give you a light from my torch."

As the dead man was turned over, Loxton gave an ejaculation of surprise.

"Why, it's Oakley, sir! The man I mentioned in my reports on the Pickford affair—the assistant-librarian."

"Ah, indeed!" said Sir Clinton, apparently unperturbed by this. "Then I'm afraid you won't have the pleasure of putting him in the dock after all, Inspector. A nuisance, isn't it? Well, we must take things as they come."

Something seemed to catch his attention, and he stooped down, shining his torch at close range upon the dead man's face. When he straightened himself up again, Wendover in turn bent to see what had attracted the Chief Constable's attention.

"See some red on his lips, Squire?" Sir Clinton inquired. "Lipstick, obviously. Was he an effeminate type, by any chance? What do you think, Inspector?"

"I never heard anything of the sort about him, sir."

"I shouldn't expect it, after the report you made. Besides, that lipstick stuff wasn't deliberately put on. It came there accidentally, by the look of it. He may have been kissing a girl, perhaps. However, we needn't bother about it just now. You'd better go through his pockets."

Loxton obeyed, kneeling down by the body and naming each article as he came upon it.

"Right-hand breast pocket: identity card, James Oakley. Note-case: two one-pound notes and three ten-shilling notes. No other papers of any sort. . . . Left-hand breast pocket: handkerchief. . . . Left-hand outer pocket of jacket: briar pipe; tobacco pouch. . . . Right-hand pocket: empty. . . . Waistcoat pocket, top left-hand; fountain-pen in clip. . . . Waistcoat pocket, lower left-hand: an old pocket-knife, three-bladed. . . . Right-hand upper waistcoat pocket: one of these pocket inhalers. . . . Right-hand lower waistcoat pocket: a lighter, large size, and the stub of a pencil with rubber on the end, and a bus ticket for the route between Ambledown and here. . . . Trouser-pocket, left-hand: a half-crown, two florins, a shilling and two sixpenny-bits. . . . Right-hand trouser-pocket: five pennies and two halfpennies, and some keys on a ring. . . . That's all, sir. There's no hip-pocket. That collection doesn't tell us much," he added gloomily.

"No?" said Sir Clinton. "He had a cold in the head. The inhaler and the state of his handkerchief show that. And I don't think he murdered Pickford. But that's a mere academic point now, in any case. The immediate problem is how he got killed himself."

He stooped again and ran his fingers over a fairly wide area of the road-surface around the body.

"There's only been a single shower of rain to-day. It came driving down from the north—about a quarter past ten. I heard it beating on the window-panes of the smoking-room, Squire. Oakley was killed before that shower. Why? Because the patch of ground under his body is quite dry whilst the rest of the roadway is damp. More to the point is how he was knocked out. There aren't any footmarks. The ground was bone dry before the rain, and this road-surface is far too hard to take impressions. We'll have to look elsewhere."

Returning his note-book to his pocket, he began to cast round, pacing slowly up the avenue away from the body. The first thing to catch his eye was a stone which lay in the roadway. It was about the size of a croquet-ball, but egg-shaped instead of spherical, and it had a coat of whitewash—evidently it was one of those stones which formed a border to the drive.

"Inspector! Will you please take a measurement or two from this tree, and that one, to fix the place of this stone? Don't touch it. I want its position fixed before we move it."

He ran his eye along the files of stones by the side of the avenue, but as none was missing he moved on, glancing from side to side until he turned the next corner and disappeared. Loxton, meanwhile, pulled out a tape-measure and began to take the distances of the stone from the two trees. Wendover followed the Chief Constable round the bend in the avenue and made up on him just as he came upon a gap in the lines of stones.

"This seems to be the place," said Sir Clinton. "The recess in the ground would just fit one end of that ostrich-egg. Put your finger into the little pit, Squire. Damp, isn't it? Then evidently the stone was taken out of this cavity before the rain shower. No doubt Dundas could make us a cast of the hole if we need one, just to amuse the jury. We'll go back now, I think."

"Got the measurements?" demanded Sir Clinton. "Then we can shift this thing. No use having it knocked about by our cars as we pass. Let's see. Dundas would pack it nicely for us, but as he isn't here and we haven't his traps, we'll just have to do the best we can. Have you a bag with you, Inspector? You might bring it along, please."

Loxton had no intention of missing anything, so he dispatched the sergeant to bring the kit-bag from the police car. Meanwhile the Chief Constable produced a pair of rubber gloves from his pocket and drew them on. Then he pulled out his handkerchief and wrapped the stone in it, handling it tenderly.

"Dundas would scoff at this way of doing things; but we can do no better," he said grudgingly.

Eyre returned with the kit-bag; and Sir Clinton packed the silk-enwrapped stone delicately, wedging it carefully with some of the other contents.

"Take care of it," he said, handing the bag back to Loxton. "It's a smooth stone, and we may get finger-prints off it, perhaps. Who is that woman you have in your car? I noticed her as we edged past."

"It's a Mrs. Pickford, sir. You've seen her name in my reports. We found her hanging about near the gates; and she wouldn't give any account of herself, so we detained her."

Sir Clinton nodded.

"Let her sit in the off-side seat. There's no need for her to see Oakley's body. Put one of your constables on guard over this place. Are there any more coming? Then let them come right up to the house and picket the doors. We'll go up there ourselves now."

"Very good, sir."

13

THE EAVESDROPPER

WHILE they stood on the steps of Friar's Pardon after ringing the bell, Sir Clinton turned and looked out over the moonlit landscape.

"That must make a fine display of colour when it's in season," he remarked, pointing to the spacious arc of rhododendrons which bounded the lawn to the east and south. "Pity it's past its best."

Before Wendover could reply, the door was opened by Lizzie Sparrick. Apparently she recognised Loxton and was about to say something when she noticed Wendover behind the inspector. She stared inquisitively at May Pickford, but stifled some remark which evidently came to her tongue.

"We want to see Mr. Collingbourne," said Loxton. "This is Sir Clinton Driffield, the Chief Constable."

"Come in then, an' I can get the door shut."

She admitted them to the hall, closed the door, and switching on the lights, examined them one by one with ill-disguised curiosity. On the way up to the house Sir Clinton had said a few words to the inspector, and Loxton took things into his own hands at once. He questioned Lizzie Sparrick about the exits from the house, issued orders to his men to picket them, settled May Pickford in a chair in the hall with a constable on guard to prevent Lizzie from seizing the chance of talking to her; and then waited for the Chief Constable to take charge.

"You're Lizzie Sparrick, I think," Sir Clinton began. "Have you been in the house all this evening?"

"I've been in all day, sir."

"Who lives on the premises? Don't bother about visitors just yet."

"There was Mr. Collingbourne, Mr. Fearon, an' Miss 'Erne at dinner, sir. Besides that, there's the cook an' me."

"Have you had any telephone calls or telegrams to-day?"

"There was a phone call for Miss Diana just before dinner. A man's voice, it was. 'E gave no name an' I didn't know the voice. I just called Miss Diana an' she gave me some message to the cook an' shut the door on me. The telephone's in the cloakroom an' the kitchen's a good way off, so I didn't 'ear w'at she said over the phone."

"What happened after dinner?"

"Give me time to think, an' I'll tell you. A lot o' things 'appened, an' I want to get 'em right in my mind to start with."

After a pause to consult her memory, she continued:

"This is the w'y of it, so far's I can call to mind. After dinner, Mr. Collingbourne an' Mr. Fearon went into the study. Miss Diana went upstairs to 'er room—I'll tell you about that, by an' by. I was busy clearin' aw'y the dinner things. W'en I'd done that, cook said she'd an 'eadache an' was goin' up to lie down on 'er bed once she'd finished washin' up. So I give 'er an 'and an' told 'er to go off, an' I'd see to the rest. W'ich she did. I 'ad the kitchen wireless to keep me company. I was just listenin' to the nine o'clock news—Big Ben 'ad just struck, I remember—w'en the front door bell rang, an' I went to answer it. It was a man Oakley, 'im that 'as a job at the Mitcham Library."

"That's very clear," said Sir Clinton, encouragingly. "You're quite sure about the time?"

"Abso*lute*ly, sir. Do I go on? Well, w'en I opened the front door, I recognised this Oakley at once, 'avin' seen 'im often at the library w'en I was doin' paper-salvage work. I expected 'im to ask for Miss Diana, seein' they've been so much mixed up together in this book-collectin' stunt; but it was Mr. Collingbourne that 'e wanted to see, an' that surprised me a bit, for 'e 'ad never put 'is foot over the doorstep of this 'ouse before, an' I didn't suppose 'e even knew Mr. Collingbourne."

"Did you notice anything particular about him?"

"'E seemed a bit nervous an' excited-like, I thought; but p'r'aps that was just my fancy," said Lizzie, honestly. "'E gave me 'is visitin'-card, very formal; an' I showed 'im into the study. Mr. Collingbourne seemed to be expectin' 'im. Mr. Fearon was there as well . . . I—I 'appened to 'ave somethin' to do in the 'all just then . . . an' I over'eard some things they said."

"You listened at the door," paraphrased Sir Clinton, equably. "Quite so. What did you hear? That's the point."

"Nothin' I could make much out of," Lizzie confessed

candidly. "Just scraps 'ere an' there w'en they raised their voices. There was somethin' about old manuscripts; Mr. Collingbourne's always talkin' about old manuscripts; 'e's got a bee in 'is bonnet about 'em, it seems to me. An Oakley said somethin' like: 'If I 'ad a 'undred thousand pounds, would it make any difference?' 'E seemed to be sneerin'-like. . . . No, not that, ezackly. I took it they'd been tellin' 'im that 'e didn't add up to tuppence—w'ich was quite true—an' 'e didn't like it. Any'ow, they seemed to lose their tempers over somethin' —leastways, Mr. Collingbourne did."

"And did you hear any more?"

"Not at that time," said Lizzie, quite unabashed. "Miss Diana came downstairs an' I slipped away. She'd changed w'ile she was upstairs. At dinner she was wearin' a light evenin' frock, a very nice one it is; but w'en she came downstairs again she 'ad on a coat an' skirt, more like the sort o' thing to go outside with, on a chilly night like this. She went out by the front door."

"About what time was that?" demanded Sir Clinton.

"That would be about twenty or twenty-five past nine, I think, but I didn't look at the clock. After Miss Diana went out I began to think about doin' some darnin' to pass the time; an' I started to go up to my room to see if I could fix up a ladder in a pair o' stockin's. I opened the kitchen door quietly; an' just as I was doin' that, Mr. Fearon came out o' the study an' went upstairs. I knew w'ere 'e was goin'; 'e goes up to the dome w'ere the telescope is almost every night w'en the sky's clear an' there's an 'alf-moon. 'E's doin' some drawin's o' the moon, it seems. I've 'eard them speak about it at times, 'im an' Mr. Collingbourne an' Miss Diana."

"You saw Mr. Fearon come out of the study," said Sir Clinton, patiently.

"Yes, 'e went upstairs. I waited a bit an' then I went up myself; an' I seen 'im at the end o' the passage that runs along the west wing to the door that leads into the dome. Once 'e was inside an' the door shut, I followed along. My room's on that passage, third door on the left; an' I went to it to get this silk to darn the ladder in my stockin'. I could 'ear Mr. Fearon in the dome. 'E was openin' the slit in the roof an' turnin' the dome. 'That won't do cook's 'eadache much good,' I sez to myself. It makes a terrible rumble. Often 'e's waked me up in the night, turnin' the thing into position. Cook complains of it, too. She sleeps in the room next me. It must be a cold job in the winter-time, sittin' up there for hours together, but Mr. Fearon keeps an old overcoat in the dome to slip on if 'e gets chilly."

"Don't bother about Mr. Fearon," said Sir Clinton. "What did you do yourself?"

"I got w'at I wanted—the silk an' the stockin's—an' I was comin' back to the stair-head w'en the study door opened, an' then from the 'ead o' the stairs I 'eard Mr. Collingbourne lettin' Oakley out at the front door. Oakley stopped on the step an' 'e said: 'That's your last word? You won't change your mind?' An' Mr. Collingbourne, 'e laughed; not amused-like but t'other way, if you know w'at I mean; an' 'e said: 'W'ere did you pick it up? That's w'at I'd like to know.' An' that was all I 'eard before the door shut."

"What time was that?" asked Sir Clinton.

"Round about 'arf-past nine, I think, sir; but I can't be sure to a minute."

"Mr. Collingbourne went back into his study after that? He didn't go out with the man Oakley?"

"Oh, no, sir. I didn't see 'im, bein' round the bend o' the stair; but I 'eard 'is steps in the 'all after the front door closed, an' I 'eard 'im shut the study door be'ind 'im."

"What happened after that? You make an excellent witness, I must say."

Lizzie Sparrick almost visibly glowed at this compliment. She threw a glance at Inspector Loxton which indicated plainly what she thought of his methods as compared with those of the Chief Constable.

"I sat in the kitchen for the best part of an hour, sir," she continued. "I was busy with darnin' and so on. I'd 'ave gone to bed, but Mr. Collingbourne was expectin' a visitor, 'e told me; so I stayed up. Then the door-bell rang again, an' I went to answer it. As I passed the foot o' the stairs, I see Mr. Fearon at the top of 'em, comin' down; an' so I 'ad to wait till 'e got to the study door before I could switch off the 'all lights an' open the front door. As soon as I 'eard the study door close, I put the 'all lights out an' let in this Dr. Goldsmith—'im they was expectin', you understand. 'Is room was ready for 'im, but 'e wouldn't go there; 'e just wanted to 'ang up 'is 'at and coat in the cloakroom and then 'e wanted to see Mr. Collingbourne at once, so I showed 'im into the study w'ere Mr. Collingbourne an' Mr. Fearon were. By an' by, Mr. Fearon came out an' ordered me to take in some refreshments to this visitor; an' then 'e went to the phone in the cloakroom. 'E shut the door, so I didn't 'ear who he rang up; I was busy cuttin' sandwiches in the kitchen. Then 'e came back an' went into the study again. I took in the tray. Then Miss Diana walked in at the front door an' went straight into the study."

Lizzie paused, as if to recall anything which she might have missed out, but evidently she was satisfied with her tale.

"W'at's it all about, sir? I'm not inquisitive, really, but——"

"You'll hear soon enough," broke in Loxton. "Meanwhile, just you keep a still tongue in your head."

Lizzie bridled at this cavalier treatment and turned to Sir Clinton; but the Chief Constable was slipping off his light overcoat and had apparently not noticed Loxton's intervention.

"Please show us the cloakroom," he said. "I want to hang up this coat."

With a huffy glance at the inspector, Lizzie led the way down the hall to the foot of the stairs. As they reached them, Sir Clinton paused before a table on which, beside a salver and some flower vases, lay a pair of yellow chamois gloves. An umbrella stand, in which stood several heavy sticks, flanked the table. Sir Clinton picked up the gloves, examined them for a moment, and retained them in his hand.

"Just a moment," he said to Lizzie. "When you saw Miss Herne go out, did you notice if she took a stick with her?"

Lizzie pondered deeply for a few seconds; then she shook her head.

"I don't remember rightly w'ether she did or not, sir. Reelly, I can't think."

"It doesn't matter," Sir Clinton reassured her. "Lead on."

The cloakroom was at the end of a side-passage off the hall. Sir Clinton hung up his coat and hat and, as Wendover copied him, the Chief Constable turned again to Lizzie.

"Which is Dr. Goldsmith's coat?"

Lizzie pointed it out and Sir Clinton examined the contents of the pockets; but he found nothing to interest him except a pair of gloves and a sheet of paper, much-folded and worn, which he studied for a time before placing it carefully in his own pocket-book. Then he turned once more to Lizzie, who had been watching his proceedings with unashamed inquisitiveness.

"I want the fingerprints of everyone in the house," he explained to her. "Just a formality, in your case, of course. That's why I'm going to begin with you. After you have had yours taken, no one else can very well object to letting me have theirs. You see?"

"I see, sir," said Lizzie, highly flattered by being thus taken into the confidence of the Chief Constable.

Already she saw herself as the heroine of the evening, helping the authorities, indispensable, "in the know." That would make a fine story to tell, by and by.

"And cook's fingerprints, too, sir?" she asked.

"She has a headache, hasn't she?" said Sir Clinton. "I think we'll respect her rest for the present. We can get her prints later, if we need them. And now will you go with Inspector Loxton and let him make a record of your prints? Run along now, there's a good girl."

When Lizzie and Loxton had gone, Sir Clinton turned to Wendover.

"I can tell you one thing, Squire. I don't think you're likely to see the St. Rule's Treasure, yet a while."

"That won't keep me awake," retorted Wendover. "But what makes you so sure of that, Clinton?"

"Well, all these speculations about the discovery of the treasure by Pickford arose out of the entry in Pickford's diary—the one in which he spoke of writing to a goldsmith. You remember that? My impression is that the only Goldsmith of any importance to us is under this roof at the present moment; and he's not a dealer in precious metals."

"I never believed in the existence of the St. Rule's Treasure," declared Wendover. "By the way, you seem very friendly with that maid. She's a nasty little thing to have about a house, listening at doors and prying around generally."

"If I had bullyragged her," pointed out Sir Clinton, "it would have taken me twice as long to extract her news; and perhaps she might have left out some of the details. I wouldn't have her in my own house for an hour; but there's no room for personal prejudices in my line, Squire. As it is, we've got quite a lot from her to think over. But now we'll go back and see how Loxton gets on with his fingerprinting. Then she can show us in. I want to have a look at this American. You know his name, of course. One sees it mentioned at lots of big auctions."

14

"SABRINA FAIR . . ."

As the three newcomers were shown into the study by Lizzie Sparrick, Collingbourne blinked at them uncertainly in turn, winding up with a nod of recognition to Wendover, who thereupon took it on himself to introduce Sir Clinton and the inspector, lest their involuntary host in his blindness should mistake one for the other. This seemed to remind Collingbourne of his social duties, and he did the like for Diana, Fearon, and the American.

"Now we all know each other," he ended, fatuously. "I've heard your name often, Sir Clinton. Curious that we've never seemed to run across each other before, very curious. This is a troublesome business, a most regrettable affair, isn't it? The poor fellow—it's Oakley, isn't it?—was here in this room not so long ago. Strange. Very strange indeed. Of course, if there's any help we can give . . . very glad indeed . . . naturally. . . ."

His speech tailed off into incoherent ejaculations.

Sir Clinton pointedly glanced at his watch. Evidently he had no intention of wasting time.

"I'm afraid I shall have to bother you with some questions. Nuisance, isn't it? It will be more convenient to take you one by one, if you don't mind. Saves getting things mixed up. So if there's a room which could be used . . ."

"This one will do," Collingbourne hastened to suggest. "We can all go somewhere else just now, and you can send for us one by one when you want us, if that will suit. There's a desk with plenty of note-paper, and if you need anything else—anything—just ring the bell and let us know. We're only too anxious to help in any way, you understand. . . ."

"Thanks," said the Chief Constable. "Then I think I'd like to hear Dr. Goldsmith first."

The inspector ushered the rest of the party out into the hall, and then came back to the desk, ready to take notes.

"I'm sorry for all this fuss," said Sir Clinton, turning to Goldsmith. "It's a poor reception for a visitor from overseas in these days; but I am afraid we must go through the formalities. Would you mind letting me see your identity papers, please?"

The American produced a passport and one or two other documents which he handed to the Chief Constable who, after a glance at them, passed them to the inspector.

"What brings you over to England just now? It's hardly a pleasure resort in these days."

"I collect old books and manuscripts. I deal in them, too; that's my trade. You can easily identify me; I'm pretty well known in the auction rooms, both in London and New York. A lot of interesting stuff has been coming to light in this paper-salvage business you've been running on this side, so I came over to look round, on chance. I've been moving about your country, keeping my eyes open."

"But what brings you here, Dr. Goldsmith? This isn't a very promising field, surely."

"Mr. Collingbourne has corresponded with me from time to time," the American explained. "When he heard I was over on this side he invited me to look over his collection. He claims to have some fine stuff. I wanted to see it. I might even make him an offer for anything that takes my fancy. And there's a man in Ambledown I want to look up. He sometimes gets hold of good things. Tibberton is his name—a second-hand bookseller."

"If you want to see him," said Sir Clinton grimly, "you'll have to book another passage—with Charon instead of the Cunard. He was killed on A.R.P. duty not long ago."

"I'm sorry to hear that," said Goldsmith, evidently taken aback by this news.

"You had some communication with another local man, I think," Sir Clinton went on in a casual tone. "Pickford's the name."

"How do you know that?" demanded Goldsmith, in a tone of suspicion. "I gathered from his letter that the matter was strictly confidential; but since he seems to have been talking about it himself, there's no harm in telling you. He wrote to me hinting that he had some stuff which might be saleable. If I did not want it for myself, he said he'd like my opinion on it."

Wendover pricked up his ears at this, and decided to break into the conversation.

"Can you tell me, Dr. Goldsmith, if this book, or whatever it was, belonged to the Mitcham Library? You see, I'm a trustee for that institution. Pickford was librarian, but he had no authority to sell anything out of it. He was hard up and might have been tempted. One would like to know. It's not a matter of idle curiosity, as you can understand."

"I'm not a receiver of stolen goods," Goldsmith assured him with a faint smile. "I should want to see a good title to the thing before I touched any transaction of that sort. But thanks for putting me on my guard. I'll look after that when I meet Pickford."

"You'll need to cross the Styx to do that," interjected Sir Clinton. "Pickford's dead. Book-collecting seems to be one of the dangerous trades, hereabouts."

He glanced keenly at the American, but Goldsmith's face betrayed nothing, not even a faint surprise at the news.

"D'you tell me so?" he said, evenly.

"You never met him?"

"No, I never met him. I can let you see his letter, if you like. I haven't it with me, but I can easily look it up for you."

"I should like to see it later on. You've never been in Ambledown before, Dr. Goldsmith?"

Goldsmith shook his head decidedly.

"Never before this evening."

"Would you mind telling us about your movements since you arrived to-night?"

Goldsmith paused before beginning his tale, as though considering carefully what he had to say.

"I came down on the Birmingham train and changed at

Trendon. I thought someone from Friar's Pardon might meet me at Ambledown, but no one turned up, so I took a taxi. It broke down, though, some distance from here; and as I had only a light suit-case, I walked on. The taxi-man directed me. As I was coming up the avenue I saw something lying on the ground. The moon was behind a cloud and my torch-battery wasn't very good, but I examined the body. No, I didn't touch it or move it. That's your job, of course. But the man seemed dead. I saw no blood except a trickle from his ear. He was lying on his face. I never touched him, just knelt down beside him. Oh, yes, I did try to feel his pulse, but there was no sign of one, so far as I could make out. Then there was a sharp shower of rain, very short, as I got to my feet again. I didn't look at my watch. I suppose I ought to have done, but I never thought of it."

"You don't know the man?" asked Sir Clinton.

"I don't know anyone hereabouts. Even Mr. Collingbourne I hadn't met till I came in here to-night."

"Did anything catch your attention as you stood there?"

"I saw a white stone—quartz, likely—lying on the roadway near the body. I examined it, but didn't touch it. It was about the size of a small coco-nut."

Sir Clinton made a slight gesture and the inspector opened his bag and produced the stone from the avenue, which he placed gingerly on the desk.

"This it?" he inquired.

"There were some red spots on the one I saw," explained Goldsmith, moving over to examine the exhibit. "I took them for blood. Yes, this seems to be the stone. You can see the red on it."

"Don't touch it, please," said Sir Clinton. "Did you

notice any gap in the border where it might have come from?"

Goldsmith shook his head decidedly.

"No, I remember glancing round, wondering where the thing had come from; but I saw no gap."

At a gesture from his superior, the inspector covered up the stone again. Sir Clinton turned back to the American.

"As you were coming up the avenue, did you hear any sound that caught your attention?"

"I suppose you mean a cry, or something of that sort? No, I don't remember anything except the barking of a dog, far away in the distance. I certainly heard no footsteps in the avenue; and nobody met me or passed me while I was on my way up from the gate. The first person I saw was the maid who opened the door to me. . . . Oh, yes, just before that, while I was waiting on the doorstep, I did hear something—a long rumble like a distant peal of thunder that lasted for some seconds. I wondered at the time if it was a bomb—I've not been in an air-raid, so far—but there was no flash or anything of that sort. That's really all I can say."

Sir Clinton felt in his pocket, produced his pocket-book, extracted a worn sheet of paper which Wendover recognised. He opened it out on the desk, with a cautionary gesture.

"Here's something I want you to look at and give me your expert opinion about," he said. "Don't touch it, please. Just examine it."

The American seemed slightly surprised by the request, but he leaned over and scrutinised the document deliberately.

"Well, what do you make of it?" asked Sir Clinton after a time.

"'*Sabrina fair*,'" read Goldsmith aloud. "'*Listen where thou art sitting*. . . .'" It's the invocation in *Comus*, of course. This seems to be a letter from John Milton to his friend Lawes about the arrangements for the Ludlow Castle masque. It seems to be an early draft. See the corrections? He wrote *Hear me* to start with, and then changed it to *Listen*! And he had *limpid* to begin with, and altered that to *glassy*, finally. This is interesting."

Loxton pricked up his ears. Here was a chance of learning something about the value of these old books and scraps of paper.

With a glance of deprecation in Sir Clinton's direction, the inspector put in his oar.

"What would you say that bit of paper was worth, sir?" he asked the American.

Goldsmith's face remained inscrutable. He had attended too many auctions and played too many games of poker to betray the slightest indication of his thoughts. Nor did he seem inclined to speak in a hurry.

"I should say that its price would depend on just how much somebody wanted it," he said after a pause.

"How's that?" retorted the inspector, obviously nettled by what he took to be mere fencing. "It must have some sort of definite value, surely?"

"You're thinking of buying a stamp over the post-office counter," rejoined Goldsmith, with a flicker of a smile. "That's about the only kind of document which has a fixed value. If you put this"—he indicated the letter —"up to auction, the price it would fetch would depend on the people who attended the sale, the money they had to spare, and the eagerness they felt to buy this particular piece of paper. Hardly anything fluctuates so much in price as old books and manuscripts. Now, for instance, would you yourself pay £100,000 for an old manuscript?"

"I'd have to get the £100,000 myself first," said Loxton glumly. "And if I had it, there's a lot of things I want more than an old manuscript."

"Exactly my point," retorted Goldsmith. "But the B.M.—the British Museum, I mean—bought a manuscript not so many years ago and paid £100,000 for it."

Wendover was surprised by the expression which flitted across Loxton's face. Evidently Goldsmith's words had suggested something to the inspector, something which had enlightened him and annoyed him simultaneously.

"That was the Codex Sinaiticus. They bought it from the Russians, before the war. I don't suppose you'd have offered a fiver for it, yourself—if as much. Now you see why one can't tell what an old manuscript is 'worth.' It all depends. I certainly don't propose to give you a guess at the value of this *Comus* affair. I'd need to examine it a good deal more carefully before I could do that. Even then, I might be wrong, and that would do my credit no good. No, Mr. Loxton. Take it to an English expert if you want that sort of thing; he'll give you an honest opinion. But I'm not going to say anything about it."

"You've never seen it before?" asked Sir Clinton, carelessly, as though he felt it was time to change the subject.

"No. And I never forget a manuscript that I *have* seen, I may tell you. After all, it's my trade."

Sir Clinton carefully folded up the letter and returned it to his pocket-book. Then he made another slight gesture to Loxton who dived into his bag and produced a pair of gloves which he laid on the desk.

"These yours, sir?" he demanded.

"Yes, they're mine," admitted Goldsmith after a glance at them and another at the face of the inspector.

"Were you wearing them to-night?"

"No, I haven't had them on for days."

"Now would you mind telling us the rest of your story?"

Goldsmith did so, in the fewest possible words, bringing his narrative up to the point when the police arrived.

"Thanks," said Sir Clinton. "I think that covers all the ground except for two things. We're taking the fingerprints of everyone in the house. Do you mind having yours taken? You can refuse if you like, you know."

"I don't mind in the least."

Loxton dived into his bag and laid out the necessary things on the desk. When the process was over, Sir Clinton made another request.

"Would you mind if Inspector Loxton brushed you down? To be quite frank with you, it's the merest formality; but I'm going to ask some other people to go through it too, and it would make things easier if everyone agrees to it."

"Oh, certainly," Goldsmith conceded at once. "Go ahead."

He stood patiently on an outspread sheet of paper whilst the inspector brushed down his trousers and collected the results.

"I'm sorry to have put you to all this trouble," said Sir Clinton. "It's just routine, you know. We may want to ask you a question or two more, after we've seen the other witnesses. In the meanwhile, would you mind not discussing this business with the rest of them? Once people start talking a thing over, they're apt to get muddled up; and I'd rather run no risk of that. And now, if you'll read over the notes that Inspector Loxton has made of your evidence and sign them, that finishes the matter for the present."

When Goldsmith had left the room, Sir Clinton turned to the inspector.

"Are we going too quick for you? I saw you were taking it down in long-hand."

"I can manage it all right, sir, if you keep to that speed. That American's a cool card, sir. He denied all knowledge of that paper without moving a muscle, and yet I saw you take it out of his overcoat pocket not a quarter of an hour ago. That's a rum start, that is."

"Very curious," agreed Sir Clinton. "But not beyond conjecture, as one of Mr. Wendover's favourite authors would say. Think it over. In the meanwhile, we'd better hear what Miss Herne has to say for herself. Do you mind moving to another seat? I want to take her fingerprints myself. And put a chair for her at this side of the desk. Thanks. You might ask her to come in now."

The inspector ushered Diana into the room and Sir Clinton invited her to take the chair which had been arranged for her, across the desk from his own.

"I understand, Miss Herne," he began, "that you had some acquaintance with this unfortunate man Oakley?"

"I knew him casually," Diana admitted, after a slight pause.

The inspector frowned as he noted the momentary hesitation. Witnesses who played that game generally had something at the backs of their minds. The girl was obviously nervous, but she was holding herself well in check, and plainly she had no intention of answering even the simplest question until she had thought it over and seen its bearings. Not a good witness—one of these fencers who think themselves so smart. "Pity the Chief didn't leave her to me," he reflected, sourly. "I know how to handle that type. He's too kid-gloved." He wrote down Diana's answer and gloomily waited for the next question.

"You met him first in connection with this local paper-salvage scheme, I think?" pursued Sir Clinton.

"Yes."

"Merely a sort of official acquaintance then?"

A faint smile flitted across Diana's lips at this definition.

"Well ... Yes, I don't think you could put it better," she agreed. "We were both kept busy, and naturally we ran across each other frequently."

"You met him at the library, of course, amongst a number of other people. You wouldn't learn much about him under those conditions." Sir Clinton paused for a moment and then continued with an air of complete frankness. "My difficulty is that I know so little about him. Now I'm told that you used to drive about in your car with him on this salvage work. You must have got to know him to some extent; you could hardly help learning something about him, and you can help me here."

Diana seemed in no haste to enlighten Sir Clinton. She knitted her brows, and seemed to ponder a good deal before she answered. But her first words went some way towards accounting for the delay.

"It's not very nice, discussing the poor man just now, is it?" she began. "But if I say nothing, you might get a wrong idea of things; and it can make no difference to him now, so perhaps it doesn't matter. He was a common little man, quite unattractive—to me, at least—with a dreadful accent and no ... well, no poise. I mean he was either boasting or else cringing and over-polite in an underbred sort of way. That side of him set my teeth on edge. He talked quite a lot, while I was driving him round, mostly about himself. He seemed very ambitious, and he hadn't got on as well as he thought he ought to have done, if his merits had been recognised. He'd been kept down, he said. Really, he was a bit of a bore, poor little man, but rather pathetic, in a way. I was sorry for him. But lately . . ."

She pulled herself up sharply.

"Lately?" prompted Sir Clinton.

"Lately?" repeated Diana, evidently to gain time for thought. "Oh, lately, I noticed a change in him. He got cocky and overpleased with himself, and I didn't like him a bit. I meant to get someone else to take over this business of driving if I could."

Inspector Loxton nodded to himself. In his own mind he was quite certain that this last speech was something quite different from what she had originally intended to say. She was hiding something, and desperately eager to hide it, too.

"You don't know anything about Oakley's family?" Sir Clinton asked.

Diana shook her head.

"He never mentioned them to me. I don't even know if he had any relatives alive."

"Did he ever say anything to you about his relations with the librarian, Pickford?"

"Nothing worth remembering. In fact, now I look back, he seemed rather to avoid talking about Mr. Pickford to me. I mean, if I mentioned Mr. Pickford, he rather shied away and changed the subject. Perhaps I'm just imagining it, but I got the impression that the two of them did not get on very well together."

"You can't recall anything which might throw some light on what happened to-night, Miss Herne? No? Well, there's just one thing more, a mere formality. We're taking the fingerprints of everyone in the house. It's merely a matter of routine. Would you mind letting me have yours along with the rest? I've got the maid's, and Dr. Goldsmith's; and I shall ask Mr. Collingbourne and Mr. Fearon, by and by. You can refuse, if you wish, of course."

This time, Diana's hesitation was unmistakable. Ten seconds or more passed before she replied.

"I don't see what good it could do."

"Neither do I," said Sir Clinton, with a slightly bored gesture. "But when I send in my report on this affair, some people are sure to ask if I secured all the finger-prints available; and if I say no, then they'll want to know who objected, and why. Some people are too clever by half, at times," he went on, in a reflective tone. "It gives a lot of trouble."

Diana apparently came to a decision, though not without difficulty.

"Oh, if it is going to lead to any trouble, I won't refuse," she said. "Do just as you please about it."

"Thanks," said Sir Clinton, without any particular gratitude in his tone. "It'll help to keep our finger-print expert busy, and that's always something. Would you mind letting me see your hands? Backs upward, first. Thanks. And now the palms, please."

Diana turned her palms upward, and as she did so she gave a start which not even her self-control could conceal. Then she bit her lip as though to stifle some ejaculation. Across the end of the first two fingers of her right hand lay a broad faint streak of red. Sir Clinton noticed it, but seemed to give it very little attention.

"Lipstick," he commented indifferently. "You've been rubbing your hand across your mouth probably, and never noticed it. I'll have to get that off before I can take the prints."

From the desk he picked up a small bottle of benzene

and some cotton-wool; and with their help he proceeded to swab away the colouring matter with the air of a man who finds extra trouble injected into an already wearisome task. When he had finished, he laid the pink-stained cotton-wool on the desk beside him, and began to record Diana's fingerprints, with a running commentary of small talk.

"That should make a good job of it.... We sometimes have to clean people's fingers like this.... Some people have sweaty hands, and that makes a mess of the record. ... It's best to be on the safe side ... Benzene clears the perspiration away, so we always have some of it handy.... And now the other hand, please.... Lipstick reminds me of another case, a while ago.... It turned on whether two samples of lipstick were identical or not.... You wouldn't think that easy to prove, would you?... But our friends the chemists, they seem able to tackle anything.... Or, at least, they'll swear to anything in the box, and convince a jury easily enough ... I'm no expert on these things.... Thanks, Miss Herne, that finishes it."

He seemed as though about to release her when another idea appeared to strike him and he lifted the handkerchief from the white stone, manœuvring it as though aimlessly until the red streaks on it were towards the girl.

"Have you any idea where that could have come from?" he asked casually.

Diana seemed to have regained complete control of herself.

"It looks like one of the stones from the border of our avenue," she said composedly, ignoring the red marks. "My uncle had them laid down when the black-out started to make it easy for people coming up to the house after dark."

"I rather thought that was where it came from," agreed Sir Clinton.

He replaced the handkerchief over the stone; then, from Loxton's bag he took a clean, wide-mouthed stoppered bottle. Waiting until he was sure that this had caught Diana's attention, he picked up the red-stained swab of cotton-wool, pushed it into the bottle, replaced the stopper, and returned the bottle to Loxton's bag.

"There's just one thing more, Miss Herne. Would you mind standing on a piece of paper and letting Inspector Loxton brush you down? It's just a matter of routine again; Dr. Goldsmith let us do the same for him."

"Oh, I don't mind," said Diana; but Wendover thought that there was a curious reluctance in her tone. She submitted to the process with a good grace, however. When it was over, Sir Clinton thanked her with an inscrutable expression on his face.

"That finishes us . . . at least for the present," he said. "Think over things, Miss Herne; perhaps you will remember something else which might help us. I may want to see you again, later on, when I've seen the other witnesses. You won't go to bed just yet? Thank you."

He opened the door for her and ushered her out into the hall. As he came back to the desk he glanced at the inspector.

"And what's troubling you?" he asked, with a certain amusement.

"I don't follow your game, sir; that's all. It's as plain as a pikestaff that she was holding something back. To my mind you had her a bit rattled. You'd got her into a corner and you could have done what you liked with her."

"Sounds almost like a description of a criminal assault," said Sir Clinton, with an impish smile. "But I see what you mean. You think she was hiding something? So do I. But she wasn't rattled nearly so much as you suppose; and if I'd gone straight on, she'd probably have shut up like an oyster. I let her see I knew more than she had imagined, and now I've sent her away to let that sink in. Nothing like a touch of misgiving for clarifying the wits. She's probably wondering just now how much I know and why I didn't ask her where she went when she left the house after dinner."

"But you don't suppose she knocked Oakley on the head, surely," broke in Wendover. "She wouldn't have the strength."

"I don't suppose anything," retorted the Chief Constable. "I'm trying to find out. And the next step is to interview your talkative friend. Will you bring in Mr. Collingbourne, please, Inspector?"

15

A PROPOSAL OF MARRIAGE

COLLINGBOURNE took the initiative almost before he had settled himself in his chair.

"Well? Well?" he demanded, fussily. "Have you got to the bottom of this business yet? Have you made any progress?"

"We are doing our best," Sir Clinton assured him. "But we need facts. Can you tell us what brought Oakley here this evening? Was he an acquaintance of yours?"

"I hardly knew the man," declared Collingbourne. "I'd met him at the Mitcham Library once or twice; that was all. Shabby little fellow with a dreadful accent

and no *savoir-faire*. Not a scrap. Not out of the top
drawer, by any means. So when I got his note this
morning I was very surprised indeed."

"A little slower, please," suggested Sir Clinton.
"Inspector Loxton has to take all this down. You got
a note from Oakley?"

Collingbourne moderated his torrent of explanation
temporarily, though it soon got out of hand again.

"Yes, it came while we were at breakfast—the post
was late—and I read it to my niece and my nephew, it
sounded so peculiar. None of us could make out what
he was driving at."

"Have you got this note of his?" asked Sir Clinton.

"No, no! I threw it into the waste-paper basket.
It'll be in the paper-salvage sack, if you want it. We
never burn any paper here, nowadays, except for lighting
fires. You can easily fish it out. But the gist of it was,
so far as I could make it out, that he wanted to see me
to-night at nine o'clock, on business. 'On an urgent
matter of great importance to both of us.' That's what
he wrote; those were the words. Very mysterious, we
thought, naturally; for what sort of urgent and important
matter could he have with me, when I hardly knew him
by sight? It puzzled me."

"And he turned up at nine o'clock?" Sir Clinton cut
in, to stem this flood of needless speculation.

"Yes, he came about nine o'clock. I was in this room,
and my nephew was with me at the moment. Oakley
seemed to me nervous and excited when he came in;
but he never had any ease of manner, you know. He
was obviously taken aback when he saw my nephew,
quite put out, I noticed. That rather set my back up,
I admit. Wasn't one of my family good enough for him,
I'd like to know. He began by saying that he wanted a

private conversation, entirely private, and so on; and he looked at my nephew as if he expected him to leave the room. This annoyed me, I confess, annoyed me very considerably. I've every confidence in my nephew's discretion, and I was vexed, very vexed indeed, that a stranger should be throwing any doubt on it. Besides, I wasn't going to allow this underbred fellow to lay down the law in my own house. I told him I wished my nephew to be present; and if that didn't suit him, there was an end of the matter. I wasn't really interested in the man or his business, so I was firm. He gave way, finally, in some ill-humour. I told you he had no *savoir-faire.*"

"And what *had* he to say, after all this?" asked Sir Clinton rather testily.

"He began by asking me how one could find out the value of a very rare manuscript. I told him to apply to the B.M.—the British Museum, you know. But I advised him not to bother them unless the thing was really important. Naturally, they don't want to be troubled by Tom, Dick and Harry about a signature of Marie Corelli or a postcard written by Hall Caine. I suppose I may have seemed a little contemptuous about the matter, for he seemed to get annoyed and rather excited. Evidently he had the thing on him, for once he made a movement towards his breast-pocket as if he was going to bring it out, but apparently he thought better of that. I offered to buy it myself, if it was any good. At that, he grew positively insulting, downright offensive, I may say. Did I imagine that *I* could buy a really valuable manuscript, something worth having, a rare treasure? And he mentioned the *Codex Sinaiticus* as an example. Did I know that it had been bought for the British Museum for £100,000? I said I knew that quite well, but I didn't think there were many things like that floating about. That nearly made him bring the thing out of his pocket, but he thought better of it again."

"So you got no clue to what it actually was?" asked Sir Clinton.

"Not the least," said Collingbourne. "Probably it was something of no value at all. What did a man like that know about real rarities? But all of a sudden he changed his attitude completely, made a cringing apology for 'having shown a little heat' in his conversation, and so on. He assured me that what he'd got was something extremely rare—unique, in fact. It would make him a rich man, and so forth. Rubbish, of course, but it's no use arguing with an ignorant fellow like that, no use at all. And I couldn't have advised him, even if he had shown me the thing. My eyes are so poor now that I can't see to read."

"I'm sorry," said Sir Clinton sympathetically. "It must cut you off from a lot of enjoyment, especially a man of your tastes. But what happened after that?" he added hastily, to forestall a ramble into side-issues.

"After that?" repeated Collingbourne. "Oh, that was really amusing, quite funny, indeed. He asked me if I was my niece's guardian. Where he picked that up, I don't know; but as a matter of fact I am. Her father in his will appointed me to look after her until she was twenty-five. He'd nothing to leave her but a pittance, so that was his way of providing for her, I suppose, throwing the expense of her keep on me. But . . . guardian! As if anyone could be expected to control any girl up to twenty-five nowadays! Absurd, isn't it? She does just as she pleases. But the Oakley fellow apparently took this guardian business seriously. He didn't belong to our class, of course, and he must have got his ideas of it mostly out of mid-Victorian novels, or so one would think. Anyhow, he solemnly inquired if I had any objection to his paying his addresses—his very words, I assure you!—to my niece. I kept a straight face, but with difficulty though, as you can imagine. My nephew evidently found the situation too much for him, for he abruptly left the room. I suppose he wanted to have his laugh out. Anyhow, he muttered some hasty excuse about going up to the dome—the observatory, you know—and left us together. So I was left to handle this absurd situation. I told Oakley it was no business of mine; he could present a dozen addresses—illuminated ones, if he liked—for all I cared. It was the girl's affair, not mine. But if he imagined that he could keep her on a third-rate librarian's screw, he'd a lot to learn. And I didn't propose to finance love-in-a-cottage no matter what happened. I wanted him to understand that clearly. I thought it might choke him off, once and for all. But instead, he got as red as a turkey-cock and lost his temper completely. I won't repeat what he said: the poor creature's dead now. But he talked as if he were a perfect Crœsus and I, by comparison, was a poor devil without one penny to rub against another. To tell you the truth, I thought he was a bit touched, rats in the garret. As if my niece would look at him! Amazing! Amazing! After that, there was nothing to do but show him out, and I did so."

"What did you say to him at the door?" interjected Sir Clinton.

"What did I say? . . . Oh, I offered him a fiver for his find, on spec. A pig in a poke, pure and simple. And I think I asked him where he'd come across this precious treasure. I was quite courteous about it, perfectly polite, you know; but he was in a furious temper and went off, saying something about having given me my chance, or some silly thing like that. I was really quite glad to be rid of him."

"What time did he leave you?"

"It was about half-past nine, or a little later. I came back here and was going to switch on the wireless for some item I wanted to listen to, but when I looked at the clock I found I'd missed it."

"You can see the clock-face, then?" asked Sir Clinton.

"Well, I've dropped some atropine—belladonna, you know—into my eyes this evening because I wanted to look at the newspaper headings."

"Where does that door lead to?" demanded Sir Clinton, pointing to one on the south wall of the room.

"Out to the garden," Collingbourne explained. "There's a sort of pantry there, where we keep camp-chairs; and there's a sink that my niece uses when she brings in flowers to decorate the house."

"You didn't go out of the house, did you?"

"I?" ejaculated Collingbourne in a tone of astonishment. "What would I run about outside for? Admiring the beauties of Nature, I suppose. Why, man, I can hardly see well enough in broad daylight to recognise a man passing me in the street. You wouldn't catch me stumbling about after dark, even if there is a moon."

"Mr. Fearon came downstairs later on, didn't he?"

"Yes, he did. He'd been making a drawing of the moon, he told me. He's very good at that kind of thing, very quick and very neat. You should ask him to let you see some of his lunar sketches, if that kind of thing interests you. I used to look them over myself, at times, before my eyes went. Not that it really interests me much."

"What time did Mr. Fearon come back here?" interrupted Sir Clinton, evidently intent on keeping Collingbourne to the main track.

"Oh, shortly after ten, just a minute or two before Dr. Goldsmith turned up and gave us the news of Oakley. Though, of course, we didn't know it was Oakley then, you know."

"What were you and Mr. Fearon talking about when Dr. Goldsmith arrived? Can you remember?"

"We were having a laugh over Oakley's visit. It sounds callous, doesn't it? But, of course, at that time we'd no notion he'd come to grief. My nephew was much amused over Oakley 'paying his addresses.' He had to leave the room, he told me, lest he should laugh in the man's face."

"When Dr. Goldsmith arrived, was he excited?"

"Not more than you'd expect, considering he'd just found Oakley's body. But you'd better ask my niece or my nephew. You must remember that I can't see well."

Sir Clinton acknowledged this with a slight nod, watching his witness as he did so; but Collingbourne showed no sign of having noticed the gesture.

"What is the value of a manuscript in the handwriting of John Milton, can you tell me?"

"It might be anything," replied Collingbourne. "I have some Milton MSS. myself. I paid £25 for one of them at an auction; some others I got through Tibberton, quite cheap, considering what they were. It all depends."

"I see you have a fire in the room, though it's summer."

"Oh, yes. Yes. I've got a poor circulation nowadays. I get no exercise to speak of, with these eyes of mine."

"Do you wear gloves outside, Mr. Collingbourne?"

"Gloves? Gloves?" retorted Collingbourne, rather ruffled apparently. "No, I hate gloves. I haven't worn any for years. The last time I had a pair on was at a funeral. I can't see why people wear gloves; effeminate things, I think."

Sir Clinton seemed to have asked all the questions he thought necessary, and he ended up with the routine request for permission to brush down Collingbourne's clothes, which met with no objection though it seemed to surprise Collingbourne somewhat. Then, after the inspector's notes had been signed, Sir Clinton dismissed his witness.

"He can't have been outside in the dew to-night, sir," Loxton reported when the door had closed behind Collingbourne. "I felt his pumps when I was brushing them, and they were bone-dry."

"You're not suspecting *him*, are you?" said Wendover. "He's as blind as a bat. You could see that for yourself. And in any case, dry shoes prove nothing. He might have walked down the avenue all the way and back, and then there would be no dew underfoot."

Sir Clinton intervened, covering the inspector's obvious mortification.

"You saw no red stains on his hands, did you, while you were taking his fingerprints?"

"No, sir. I looked carefully for that."

"Neither did I. Now I think we'll take Mrs. Pickford. You might bring her in, please."

Wendover's mental portrait of May Pickford had been based on the colourless phrases of Loxton's report, slightly amplified by the glimpse which he caught earlier in the evening; but when she came into the full light of the study, he found an explanation of some things which had been obscure to him before.

"Her looks are hardly above the average," he reflected in slight surprise. "She's a common little thing; but somehow she has an almost uncanny physical attraction —a regular aura of it. No wonder she managed to collect such a crowd of admirers. A woman with a gift like that might be a dangerous type. Perhaps she is."

From the inspector's report, Wendover had expected to see a cool, collected young woman, sufficiently clever and ready-witted in verbal fencing—a bad witness by the Loxton standards. Instead, he was surprised to see a very perturbed and anxious girl, who seemed at her wits' end.

With a gesture, Sir Clinton invited her to take the chair which Collingbourne had just vacated.

"Don't be worried because we have to ask you some questions," he began in a tone which, to Inspector Loxton's ears, failed to strike the proper official note. "You've had a trying time lately, I know, between to-night's experience and the death of your husband not so long ago. We haven't got that cleared up yet, I'm sorry to say; and I'd like to know one or two things which might help us. You and he weren't happy together. Quite unsuited to one another, I gather. Then why did you marry him?"

May Pickford hesitated for a moment, looking at Sir Clinton's face as if to read something from his expression.

"I wasn't in love with him, if that's what you mean. Shall I tell you how I met him?"

"If you please."

May Pickford seemed encouraged by his tone. She crossed her knees, smoothed down her skirt, settled herself in her chair with an unconsciously graceful movement, and, after a glance at Wendover, began her tale.

It was a dingy little story. Orphaned in her teens, she had fallen to the care of a grandmother living on a scanty annuity, and had drifted from one unskilled employment to another, never interested in any of them, never retaining a post for long, and never learning anything which might lead to better things. When her grandmother died the annuity ceased, and May was left alone in the world, dependent on what she could earn herself. It was not much. And by this time she was obsessed by a desire to get some share in life's enjoyments, some escape from the drabness of the existence she was leading. Finally, she drifted in employment as waitress in a café at a summer resort, and her looks made her popular with a certain type of male clientele, here to-day and gone to-morrow. By that time, her philosophy of life had become crystallised. "Men want just one thing from a girl. Make them pay as much as they can afford, and give them as little as possible in exchange. Have a good time; one's only young once."

Then appeared Pickford on holiday, a casual visitor to the town, where he had not a single acquaintance. Time hung on his hands. He was feeling lonely. Then one day he drifted into the café. She fascinated him at first sight; and she found it amusing to excite him and make him jealous of some of her younger hangers-on. He was open-handed so long as he could secure her to himself; and she got the idea that he must be well off, not realising that he was spending beyond his means merely for the sake of her company. She had no interest in him as a personality and asked no questions about who or what he was. To her, he represented merely an ever-open purse, ready to gratify her whims and to give her expensive presents without getting anything in return.

Suddenly, disaster broke upon her. She had been over-friendly with her employer; his wife surprised the two of them at an awkward moment; and May found herself dismissed towards the end of the season, when she had not the slightest chance of securing a new place. She had never saved a penny—money slipped through her fingers—and she was turned adrift without a character, without even enough in hand to pay for a week's lodging. And at that juncture, Pickford's infatuation came to a climax and he proposed to her. In her panic she grasped at the offer. He had been generous and seemed to have plenty of money. "Besides, nobody else would come up to the scratch," she explained artlessly. She thought of possible alternatives, accepted Pickford, and they were married at a register office almost before she had realised what she was doing.

A week's honeymoon enlightened both of them. Her looks still obsessed him, but to her his exigencies grew more and more distasteful as time went on. They had nothing in common. His life was a bookish one, and she had never read anything except a few cheap novels. Greatest disillusion of all, she found that he was a poor man. Now that he had got her, he grudged every penny spent for her pleasure. She missed the little attentions which other men had lavished on her: suppers after a theatre, gifts of flowers, evenings at the cinema or music-hall, drives on a Sunday, presents chosen with special care for her tastes. And, as she soon realised, he would never change nor would he better himself in the world. He was a natural drudge, and he looked to her to run with him in double harness, content with her lot.

"I should never have married him," she said, bitterly. "He was too old for me and far too dull. He had no idea of amusement. He never wanted to go to a show; I had to drag him out almost by main force, even at the start; and later on I gave that up and went by myself. He was always poring over books and talking about Shakespeare. Shakespeare! It made me scream at times, the sheer dullness of it. We never gave parties. The women round about didn't take to me. I wasn't their sort. They did their best to find out who I was and where I came from, but I kept my thumb on that, and I made Pickford keep quiet, too. No parties means no amusing men coming about the house, nobody to make you laugh and cheer you up and talk nicely to you. It was . . . sort of stifling. And he never gave me any money to spend. A girl needs pretty things. That's natural, isn't it? We had terrible rows over that almost from the start; and things got worse when the war came. He was pinching and scraping all the time. And he began to drink, too. It was unbearable living with him."

She clasped her hands about her knee, and her rings sparkled.

"That's a pretty solitaire," said Sir Clinton. "May I look at it?"

She took it from her finger and handed it across the desk.

"It's a good stone," he commented after examining it with care. "A South African one, I'd say. I held a post out there at one time and had to know something about diamonds. An heirloom, perhaps?"

May Pickford looked slightly confused.

"No, it was a present."

"From your husband?" asked Sir Clinton in a tone of surprise.

"No, not from him; from a friend."

"And these other rings—were they presents, too?"

"Yes," May admitted, reluctantly.

"You've been very fortunate in your friends," said Sir Clinton, dryly, as he handed back the ring. "Did your husband approve of your taking valuable gifts from friends—from male friends, perhaps?"

"I told him I bought them myself. He thought they were artificial, cheap stuff."

Sir Clinton leaned back in his chair and ran his eye over the get-up of his witness: expensive shoes, sheer silk stockings, a skirt cut by an expert, a bag better than the common run, and a very smart hat.

"Your husband grudged you money, and yet you seem to dress very nicely. How did you manage?"

"Sometimes I put things down to the account, and then there was a row when the bills came in. Sometimes I borrowed money."

"From these generous friends. By the way, who were these people?"

"Well, I knew Mr. Quinton, and Mr. Grindal, and Mr. Oakley, and some others. They lent me money."

"Did you mean to repay them?"

"Well . . . if they asked me, of course."

"But you didn't expect them to ask. Did you give your husband any cause for jealousy?"

"Well . . . He was jealous, anyhow."

"With good grounds?"

"Well . . . perhaps."

"We may as well speak plainly, Mrs. Pickford. Was Oakley your lover?"

May Pickford evidently saw that she had already admitted so much that it was not worth while denying a clear inference.

"At one time he was," she acknowledged candidly. "But he soon ran out of money. Then, not long ago, he hinted that he might have more money coming in, quite a lot of money."

"Ah! Did your husband ever talk in the same way?"

May Pickford's expression changed at this question, as if some new light had dawned on her.

202

"How did you guess that?" she asked, in obvious surprise. "I never put two and two together till this moment when you asked that question; but Pickford *did* talk about his ship coming home. I paid no attention to him. I'd never taken his talk about the St. Rule's Treasure seriously; it seemed to me just a silly fancy he had. But now I remember, he seemed very confident—they both were."

"On the night of your husband's death Oakley went to your house? What did he want?"

"I think he meant to break things off between us. I had the feeling that he was after another woman and wanted to drop me. It wasn't altogether a surprise. His story was that he didn't want any risk of a row with Pickford just then; but I was pretty sure that he was really after Diana Herne and wanted to get rid of me to make way for her. Something Pickford said, sneeringly, put me on that track. We parted on rather cool terms that night, though I never mentioned that Herne girl to him at all."

"Thanks," said Sir Clinton. "That clears away one possible suspicion. Some people may have thought that Oakley murdered your husband with the idea of stepping into his shoes, so far as you were concerned. There was nothing in that, of course?"

May Pickford seemed genuinely surprised by this hypothesis.

"I never thought of that," she said. "If these people had known the inside of the thing, they'd never have imagined anything of the sort. As a matter of fact, Pickford's death landed me in Queer Street. His income stopped . . ."

"And creditors began to worry about their bills? But no doubt these generous friends of yours rallied to help you?"

"Did they?" retorted May Pickford, bitterly. "I'll give you a specimen of *that*. I'd borrowed money from time to time from Mr. Grindal; and I'd signed a lot of papers. I never expected him to ask for the money back. I thought it was just a sort of formality and I'd hear no more about it, considering everything. So I went to him in this trouble and asked him to help me with some more money to pay some of the shopkeepers. He's a brute, that man. He refused to lend me a penny. What's more, he turned nasty and told me it was time I was thinking of repaying what I owed him already! In fact, though I could hardly believe it, he had the nerve to tell me that he would sell me up if I didn't pay! And he meant it, too; I could see that plain enough. I dare say he was tired of me. Still . . ."

"Was this recently?"

"Only a day or two ago," May Pickford explained. "So there I was—landed! I tried to see Mr. Quinton; he's got plenty of money, you know. But it seems that he's gone off somewhere, yachting, perhaps . . ."

"Hardly in war-time," interjected Sir Clinton.

"Well, I don't know where he's gone—on holiday anyhow, and left no address. So I couldn't get hold of him. I'm nearly desperate; for I won't have a penny. It's worse than the time when I married Pickford, and that was bad enough. There was only Oakley I could turn to. If his ship *had* come home he owed me something, even if we hadn't parted on very good terms. So to-night I went to his house. I missed him by just a minute or two, and they told me he was coming to Friar's Pardon. He'd let that slip out to his landlady. I knew he'd have to go by bus, so I hurried off to the nearest stop on the route, and I saw him board a bus and go off, leaving me to wait for the next one."

"What bus did Oakley catch?" asked Sir Clinton.

"It was one that passed that stop at 8.45; I had to wait for the 9.15 one. That didn't matter. I could wait for him in the avenue, here, after he'd been up to Friar's Pardon. The way I worked it out in my mind was this. Diana Herne was the only person that would draw him to Friar's Pardon. But he wouldn't be going to see her at that time of night unless he had some very special reason. That meant that he'd come into this money he had talked about; at least, that's what I thought. She'd never look at him except for money and it would want a lot of it to make her look at him at all. If he had money, then he owed it to me to get me out of the hole I was in. And if he wouldn't do it pleasantly, then I'd put the screw on him by threatening to tell Diana Herne all about him and myself. *That* would upset his plans for her, you see. She's not the sort to take a second-hand article from all I've heard about her."

"Blackmail, in fact?" said Sir Clinton, bleakly.

"Well, you can call it that if you like. I never had the chance to try it on, so you've nothing against me on that count," said May Pickford, angrily.

"You caught the 9.15 bus. Did you see anyone you knew among the passengers? Anyone who could corroborate that tale?"

"I saw young Mr. Hicks of the factory. I don't know him to talk to; but I recognised him because I'd once seen him at a war meeting. There's no bus stop exactly at the gate of Friar's Pardon, so I went on to the next one; but when we got there, young Mr. Hicks got down, and I stayed on the bus till it came to the stop after that. You see, I know the lie of the land about here, and I meant to get into the grounds and cut across the fields, and I didn't want young Mr. Hicks to see me getting in.

There's a stream in the grounds, but there's a plank bridge over it, and I aimed for that, as well as I could; for there was no path on the line I took; and in the dusk I blundered into a patch of wild garlic. You can smell it off my shoes, I expect."

"Easily enough," Sir Clinton assured her, glancing up at Collingbourne's map on the wall. "And after you had crossed the bridge?"

"I came up against some fencing that wasn't there the last time I was over that ground. Wire-netting, some of it, so I suppose they want to keep out rabbits. That was before I came to the bridge. Then I struck a barbed-wire fence. I suppose they graze sheep and wanted to keep them off that bit. Then I came to the avenue and struck another barbed-wire fence. I was just trying to get through that when I heard voices. There was a sharp bend in the avenue to the left of me, and the people were just round the corner, so I didn't see them—there's undergrowth just there—and I couldn't make out what they were saying. But I recognised Oakley's voice, and the other was a girl. I guessed it was the Herne girl; who else could it be? They sounded as if the girl wasn't pleased over something. Then I heard a sort of exclamation from her, and by the sound of their steps it seemed to me as if there was some sort of a struggle. And after that there was dead silence. I waited a while, expecting the Herne girl to come back up the avenue towards the house; but she didn't pass where I was. I didn't want to risk meeting her—of course I'd no business there—so I made up my mind to get across the avenue and strike straight for the gate across the fields. The avenue has a lot of bends in it, and I thought I'd get to the gate and wait there for Oakley; he'd take longer, walking down the avenue. It took me some time to get through the barbed wire on to the avenue; my skirt caught, and gave me some bother. And I got caught again by a prickly thing—a bramble branch or something—as I was crossing a stile. But I'm sure I managed to get to the gate before anyone could if they went down the avenue."

"You didn't see Miss Herne or anyone else, did you?"

"No, I saw nothing of her; but I did see a man walking up the avenue. That was after I got to the gate and was waiting under some trees till Oakley came along. This man didn't seem to know the place. He used a torch now and again and he was carrying a bag or a suit-case."

"What time did you see him?"

"Oh, I don't know. It was before the rain-shower; that's all I can tell you."

"Did you get wet by that shower?"

May Pickford shook her head.

"No. I was standing under some thick trees when it came on, and I just stayed there until the police came along and took me up. My shoes may be a little wet with the dew on the grass, but that's all."

She made no objection to having her fingerprints taken and her skirt and stockings brushed down. In fact, she volunteered to be searched, if necessary, though her offer was not accepted. Then she signed Loxton's notes of her evidence.

"Are you detaining me for the night?" she asked, after a glance at her watch. "The last bus has passed here long ago, and I don't know how I could get home."

"We'll send you in a car, by and by," Sir Clinton assured her. "That's all we want from you at present."

Loxton opened the door and showed her out. When he turned back Sir Clinton was scribbling a note.

"You've got a fingerprint expert, haven't you, Inspector?"

"Yes, sir—Fleming. He's outside."

"Good! Then as soon as we have got Fearon's finger-prints I want you to give Fleming this note and all the fingerprints we've taken, as well as that white stone and this Milton MS. And, by the way, you'd better take my own prints as well now, and give them to Fleming along with the rest. After that we'll take Fearon's evidence and then the set will be complete."

16

"*QUEEN AND HUNTRESS* . . ."

WHEN Fearon came into the study he turned an accusing eye on Loxton and, without waiting to be questioned, began a mock-complaint.

"As a mascot, I don't think much of you, Inspector. You're a complete washout in that line of business. I saw you officially a while ago. What's the result? I went down with a dose of gastric flu straight off—that very day—and I haven't been able to get across the door-step since then. And now, just when I'm struggling back to normal again, you come bustling in here to pay me a return visit. What's going to happen next? Mumps, scarlet fever, ingrowing toe-nails, or cancer of the top-knot? Give it a name and let me know the worst. Mean-while, I'll sit down, if you don't mind. Better able to bear the news that way, perhaps. I still feel a bit shaky."

"If you feel as superstitious as all that, Mr. Fearon, perhaps I'd better take the inspector's place," said Sir Clinton affably, disregarding Loxton's scowl at Fearon. "I want to ask you a question or two. You were in this room when your uncle interviewed Oakley to-night, weren't you?"

"For part of the time," Fearon rectified, dropping his facetiousness. "I left, after a while. It was no business of mine, really."

"Tell me what passed between Oakley and your uncle, please."

"Checking it up, are you?" said Fearon, with a slight return of his bantering tone. "No need, really. My uncle is strictly truthful; and as for myself, my veracity is the talk of both hemispheres—at least, when my name happens to crop up in conversation."

When it came to giving his actual evidence, however, Fearon dropped his persiflage, and his account tallied almost exactly with what Collingbourne had already told. When he had finished, Sir Clinton put a question.

"Did Oakley give you the impression that Miss Herne had encouraged him in any way?"

"No, he didn't," said Fearon, bluntly. "He asked for 'permission to pay his addresses,' as he put it. That means, I take it, that he hadn't started. Besides, my cousin would never encourage a rank little outsider like that. What would be the good of encouraging him? His looks would hardly carry her off her feet. And he had no money. Both she and I know what it is to be hard up. We've been kept short for years, while my uncle scattered thousands on that wretched collection of his. When she marries, she'll take somebody with enough cash to give her a good time. No one knows that better than I do," he ended, with a tinge of bitterness.

"But, judging from this interview to-night, he'd got hold of something worth a small fortune," objected Sir Clinton. "That knocks the prop from under half your argument."

Fearon laughed and tapped his forehead meaningly.

"Bats in the belfry, my dear man. Off his rocker, if you ask me. I didn't believe a word of it. Nor would you, either, if you'd heard him. I dare say he believed it himself. Loonies always believe their own tales."

Sir Clinton mused for a moment, while his fingers beat the devil's tattoo on the desk.

"I'd like to see some trace of a motive," he said reflectively. "After all, Oakley's dead. There must be some reason . . ."

"Suppose he's been bragging to other people about his wonderful treasure," said Fearon, shrewdly. "My uncle and I had no use for his yarn; but some ignorant devil might have swallowed it, and done him in to get hold of the thing."

Sir Clinton seemed more impressed by this than Wendover had expected.

"That's worth considering," he said, reflectively. "You haven't anyone in your mind?"

Fearon shook his head.

"No, nobody," he said candidly. "I knew next to nothing about the man, much less about any friends he had."

"Well, it can't be helped," said Sir Clinton with a shade of disappointment in his tone. "Any objection to my taking your fingerprints, Mr. Fearon? We've got everyone else's and it might raise talk if we didn't take yours also."

"It's all the same to me," said Fearon. "Go ahead."

Sir Clinton began the work immediately.

"Miss Herne went out after dinner, didn't she?" he asked as he took the first print.

"She went up to her room after dinner; then she must have changed into a coat and skirt and gone out. The next I saw of her was when she came in again. That was after Goldsmith turned up—say half-past ten."

"Did she look just as usual when she came in? (That's a nice print, isn't it?)"

"I didn't notice anything particular about her," said Fearon. "One never does look carefully at people one's meeting at all times in the day. At least, I know I don't."

"You didn't notice if she looked excited, or agitated, or anything of that sort?"

"Not a bit," said Fearon. "But she's not that sort, anyhow. Showing her emotions is not her long suit. I remember, once, when her favourite dog got run over. She never turned a hair—on the surface."

"I suppose you're right," Sir Clinton agreed. "Now I'll take the next finger, please. . . . You didn't hear the end of the interview between your uncle and Oakley, I believe. You went upstairs, didn't you? What were you doing up there? We have to account for everybody's time, you know," he added, half-apologetically.

"There's a five-inch telescope up there," Fearon explained. "It belonged to my grandfather. My uncle takes no interest in it, so I'm the only person who ever goes near it. The moon's clear to-night, and I was making a sketch of it. One can't do much planetary work with an old-fashioned five-inch aperture, but it's good enough for the moon."

"I remember the moon in South Africa," said Sir Clinton. "One can see quite a lot with the naked eye out there; the air's so clear, compared with our climate at home. . . . Now I think we'll take the other hand, please. . . . Still, even on this side of the world one must see a good deal even with a small telescope. It's a nice clear night. . . ."

211

"Care to see it?" asked Fearon. "It won't take five minutes!"

Sir Clinton seemed torn between two inclinations. He glanced at his watch and then made up his mind.

"Well, I *would*," he confessed, reluctantly. "Now this finger, please. . . . It won't take long, as you say. . . . That's an excellent print, isn't it? I shan't have to repeat any of these. . . . Suppose we go up after I've got the set done? But only for a minute or two. . . . There! That's the lot, thanks. Now I'd like to have a look at the moon. But only five minutes, please. You can follow us up, Inspector."

Fearon led the way through the hall and up the staircase. Coming behind with Sir Clinton, Wendover noticed a tiny rectangular cut on Fearon's dinner-jacket, just behind the right shoulder, but it was so small that it was hardly perceptible. At the top of the stairs they turned left along a corridor.

"Which rooms do Sparrick and the cook sleep in?" asked Sir Clinton.

"This is Sparrick's," replied Fearon, pointing to one door, "and that's the cook's room, next door. The maids sleep in this wing; my uncle's room is in the other wing, so is mine, so is my cousin's. Goldsmith is there, too, just now. We look out on the front, just as the maids do. This is the door into the dome."

He opened the door at the end of the passage, and ushered his companions into the observatory.

"I always keep the maids out of the dome," he explained, except when I let them in to clean the place up, once in a while, under my own eye. If they had the run of the place they might tamper with the telescope or jar up the sidereal clock. It's safer to do my own dusting"—he pointed to some dusters on a shelf—"but that's not often.

If you happen to rub against anything there's a brush over there. And now I'm going to put this ulster on. I got a relapse in that gastric flu by coming up here in the cold nights, so I have to take precautions."

Wendover had never been in the dome before and he looked about him inquisitively. The telescope, equatorially mounted on a stone pillar passing through the floor, pointed to the closed slit on the southern side of the dome. At the eye-piece end stood a ladder seat for the observer, and on one of the arms of this was bracketed a board carrying sketching implements and an unfinished lunar drawing. In one corner of the room the sidereal clock was ticking and in the opposite corner the floor opened on to the beginning of a narrow spiral stair leading down to the ground-level. In the daytime, light came through a series of lancet windows too narrow for a man to pass through and now covered by black-out curtains.

"Care to have a look at the moon?" asked Fearon.

"If I may," said Wendover, after consulting Sir Clinton with a glance.

Fearon, after switching off the lights in the dome, opened the slit and then, going over to the northern side of the room, began turning a heavy wheel which moved the dome round.

"A bit noisy," he apologised. "It's all very old-fashioned, you see. The slit was in position when I left it, but the moon has moved on since then, of course."

Sir Clinton gave a sharp ejaculation of annoyance and began to grope on the floor round where Fearon was standing at the wheel.

"Sorry!" he explained. "I've dropped my pencil. . . . Ah! Here it is."

He recovered it after a few moments and stood up again, rubbing his fingers together.

"May I use one of your dusters?" he asked Fearon. "Your floor's rather dusty, if you'll excuse my saying so."

He picked a couple of dusters from the shelf, scrubbed his hands with them, and put them back in their place. Fearon, meanwhile, had got the dome into position so that the slit bore upon the moon; and, sitting down on the ladder-seat, he brought the telescope to bear.

"Have a look," he said, moving aside so as to let Wendover sit down. "That's Copernicus, the biggest ring-crater on the moon. The ring's fifty miles across, and the walls are about as high as our Alps."

"Is your interest in these things purely æsthetic?" Sir Clinton inquired, as Wendover stared through the eye-piece.

"Oh, no. I'm a member of the Lunar Section of the B.A.A.—the British Astronomical Association, I mean. There's been some talk about slight changes in the lunar surface near Copernicus, and we've been asked to make as many drawings of the spot as we can, when the sunlight's falling on the moon at a particular angle. That sketch on the drawing-board was what I was working on to-night. It's a laborious business. Here are some of the drawings I've made already."

He took down from a shelf a fat portfolio containing some dozens of lunar pictures which he leafed over as he held them out for Sir Clinton to see by the light of the moon.

"It's too dim to see them properly," said the Chief Constable. "I'd like to have a look at them when you've shut the slit and got the lights on again. I see you write the date and time up in the corners."

"Always. They're not much good without that—at least, they are better with it. One always puts these figures on any astronomical drawing. I've dated this one on the drawing-board; but I hadn't time to finish it."

"Where does that stair in the corner lead to?" asked Sir Clinton, with no particular sign of curiosity.

"There's a room below this," explained Fearon. "It's been a store-room at one time and it's cluttered up with rubbish. I haven't been down there for ages. Care to have a look round?"

Without answering, Sir Clinton pulled out his torch and made his way down the stair, followed by the inspector. At the foot they found themselves on a level with the ground outside and surrounded by old furniture, bits of old iron, and all the rubbish which had accumulated there over many years. On the northern side was a door with glass panels in its upper half. Sir Clinton picked his way to it, but found it locked with the key on the inner side. He tried to turn the key in the lock, but it was evidently rusted up and refused to move.

"See if you can get it out, Inspector."

Loxton manœuvred for a time, whilst Sir Clinton turned the beam of his torch on the glass, revealing outside a deep little portico which evidently opened on to the moon-lit garden.

"Here it is, sir. I've got it loose," said the inspector, holding out the key which he had managed to extract from the lock. "It's covered with rust; it doesn't seem to have been turned for ages."

"So I thought, from the feel of it," Sir Clinton confirmed. "You can put it back in the keyhole now. We'll go upstairs again."

They climbed up into the dome. Wendover was still gazing through the telescope.

"Time's up, I'm afraid," said Sir Clinton. "We'll need to get back to business."

Wendover rose from his seat rather reluctantly.

"Lovely sight, that," he said. "Some of it's just like very delicate silver lace-work."

Fearon closed the slit and switched on the lights in the dome.

"There! That's all shipshape," he said. "One never knows when it will rain, and the water would damage the telescope if it got through that slit. By the way, I don't want to be inquisitive, but I'd like to ask you a question. You went through Oakley's pockets, I suppose. Did you find this marvellous affair that he boasted to us about?"

Sir Clinton shook his head.

"No, nothing of the sort."

Fearon's surprise at this answer was obviously genuine.

"I thought as much," he said after a pause. "The man must have been moon-struck, just as I guessed. Outside his imagination I don't suppose the thing existed at all. But that gesture he made—as if he meant to take it out and show it to us—well, it made me wonder, when I thought over the business; and I was almost convinced there might be something in his yarn. Shall we go down now?"

When they got back to the study Sir Clinton produced the yellow chamois-leather gloves which he had taken from the hall-table.

"You recognise these, of course?" he asked, indifferently, throwing them backs uppermost on the desk.

"They're mine," Fearon admitted without hesitation.

"Do you think Miss Herne could wear them?" asked Sir Clinton, sharply.

Fearon pondered for a moment. Evidently the suggestion puzzled him.

"She *could* put them on, of course," he answered slowly.

"That's to say, she could get her hands into them easily enough. But they'd be miles too big for her."

"Yes, she's got small hands," admitted Sir Clinton rather grudgingly. "And yours are about normal for a man of your size. Well, never mind that. It's not important. Now the inspector will read over the notes he's taken of your evidence, and you might sign them."

Loxton read his notes in an expressionless drone, while Fearon listened critically, as though anxious to catch the inspector in some error.

"That seems all right," he declared when the recital ended. "Where do I sign? Here? Then that's that."

When Loxton had ushered Fearon out of the room, Wendover turned to Sir Clinton.

"You forgot to brush him down, didn't you?"

The inspector looked startled when he was reminded of this, but the Chief Constable was quite unruffled.

"You were so interested in the moon, Squire, that you missed a point. I dropped my pencil, if you remember. In groping round for it I brushed against the bottoms of Fearon's trousers. They were bone-dry. So were his pumps. That seems interesting, doesn't it?"

"It looks as if his tale's true," said the inspector reluctantly, as Wendover kept silent. "If he'd been outside amongst the dew he couldn't help getting the ends of his trousers wet."

"That was one of the things that took me up to the dome to find out," explained Sir Clinton. "I'm not so keen on the moon as you are, you know, Squire. But time's getting on. Will you see what Fleming has made of things, Inspector? He ought to have a note for me by this time."

Inspector Loxton went out of the room and came back almost at once with a sheet of paper which he handed to Sir Clinton. The Chief Constable glanced at it and then handed it to Wendover who read it in his turn.

FINGERPRINTS

On Stone: One clear print in red pigment certainly made by Miss Herne. Several other prints smudged, some probably made by her.

On MS.: Three clear prints made by Sir Clinton Driffield. All others made some time ago. Dim and imperfect. Three look like Collingbourne's prints and two resemble Miss Herne's prints.

Wendover, aghast, passed the paper to Loxton, who read the message and smiled.

"Getting warmer, sir. This looks very promising."

"I think we'll put a question or two to Miss Herne," said Sir Clinton. "She's had time to think things over by now. Please bring her in, Inspector."

"There's something fresh, sir," said Loxton. "Our men have been searching the grounds; and in the summer-house beyond the avenue they've picked up young Hicks of the dynamo factory—the man who was lurking about in Goodman's Row on the night that Pickford was murdered in the garage. He's been detained, if you want to question him. So far, he's said nothing."

"I'll see him later," Sir Clinton decided. "Meanwhile, please bring Miss Herne in here."

While they were waiting for the girl Sir Clinton picked up the gloves from the table and held them out to Wendover.

"You see the faint red spot on the palm of the right-hand one? It matches the colour of Miss Herne's lipstick, doesn't it?"

- - -

218

17

DIANA HERNE

WHEN Diana Herne reappeared with the inspector, it seemed to Wendover that she had lost some of the coolness which she had shown at the first interview with Sir Clinton. Evidently she had been "thinking things over" and the process had not been good for her nerve.

"Please sit down, Miss Herne. I want to ask you a few more questions. First of all, do you recognise these gloves?"

This opening seemed to surprise Diana. She looked at the gloves which were still lying, backs upward, on the desk.

"I've seen my cousin wearing a pair like them."

"Have you ever worn this particular pair yourself?"

Wendover could see that this question perplexed Diana.

"No, I haven't," she said after a slight pause. "These things are at least two sizes bigger than anything that would fit me. Look!"

She spread her own right hand on the desk opposite the right-hand glove, and the disparity in size was obvious.

Sir Clinton dismissed the subject of the gloves at once. He sat silent, sphinx-like, and scrutinised the girl as though he expected to have to pass an examination on her appearance.

"When I saw you before, Miss Herne," he went on after a pause, "you told me one or two things. Finally, I asked you if you could think of anything else which might throw light on this affair. You said no. Have you any objection to telling us now, what you were doing while you were out of the house between half-past nine and half-past ten to-night?"

"I was meeting a friend," Diana admitted after a moment's hesitation.

"A Mr. Hicks?"

Diana was evidently staggered by this question.

"Yes, it was Mr. Hicks," she confirmed after another momentary hesitation.

"And that's all you can tell me about your doings?"

"That is all."

Sir Clinton again seemed to be studying the girl from head to foot, and Wendover could see that this silent scrutiny was making her nervous.

"We know more about you than you think, Miss Herne," said the Chief Constable, warningly. "Of course, I say that to a good many witnesses; but in your case it happens to be true."

"Are you suggesting that I'm not telling the truth?" demanded Diana angrily.

"I'm suggesting that you haven't told us the *whole* truth yet," said Sir Clinton icily. "Did you meet Oakley this evening? Yes or no."

Diana evidently reflected carefully before replying, knitting her brows in perplexity. Finally, she seemed to make up her mind.

"Yes, I met him."

"Accidentally or by prearrangement?"

"He asked me to meet him," admitted Diana with marked reluctance. "Why are you putting these questions?"

There was no relaxation in Sir Clinton's sternness.

"So long as I go on asking questions, Miss Herne, you may think yourself lucky. If I were to stop short, it might mean that I'd decided to bring a charge against you. After that, I'm not allowed to ask you a single question. It hasn't come to that *yet*. Now, when had you arranged to meet him?"

"He asked me to meet him in the avenue at half-past nine," Diana confessed, evidently in perturbation at the Chief Constable's statement of the rules. "But you wouldn't understand, unless you knew what led up to that."

"Suppose you tell me then," said Sir Clinton, with a touch of impatience.

"Well, if you must know," she began, "he fell in love with me. We were thrown together a bit during this salvage business, and I could see it coming on. Naturally, I did what I could to put him off. I was sorry for him in a way, and I didn't like to snub him brutally. Perhaps it would have been better if I had done so at the very start. But I shirked that. I thought he'd see for himself how ridiculous it was. He didn't though. It began to grow rather awkward, because he was so stupid about it. I told you before that lately he took to boasting—got a bit above himself, in fact. This morning I got a note from him. I've torn it up, so I can't show it to you. It hinted that things which weren't possible at one time might be more possible now. I guessed he meant money—as if I'd ever have married him even for a fortune. Practically, it was an invitation to meet him and listen to a proposal of marriage. I didn't feel particularly honoured. In fact, I was rather angry at not having been able to check him, in spite of all the discouragement I'd put in his way; so I determined to meet him and finish the business, once for all, even if I hurt his feelings badly. He'd no business to be so thick-skinned and obtuse. So I met him down the avenue as he asked me to do."

"Was he up to time?" asked Sir Clinton.

"No, he wasn't. He kept me waiting for five minutes

or more, and that made me angry. I'm not accustomed to hanging about when I make an appointment with a man. When he did arrive, coming down from the house, he seemed to be in a bad temper, and that ruffled me a bit more. So I asked him sharply what he had to say for himself. He began a long rigmarole about how a fortune was within his grasp—these were the very words he used—and how this would make all the difference, and so on. I congratulated him, of course; what else could I do? That made him go off into a lot of boasting, which didn't interest me a bit. All I wanted was to get the thing over. However, he came to the point at last. I've had a few proposals in my time, but nothing like that one. I got the feeling that he imagined he was overwhelming me by offering me the chance of marrying him. *King Cophetua and the Beggar Maid*, second edition, if you understand what I mean. By this time I was downright angry with the man. It was a bit steep, you know. So I told him bluntly that anything of the kind was out of the question. Perhaps I didn't wrap it up nicely enough, but he'd exasperated me by his conceit and his thick hide."

She paused for a moment and glanced at Sir Clinton as though to see if he appreciated her feelings.

"Go on, please."

"He seemed completely dumbfounded. I suppose he must have rehearsed that speech a good many times—it sounded like it—and he must have persuaded himself that I'd snap at him. Some men do work themselves up into that state by brooding in advance. I've seen it more than once. Evidently he couldn't believe I meant what I said. He must have thought it was my maiden modesty or coyness or something of that sort. He just stood and looked at me for a moment or two. Then he stepped forward and flung his arms round my neck; and before I knew what he was doing he kissed me several times."

She halted, as though recalling the scene and her own reactions. Then she pursued her story in a quieter tone.

"I don't mind a man kissing me, if I happen to like him. But I did not like this man Oakley. I was furious with him. He seemed to think his kisses would work wonders: the Sleeping Beauty and Prince Charming and all that sort of thing. And he had a wet mouth . . . Ugh! . . . I pushed him away from me and stood back, wiping away the wetness of his kisses. I suppose that was what blurred my make-up and left some of my lipstick on my hand."

"There were traces of lipstick on his mouth," commented Sir Clinton. "That confirms what you say, Miss Herne. Now go on, please."

"We stood watching each other for a moment or two," Diana continued. "The moon gave light enough for me to see him fairly well. He looked baffled, like a man whose plans have gone completely out of gear; but I could see that he hadn't given in, and I expected him to attack me again. He looked really ugly—dangerous, I mean. I didn't know what might be in his mind, so I stepped back a little and picked up one of the white stones that border the avenue. That checked him. He cringed, just as you see a dog cringe when you threaten it with a stone. He began to apologise for what he'd done. 'His passions had overcome him,' he said, and he was 'very sorry to have lost control of himself.' Oh, yes, those were the words, I remember them quite well. He must have found them in some book or other; nobody ever talks like that, and nobody but a fool would have apologised in that way. I felt inclined to say: 'Begone!'

It's what the heroines of his reading said, I expect. However, I just told him I'd had enough of him and he'd better go. And I made it quite plain that I'd hit him with the stone if I had any more trouble with him. He gave me a long look. Perhaps he imagined I'd weaken if he persisted. I wasn't really frightened; it wasn't far from the house; and I could have screamed if the worst had come to the worst. However, he evidently realised that the cave-man business cut no ice with me, and he turned away off towards the avenue gates. Then I dropped the stone and went through the trees towards the summer-house."

"What time was that?" asked Sir Clinton.

"It was ten minutes to ten," Diana replied without hesitation. "I looked at my watch in the moonlight. You see, I'd another appointment to keep."

"With Mr. Hicks? How would he reach the summer-house? By coming up the avenue?"

If Diana Herne saw the implication of this question, she showed no sign.

"No," she explained. "He usually takes a short cut through the grounds when he comes to meet me."

"You met him at ten o'clock, I suppose?"

"Yes, he was there when I reached the summer-house. He's usually early when I meet him."

"Was he wearing gloves?"

"No, he wasn't. And he hadn't been wearing any. I noticed that his hands were very cold."

"He was with you in the summer-house until you came back here, about 10.30? And between the time you left Oakley and the time you reached here, you heard nothing—no sound, I mean, that caught your attention, no cry or anything like that?"

"Nothing whatever."

Wendover was relieved to see that Diana seemed to have got over her trepidation as the interview went on. Now she appeared to have recovered all her normal coolness. Sir Clinton produced the Milton MS. and spread it on the desk so that she could see it without touching it. At her first glance, she gave a faint ejaculation of surprise.

"Why, that's from my uncle's collection! He bought it not so long ago, and I remember cataloguing it for him."

"You're quite sure about it?"

"Absolutely certain. If you'll look at the top right-hand corner you'll find a very faint set of figures in pencil. That's the catalogue number which I put on it myself. I don't know if my uncle could identify it. I noticed that it was on the market and when I mentioned that to him, he told me to buy it and catalogue it. I don't remember if he even looked at it when it came, owing to his eyesight."

Sir Clinton folded up the manuscript and put it into an envelope from one of the desk drawers. His next question evidently came as a surprise to the girl.

"What, exactly, are your relations with your cousin, Mr. Fearon?"

"I don't quite understand that . . . Oh, I think I see what you mean. Any love-passages between us? No, none, so far as I'm concerned. My cousin hasn't the slightest ground for interfering in my affairs, if that's what you want to know."

Sir Clinton pondered for a moment as though trying to think of any other points to be elucidated. Then he put a final question.

"That's the *whole* truth, now, Miss Herne?"

"I've told you everything now, exactly as it happened."

"Thanks. Then I needn't trouble you any further, if

you'll be good enough to sign these notes which the inspector has been taking."

When she had done this, Sir Clinton ushered Diana out and dispatched Loxton to fetch Collingbourne.

"Just sit down, Mr. Collingbourne," said Sir Clinton when his witness appeared. "I won't detain you long."

"Have you cleared up this business?" demanded Collingbourne. "Have you got to the bottom of it? It's most perplexing. I can't make head or tail of it myself."

"Not yet, I'm afraid," said the Chief Constable. "I'd just like to ask a question or two. Your eyes let you move about the house, but you can't read?"

"Hardly at all, hardly at all. With atropine, I can just make out the headlines in the newspaper."

"But you still buy manuscripts occasionally?"

"That's quite true. You're perfectly right there. I do buy a few. My niece keeps an eye on the catalogues for me and tells me about anything that's going, and I buy only from reliable dealers, so there's not much risk, really."

"Did you buy a letter from John Milton to his friend Lawes about plans for the Ludlow Masque?"

"Yes, yes, I did. A while ago, it was. My niece managed that for me. I haven't even looked at the thing. Once I get this operation over and can see again, I've got quite a lot of treats like that waiting for me. It will be very pleasant to go over all these things I've been buying."

"Now, another point," said Sir Clinton, dismissing the problem of Collingbourne's prospective joys. "I think you bought a coil of rope a while ago. What did you want it for?"

"A fire-escape, a fire-escape. This house is just

tinder, with all this old wood as dry as it can be. And these raids, you know. A single incendiary and the place would be a furnace in no time. I'm terrified of fire. Wendover can tell you about that, if you ask him."

"You keep this rope upstairs, I suppose? I'd like to have a look at it."

Collingbourne stared at the Chief Constable in apparent surprise.

"What do you want that for?" he asked. "This case has nothing to do with ropes."

"Did I say it had?" retorted Sir Clinton, innocently. "No, I don't mind telling you, Mr. Collingbourne. I want a word or two with that maid of yours—Sparrick—and I prefer to ask my questions when she's off her guard. You see? So if you will be good enough to ring the bell and tell her to show me where you keep this rope, that will do very well. You'll stay here, of course."

"Oh, very well, very well," said Collingbourne fretfully. "Do just as you please. The rope's in the housemaid's closet upstairs, across the corridor from my bedroom."

He rang the bell, and in a moment or two Sparrick made her appearance, evidently burning with curiosity. Collingbourne gave his orders and Sir Clinton, with Loxton and Wendover in attendance, followed the maid into the hall and up the staircase. At the top they turned to the right.

"That's Mr. Collingbourne's bedroom," explained Lizzie, pointing to the closed door. "An' 'ere, just opposite, is w'ere this rope's kept."

She threw open the door of a small room. On one wall were shelves: one shelf with an orderly row of bottles of polishes, cleaning fluids, and the like; another on which folded dusters and cleaning cloths were trimly stacked; and a third holding a long line of boots and shoes. Brooms, mops, and brushes were suspended from pegs. Some rugs lay on the top of a cupboard. On the floor were a vacuum-cleaner and a couple of dustpans. Leaning against the wall in one corner were two golf-bags and a couple of fishing-rods in their cases. A heavy coil of rope hung from two pegs in the wall.

"You keep things nice and tidy," said Sir Clinton approvingly. "Whose rods are these?"

"One belongs to Miss Diana, the other's Mr. Fearon's. The golf-clubs are Mr. Fearon's and Miss Diana's; she prefers to keep them up 'ere."

"She didn't take one of them with her to-night when she went out?"

Lizzie Sparrick looked both surprised and puzzled by this question.

"Nossir! Not as I see'd, any'ow."

Sir Clinton glanced along the shoe shelf.

"You keep things very neatly," he remarked, idly.

"Yessir!" Lizzie confirmed, proudly. "These are all Mr. Fearon's on the left; then Miss Diana's; and then Mr. Collingbourne's lot on the right. I clean the lot of 'em; every night I clean the ones they've used that day. That's one thing I never put off, unless they're too wet to clean, and then I do it first thing in the morning."

"Do you?" asked Sir Clinton, chaffingly, as he picked up a pair of brown shoes from Fearon's section. "What about these? They haven't been cleaned, have they?"

Lizzie looked slightly chapfallen.

"There's a reason for that, sir. You're quite correct, sir. The last time Mr. Fearon wore these was on the day when 'e an' I went to give evidence to Mr. Loxton, 'ere; an' they weren't cleaned that night—nor since. But w'y? 'Cause we've run out of brown boot-polish an' I'd nothin' to put a shine on 'em, so I just left 'em alone till I got some more o' the stuff. You can't get it for love or money these days."

"I apologise," said Sir Clinton, gravely, putting the shoes back on the shelf.

He said a word or two in an undertone to Loxton, which Wendover did not catch and then he turned and unhooked the rope from the wall. After examining it he handed it to Wendover.

"You'd better have a look at it, Squire. And now "—he turned to Lizzie Sparrick—"I want to see Mr. Cóllingbourne's room—and your room, also, if you don't mind. You might bring the rope with you," he added to Wendover. "We may want to look at it in a better light."

Leaving the inspector behind they visited the bedrooms of Collingbourne and the maid, both of which looked out on the avenue side of the house. Sir Clinton asked a number of questions which seemed to Wendover a mere waste of time. When they went downstairs to the hall again they found Loxton talking to one of his subordinates.

"You needn't carry that rope about," said Sir Clinton, taking it from Wendover and handing it to the constable.

Glad to be rid of his encumbrance, Wendover pulled out his pocket-handkerchief and fastidiously wiped his palms, which were rather clammy after handling the coil. As he did so, Collingbourne, evidently attracted by the sound of voices, put his head out of the study, saw his rope, and came forward to protest.

"You're not going to take away my fire-escape, are you?" he demanded in an anxious tone. "That would leave me quite helpless if a fire broke out in the night; and an incendiary might fall in the place while we're asleep. That staircase is all wood; it would go up almost in a flash; and then where should we be, all cut off in the upper story?"

"Surely you're exaggerating a little," said Sir Clinton, reassuringly. "Your house can't be so dry as all that. Why, that housemaid's pantry seemed to me rather damp, if anything."

"Damp? Damp? Nonsense! Driest place in the house. On one side of it there's the hot-water tank. The bathroom's on the other side, and I take a hot bath every night. Besides, it's just over the kitchen and gets all the heat from there. Dry as a bone, I tell you, dry as tinder! If you dropped a lighted match there, the place would be ablaze in five minutes."

"I'm sorry, Mr. Collingbourne, but we must take charge of this rope," said Sir Clinton inflexibly. "You'll be able to get another one to-morrow morning; and we're half through the night already."

He cut short further argument by turning to Loxton.

"I'll see Mr. Hicks, now. Bring him along to the study, if you please."

18

PROMISES AND PIE-CRUST

WHEN Cyril Hicks was shown into the study he did not wait to be questioned, but immediately took the offensive himself.

"You're the Chief Constable, I believe," he said, truculently. "Will you kindly tell me why your subordinates have detained me?"

Sir Clinton ignored the intentional discourtesy of Hicks's tone.

"Please sit down, Mr. Hicks; this may take a little time. You've no idea why you've been asked to come here? None at all? Then I'll explain. Miss Herne has given us an account of her doings to-night. You may be able to confirm part of her story. That's why you're here."

Hicks was not in the least placated by this.

"Can't you take her word for it?" he demanded, angrily. "Do you imagine she's not telling the truth?"

"I'm not paid to imagine things," Sir Clinton pointed out in a colder tone. "I'm paid to find out the truth if I can. Of course, if you can't confirm what Miss Herne has told us, there's no more to be said; and I shall merely make a note of the fact. I've no power to extract information from you if you decide not to support Miss Herne's evidence."

Wendover, watching Hicks's face, saw some of the truculence fade from its expression.

"I'm no good at riddles," Hicks retorted. "If you'll tell me what all this is about I might understand better."

"I'll put it in a nutshell," said Sir Clinton. "A man Oakley was found murdered in the avenue here to-night. So far as we know, the last person to see him alive was Miss Herne. She has told us a story about her doings to-night. You may be able to confirm part of it. If you can't do that, what reliance would you expect us to place on the rest of her tale?"

The news of the Oakley murder seemed to take Hicks completely by surprise, so far as Wendover could see; but he was astonished by Hicks's reaction to the news. Instead of asking about the murder he seemed to be thinking about something else.

231

"Well, what did she say?" he demanded, with all his truculence gone and a very real anxiety replacing it in his tone.

"And then, when I tell you that, you'll support it?" said Sir Clinton, frigidly. "I'm afraid that kind of confirmation would be of no use to us."

Wendover expected Hicks to flare up again at this very plain insinuation; but instead he paused for consideration; and when he did speak it was in a tone of restraint.

"Then what do you want me to say?"

"I want to know details of your own movements to-night, both before and after you met Miss Herne. You don't need to say anything unless you choose. That's the position. Do as you please."

Sir Clinton's tone had become completely indifferent, and this appeared to have some effect on Hicks. Again he seemed to be thinking hard, keeping his eyes on the carpet at his feet. Finally, he made a slight gesture with his hand as though conceding the Chief Constable's demand.

"Very well," said Sir Clinton, interpreting the gesture. "Perhaps you can tell us—as carefully as you can—what you've been doing to-night. Start before dinner-time."

Hicks seemed to have made up his mind to be completely frank. In fact, Wendover was slightly surprised by the complete lack of reticence he showed once he was fairly launched. He did not even put a single question about the murder of Oakley, but seemed to concentrate his whole attention on replying to Sir Clinton's perquisition.

"Ask your questions. I'm quite ready to answer, and you can check me by anything Miss Herne has said."

"Naturally," said Sir Clinton, bleakly. "You used the

telephone before dinner? Start there. Give me the names of the people you rang up."

"Only Miss Herne. That was about half-past seven. We arranged to meet at the summer-house here at 10 p.m."

"Is that a common practice with you and Miss Herne?"

"Sometimes we meet there."

"Are you and Miss Herne engaged?"

"Yes."

Wendover made a slight movement of surprise. If Diana was engaged to Hicks why had she not told Oakley about it and put a stop to his fancies at once? However, the next question cleared up that point.

"How long have you and Miss Herne been engaged?" asked Sir Clinton.

"Only to-night, after we met in the summer-house."

"Had you any understanding with her before that?"

"I got some news to-night which made an engagement possible."

"Perhaps we'd better have this cleared up," said Sir Clinton. "Tell us about it in your own way."

Hicks, apparently, had his story ready. Originally, the firm had been run by his father as Hicks & Co. Before the war, Hicks & Co. had fallen into financial difficulties; and Morant had supplied capital to set them on their feet again in return for a share in the firm, which then became Hicks, Morant & Co. The Hicks and Morant families had thus been brought into contact, and an attachment had sprung up between young Hicks and Joan Morant, old Morant's daughter. It was a boy-and-girl affair, Hicks explained; but it had led to an engagement and it was understood that they were to be married when young Hicks was made a partner in the firm. Then came the war. Joan Morant joined the

W.A.A.F. and was sent out to Cairo, where she was still posted.

Meanwhile, Diana Herne had taken a war-post as a secretary in Hicks, Morant & Co. and was thrown into daily contact with Cyril Hicks, who fell in love with her. Morant was a touchy old man who had never been much in favour of Cyril Hicks getting a partnership, but who had agreed to it solely on account of the Hicks-Morant engagement. If Cyril had jilted his daughter, old Morant would have taken it badly and would have made himself awkward in the affairs of the firm; and apparently Hicks senior might have sided with him. Actually, arrangements had been completed and the partnership was to be signed in the course of a week. It was an awkward situation for young Hicks.

Fortunately, that very evening, the Gordian knot had been cut in a wholly unexpected way. Young Hicks received a cable from his fiancée telling him that she had discovered that she was not really in love with him; that she had found an R.A.F. officer who suited her better; and that she would be married before the cable reached him. Evidently she was nervous about her father's reaction to this affair, and she had asked in her cable that Cyril should say nothing about it until she was able to send a letter to old Morant, explaining things in detail. This seemed to clear the way completely. At once he rang up Diana Herne and arranged a meeting at the summer-house so that they might talk over the whole affair and concert plans to meet the new situation.

"That was the meaning of the phone call," Hicks concluded.

"What happened next?" Sir Clinton inquired impassively.

"I was on pins and needles," Hicks admitted with

apparent frankness. "I started off from home far too early, so I was ahead of my time when the bus came to Friar's Pardon; and I decided to go on to the stop beyond the gates and walk across the grounds so as to put off time. I was in no hurry and took things easy."

"Can you give us some idea of the way you went?" asked Sir Clinton.

"I crossed a hayfield," Hicks explained after some moments consideration. "Then I struck a wire fence and got over it. Then there was another fence. I was making for the stepping-stones over the brook that runs there. I slipped on one of them in the gloom and got wet over the ankles."

He held out a foot for examination and Loxton stepped over and felt the soaked shoe to which some fragments of leaves and grass were clinging.

"After that," Hicks continued, "I crossed the avenue and made straight for the summer-house."

"Did you meet anyone on the way?" asked Sir Clinton. Hicks shook his head.

"No one met me, and it was getting too dark to see far. I don't even remember hearing any noise out of the common, except a dog barking away in the distance."

"When did you get to the summer-house?"

"I looked at my watch to see if I had hit off my appointment. It was just a quarter to ten when I got there. Miss Herne came just on time—ten o'clock. She was a bit, a little bit, more excited than usual. That was natural enough, of course, considering my phone message. I was excited myself, too."

"Did she mention that she had seen Oakley this evening?"

"No, she never so much as mentioned his name. We had plenty to talk about without that. We discussed the thing in all its bearings and we finally settled that we'd better say nothing about an engagement—not publicly—until the deed of partnership was actually signed. For one thing, I had to wait till old Morant got Joan's letter telling him about her marriage. For another, if Miss Herne and I had announced any engagement before the partnership was fixed up, old Morant would have smelt a rat and guessed that something had been going on between the two of us at the time I was engaged to Joan Morant. With his touchiness that might have raised trouble. He's none too keen on my getting a partnership anyhow."

"How long were you in the summer-house with Miss Herne?"

"About half an hour, I think," said Hicks after a moment's consideration. "She wanted to get home quickly, once we had things arranged. We didn't want any risk of our meeting leaking out, lest it led to trouble; and we arranged not to see each other again until after the deed was signed, so as to cause no talk. No use getting wrecked in sight of port, is there?"

"Is there anyone who could give any evidence confirming this story of yours?" asked Sir Clinton.

"Well, the bus conductor knows me by sight, as I've been to Friar's Pardon often enough. He might remember me. And, of course, Miss Herne could confirm seeing me at the summer-house."

"Do you know Mrs. Pickford—the wife of the Mitcham Library librarian who was murdered some time ago?"

Hicks shook his head definitely.

"Not even by sight."

"Another point," continued the Chief Constable. "You're on very familiar terms with Miss Herne. What do you call her, when you're alone?"

"Diana, sometimes; usually Di, though," Hicks answered without hesitation.

"That telegram you got on the night of Pickford's murder was signed 'Di,' wasn't it? Did Miss Herne send it?"

"No, she didn't. It puzzled both of us completely to know who sent it. It must have been written by someone who happened to overhear us accidentally. It couldn't be anyone at the factory, for we were particularly careful there, naturally. I never called her anything but Miss Herne, there."

"When you were hanging about Goodman's Row that night, did you see anyone you recognised?"

Hicks evidently racked his memory.

"I think I remember seeing one of our lorry-drivers: a man called Bartram. He was on duty as an air-raid warden. And I caught a glimpse of this man Oakley, too. Nobody else. If it's Miss Herne you're thinking of, she wasn't anywhere near the place that night. I was waiting for her and I couldn't have missed her. Besides, she knew nothing about that supposed appointment. The wire wasn't from her. We've talked that over often enough, for we were very worried about the affair, owing to all this secrecy business and my engagement to Joan Morant. We were a bit troubled, as you can guess, at the idea that some third party knew more about Miss Herne and myself than was safe, by our ideas."

"You and Miss Herne parted at the summer-house about half-past ten. What did you do with yourself after she had gone?"

"I went back to the summer-house and had a smoke. I'd a lot to think about, one way and another."

"No doubt," agreed Sir Clinton.

He leaned across the desk and ran his hand down Hicks's jacket from shoulder to cuff. The gesture puzzled

Wendover for a moment; then he remembered the sharp shower of rain which had fallen about ten o'clock. Sir Clinton's face betrayed nothing of what he had learned. He sat back in his chair, with a slight sniff which might have indicated contempt. Apparently he had come to the end of his investigation.

"Any objection to the inspector taking your finger-prints and brushing you down, Mr. Hicks?" he asked. "Everyone else has gone through it, and it might look strange if we omitted it in your case."

"Anything you like," Hicks conceded, indifferently.

After Hicks had gone, Sir Clinton turned to the inspector.

"I'm leaving the awkward part to you now," he explained. "Get the shoes, socks and trousers of all the male witnesses; and Miss Herne's shoes, stockings and skirt. Also, when you take Mrs. Pickford home, make her change and give you the shoes, stockings and skirt that she's wearing now. You can say it's an order from me. I shall be off the premises by then and they can't argue about it. See that Professor Dundas has these things and the rest of the specimens at the earliest possible moment. Oh, yes, you'd better take that map on the wall for him also; it'll save him some trouble. Tell him I want his report at the very earliest possible moment. His vacation's on just now, so he can give his whole time to the business. And now, Squire, we might get back to the Grange."

"There's just one thing," said Wendover. "It must be rather awkward for Goldsmith. I mean, being landed amongst a lot of strangers in a house that's got this affair hanging over it. Would there be any objection to my inviting him to stay at the Grange, if Collingbourne doesn't mind?"

"That would be very convenient," Sir Clinton agreed, in a rather cryptic tone. "I've no objection, if you can persuade Collingbourne to let you take over his guest. I leave you to fix it up now. After that, I'll bid Collingbourne good night and thank him for lending us his study. *Toujours la politesse!*"

19

COMMON SENSE AGAIN

"Here are a couple of notes for you to add to your dossier on the fauna of this neighbourhood, Squire," said Sir Clinton chaffingly. "I've got in touch with the Eire Civic Guard. You remember the girl Rachel Murneen whom Inderwick got into trouble? That seems to run in the family. Her mother was the daughter of the Castlecarney lodge-keeper whom you told me about not long ago. That seems interesting. I've asked for more information, but I can guess the reply already, I think."

"What are you asking?"

"You really mustn't let your brain rust in this way, Squire. Just think for yourself. It's good for the grey matter."

"Well, what's your second nature note?" demanded Wendover, crustily.

"I've had Grindal the moneylender on the carpet and extracted quite a lot of news from him about his dealings with Pickford, Mrs. Pickford, and young Fearon. Between ourselves, I didn't find Grindal a very likeable creature . . . Oh, no! He's quite within the law; there's no fault with him in that matter so far as I know.

It's just that I don't like his type. He let me look through his books. On 9th June, young Fearon repaid Grindal £50 on a debt, and he did the same on 17th June. It seems a good deal for a young man with a small income, so I suppose he must be betting. One can go on at that rate so long as one can spot winners, but a run of bad luck would make a difference. He's evidently not perturbed by risks."

"He's a young ass," growled Wendover. "Always was. By the way, Clinton, have you had any results from Dundas since you sent him all that stuff to examine?"

"He's not quite finished yet, but here are some of his conclusions to go on with, if you're interested. They do suggest one or two points."

Sir Clinton drew a long envelope from his pocket, extracted a foolscap document and opened it out.

"I'll take his subjects in the order he mentions them himself. In the first place, there's the matter of type-writing. He's compared the types in the blackmailer's note to Inderwick, the telegram signed 'Di,' and Loxton's office reports. These three things were all written on the same Imperial machine. It has been used by a lot of different people, and has got knocked about by unskilful typists, so the spacing and alignment of some of the letters have got out of adjustment. You know how the amateur typist clashes his keys and displaces the type slightly. Dundas has enough evidence to establish that all these documents were written on the same machine. Of course, the type face was cleaned from time to time, but that makes no difference when it is a matter of spacing or alignment. Well, that's that.

"Then in the matter of the fingerprints Dundas confirms Fleming's opinion. There's not the slightest doubt that the fingerprints on the time-table left behind by the blackmailer on Inderwick's table are Oakley's prints. They're quite unmistakable. So much for that.

"The third point's interesting. We got hold of Oakley's shoes after he was murdered. He only had two pairs in his possession. One pair are quite clear of any clay. Out of the second pair, one shoe has tourmaline and tarmac particles adhering to it. The other one has nothing of the sort."

"That merely shows that he stepped on the clay with one foot and stepped on something else with the other when he was at the bomb-crater," Wendover objected.

"That may be, for all I can tell," admitted Sir Clinton. "Dundas noticed that Fearon's shoes show only very slight traces of both stuffs; in fact, Dundas seems to have had some trouble in finding any.

"Now he comes to the rope question. We've checked the length of the rope that Collingbourne bought. It's now short of that by exactly the length of the halter that hanged Pickford. Dundas has examined the ends of the two portions, and he's prepared to swear that they are two bits of the same stretch of rope; so it's clear that the Pickford halter was cut from Collingbourne's fire-escape."

"What about the burned rope that was found in Oakley's dustbin?" asked Wendover.

"It comes from the same shop and it's the same kind of rope. But it doesn't seem to have any connection with the other two, so far as Dundas can make out. You must remember that a number of people bought this kind of rope for fire-escapes, just like Collingbourne. We can't trace that any further, so far as the rope itself goes."

"And what next?" asked Wendover.

Sir Clinton took a rough sketch-map from his pocket and handed it across to Wendover.

"You'd better look at that while I read you what Dundas found amongst the things from the clothes of the various people. Take Miss Herne, first of all. There was a faint streak of wet paint on her skirt, which might have come from brushing against that newly-painted gate marked on the map. The paint's the same in both cases. Her skirt had a whiff of the smell of Douglas fir; and there's a young plantation of Douglas firs marked on the map. Then there were tiny fragments of fern-leaves. To get into the wood marked on the map, she would have to scramble up a sunk fence on its northern side; and there are plenty of ferns there which would serve as hand-holds and get broken in the process. Dundas finds the ferns and fern-fragment match. And, finally, he found tiny bits of broken toadstool on her shoes; and the wood is full of toadstools."

"Now for young Hicks's doings. It was lucky for Dundas that I sent him Collingbourne's framed map with its *hortus siccus* gummed on to it; otherwise he'd have had a lot of bother hunting up botanical information. As it was, he had specimens of the plants to help him in his identifications. The Hicks collection amounts to this: some hay seeds, traces of *Spiranthis stricta*, some bits of *Erica ciliaris*—Fringed Heath is the ordinary name—caught in the welt of his shoe, and a smell of spearmint about his footgear. Add to that the fact that his socks were wet owing to a slip at the stepping-stones, and you have the tale complete.

"Mrs. Pickford's case is even more fully represented. Like Hicks, she carried away some hay seeds. Her shoes, you remember, smelt strongly of garlic. There were a couple of prints of her shoes in some muddy ground near

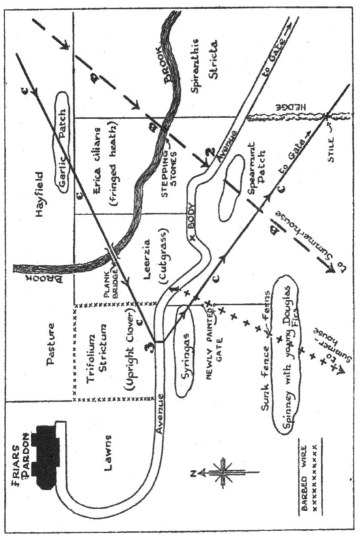

DIAGRAM 4

FRIARS PARDON

Lawns

Avenue

Pasture

Trifolium Strictum
(Upright Clover)

Hayfield

Garlic Patch

Erica ciliaris (fringed heath)

BROOK

BROOK

PLANK BRIDGE

Leerzia (Cutgrass)

STEPPING STONES

Spiranthis Stricta

to GATE

HEDGE

STILE

Avenue

to Gate

Spearmint Patch

BODY

Summer-house

Syringas

NEWLY PAINTED GATE

Sunk Fence

Ferns

Spinney with young Douglas Firs

to Summer-house

Summer-house

N

BARBED WIRE
xxxxxxxxxxx

the plank bridge. Dundas thinks he has spotted some traces of some plant he calls *Leerzia oryzoides*—Cutgrass is its common name he says—and he is quite definite about a petal or two of *Trifolium strictum*, which sounds more familiar as Upright Clover. Then there's a tear in one of her stockings which probably came from barbed wire. A syringa petal was clinging to her shoe. And, finally, there was a tiny fragment of bramble attached to her stocking. That's all."

"Dundas seems to have spotted a lot," commented Wendover, half-ironically.

"Most of the things were almost microscopic—that paint stain on Miss Herne's skirt, for example. Dundas is very thorough. But take the map, Squire. You see the line marked by crosses? Miss Herne walked down the avenue from the house, leaving no traces on the roadway, until she reached the point marked 1, where she met Oakley."

"How do you know she met him there?" demanded Wendover.

"Because that's the point where the white stone was lifted from its place at the side of the avenue. At the end of the interview, she left the avenue and took to the fields following the line of crosses. It's drawn as straight on the map, but that's only for convenience. The point is that she didn't go near the clump of syringas, so far as traces show. The rest of her route fits neatly on to Dundas's finds."

"Pass that," decided Wendover, relieved to see that Diana Herne's movements seemed to clear her of any connection with the murder.

"Take Hicks, next," Sir Clinton continued. "According to Dundas he must have followed the line marked BBB, which concords with his own evidence. He crossed the avenue at the point marked 2, which is out of sight and hearing of the spot where the body was found. If one accepts Hicks's evidence he must have been well on his way to the summer-house when the murder occurred.

"This map's only a sketch, I suppose," said Wendover. "It's not to scale even approximately?"

"No; it's only a rough sketch," Sir Clinton confirmed. "Now, to finish with it, CCC represents the route that Mrs. Pickford followed. She must have crossed the avenue near the point marked 3, if you believe her evidence; because although she could hear the voices of Miss Herne and Oakley, she could not see them nor was she near enough to catch their words."

Wendover stared for a time at the sketch-map in silence and then said, with obvious relief:

"That seems to clear all three of them."

"It supports their evidence up to a point," Sir Clinton amended. "You mustn't forget that once they got on to the hard ground of the avenue they could walk up or down it and leave no trace, so long as they came back and left it opposite the place where they came on to it. So far as this evidence goes, Miss Herne might have followed Oakley down the avenue, murdered him, and then retraced her steps to the point 1 and left the avenue there. Don't let sentiment sway your judgment, Squire, even if she is a good-looking girl."

Wendover shrugged his shoulders without answering this.

"Well, is that all Dundas has to say?" he asked.

"There's just one more point—the lipstick business. You remember that there were traces of lipstick on Miss Herne's hand, on Oakley's mouth, on the white stone, and on the palmar surface of that right-hand chamois-leather glove from the hall-table? Dundas has made analyses of the lot, and the stuff's the same in all cases, so one can infer that all the specimens originated with Miss Herne's lipstick. She lays it on thick enough to spare some of it. That's the end of Dundas's report, so far."

Sir Clinton paused for a moment and then, as though musing to himself, he added:

"If one were going to use a golf-club as a weapon, which would one choose, I wonder: a niblick or an iron? And iron would make a better walking-stick, certainly."

Then, before Wendover had time to put a question, the Chief Constable went on, briskly:

"There's another point that has to be kept in mind, Squire. That interview between Oakley and Collingbourne suggests that Oakley must then have had some valuable document in his pocket. Both Collingbourne and Fearon concur in that. Well, where is it? It wasn't on the body when we searched it. There seem to be only three likely explanations. It must have been given up by Oakley to someone before the murder; or it must have been removed from the body by the murderer; or else it must have been taken by someone who found the body. That links up with the Milton MS. How did it come into the affair? It might have been put into Oakley's pocket as a blind, after the murder, and removed by somebody before we examined the body. The thing came from Collingbourne's collection apparently. Who had access to it? Collingbourne himself, for one. He talks a lot about being as blind as a bat, but atropine seems to let him see well enough to recognise a document, or he wouldn't be able to read the headlines in a newspaper. Fearon could have got access to the collection at any time. Miss Herne knew all about it, for she filed it for Collingbourne. And I understand that Goldsmith was looking over the collection, too, though that was after the murder. Still, he might have pocketed it then for all we can tell. There were no fingerprints of his on it, of course. In fact there were no recent prints on it except my own."

Sir Clinton paused and threw a quizzical glance at Wendover.

"All has been laid before you, up to date, Squire. You've seen everything I've done, and you've read all the evidence, Loxton's and Dundas's reports, and so on. 'Common sense is all you need,' as Dundas says. I leave it to yours. But if I were a betting man like young Fearon, I think I'd be inclined to lay long odds on one point."

"And what's that?" demanded Wendover.

"That Loxton won't be very pleased when the matter's cleared up finally. But life is a mixture of action and reflection. You can go on with the reflection, Squire; I'll manage the action in the next stage. May I use your phone? Thanks."

The instrument was standing on a table in the corner of the room. Sir Clinton dialled a number and Wendover listened as he spoke.

"I gave you an envelope; have you got it? . . . Open it, and detain the person whose name you'll find inside . . . Now this is important—vital. Don't allow your prisoner to communicate with *anyone*—anyone at all— until I've seen you. You understand? . . . Yes, in a cell; that would be safest . . . No, you'll have to curb your curiosity for a little while; I haven't time to explain just now . . . Ring me up here at the Grange as soon as you've put the thing through. That's all for the present. Good-bye."

Sir Clinton laid down the receiver and turned to Wendover.

"Sorry to cut short your meditations, Squire, but it's your turn for action. Do you mind bringing your car round? I have to stand by the phone for the present."

Rather unwillingly—for he was afraid of missing a single link in the chain of events—Wendover went off hastily to his garage and brought the car to the front door of the Grange. By that time, however, Sir Clinton had received his message over the telephone, and he left Wendover to speculate on its nature.

"We may as well start now, Squire, if you're ready."

"Where to?" demanded Wendover. "Ambledown?" Sir Clinton shook his head.

"No," he explained. "There's still one bit of evidence I want to collect. We'll go to Friar's Pardon first, if you don't mind. Ambledown will keep for the present. Don't be in a hurry. We've plenty of time."

At the Friar's Pardon gate, Loxton and two constables were waiting in a police car which, at a sign from Sir Clinton, dropped in behind Wendover's motor as they drove up the avenue. At the house door, Loxton left his subordinates in the car and joined the Chief Constable and Wendover. Sir Clinton rang the bell, and when Lizzie Sparrick appeared he asked to see Fearon. They were shown into the study.

"Phew!" exclaimed Wendover as the door closed behind them. "I don't hold with this fad of Collingbourne's. A fire in this weather!"

He nodded towards the hearth in which a few coals were smouldering, and sat down as far away from it as possible. Fearon did not keep them waiting long. He came into the room with his usual jaunty air, glancing at his visitors in turn.

"Ah! Here we are again: the old familiar faces once more assembled. What's brewing in the witches' cauldron this fine morning?"

"Casting yourself as Macbeth, are you?" asked Sir Clinton, with a smile. "I can't rise to those heights. This is just a piece of routine. You've got two bags of golf-clubs upstairs, I think. Do you mind bringing them down and letting me have a look at them?"

"Mind? Not a bit! Pleasure to do anything for such distinguished visitors. I'll e'en do it now, if you'll excuse me."

He left the room and soon returned with the two bags.

"These ones are mine," he pointed out, "and these are my cousin's."

"I'd almost have suspected that from the initials on the bags," said Sir Clinton, mildly. "But I'm glad to have your confirmation. Nothing like being sure of a thing, is there?"

He took Diana's bag from Fearon and began a very careful examination of the clubs, paying special attention to the heads of the niblick and the irons, and at one point taking a magnifying-glass from his pocket to assist him. Then he examined Fearon's clubs, but only cursorily, as if they were of little importance.

"I'm afraid we shall have to take both sets away with us," he said, looking up at Fearon. "Do you mind?"

The suggestion seemed to surprise Fearon, but he made no objection. Wendover was also surprised, since, so far as he could see, both sets were perfectly ordinary, right-handed clubs.

"I want to tie the two bags together," explained the Chief Constable. "Could you let me have some twine, please? I see you have a string box on the desk over there."

Fearon stepped over and picked up the box, while Sir Clinton held the bags together, ready for tying.

"There's another point I want to ask you about," the Chief Constable went on. "You'll remember that about the end of last month—(Thank you, would you mind tying these things together *here*?)—you were in a bus which collided with a small car. One of our constables took your name as a witness of the accident. There's been some conflict in the evidence—(Shall I put my finger on the knot?)—and I'd like to hear what you have to say about it. (And now, I think, if you put another bit of twine round the other end, it would hold things together.) The driver of the small car says he skidded and that it wasn't careless driving. The bus-driver swears that it was entirely the fault of the other man, and our constable seems to favour that view. (Shall I put my finger on this knot?) The road surface was like iron, and it's difficult to prove anything from the tyre-marks, such as they are—(Thanks, that seems shipshape now)—so if you can remember anything clearly about the affair, it would be very useful in clearing the business up."

Fearon considered for a moment or two before replying.

"Difficult to recall exactly what happened," he confessed. "I was in the front seats, and the glass went with the shock, and most likely I shut my eyes at the crucial moment. I don't remember seeing the small car skid, though. My impression was that it came round the turn far too fast, cutting the corner and landing into the bus."

"That's what the bus-driver says," said Sir Clinton, laying the golf-bags against a chair. "And now, Inspector, will you arrest this man for the wilful murder of James Oakley?"

Before Loxton could step forward, Fearon thrust his

hand into his breast pocket, pulled out a paper, crumpled it up, and flung it into the fire. The inspector dashed forward, thrust his hand among the embers, and rescued the sheet before it was well ablaze. At the same moment, Sir Clinton gripped Fearon.

"No use making a fuss. I'll break your wrist if you give any trouble," he said quietly. "Now, Inspector, go ahead."

Loxton made the formal arrest and added the usual caution, though he deprived the ceremony of any dramatic effect by licking his fingers, which had been slightly scorched when he rescued the document from the flames.

"I've nothing to say," snarled Fearon. "You'll be sorry for this bungle yet."

"If it's loyalty that restrains you, you needn't be so scrupulous," Sir Clinton pointed out, coolly. "We have your confederate under lock and key already."

Loxton handed over the fire-damaged sheet of paper to the Chief Constable, who placed it carefully in a large envelope from the stock in Collingbourne's desk.

"Now you'd better put this man in the charge of your constables, Inspector, and go yourself to search his room upstairs. The following are what I particularly want you to look for: a flask with one of these sliding-on cups, or a collapsible cup; a theatrical eyebrow pencil and any other make-up you find; all the mufflers that are lying about; and . . . oh, yes! a packet of permanganate and a packet of sodium sulphite or something of that nature. And you can take these golf-clubs with you also when you leave, just as they are. Bring away anything else that looks like being useful, of course."

He considered for a moment or two, but seemed to have given all the necessary directions.

"That's all, I think. You can ring me up at the

Grange later and let me know how you've got on. Coming, Wendover?"

On the way home Wendover turned to Sir Clinton.

"What did you drag me into that business for?" he demanded. "You landed me in a most awkward position. After all, I know that family."

"Why?" echoed Sir Clinton, with an air of the utmost innocence. "I thought I was doing you a favour, Squire. You know you like to be in at the death always."

Then, seeing that Wendover was seriously offended, he changed his tone.

"I needed you for camouflage, Squire. If I'd gone there as the complete High Panjandrum, our friend would have smelt a rat and things might not have been so easy. For all I know, he may have a revolver on the premises and I've no desire to see one of my men shot, even in the most excellent cause, if that can be avoided. As it was, your face was my fortune, so to speak. If I had warned you beforehand you'd have given the show away by your looks. You're too honest to conceal your feelings. I apologise—quite sincerely—but I plead that I acted for the best, and it came off."

Wendover's only response was an inarticulate grumble, for his feelings were still raw. After a silence he spoke again.

"Who's this confederate you've arrested?"

"Our zealous friend, Sergeant Eyre. I told you Loxton wouldn't be pleased. He thought a lot of Eyre —most efficient officer and all that, you know. Loxton prides himself on being a judge of character; but he fell down badly this time."

20

THE PICKFORD MURDER

"THE key to the whole affair, Squire, lies in one detail: the fact that the blackmailer did not return to visit Inderwick on the prearranged date. Only one thing would prevent him coming: the knowledge that Inderwick had gone to Loxton and that if he went back to Chastelnau he risked walking into a trap. The inference is obvious. He had a confederate in the police force."

"That seems obvious enough once it's pointed out," admitted Wendover, "but I may as well be honest and say that it didn't occur to me at the time. And I remember you dropped a hint that Loxton wouldn't like it when the facts came out."

"As soon as the idea of a police confederate occurred to me," continued Sir Clinton. "I looked about for confirmatory evidence. The first thing that suggested itself was Inderwick's description of the man—*not* the blackmailer—who used to pay visits to Rachel Murneen when she was at Chastelnau. 'He might have been in the Army, by his manners.' That was the impression he made on Inderwick. But a man in the Army, nowadays, wouldn't be going about in plain clothes. It sounded to me more like a constable or a sergeant off duty."

"That's only suspicion," objected Wendover. "It doesn't prove much."

"There wasn't much difficulty about proof," retorted Sir Clinton. "You'll remember that the blackmailer's letters and Loxton's reports were typed on the same Imperial machine. *Ergo*, either the blackmailer or some confederate of his had access to the Imperial typewriter at the Ambledown police station; and that fitted in neatly with the fact that the blackmailer learned at once that Inderwick had complained to Loxton. I remember, Squire, how amused you were when I told you there was a link between the Inderwick affair and the Pickford case. Like to have another laugh on the subject?"

"What came after that?" asked Wendover, rather shamefaced.

"The next thing was to fasten on the confederate, of course, since we knew where to look for him. Then I remembered about my fishing at Waterville, and how useful my good friend Sergeant Eyre had been, with his local knowledge. He came from that part of the country. So did Rachel Murneen. It seemed not unlikely that he was the man who visited her at Chastelnau and learned that she was in trouble. Naturally, I began to pay particular attention to the affairs of Sergeant Eyre.

"The possibilities were suggestive. Eyre had access to the station typewriter on which the blackmailer's letters were typed. The 'Di' telegram was typed on the same machine. Again, Eyre knew all the routine of the station and could say when the constables on that beat would pass the garage in Goodman's Row, and when the coast was clear. Somebody sent a faked specimen of scrapings from Oakley's shoes to Dundas; and the only people who could have made that substitution were Eyre or Loxton, so far as one could see."

"I ought to have seen some of these points myself," Wendover interjected candidly.

"Of course you should: you knew all the facts. But let's go on. Who was the man who did the actual blackmailing? He was—on the face of things—Eyre's confederate. Now Eyre gave Fearon a very firm alibi on the night of the Pickford murder. Not only so, but he suggested to Fearon that he should give evidence about the alibi to Loxton, though there was no need for volunteering anything of the sort. And when young Fearon did go to Loxton, he went with a sheaf of notes in his pocket to back up his plain tale. Do you think an honest man would do that? He'd wait till he was asked for them. It was this sort of thing which made me say that Loxton wouldn't like the solution. He rather prides himself on being a judge of character, and he thought a lot of Eyre. Then I asked myself: Why should Eyre and Fearon be hunting in couples—a young squire and a police sergeant? Not a very likely combination. Then I reflected that Rachel Murneen, Eyre and Fearon all come from the same district and might have known each other years ago in Eire."

"I see it!" interjected Wendover. "Eyre may be that half-brother of young Fearon—old Fearon's illegitimate son who played with young Fearon when they were boys."

Sir Clinton nodded.

"That's what I guessed a while ago, after I thought over the story about the Fearon *ménage* at Castlecarney. And I guessed also that the girl Rachel was perhaps a half-sister of Eyre's. Like her mother, she's been seduced by her employer. It seems to run in the family. That cleared things up a bit. Just to be on the safe side—though it really wasn't necessary at that time—I got some of my friends in the Civic Guard to look into things over in Kerry; and it turns out that my guess was right. Old Fearon seduced Martha Eyre, the daughter of his lodge-keeper, just as you told me. The result was Eyre. Then Eve Fearon gave birth to a son, young Fearon. Finally, Martha married a man Murneen and produced, among other offspring, Rachel Murneen, who was seduced by Inderwick. So Eyre is a blood-relation of both Rachel and young Fearon. The friend who visited her at Chastelnau was obviously Eyre in plain clothes. But I learned all that a while after my suspicions had turned on Sergeant Eyre and his doings."

"But what tempted young Fearon into the blackmail business?" demanded Wendover.

"I don't know for certain which of them was the brain of the partnership," said Sir Clinton. "In the blackmail affair, Eyre was the man with the information, obviously; and he couldn't afford to do the blackmailing himself, for Inderwick knew him by sight, which would have made disguise rather difficult. As for Fearon's motive, it's plain enough. That moneylender must have been pressing him for repayments of some debts. He must have been pressing pretty vigorously, too; for if you remember the dates I gave you from his books, young Fearon rushed off to pay something on account each time he blackmailed Inderwick. I don't know how he got into debt with Grindal; probably by spotting winners that didn't win and backing them beyond his means. It's no great matter."

"Did they plan to throw suspicion on Oakley at the very start, do you think?" asked Wendover.

"I can't say. Perhaps they were just trying to give Inderwick something to take hold of in his description, if he did cut up rough. After all, dark heavy eyebrows are things which attract attention to themselves. Look at Hess. If you photographed him with his eyebrows clipped short, how many people would recognise him? And his portrait's one of the best-known in the world. As to the swarthy skin, that's easily fixed. A weak solution of permanganate of potash will darken your skin to any extent you please; and, what's more important, you can get rid of it by washing your face in a solution of sodium sulphite. You can buy both stuffs at the nearest druggists. We found packets of them in Fearon's room when we searched it. But that seems enough about the blackmail affair. I'll turn to something bigger: the Pickford murder."

Sir Clinton took out his case and lighted a cigarette.

"In that case," he began, "there seems no doubt that they planned to throw suspicion on Oakley. The affair started at the time Lizzie Sparrick overheard that discussion between Oakley and Pickford at the library. You read her evidence, and it's clear from it that Fearon had just the same chance of overhearing it. She didn't make much of it, you'll remember; but Fearon was better educated, and probably he understood references which meant nothing to her. Even she was able to spot that they were talking about a valuable document; and no doubt Fearon got a glimmering of what the thing actually was. It was the thing that Pickford in his diary referred to as 'It.'

"Within a week, they seem to have laid their plans; and they definitely made up their minds to throw suspicion on Oakley. Not altogether a bad selection, for he had been mixed up with Mrs. Pickford, which suggested a motive. Stupidly, however, they decided to shuffle off the blackmailing affair on to his shoulders as well; and so you get the time-table with Oakley's finger-prints on it left behind at Inderwick's by the blackmailer."

"I don't see how they managed that," said Wendover. "The prints *were* Oakley's, weren't they?"

"I can't swear to the exact method, of course," replied Sir Clinton, "but here's a suggestion for you. You know what they were doing at the Mitcham Library—sifting the grain from the chaff in all the books and papers that were pouring into the place during this salvage collection. Imagine Fearon giving a hand, as he did. He comes to Oakley with a collection of dirty old papers and asks him to look over them; and amongst some valuable stuff he has this time-table. Oakley takes them up, one by one, and when he comes to the time-table he throws it into the discard whence Fearon recovers it later on. Everyone's hands were dusty just then, and Oakley would leave his prints on the thing clearly enough for our purposes. But it was there that they made a mistake which put me on the alert at once when I saw it and made me quite certain that Oakley was not the man who blackmailed Inderwick. Too clever by half, like a good many criminals."

"I don't see it," confessed Wendover, after thinking carefully.

"When did the blackmailer fix his first appointment?" asked Sir Clinton. "At 11 a.m. on Tuesday, 8th June. That was in his first letter. Do you suppose that Oakley could have got away from the Mitcham Library—where they were working at full steam—at 11 o'clock in the morning to go up to Chastelnau? Hardly likely. And if he had been away from the library at all, at that time, he'd have been out book-hunting with Miss Herne in her car, and she could have given him an alibi. That suggests to me that they didn't think of really trying to incriminate Oakley until the murder problem arose; and when they did decide to throw the blame on Oakley, they clean forgot that little touch."

"I never noticed that point," Wendover confessed, frankly. "Nor did Loxton, either," he added to salve his pride.

"No, you would insist that the blackmailing affair was quite separate from the murder. 'All are but parts of one stupendous Whole,' as Satan Montgomery remarked. You don't read enough poetry, Squire."

" Get on with the murder," said Wendover, impatiently.

"It's simple enough to fit a story to the evidence," Sir Clinton assured him. "Here are the bones of the business; you can fill in any further details for yourself. Fearon arranged to meet Pickford at the garage to give a hand in laying up that car, and he chose a time when, as Eyre could tell him, no constable was likely to be in the neighbourhood. The air-raid was a bit of bad luck, coming just then; but at least it cleared the street of the usual passers-by. Fearon and Eyre put their heads together and concocted that tale about Fearon wanting information about police technique, which was to serve as an alibi. As an additional complication they arranged the telegram signed 'Di' which Eyre typed on the station machine and handed in over the post-office counter at the right moment."

"What did they want that for?" demanded Wendover.

"Evidently Fearon had overheard Hicks talking to Miss Herne, probably that day at the library when Hicks went there about the paper-salvage business. The ordinary person wouldn't have noticed that Hicks called her 'Di'; but Fearon was jealous of anyone coming near his cousin, so he'd notice it at once if he overheard Hicks. I suppose the idea behind the wire was to bring Hicks to the neighbourhood of the garage at the crucial time and probably they hoped to throw some suspicion on him by some means or other—anyhow, in the matter of suspects, the more the merrier was their idea, probably. They weren't as clever as they thought themselves, you know; and perhaps Fearon's idea was to throw some mud on Hicks, on the chance of it sticking. For one thing, he could be pretty sure that Hicks would refuse to say anything about the telegram, on Miss Herne's account; and that in itself would look suspicious.

"Eyre's business was to stay at home—he lives alone —and see that no one got into his house, so that there could be no contradiction of the alibi. He was off duty at that period of the day."

"Meanwhile, Fearon cut a length off Collingbourne's fire-escape rope and took it with him into Ambledown. I don't suppose he wound it round himself under his waistcoat, so presumably he carried it in a parcel, since one could hardly set off to hang a man with the rope in plain sight. But I haven't been able to get a reliable witness who saw him carrying a parcel, which is a pity. However, it hardly matters, for these clever fellows make mistakes; and Fearon's mistake was to leave a halter in the garage which exactly made up the original length of Collingbourne's fire-escape. He ought to have at least gone the length of cutting an extra bit off Collingbourne's section. But one can't think of everything, I suppose.

"He had a bit of bad luck in the matter of the bus collision which made him get out and walk past the bomb-crater, so that he got clay on his shoes. Probably he was too busy rehearsing the murder to notice a trifle like that. Anyhow, he arrived at the garage a bit behind time and left his traces there on the floor."

Sir Clinton threw away the end of his cigarette and helped himself to a fresh one before continuing.

"I forgot to mention that he must have brought away a flask from Friar's Pardon, and in the flask he had whisky doped with paraldehyde. He offered Pickford a drink out of the flask-cup and, of course, Pickford never refused a drink in those days. So, in a few minutes, Pickford was drugged and fit for the hanging."

"Why didn't Fearon merely drug him and get the

document from him while he was unconscious, instead of murdering him?" Wendover put in.

"Because if Pickford woke up to find that the document had gone he'd have known who stole it; and then the fat would have been in the fire. Besides, I expect that Fearon had his programme all arranged, and didn't bother to search Pickford's pockets until he'd got him strung up. Anyhow, he must have got a nasty surprise when he found he'd committed a murder for nothing, and that someone else had the document. Of course, knowing what he knew, he must have guessed at once that Oakley had got it. But he's not a very careful fellow at the best, or he'd have avoided tying that clove-hitch on the car-bumper. It's not the kind of knot that the ordinary man ties; and it pointed fairly straight to somebody who had handled a boat until a clove-hitch came natural to him. And, of course, you told me about Fearon's hobby with his coble in his young days.

"Next day, according to plan, he forced himself on Loxton as a voluntary witness, partly with the idea of turning suspicion on Oakley, and partly to establish his alibi with Eyre. Here, he overdid it, coming with all his faked notes in his pocket to reinforce his alibi. No honest man would have done that. But he did get something out of his interview with Loxton, for Loxton mentioned 'a goldsmith' and Fearon would see the meaning of that at once, since he knew that Goldsmith was coming to Friar's Pardon in a few days. An innocent man might have blurted that out but Fearon kept it to himself. Why? Because, probably, it gave him definite information about the document. Up to that point, he could hardly be sure that it wasn't something dealing with the St. Rule's Treasure; but when Goldsmith's name came in, it was clear that the document was intrinsically valuable. So at that stage he knew that it was worth while getting hold of 'It' for its own sake; and he probably guessed that Oakley had it in his possession.

"Meanwhile, Eyre had been doing his bit by substituting some of the garage clay for the stuff which he had scraped from Oakley's shoe. Probably all that had been arranged between the two of them beforehand. They were really a very clumsy pair of lubbers."

"Why?" asked Wendover. "I mean why do you say that at this particular point?"

"Because if they had managed to throw suspicion, real suspicion, on Oakley, he'd have been arrested—and what chance would they have had then of getting hold of 'It'? It's no great pleasure to track down such a pair of louts, Squire. They made too many mistakes."

"It's a pity you can't connect Eyre directly with that murder," said Wendover.

"I can connect him quite directly enough to earn him a hanging," said Sir Clinton. "What more do you want? The 'Di' telegram was typed on the station machine. That makes him an accessory before the fact."

"So it does," agreed Wendover. "That's satisfactory, anyhow."

21

THE MURDER AT FRIAR'S PARDON

"You've made the Pickford affair plain enough," said Wendover, picking up the sketch-map of the Friar's Pardon ground.* "Now what about the Oakley murder?

* See p. 249.

These routes marked on this sketch seem to clear all the people who followed them."

"As a matter of actual proof, they clear nobody," retorted Sir Clinton. "Every one of these people stepped on to the avenue at one time or other, and the avenue shows no footprints. For instance, Hicks might have taken the route ascribed to him on the sketch; but in addition, after getting on to the avenue at the point marked 2, he might have turned to his right, walked up the avenue, met Oakley and killed him, and then walked down the avenue again to the point 2 and after that made the remainder of his track. The same for all the rest of them. Let's take things as they come, Squire."

"Well, how *do* they come?" demanded Wendover, impatiently.

"In due order," rejoined Sir Clinton, placidly. "We'll start with the lipstick. Traces of it were found on Oakley's lips, on Miss Herne's palm, on the white stone, and on those chamois-leather gloves. That girl really does spread it too thick—like the Carpenter's butter. Now the first three confirm Miss Herne's story that Oakley kissed her and she fended him off by threatening him with the stone. The traces on the chamois-leather glove are very faint. In fact, without Dundas and his microchemical analysis, I doubt if we could have proved the identity between the glove-stain and the rest of the lipstick pigment."

"Check!" interrupted Wendover. "You're assuming that Miss Herne left some pigment on the white stone when she picked it up to defend herself against Oakley. I'll pass that; it agrees with her evidence. Then you assume that someone wearing the chamois gloves picked up the stone and got a trace of the pigment on the leather off the stone. And I suppose your next link in the chain will be that this person was the murderer of Oakley? And that the gloves were to avoid leaving any finger-prints?"

"You follow me like a bloodhound, Squire. That was precisely what I intended to suggest."

"Indeed!" said Wendover ironically. "But you seem to have overlooked one or two trifling matters, Clinton. First, the red stain was on the right-hand glove, which meant that the murderer picked up the stone with his right hand. Second, Oakley was killed from behind by a blow on the right-hand side of his head. That implies that he was killed by a right-handed man. It couldn't have been Eyre, for he only came upon the spot in Loxton's car and must have been at the police station before that. And yet Dundas made out that it was a left-handed man who killed Pickford. Where are you now?"

"Just where I was before you butted in, Squire. *J'y suis, j'y reste*, since I see no valid reason why I should shift. The trouble with you is that you want everything to be either white or black; you're mentally blind to greys. Have you never heard the saying that a left-handed bowler is nearly always a right-handed bat? Surely you've seen a man playing golf with left-handed clubs and yet signing cheques with his right hand. A person may be left-handed so far as arm movements go and yet employ his right hand when he uses a screwdriver. Or vice versa. My point is that the arm and the hand movements may differ in their dextrality or sinistrality, if you will allow me the terms. And some people are even ambidextrous, or you wouldn't find the word in the dictionary."

"Oh, of course, you've got a loophole to wriggle

through, always," declared Wendover. "Go on with your harangue."

"Harangue?" echoed Sir Clinton. "Dialogue's more accurate; for, after all, I do get a word or two in occasionally in the middle of your carping. But don't let's differ over such niceties. Next point. As we were going upstairs to the dome at Friar's Pardon, did you notice that Fearon had a small tear in his dinner-jacket, near the shoulder?"

"I did notice it," Wendover claimed. "But when I saw the walls of the dome, all over nails to hang things on, I put it down to his rubbing against one of them. I wasn't thinking of young Fearon as a murderer just then, you see."

"I *was*, by that time," said Sir Clinton. "To me it suggested a man creeping through a barbed-wire fence; and as I'd just been looking at the map on Collingbourne's study wall, I recalled the barbed wire round the enclosure containing *Trifolium strictum*, or Upright Clover, if you like that better. You can see it marked in the sketch. I found it suggestive. But at that stage Fearon seemed to have a perfect alibi. He'd been in the dome when the · murder was committed, according to his story; and I hadn't a scrap of evidence to break that story down. From Lizzie Sparrick's evidence his tale seemed sound. So at that stage I set my mind to work to break that alibi if possible."

"I suppose he must have got out, somehow."

"Easy to say; but difficult to prove beyond dispute, Squire. That was my trouble. Then I recalled Goldsmith's evidence. When he came to the door of Friar's Pardon he heard a *long* rumble—longer than the usual peal of distant thunder. That was the dome being turned by Fearon—*after* that sharp shower of rain. As the rumble was a long one, it meant that the dome was being turned through a big arc. Now when we got up to the dome we found the slit in the dome on the south side— the side where the moon was."

"I see your point," interrupted Wendover. "A *long* rumble meant that the dome was turned so that the slit was shifted from the north side to the south, through about 90°?"

"Quite so. But if the open slit was on the north side before that, it must have been open to the rain driving down on the north wind. That was why I dropped my pencil and groped about for it on the floor. I wanted to learn if the floor was wet on the northern side and not on the southern side. It was. That proved that the slit had been open and turned to the north during that burst of rain, although the moon was in the south. Further, no astronomer, amateur or professional, would let rain blow on to his telescope when he could prevent it by closing the slit. Therefore, at the time of the rain-burst, there was no astronomer, amateur or professional, actually in the dome. *Ergo*, despite his neat alibi, friend Fearon was not in the dome at that stage of the proceedings. I looked at the slit. Fearon might have got out of the dome by squeezing through it. A tight fit, but he could have managed it. So I'd learned something by my bit of by-play with the pencil. Did you spot what I was after, Squire?"

"No, I didn't," confessed Wendover, crestfallen. "I thought it was just a bit of clumsiness on your part."

"How well you know me, Squire," said Sir Clinton, admiringly. "Not a thing escapes you. But to continue. I did rather more than that by my groping about. I managed to feel Fearon's trousers and pumps, *en passant*. They were quite dry. That was rather a facer; for if he'd been out in the *Trifolium strictum* enclosure—as the tear in his jacket suggested—then his pumps and the hem of his trousers would have been wet with dew. But there's aye a way, if you look carefully enough. So when I got up to my feet again, I borrowed his dusters, ostensibly to wipe the dust of the floor off my fingers. You saw that, Squire, but you don't seem to have drawn the proper inference. What I wanted to learn was whether these dusters were moist. They were. He'd used them to dry his pumps after he returned from his little expedition. And he'd turned up his trousers pretty far, so that they weren't wet with dew. But his socks were wet at the insteps, as I found in the course of my clumsy groping after my pencil. He ought to have changed his socks. He's really a lubberly fellow in the murder line."

"Wait a bit!" interrupted Wendover. "If he'd been out of the dome then, he'd have been wet all over by that driving shower. He wasn't. His clothes were quite dry. I saw them close at hand."

"So did I, and I even rubbed against him 'accidentally.' You're quite correct, Squire. His jacket was quite dry. A bit of a puzzle, isn't it? That was one reason why I went down and had a look at that lumber-room under the dome. Naturally, I didn't expect to find an exit down there. I knew he'd got out of the dome through the slit, and no man would do that, in his senses, if he could have got out by walking through a door. What I wanted was to see outside, without raising Fearon's suspicions too much. And, of course, there was the little portico in which he could shelter until the rain shower passed."

"He showed us the lunar drawing he'd made that night," objected Wendover. "It was half-finished, you remember. I suppose you thought I was a bit childish in wanting to have a look at the moon through his telescope, Clinton; but what I really wanted was to have a chance of comparing the actual face of the moon at that time with the drawing he'd made. They were exactly the same. And yet, if he'd been scampering about the grounds as you make out, he wouldn't have had time to make that drawing. It's a full half-hour's work, if I'm any judge. Longer than that, if anything. How do you account for that?"

Sir Clinton looked at Wendover with an approval which was quite unfeigned.

"Now that was clever of you, Squire. You completely took me in there. I thought you were merely in the 'penny-a-peep' business and taking a look through the telescope on the cheap. But, alas! the results aren't up to the level of the technique. Fearon told us that he was a member of the Lunar Section of the B.A.A. and that his job was to watch the moon's surface at the time when the shadows on it were in one particular position. They're in that position roughly once a month. He's got a dozen or two of drawings in that portfolio of his, and they're all very much alike. All he had to do was to take out one of the old ones and put it on his drawing-board. I don't suppose he drew a stroke that night."

"Oh!" said Wendover. "I forgot that part of it!"

Sir Clinton turned away from the subject at once.

"You remember what happened after we came out of the dome? I made a fuss with Collingbourne and insisted on seeing his fire-escape rope. Of course, that was what Fearon used when he slid down from the slit in the dome. Did you notice anything about it when I handed it to you?"

"It was clammy, I remember."

"Naturally, since it was hanging down from the dome during the shower. That was what I was looking for; and that's why I asked about the dampness of the house. But I killed two birds with one stone by getting hold of the shoes Fearon had worn on the night of the Pickford murder. He'd cleaned them before handing them to Lizzie Sparrick; but it would take a better cleaner than Fearon to get rid of all traces of that bomb-crater clay once Dundas was on his trail. The point is that he *tried* to clean them. Why? We knew he was in that bus accident; my constable took his name as a witness. He couldn't conceal that part of the story. But the crucial thing—he probably learned about it from Eyre—was the actual clay itself, because that was connected with the Pickford murder. So he promptly cleaned that off his shoes to the best of his ability. No innocent man would have bothered to do that, so by cleaning his shoes he merely added another item to the evidence against him."

"He seems to have put his foot in it, again and again," Wendover conceded. "Too clever by half, as you say. But go on."

"I've told you already that the halter in the Pickford case was a bit cut from Collingbourne's fire-escape. As to the pieces of charred rope in Oakley's dustbin, I think that Eyre probably put them there with the idea of strengthening the suspicion against Oakley. But that's not very important, since we can hang Eyre anyhow, on the strength of the police typewriter. Do you remember what we did after I'd picked up the rope?"

"We went and examined Collingbourne's bedroom, and you spent some time in asking that Sparrick girl a lot of questions about some things in it—pointless questions, they seemed to me."

"Who are 'we'?" asked Sir Clinton. "'Us,' I

suppose, eh? If you tax your memory, Squire, you'll recall that Loxton had left the party. I'd tipped him off to go back to the dome; and our visit to Collingbourne's bedroom was merely intended to occupy the attention of that little chatterbox, Lizzie Sparrick, while Loxton was getting hold of these dusters. They were sent to Dundas; and he detected traces of Upright Clover and Cutgrass which had stuck to Fearon's wet pumps and been transferred to the dusters when he used them to scrub his pumps dry, after getting back into the dome. That establishes the route he took when he got out: down from the dome, along the north side of the house, across the corner of the pasture, then through the barbed-wire fence—probably tearing his jacket in passing—and so over the Upright Clover and Cutgrass plantings to the avenue, somewhere about the point marked 1, where he lay in wait for Oakley."

"He had the gloves on then, to avoid fingerprints, I suppose," said Wendover, examining the map. "He must have seen the interview between Oakley and Diana Herne—which wouldn't improve his temper—and he had to wait till Diana went away. And there was the white stone, ready for him as a weapon. But what about the Milton letter, Clinton? You haven't got that into the story."

"The Milton letter?" echoed Sir Clinton. "My impression is that the Milton letter affair was an afterthought, an impulsive notion which looked well on the spur of the moment. Consider Fearon's position when he got back into the dome. He'd achieved his murder. He'd got what seemed—to him at any rate—an unshakable alibi, for Lizzie Sparrick would swear quite innocently that he'd never come out of the dome since he hadn't passed the door of her room. He robbed Oakley's body and secured 'It,' the object of the whole affair. Excellent business! Then, suddenly, it must have flashed on him that there was one gaping hole in the case. Colling-bourne is an old babbler. He'd be sure to gabble out the story about Oakley having a valuable document in his pocket. And where was the valuable document? Not on the body. That was the weak point. Once people began asking questions about the document, one couldn't say where it would all end, especially if he wanted to sell the thing—as he obviously meant to do."

"There's something in that," Wendover admitted. "But why take the Milton MS. from his uncle's collection?"

"I said the idea was an after-thought which occurred to him after he got back into the dome. Where was he going to get an old document of *any* sort then, except out of his uncle's collection? It was that or nothing. And he couldn't risk going back to the body to slip a paper into Oakley's pocket. That was too risky. Bright idea! He knew that Goldsmith would arrive very soon. In fact, the arrival of Goldsmith must have been in his mind, for he must have been afraid that the American's taxi would come up the avenue and catch him in the very murder. So why not wait and see if Goldsmith brought the news of the murder—as he actually did—and then slip a compromising document into Goldsmith's pocket? That would throw suspicion on Goldsmith and confuse the trail still further. It must have seemed to Fearon, on the spur of the moment, quite a brilliant notion. So he stole the first thing he could remember from the collection: the Milton MS. And when he went out of the room to order refreshments, he went along to the cloakroom and stuffed it into Goldsmith's overcoat

271

pocket where I found it, just as Fearon hoped. Colling-bourne would never notice what Fearon was doing; he's half-blind, anyhow. I don't say that's exactly what happened, for I've no real proof; but it seems to be the only explanation that covers the facts. There were no fingerprints of his on the Milton MS. so probably he slipped on his chamois gloves while he was handling it and then put them on the hall-table afterwards to get rid of them."

"There's another point you haven't mentioned," said Wendover, "but I think I can guess what you were after. The two sets of golf-clubs, I mean."

"Oh, that? What I wanted was an excuse to make Fearon tie a couple of knots in a piece of twine; and I had to distract his attention while he was tying them, so that he'd follow his natural bent without thinking about what he was doing. Hence my minute inspection of Miss Herne's clubs and all the chatter about that bus accident. Actually, he tied a couple of *left-hand* granny knots, the same as the knot in the Pickford halter. It's always another bit of evidence against him."

"What did Loxton find when he searched Fearon's room?" asked Wendover. "You seemed pretty sure when you gave him his orders."

"He found a big flask with a cup attached. That was what Fearon took to the garage to drug Pickford. He also found an eyebrow pencil and some other make-up things. It was easy to guess that they'd be there, when one thought of the blackmailer's get-up. The permanganate and sulphite were long shots, though they came off. Permanganate makes your skin look swarthy, and the result will stand examination in daylight, which grease-paint might not do; and you can clean off the stain with sodium sulphite quickly and easily. And there was a muffler which Inderwick has identified as very like the one the blackmailer used to wear."

Wendover tried to recall other points, but there seemed to be nothing worth asking about except for one question.

"All this is Hamlet minus the Prince of Denmark," he said at last. "The real centre of the business is this thing that Pickford called 'It'—the thing that was worth £100,000. I suppose it was done for when Fearon pitched it into the fire? But what was it? I'd like to know that."

"It's completely off my beat," said Sir Clinton, candidly. "But Goldsmith will be back shortly—he's gone down to the Mitcham Library to look over the salvage finds for us and see if there's anything really valuable amongst them—and when he turns up here again I'll show it to him and we'll hear what he has to say about it."

22

"*IT*"

"You seem to have cleared up most of the business, Clinton," said Wendover, ruminatively. "But there are still one or two points you haven't touched on. I mean some of those phrases that Lizzie Sparrick declared that she overheard when she was listening to the talk between Pickford and Oakley at the library: 'That cod Hicks'; 'the new place'; 'B.M.'; 'Testament'; '£100,000'; 'second-best bed'; 'Russians,' and 'Anathema.' You haven't worked them into the story."

"Some of them aren't very difficult," said Sir Clinton, in a lazy tone. "To take the first one, you've got to remember that the Sparrick girl has trouble with aspirates. What she actually reported was: 'That cod 'Icks.' Allow for a slight misunderstanding on her part, and 'cod 'Icks' becomes 'codex.' What's a codex, do you remember, Squire?"

"It's a manuscript book, isn't it? I remember once reading an article about manuscripts of the Bible, and some of the names seem to have stuck in my mind: Codex Alexandrinus, Codex Bezae, Codex Regius, and Codex Vaticanus."

"You've forgotten the only one that matters to us. 'Synie-something.' Doesn't that suggest Codex Sinaiticus? And what does that remind you of?"

"Of course!" ejaculated Wendover, suddenly enlightened. "Now I remember! Not long before the war, the Russians sold the Codex Sinaiticus to the British Museum for £100,000. That's what you mean, isn't it, Clinton?"

"It suggests that they were talking about rare MSS.," said the Chief Constable, cautiously.

"You mean they'd got hold of something themselves, equally rare? 'It,' in fact?"

"That's one way of looking at it; but rare MSS. are off my beat, Squire. They're Goldsmith's speciality, not mine."

"That must have been the thing that Fearon tried to burn when you arrested him. Is it much damaged?"

"I'll let you see it," said Sir Clinton. "You can judge for yourself."

He left the room, and in a few minutes returned with two sheets of glass bound in *passe-partout*, between which lay a scorched sheet of paper.

"There it is," he said, handing it to Wendover. "You can read both sides of it through the glass."

Wendover examined the upper side with knitted brows.

"What a fist!" he complained. "I can hardly make it out. Whatever the value of the thing may be, it wouldn't take first prize in a writing competition for five-year-olds."

He fell to deciphering the document, but between the difficulty of the handwriting and the hiatuses due to the flames, he could only make out a phrase here and there.

"'Ye that on the sands with printless foot'. . . . 'And 'twixt the green sea and the azured vault' . . . 'the pine and cedar' . . . 'certain fathoms in the earth' . . . Is it . . . ?"

Sir Clinton bent over his shoulder and laid his finger on a spot in the MS.

"That ought to make it clear, surely, Squire."

Wendover puzzled for a little longer and then gave an exclamation:

"Ah! . . . 'I'll drown my book' . . . Why! It's a page of a MS. copy of *The Tempest*!"

"Try the other side, Squire."

Wendover reversed the *passe-partout* and began to study the back of the sheet.

"A quarter of this is upside-down," he complained, "and the writing is almost indecipherable. He seems to have started off by trying his pen. I can make out: 'Will' . . . 'Willm' . . . 'William.' And one would think he'd been trying different spellings of his name to see which looked best: here's 'Shakspere.' Then in the other corner is 'Shakespear' and . . . over here . . . he spells it 'Shakespeare.' It would be hard enough to make head or tail of it even if we had the whole of it, but just when it seems to make some sense there comes a burnt patch. I give it up. It's more in Goldsmith's line than mine."

"*Nil desperandum*, Squire. Just follow the point of

my pencil and I'll show you a thing or two. Look here! 'Will and Testament.' See that? And here! 'Susanna . . . New Place.' And over here: 'Anne Hathaway, second-best bed.' Now recall what Lizzie Sparrick overheard: 'Testament' . . . 'New place' . . . 'Anathema' . . . 'Second-best bed.' 'Anathema' comes near enough to 'Anne Hathaway,' doesn't it, if you don't catch the exact words? There's not much doubt in my mind that this was the document Pickford had in his hand when the Sparrick girl overheard that discussion between him and Oakley. And when Oakley lent Pickford some money, he insisted on holding this bit of paper as a security. That's why Fearon didn't find it on Pickford's body and why he finally got it out of Oakley's pocket when he murdered him in the Friar's Pardon avenue that night."

"Now I see!" exclaimed Wendover. "These are notes that Shakespeare made when he was thinking of drawing up his will; just a set of jottings lest he should forget anything when the thing was finally put into shape by his lawyer. That fits in with the local tradition that Shakespeare was in this neighbourhood after he retired from the theatre. Why! This must be priceless, Clinton!"

"Quite—so far as I'm concerned," returned Sir Clinton dampingly. "What puzzles me is who should get the money. Neither Pickford nor Oakley had any proper title to the thing. I suppose the Mitcham Library has as good a claim as any. But that's a matter for lawyers."

"I wonder why he made his notes on the back of a page of a manuscript of *The Tempest*," said Wendover, in a speculative tone.

"Evidently an economical bird, the Swan. Waste not,

want not. He was a saving soul, pressing people for small debts, and so on. He may have been conducting a paper-salvage campaign on his own, in those days. But there's the door-bell. That must be Goldsmith back from the library, I expect."

In a few minutes the American entered the room and Wendover questioned him about his visit to the library.

"I can't say I found much that interested me," Goldsmith admitted. "But one or two things seem to have turned up in the course of your salvage collection. Nothing very rare, though."

Sir Clinton evidently had little interest in this.

"There's one point I want to ask you about," he said. "You got a letter from Pickford the librarian before you came here?"

"We spoke of that before," said Goldsmith. "Actually, I did get a rather mysterious note from him. In fact, in coming to Ambledown I was going to beat the record by killing three birds with one stone: see Collingbourne's collection; pay a visit to Pickford and see what he wanted; and drop in on that bookseller Tibberton. But now both Pickford and Tibberton are unavailable, and I haven't found much in Collingbourne's job lot of stuff."

"Have you the letter Pickford wrote to you?"

"Not here," replied Goldsmith. "But I can give you a rough idea of its contents. He said he had come into possession of a very valuable manuscript, a great rarity; and he'd value my confidential opinion on it. That made me inquisitive. I'm always open to a deal in something that's really rare. You don't know what's become of the thing, do you? I suppose his executors must have all his property."

"I think I can show it to you," said Sir Clinton,

picking up the *passe-partout* and handing it to the American.

Goldsmith examined it minutely for a time in silence. Then he took out a glass and scrutinised some parts of the paper minutely, still without saying anything. Wendover gazed at his guest's face, but Goldsmith's features were set in impassibility and nothing could be gathered from them.

"Well?" said Sir Clinton at last.

Goldsmith looked up from the document.

"This is a most interesting exhibit," he said, without any indication of his feelings in his tone.

Wendover could not restrain himself any longer.

"You see what it is?" he demanded. "A page of *The Tempest* and a lot of notes scribbled on the back of it— notes for Shakespeare's will. You must be pretty well acquainted with Shakespeare's handwriting, so far as specimens are extant, I suppose. Is this thing genuine?"

Goldsmith laid the *passe-partout* carefully on the table.

"You can't expect me to reply to that on the spur of the moment," he pointed out with a smile. "But I'd be surprised to find Shakespeare using a steel pen."

"How do you know he used a steel pen?" demanded Wendover, rather taken aback.

"I don't. That's the trouble. But the man who wrote *this*"—he tapped the *passe-partout*—"used one."

"Can you tell us why you're so positive about that?" asked Sir Clinton.

"If you had a trained eye, I could do it more easily," said Goldsmith. "But here are a couple of points or so. If you write with a stylographic pen, you produce lines which all have the same breadth, no matter whether your pen is moving up or down the paper. With a steel nib, you can make lines which are thick or thin—what's technically called 'shading'—but as a general rule your 'down' lines will tend to be thicker than your 'up' lines; and if you write without thinking, your horizontal lines will be slightly different in thickness from your vertical ones.

"Now a quill pen is more flexible than any steel nib; and with it one gets a variety of shading which is impossible with a steel pen unless the pen is shifted in the hand during the actual writing. Then, again, owing to the comparative inflexibility of a steel nib, its points leave 'nib marks' on the paper, so that under a microscope—or even in some cases with the help of a magnifying-glass—the ink line looks rather like a road bordered by hedges: two heavy lines with a lighter tract between them. And, owing to its stiffness, a steel pen is apt to tear some kinds of paper and so leave traces which a quill pen never makes because it is so soft and frail.

"These are only some of the points of difference between a steel nib and a quill; I'm not giving you a lecture on the subject. But I notice all these characteristics in this document, so I feel pretty safe in saying that it was written with a steel pen. And as steel pens weren't invented until 1803 and didn't come into general use until about 1830, it's a fair inference that Shakespeare didn't use one in the sixteenth century."

"You mean it's a forgery?" asked Wendover.

"Of course it is. It's very clever, and all that. It would perhaps take in some people; but no real expert would be deceived by it for a moment."

Goldsmith picked up the *passe-partout* and examined it for a few moments in silence.

"Where did this thing come from?" he asked curiously.

"I think I can account for it," said Sir Clinton. "Tibberton the bookseller was killed in an air-raid. His relations knew nothing about books and they simply sold his stock on the shelves. But there were a lot of loose papers also, and they sent these to the Mitcham Library for salvage. This sheet may have been amongst them."

Goldsmith gave one of his rare laughs.

"Well, the man's dead, so it doesn't matter. But it was on this very kind of business that I wanted to interview him. I've had suspicions—in fact, more than suspicions—about some stuff which I could trace back to Tibberton; and I was going to pay him a visit and force the truth out of him, if I could."

"You mean, he made a practice of forging old documents?" asked Wendover in some surprise. "But surely he'd have been spotted at once. Besides, he couldn't have floated enough of the forgeries to make it pay."

"It depends on what you call 'making it pay,'" rejoined Goldsmith. "There's the case of 'Antique Smith,' for instance. He specialised in producing what he pleasantly called 'facsimiles' which he disposed of through intermediaries. One of my own countrymen, a wealthy banker, paid £750 for a collection of over 200 documents. It subsequently turned out that only a single one of them was genuine; the rest were forgeries. And when the experts went into the matter they discovered that epistles by Mary Queen of Scots, John Graham of Claverhouse, and Rob Roy were all written on the same make of paper! It's all a matter of finding the right kind of customer, you know. The classic case is Michel Chasles, a distinguished mathematician, member of the French Academy. In nine years, he bought no less than 27,000 forgeries concocted by a man Vrain-Denis Lucas, and for this mass of rubbish he paid over £6,000! It included letters written by St. Luke, Plato, Pliny and Cleopatra. There was even one from Lazarus to St. Peter. All these worthies, it seems, wrote on paper—not parchment—and they were so thoughtful for posterity that every man jack of them wrote in *French*. Vrain-Denis Lucas must have been a hard worker. If he took Sundays off, he must have turned out about nine forgeries per diem for nearly a decade. And yet he managed to sell the lot to one man. As I said, it's a matter of finding the right customer. Take your friend Collingbourne. My impression is that his collection is crammed with Tibberton's output. I spotted some of the stuff myself when I was looking casually over the Friar's Pardon papers after Collingbourne had been bragging to me about Tibberton's acuteness in finding documents for him. I think you underestimate the possible profits of the trade, Mr Wendover."

Sir Clinton got up from his chair.

"If you'll excuse me for a moment, I'd like to have your opinion on another point."

He left the room and returned after a few minutes with a book which Wendover recognised as Pickford's copy of the *Annals of the Abbeys*. Goldsmith examined it minutely for some time before offering any opinion. At last he seemed satisfied.

"So far as the book itself goes," he said cautiously, "I see nothing suspicious about it. I happen to know the make of paper it's printed on, and that agrees with the date on the title page. But if you want a really reliable opinion, I'd have to make inquiries and, if possible, get hold of other copies to collate with it."

"The annotations are what interest me," explained Sir Clinton.

"Oh, that's quite a different matter," said Goldsmith. "They purport to date back at least a couple of centuries, and yet they're written with a steel pen. From one or two idiosyncrasies in them, I'm inclined to put them down as Tibberton's work, done with the idea of enhancing the value of the book. Did the thing pass through his hands?"

Sir Clinton nodded.

"He sold it to Pickford, and probably knew his customer's interest in the St. Rule's Treasure; so he took the opportunity of 'enhancing the value' of this copy by inserting a lot of spoof notes."

Wendover reached out and picked up the *passe-partout*.

"And what is this thing worth?" he asked, turning to the American.

"To me?" said Goldsmith. "Not five cents. But if you can buy it for 6d. you might hand it up in the Mitcham Library as an awful example. That's its only field of usefulness."

"Steady, Doctor!" rejoined Sir Clinton. "I seem to recall your saying that the price of a thing depends on how much somebody wanted it. You're thinking too much of cash values. That bit of paper has cost the lives of two men already; and there are two more lives forfeit, if I can manage it. Quite valuable, you see, even if it's not worth twopence in the open market. One of these ironies of Fate that one hears about now and again."

THE END

>>> If you've enjoyed this book and would like to discover more great vintage crime and thriller titles, as well as the most exciting crime and thriller authors writing today, visit: >>>

The Murder Room
Where Criminal Minds Meet

themurderroom.com